...Devlin's THREE ...EN:

'...Wise Men is a great ...ok: well
...g, believable, compelling. This is my
...the women I know, a million miles
...men traditionally have appeared in
...ctims, martyrs – I don't think so!
...draws friendship and love, with its
...rts and pains, with unflinching hon-
...the bargain, it's funny!' MARIAN KEYES

...ovel. Martina Devlin immediately grabs
...LY COOPER

MARTINA DEVLIN

BE CAREFUL
WHAT YOU WISH FOR

HarperCollins*Publishers*

This novel is entirely a work of fiction.
The names, characters and incidents portrayed in it are
the work of the author's imagination. Any resemblance to
actual persons, living or dead, events or localities is
entirely coincidental.

HarperCollins*Publishers*
77–85 Fulham Palace Road,
Hammersmith, London W6 8JB

www.fireandwater.com

A Paperback Original 2001
1 3 5 7 9 8 6 4 2

Copyright © Martina Devlin 2001

The Author asserts the moral right to
be identified as the author of this work

A catalogue record for this book
is available from the British Library

ISBN 0 00 651490 1

Typeset in Meridien by Palimpsest Book Production Limited,
Polmont, Stirlingshire

Printed and bound
Omnia Books Limited, Glasgow

For my own Molly, Molly Eccles, an aunt who's also a friend ... although infinitely better behaved than her namesake.

CHAPTER 1

'Red wine or white?' asked Helen.

'Red – our bodies need the iron,' said Molly. 'But imagine having both in stock. Helen, it's official, you're a grown-up.' She lolled on the sofa, waiting for her friend to prise open the bottle.

Despite a smorgasbord of corkscrews, Helen was fundamentally challenged in the uncorking department. Every so often she'd say wistfully, 'Isn't it a pity that Liebfrausquilch in the screwtop bottle tastes revolting? It'd be so handy,' and Molly would threaten to report her to the taste Gestapo.

'Give it here, Sharkey,' she ordered now. 'I'll die of iron deficiency if I wait for you to relieve me.' And she extracted both Merlot and corkscrew from Helen's fumbling hands. 'I thought this was supposed to be a foolproof gadget,' she added. 'Didn't the *Image* magazine testers give it the full Orion's Belt of stars?'

'Misled again,' mourned Helen. 'I read, I bought, I faltered. Fill up my glass to the brim there, Molly, this is an emergency. I need to funnel the alcohol into my bloodstream in jig-speed time.'

'You know what getting drunk on alcohol is called,' said Molly, dribbling only a few drops as she poured.

Helen waited for Molly to fill her own glass and then clinked. 'Tell me.'

1

'A return on your investment.'

They swigged in companionable silence, facing each other on Helen's somewhat mauled matching sofas from which, until she could afford two identical new ones, she wouldn't be parted. Helen favoured pairs, whereas Molly shuddered if she accidentally found herself with a double – mugs, earrings, socks, towels were all deliberately mismatched. Shoes were about all she'd concede needed to come in pairs. 'Eclectic' was the word she dredged up whenever anyone suggested her taste veered towards the idiosyncratic; nobody came right out and told her she looked like a walking jumble sale, at least not since being staffed, after years as a freelance journalist, allowed her to relax her financial guard enough to buy clothes in the Powerscourt Townhouse.

'So what's the emergency, oh inheritor of the face that launched a thousand computer blips?' she asked Helen, who was a software programmer.

The reference usually didn't fail to make her friend blush or giggle, or at least twiddle an eyebrow, but tonight she didn't react – an ominous sign. Helen took a protracted swallow that emptied her glass and said, 'Thanks for galloping around at a moment's notice.'

'You know me,' shrugged Molly. 'I'd do the Lough Derg pilgrimage if it meant a drink in the heel of the hunt.'

'I won't ask you to walk on rocks here,' said Helen, 'but you might be obliged to walk on water. I need a miracle. Or failing that, electric shock treatment.'

'So it's a red-alert emergency, sirens blaring, traffic lights contemptuously ignored and cars bulldozed aside. It can only be man trouble.'

Helen frowned and refilled her glass without topping up Molly's – which meant she was really distracted because Helen was renowned for her impeccable manners.

'Just supposing . . .' began Helen, rotating an opal heart earring in her left lobe, '. . . just supposing you fell in love with someone you weren't meant to, but it crept up on you, and before there was any chance to erect the barricades you were head over heels and resistance was futile. How do you hold the feelings at bay – feelings you're landed with whether you want them or not? Even though you refuse to meet him or return his phone calls you still think about him constantly. You can't sleep, can't concentrate on your job, and your life – which didn't seem so unsatisfactory until the thunderclap – is so sterile and empty and meaningless there's no way forward. Actually it's more of a lightning bolt than a thunderclap, but no less elemental, and it's left wasteland in its wake. God knows why I'm banging on about the weather.' Helen twisted her earring so ferociously the back dropped off but she disregarded it. As Molly bent to retrieve the sliver of metal Helen continued, 'The joy has been sapped from everything: going to work is like wading through fog; coming home to an empty house is so disheartening it's tempting to stay on the DART train to the end of the line, and a day off stretches endlessly like a prison sentence with no remission.'

Her voice dropped until it was virtually a whisper. Molly's stomach contracted at the misery on her friend's face. She leaned across the sofa and wrapped her arms around the slight frame. She'd no inkling Helen was interested in anybody, never mind running the gauntlet of thwarted love.

'Is it truly hopeless?' asked Molly.

'Yes.'

Pause.

'He's married?' prompted Molly.

'No.'

'Gay?'

3

'No.'

'A priest?'

'No.'

'In love with someone else?'

'No.'

'Indifferent?'

'No.'

'Struck down by a fatal disease?'

'No.'

'Helen, I submit. I can imagine no more obstacles. If it isn't a love that dare not speak its name, seek its flame or shriek its shame, if it isn't a love potholed by a wife and four children, or even a love with a continent, an incurable illness and a clerical collar between you, I don't see the barrier.'

At this Helen sank her head on Molly's shoulder and sobbed, while Molly furtively reached for her glass. It could be a long night, no point in it being a dry one. But after Helen had a weep and accepted Molly's offer of a cup of tea she calmed down.

'I'm being stupid,' she snivelled, juggling alternate sips of wine and tea. 'It's not love, it's infatuation. If I'm patient it will fade.'

Like curtains, thought Molly, unable to stifle the stray comparison that sneaked into her mind.

Helen continued, 'I simply have to wait for the feelings to evaporate. It's just so –' and here her composure quivered – 'dreary in the meantime. The one person to whom I could describe how confused and destabilised I feel, because he's probably experiencing something similar, is the one person I can't approach. Him.'

'You can talk to me, angel face.' Curiosity and compassion were battling it out within Molly as she wondered who this unattainable paragon could be. Helen steadfastly stonewalled efforts to probe his identity, and Molly assumed it had to be someone from work. Where else did thirty-two-year-old women meet men? It certainly wasn't in the supermarket, despite those magazine articles about checking out the contents of a man's basket in the check-out queue. Small cartons of milk, individual pizzas and a decent bottle of wine meant singles; trolleys with a rainforest of loo roll and reservoir-sized cola bottles equalled daddies. Or so the article claimed. Molly wasn't convinced it could be so self-evident. People weren't tailored from Lycra for a one-size-fits-all finish.

Whoops, Helen was talking again – concentrate, Molly chided herself. Mentally assessing other men, even mythical ones, was *verboten* when your best friend was in emotional hyperventilation.

'I know I can talk to you, you're a saint to put up with my moaning –'

'Let me have that in writing,' interrupted Molly. 'I'll never be believed unless I can produce proof.'

'You know you're a strawberry cream, not the nut brittle you like to pretend, Moll. The problem is I don't feel free to go into details here. I can't name names. This involves two people and it wouldn't be right to reveal his identity. Information leaks out – honestly, I'm not pointing the finger at you – but it could be harmful. For both of us. Least said soonest mended, as the Bible doesn't say. But probably implies somewhere.'

'Right, of course you can't say any more,' agreed Molly, monumentally disappointed. 'I expect it would be a breach of confidence if I knew him already . . .'

She looked hopefully at Helen to see if her shot in the dark had struck home but there was no response. Feck, she was longing to know the identity of this adonis who had the normally self-contained Helen sobbing into her wine glass. But after a brief internal tussle Molly acknowledged she was being selfish; the priority now was to distract Helen from her conviction that life was pointless. All this talk of staying on the DART until the end of the line had unnerved Molly with its bleakness. Depression ran in the Sharkey family – Helen's uncle had thrown himself under a double-decker after he lost his job. She wasn't about to stand by while Helen caved in to the black dog. This called for decisive measures.

What Molly liked to do when sad was to party. Also when she was happy, bored and feeling stressed. So her solution to Helen's dilemma, or the two-dimensional aspect of it she'd glimpsed, was glaringly apparent.

'We're going on the lash tomorrow night, Helen,' she announced. 'That'll take your mind off him. We'll get chatted up and flirt outrageously. It's cast-iron therapy. I'll wear my foolproof on-the-pull T-shirt, *Come, woo me, woo me; for now I am in a holiday humour, and like enough to consent* – jackpot guaranteed every time. Perhaps we'll even buy you one too, just to prove we're both the answer to a young man's prayer, cherchez la indiscriminate femme.'

'But we're not,' objected Helen.

'I know that and you know that, angel face, but no harm in stringing them along for a few drinks. So will I pick up one of my Shakespearean soundbite numbers for you? Something that intimates "Ready when you are, big boy", only in ye olde English to show you're sophisticated?'

'No,' shuddered Helen. 'What works for you wouldn't carry the same, er, conviction for me. I don't know that I have the heart for a session, Molly. The city centre's so congested, there's nowhere to sit in pubs and you can't hear yourself speak.'

'You've lost the plot, my little wounded bird. That's the whole point of Saturday nights on the town. We're both thirty-two, not a hundred and two, so let's get cracking and prove we're irresistible women in the prime of our lives. I'll meet you in the Lifer at eight and –'

'Not the Life Bar, it's too young and trendy,' complained Helen.

'So are we. And wear something jam-tarty.'

Helen looked dubious at this final injunction.

'The nearest you can manage,' amended Molly. 'Nothing buttoned up or navy.'

No point in expecting an overnight metamorphosis.

Just as well, reflected Helen, in one of her frequent reflective moments, after Molly left, that friends didn't have to share characteristics because the two of them would never have lasted the distance.

Just as well, reflected Molly, in one of her infrequent reflective moments, after she left, that friends didn't have to share characteristics because the two of them would never have lasted the distance.

Instead they had instantly formed a bond when they'd met on day one at university fourteen years ago. Admittedly they'd been thrown together as first year Arts students by mutual terror of Sarah Daly, who was acquainted with Helen from school and Molly from sharing lodgings. Sarah had been superbly informed – she'd known which bus would take them to the Belfield Campus at University College Dublin and where the bus stop was located and she'd even identified the lecture theatre location for their first session on Longfellow or some other fellow. Meanwhile

Helen and Molly had both been desperately intimidated and even more desperate not to betray it. Sarah's savoir-faire – and their discovery over coffee that they each abhorred her for it – had sparked a chemical reaction friendship.

Sitting in the taxi home, with only a sixth of an ear (and even that was probably excessive) tuned to the driver ranting about teenage pregnancies and moving on seamlessly to refugees bleeding the social security system dry, Molly decided to unmask Helen's love bug. Not to be inquisitive, God no. So she could splat him on behalf of her unhinged friend. Helen wasn't the best at romance; come to think of it she'd only had one grand passion. That had been just after graduating, with a marketing executive called Eugene. He'd been more than presentable – apart from his predilection for wearing dark shirts under beige linen jackets, which had prompted Molly to christen him the Black and Tan, although he'd insisted he preferred Gene if a nickname were essential. That relationship had juddered to a halt when he'd shown the temerity to propose. Marriage. Time for the short step followed by the long drop for Eugene.

'I'm never getting married,' Helen had insisted and Molly had concurred. Never didn't mean not ever, as Molly understood it, it meant not while you were in your twenties and could pick and choose. In your thirties, now, you might consider it. In fact Molly was actively, not to say compulsively, contemplating it. But Helen seemed curiously inflexible on the matter. One after the other their college friends had teetered up the aisle disguised as shepherdesses or woodland nymphs, surrounded by a bevy of miniature ruffians purporting to represent cherubs. Helen and

Molly, meanwhile, bought cartwheel hats because there was nothing like them for creating allure, and mouthed along to The Wedding Feast at Cana during the service. By now they were word perfect.

Lately Molly had been gazing at those brides in their ivory tower dresses and wishing she were one. Wishing she were standing at the back of a church, with a man, razor nicks on his chin from an unsteady hand, waiting in the front pew for her. Not just any man, one who made her want to bolt to the altar at breakneck speed instead of decorously swishing up.

In the meantime there were best men – and second-best men – to audition at friends' weddings. At the last wedding she'd attended, Molly had been disposed to give the best man the glad eye on the back of a spark of wit, despite his goatee beard, but a woman in a crocheted dress, complete with sausage-shaped baby-sick stain on the lapel, had swiftly signalled her prior claim.

Molly sighed. Despite fighting talk in her twenties, she wouldn't mind being the one in satin slippers for a change, hemmed in by all those aunts from Killybegs and Gortnagallon never encountered except at weddings and funerals. Being thirty-two had much to answer for – perhaps she'd have passed safely through the stage by her mid-thirties. Everyone sympathised with women over their biological clocks but what about the ones saddled with a ticking Mendelssohn's Wedding March. It left her wishing . . . wishing she were the one weighed down by Irish linen tablecloths and napkins bought in Clery's sale and stockpiled until a gift was required. Tablecloths she'd never use because they belonged to the era of laundresses and starch, but that wasn't the point – every newly-wed should have a selection. It left her wishing there was someone who regarded her as the most ravishing woman on the planet even when she couldn't be bothered sliding in her contact lenses and blinked at the world from behind glasses. It left her wishing to exchange her apartment in Blackrock, with its undernourished fridge, for a house with a bulging fridge-freezer. One of those in-your-face Smeg jobs the colour of an ice lolly.

Once or twice she'd hinted as much to Helen but the shutters had grated down and her friend had made it crystalline there was to be no backsliding as far as she herself was concerned. Wedding cake was off the menu unless it was someone else's.

Whereas Molly was finding the single life a little, well, single. She'd been in enough relationships – heck she was always falling in love; she was hooked on the adrenaline high – to know it wasn't all roses as part of a couple. But the thorns seemed less prickly the older she waxed. Sometimes she daydreamed about how agreeable it might be to have someone to cut the grass. Not that she'd much call for gardening services living in a second-floor apartment, but it was reassuring to know you had the absolute right to dispatch a male with a lawnmower to your patch when you felt inclined to exert your authority or play at being a girlie or when – and this had to be a last resort – the grass needed it. Rules were rules. Everybody knew the marriage service ran along the lines of 'do you promise to love her, honour her and cut the grass at her bidding as long as you both shall live?'

It was tricky, Molly reflected, imagining yourself immersed in marital bliss when you didn't have a boyfriend. On the contrary, disagreed her opinionated inner voice, that made it easier. There was no need to cast your eye over the current boyfriend title-holder and realise this was it: this was as good as it got. Whereas the imagination, a particularly accommodating tool, allowed you to step out with Liam Neeson, who'd just happen to be rediscovering his thespian roots with a play at the Abbey when he'd bump into you one Sunday lunchtime. You'd be reading the newspapers on a caffeine and chill-out binge, despite the contradiction in terms, and you'd drop one of the sections and bend to retrieve it just as he reached it to you, and your gazes would collide. Naturally you'd both be sitting down because otherwise you'd need a stepladder to make eye contact. And even though you always looked like a regurgitated dog's dinner on Sundays, this time you'd have bothered to wash your hair and wear something clean and pressed instead of picking over the pile of rejects on your bedroom floor and . . .

'Blackrock, what street did you want, love?'

The taxi-driver curtailed Molly's fantasy. I'm not finished with you yet, she instructed it, as she fished out her purse and advised the driver where to pull over. She debated withholding a tip in protest at his unreconstructed views on asylum seekers, hadn't the courage, and compromised by rounding up the fare by a minimal amount.

However, the interruption returned her attention to Helen. Helen, who not only never wanted to marry but seemed disinclined for a little light relief in the jiggery pokery stakes too. Her last boyfriend had been booted into touch eighteen months ago, by Molly's reckoning, the Daniel O'Donnell lookalike she'd dubbed Kitten Hips because he practised a panther walk. He had to practise it, reasoned Molly; nobody swayed naturally like that. Anyway, he went the way of all flesh that came into contact with Helen: namely she dumped him after four months when he turned serious, although her definition of too intense was his suggestion they should plant sunflowers

11

in the 10-foot square of back garden where she used to live. His subtext: I intend to be around next year to see them flower. Her reaction: Pervert. What manner of man wants to make a commitment like that?

So for Helen to fall head over neat Cuban heels for someone off limits was a manifestation of natural justice. And while Molly was sorry for her friend's palpable grief, she couldn't help thinking: Cupid's got you sorted, love, in one of those streetwise accents they use on television cop shows to portray gritty reality. Besides which, she was convinced Helen was overreacting. Too much red wine had blurred Molly's recollection of the wan face weeping against her shoulder and the dejection in tones that described how life seemed to have dimmed from colour to monochrome. Molly wasn't unsympathetic, she simply needed convincing the script was as unremittingly dire as Helen read it.

'We'll sort her out tomorrow night, Nelson,' she told her teddy bear, named because he'd spent twenty-five years in a cupboard before being liberated (she'd been frightened of him as a child for no logical reason). 'We'll canter her out in the showing ring and she'll be fighting them off with a broom handle. That'll take her mind off the fellow she can't have. And if it doesn't, at least she might tell me some more about him. I'm agog to sneak a peek at the man who can send Helen Sharkey's pulse ricocheting. Doesn't the whole of Dublin know she's the next best thing to celibate, barring lapses every eighteen months or so?'

As Molly was slinging Nelson onto the floor and climbing into bed without taking off her makeup – but remembering to collect a tumbler of water from the kitchen because

Merlot furred her tongue – Helen was washing the wine glasses and bowls she'd filled with nibbles for her perpetually peckish friend. She sat on for the longest time after Molly left, her light-hearted reassurance warming the air behind her – 'Chin up, Helen, we'll all be dead in sixty years' time.' But now that she was alone again the temperature had plummeted and the solitary allure of her terraced cottage in Sandycove, just ten minutes' walk from the seafront, seemed less acceptable – indeed, it was insupportable. She wallowed for a while, wondering why some malign fate had earmarked her for turmoil. Why couldn't she have settled for Kitten Hips or the Black and Tan, or one of the other men who'd flitted through her life? They'd have stayed if she'd allowed them but she wouldn't give them houseroom. Helen wasn't a 'settling for' type of woman, however. And her mind had been made up about love a lifetime previously.

Movement, that's what she needed. If she were busy she wouldn't be able to dwell on him. She couldn't even allow herself to think his name, although sometimes she said it aloud for the sheer pleasure of shaping her mouth around the syllables. Helen loved his name, the pattern of the K sounds in his Christian name and surname, the evenness of the double syllables in both. One time she'd been driving through Balbriggan and thought she was hallucinating because she'd passed a hardware shop and there was his name above the door. She'd had to retrace her steps to check whether there was actually a shop painted yellow and green on the corner of the main street with the name of the man she loved above it. There was. And it had made her laugh aloud with pleasure. She'd gone inside and felt herself suffused with joy as her eyes drifted along the shelves stacked with colour charts and tools whose purpose she couldn't begin to fathom. Helen had bought a paintscraper to prolong the euphoria and kept it, unused, in a kitchen drawer alongside spare batteries and scissors.

But there wasn't much gladness in her heart now as she dropped two red wine bottles into her recycling bin and recorked a third with only a glass or so eked from it. Although her feet were leaden, she knew there'd be little enough sleep that night.

'Bring some hot chocolate to bed and read the new *Maison Belle* interiors magazine you've been saving for a treat,' she urged herself. 'That'll make you feel better.'

Molly, who renamed everything, called it the *Maison Smelly* magazine, partly because Helen loved to lower her nose to the pristine scent of its unopened pages. Also because it inevitably offered free samples of potpourri refresher or fabric conditioner. Helen willed herself to believe that *Maison Belle* and a bedtime drink would reverse the decline in her flagging spirits. She knew all the tactics to manipulate a slump in mood – it was essential she did. Imagine if he contacted her on a day when she was feeling vulnerable and she succumbed to temptation and . . . Helen's face crash-landed on her hands. She wished. She hardly knew what she wished for. Careful, don't even think it, don't let the narrowest scintilla of possibility edge around your mind. She leaped up and washed and wiped, perfecting her home; she'd as soon wedge the front door open with an All Burglars Welcome Here neon sign as retire to bed leaving dishes on the worktop or CDs separated from their holders.

At the bottom of the stairs, magazine under an arm and mug in hand, she cast an eye back over her immaculate domain. At least some aspects of life were under her control. Control. It was what rendered existence manageable. When she reached the top stair the phone rang. She counted as its bells pealed twelve times. Her fingers itched to lift it but she willed them to cup her drinking chocolate, breathing suspended as she waited for the jangling to cease. When all was silent she walked into the bedroom and pressed a button to read the confirmation – he was calling. The magazine slipped to the floor and she placed the drinking chocolate sightlessly on her bedside table, toppling the alarm clock. Her uncharacteristic clumsiness flung tongues of milky liquid from the mug but Helen didn't notice the pool's inching progress towards the table's edge, or the way it dribbled onto her chrysanthemum-embroidered duvet cover. She curled, foetal fashion, with a pillow clutched to her cheek, too distressed to weep. Longing washed over her. And remembering.

CHAPTER 2

He throws himself onto the ground and subsides against a tree trunk, mute with misery. Sweating from his headlong pelt, he tugs open his shirt buttons to create a current of air against his torso. His pain is so intense she reaches out instinctively, chafing his inert hand. Helen searches for words of comfort – lies or truth, no matter so long as they soothe – but can find none. Every angular line of his body exudes desolation and it gashes her to witness it almost as much as it wounded her to watch the scene five minutes earlier between the boy and his rabid father.

Impulsively she slides onto her knees in front of him, the leaves crackling on impact, and takes his face between her hands. He's no longer sprawling, disconsolate, but watching her now, mesmerised, as she edges ever closer, bridging the gap between their bodies. Helen's unaware of what she's about to do until it happens. Her pulse is erratic, her body curves forward of its own accord; her lips sink onto his and cling there for the space of a heartbeat. There's a momentary hesitation, then she feels his lips move under hers, warm and moist.

Pinpricks of perspiration flare around the pulse-point map of Helen's body. She's tingling and the intensity of her reaction causes her to waver – she pulls back and looks at him, leaning on one hand to steady herself. An indefinable gleam in his expression touches her immeasurably. She subsides towards his mouth, even as he moves towards hers. Their lips collide, his chin rubs against hers and she experiences surprise at the grating of his stubble, then has no further conscious thought.

The two are subsumed by sentience, mouths softening into one another, captivated by the delirium of pleasure. Her hand cradling his head scrapes against the abrasive texture of the tree trunk but the pain does not register. She presses against him, winding her arms around his neck, and her body against his incites a change of mood for his mouth is no longer whispers; there's urgency in his serrated breathing and in kisses that clash teeth against teeth.

She disengages and rests her face in the hollow of his shoulder. A smattering of hairs clump in the sternum hollow between the salmon-pink nipples and her own hair tickles him as she kisses her way along his chest until she arrives at the downy belly button. And stops. She's paralysed by a mole an inch to the left of his navel which she recognises as the twin to one she has on her own body. He pulls her to him, attempting to reignite her fire with his, but it's too late. Reality has doused her and she's dripping from it. She pushes him away and runs as though flight alone can promise expiation.

'It didn't happen,' she moans, grinding to a halt. But the sensations whirling through her body are a contradiction.

'Ready to come out and play?'

It was Molly on the doorstep, encased in a calf-length black Afghan coat, collar pulled high against the wind.

'You look like Snow White in that collar,' said Helen. 'I thought we were meeting in the Life Bar. Anyway, we're not supposed to be there for another forty-five minutes.'

'I used to be Snow White but then I drifted.' Molly's hip-jutting Mae West impersonation backed Helen directly into the living room of her house – the hallway was knocked down to maximise space – and she kicked the door shut behind her with ankle-strapped heels so spindly Helen was amazed she could stand upright, let alone manoeuvre in them.

'I can tell from those shoes you're aiming for slut appeal tonight,' remarked Helen. Only half-critically.

She was still in her bathrobe, although she'd invented a face and drawn it on and her dark Cleopatra bob was blow-dried into symmetrical perfection. Throwing on clothes was always the shortest component in the exercise, providing the brain-squeezing decision about what to wear had been reached. She'd solved that conundrum lying in the bath in her seaweed solution, bought on a weekend trip to Enniscrone when she'd luxuriated in the seaweed baths that had been a tourist attraction in the seaside town since Victorian times. It had taken a few minutes to overcome her repugnance when initially she'd seen the massive cast-iron bath really was packed with seaweed; somehow she'd imagined a sanitised version. But after a while she'd stopped noticing she was sharing the water with an excess of vegetation – and it had velvet-coated her skin like no other softening agent. Helen had balked, however, at obeying the notice which invited her to empty out her seaweed into the bucket provided. It was repugnant enough floating alongside slithery black-green vines, she couldn't reconcile herself to handling them too. Skulking out, in case she were called back to clear away her detritus from the tub, she'd nevertheless paused to buy a jar of powdered seaweed because of the mermaid undulating across the front and because it promised to caress her skin.

'That's the only kind of stroking I can expect,' she'd remarked, selecting the family-sized container.

But back to Molly, beaming as she produced a half-bottle of champagne from inside Afghan folds with the flourish of a magician conjuring up a dove. 'The Lifer at eight was a serviceable plan A but it was elbowed aside by plan B. We can share a cab into town. In the meantime this will start us on the right foot, oh Helen of Athboy.'

'You know I'm from Kilkenny not Meath,' objected Helen, extracting champagne flutes from the narrow cherrywood sideboard in her living room. 'Is it cold enough?' Her tongue was already mentally capturing and splatting the bubbles and savouring their scratchy descent at the back of her throat.

'Does my granny go to confession?' responded Molly. 'Wouldn't hand over the cash until the Greek god in the off-licence immersed it in his four-and-a-half-minute cooler machine.'

'And did he chat you up during the waiting game?'

'Didn't even remark on the weather.' Molly's face epitomised mournfulness. 'His customer relations skills are non-existent.'

'Maybe he had a rush on.'

'One other person came in and bought a few cans of lager.'

'So you stood there reading wine labels and being ignored for four and a half minutes? Poor Molly, this will wash those bitter dregs away.' Helen reached her a frothing glass.

'He didn't even pretend to be stocktaking. He presented his flawless profile and stared out of the window. Impassive throughout. I might as well have been a nun buying communion wine instead of a gorgeous blonde teetering provocatively on skyscraper heels and handing over my credit card – so at least he'd know my name – for champagne.'

It looked as though Molly were fated to sin with the Greek only in her fevered imagination – 'Thought crimes again this week, Father.'

Still, there was always alcohol. She rallied, clinking glasses with Helen. 'Death in Ireland. But not just yet.'

It was her St Augustine toast. She'd acquired it during her two years working in London and still nursed a fondness for it. All the expats chanted it; some even meant it.

As she followed Helen upstairs, Molly sighed. It was just her luck to have a crush on the one Greek in the country who didn't flirt, didn't notice women and wouldn't recognise he was being given the glad eye if he found it giftwrapped in his Christmas stocking. Call himself a Mediterranean – he must have Cidona pumping through his veins.

'He probably wears a vest. All those fellows from hot countries do, for sweat containment,' consoled Helen.

'Checked again tonight: no telltale lines,' said Molly. 'Hercules' body is a vest-free zone.'

She still didn't know his name but she'd christened him Hercules because he was the strong, silent type. She was sure those capable hands of his could strangle serpents, no bother to them. But he was sturdy rather than large, her usual preference in men. Heck, here she was bending the rules for him and he still wasn't interested. She had leaned against his counter in rock-chick shoes complete

21

with peep toes on a January night cold enough for snow-drifts and he hadn't so much as looked let alone leered. It was disheartening. It was insulting. It was enough to make a woman throw away her high heels and buy desert boots. Where was the point in shimmying into a man's shop in black shoes with red heels that added at least four inches to your leg length if he didn't betray a flicker of lust? It was downright unnatural. But no one with a glass of champagne in her hand could be truly woebegone. Molly knocked it back.

'Drink it while the bubbles are still smiling at you, Helen.'

She felt the familiar rush as it hit her blood stream at warp speed and added, 'He's probably too young for me anyway; he can't be more than mid-twenties. Now, never mind my legendary Greek, make some room in your glass for the rest of the champagne and show me what you're wearing. The image we're aiming for is strumpet with a *soupçon* of class.'

Helen, who never left anything to chance, already had the clothes laid out on the bed. Molly eyed them disap-provingly.

'Dear me no, these won't do at all. These don't spell "unattainable Jezebel". There's nothing that says look but you can't afford to touch. Moleskin trousers, matching waistcoat and Chelsea boots are all very well if you're going to the pub for a few drinks and want to be left in peace but that's not what we're after at all tonight. Our mission is to have the lads fretting into their pints because we're so distracting.'

Helen stroked her charcoal-grey waistcoat. 'And how does a "Come, woo me, woo me" T-shirt strike that quint-essential note which puts us beyond their grasp?'

'Abandoned that idea. I decided to shuffle the deck and

bring on the ace – the little black number.' Molly opened her coat to reveal a dress that chastely covered everything from neck to wrist to knee but clung for dear life to each square inch of flesh between, undulating over hips and breasts with a brazenness that drew the eye, pinioned it and ridiculed the concept of allowing it time off for good behaviour.

'Janey Mac, I'd fancy you myself if I were a man,' said Helen. 'Are you sure the rabble are ready for that?'

'Ready or not, here I come. Now let's throw comfort to the wind and drape you in something equally alluring.'

'I don't have anything in that category,' protested Helen, but Molly was already rummaging in her wardrobe.

She produced a gold slip-dress, discarded its modest surcoat and handed it to Helen.

'You're a demon in female form, Molly. I can't wear a bra with that, which means my nipples will show through.' She held her champagne flute before her like a talisman.

'You're flat-chested, it doesn't matter. But your legs aren't bad,' Molly added kindly, 'and that slit up the side will show one of them off, depending on –' she swivelled the silk dress on the hanger – 'which way around you wear it. I can't tell the back from the front on this, Sharkey. Shouldn't there be a label?'

'I'm not. Wearing. A gold dress. To the pub.' Helen drained her glass defiantly. 'Since you're determined to make a harlot of me, I'll put this on.' She produced a wispy dark blue dress. 'I've had it by for an emergency. But there's no need to break the glass,' she added, as Molly flung herself on the bed, kicking over her empty flute.

'A half-bottle wasn't enough. I should have gone for the full monty,' she ruminated, waiting for Helen to morph into a seductress. She brightened. 'Perhaps I should nip back and buy another half, see if Hercules is pining without me.'

'No time, the taxi's due any minute. Pass me those suede slingbacks. I know you haven't seen them before, they're part of the emergency package too. God knows if I'll be able to totter in them. I'm only going to places that have waiter service because I intend to do absolutely no walking in these. In the interests of avoiding a visit to casualty.'

Helen struck a catwalk pose. The dress floated flimsily as a cobweb across her slim body and plummeted at the back.

'Talk about capitulation. You certainly know how to do slut when you put your mind to it,' breathed Molly. 'Even in a navy dress.'

'It's not navy, it's midnight blue.'

The doorbell punctured their quibbling.

'That'll be the cab,' said Helen. 'Let's go to a hotel bar instead of the Lifer. The champagne has given me a taste for more of the good life.'

'We'll start in The Clarence where we'll trifle with the affections of U2 fans and tourists. Then we'll check the immediate vicinity for any pop stars who might be loitering, waiting for their limousines to pick them up. Obviously we won't waste time toying with them – rock gods can have anything they want from us. Afterwards we'll plunge into the night and cause all-purpose mayhem on the streets of Dublin.'

'Promise me this.' Helen clung to the banister as she negotiated the stairs. 'We'll do it sitting down.'

Helen reeled back indoors in the early hours, giddy from laughter and wine. She dangled her shoes by the straps and plotted a route towards bed, dimly aware that every stitch she was wearing reeked of smoke but beyond caring. She was about to nosedive and only her mattress could cushion the landing.

She giggled before oblivion claimed her. A mental image of Molly on her way to the ladies in the restaurant distracted her from sleep: urbane, sophisticated and with a ladder as wide as the Liffey snaking up the back of her tights. Helen chased in after her with the replacement pair she always carried in her bag, a Good Samaritan's deed that had Molly calling her the battery-powered Little Miss Ever Ready.

But Molly admitted she was glad of Helen's taste in sheer denier when they returned to their table and found the couple next to them had bailed out, to be replaced by four South African rugby fans weekending in Dublin for a Lansdowne Road match. What a result – the craic ratio was about to skyrocket up the Richter scale, although the friends had derived a certain entertainment value from spying on the first-daters preceding the foursome. Their body language had been fascinating. They could tell from the girl's this was going to be another case of sudden-death dating; the end was as visible as if the fellow had a dagger protruding from between his shoulder blades. It was pitiful watching the polite indifference with which she treated him. Molly was prepared to gamble a month's salary there'd be no good-night kiss; that girl would be ducking for cover before the car's handbrake was on. The Boers were a distinct improvement, she mouthed to Helen, just before turning towards them, radiating a glow of invitation so brazen even the Statue of Liberty couldn't have held her torch any higher.

The friends' return from the ladies precipitated copious

eyeball slewing while the fellows tried to think of an opening gambit. Easier said than done in view of the regularity with which they'd been raising and lowering their elbows since late afternoon. Despite Molly's signals, which spelled out 'Ready when you are, boys. Form an orderly queue and I'll attend to each of you in turn', the visitors had a few false starts before they were up and running. The whole point about picking up men was the fellows had to imagine they were the hunters. So Molly and Helen ignored 'Do you always wear so much perfume?' and a burst of 'Molly Malone' when they heard her name. 'Must try harder' was the subliminal message. Finally they decided to put the lads out of their misery and asked if they could recommend any of the South African wines on the menu, offering them a shatter-proof excuse to buy a couple of bottles and push their tables together. Mingling hands and mingling glances, step one of the courtship dance.

Molly automatically chatted up a massive specimen – Hercules truly was an aberration on her usual type, best categorised as the larger the better. Obviously, she'd once rationalised, she was in the grip of some primeval instinct to select the biggest troglodyte in the tribe – what could she do? It was genetic programming.

One of the South Africans pressed dessert menus on the women and tried to cajole them into choosing the restaurant's cheesecake speciality. Molly was willing – she prided herself on being available to temptation at all times of the day or night – but Helen frowned.

'You mean voluntarily order a dessert? A high-calorific, sugar-drenched, artery-clogging pudding? Ask for it and then eat it? I think not.' Her look was withering. 'And attempting to induce someone else to do it is even more reprehensible. I call that corrupt. It's the sort of behaviour that might be acceptable in the Transvaal but it simply won't pass muster in Temple Bar.'

A study in primness, Helen signalled to the waiter and asked for a chocolate fudge ensemble that made the cheese-cake seem positively spartan. Meanwhile, Molly, not fully convinced she was witnessing a wind-up, heaved a sigh of relief and added banoffi pie – 'with ice cream as well as cream' – to the order.

The men had Irish coffees with whiskey chasers in case there was too much coffee in the coffees. Molly and Helen exchanged pitying glances at their ignorance – by the dregs of the weekend these visitors would have more faith in Irish coffees. Then Molly became engrossed in experimenting whether Hercules' place in her affections could be usurped by a Goliath of a South African with blond hair and – a million points deducted for this – a moustache that settled on his upper lip like a third eyebrow. She was inclined towards giving him a chance, when she became aware that the foot tapping against hers under the table didn't belong to . . . what was his name anyway – Pieter? . . . but to Helen. Who seemed to be suggesting, make that insisting, they adjourn to the ladies.

'How are we going to rid ourselves of the away team?' hissed Helen, surrounded by mirrors and wash-hand basins.

'I didn't know we wanted shot of them.'

'Eejit, of course we do. We don't want to go clubbing with that crew playing albatross.'

Molly brightened. So Helen was up for a stint in clubland. Usually she ended their evenings out when the restaurant staff stacked chairs around them. Molly flicked one of her corkscrew curls and waited for an escape plan to inspire her. Nothing happened.

'It's a long shot, angel face, but there's just one course of action open to us,' she said eventually.

'Name it.'

'We tell them we're tired and we're going home.'

Helen considered. 'They'll suggest accompanying us,' she pointed out. 'Should we mention our boyfriends will be waiting up?'

'Shame on you, Sharkey, depending on a man – or the shadowy outline of one – to spring the trap. So much for your feminist principles.'

Helen pulled a face. 'Fair's fair, we've been leading them on. Behaviour like that isn't in the feminist handbook. And backless dresses don't leave much room for principles. So here's what we'll do: you ring for a taxi on the mobile from in here and when it arrives we'll have our handbags and coats at the ready, leap to our feet and exit in a flurry of "wonderful to meet you and enjoy your stay" civilities, blowing air kisses two yards west of their cheeks. Deal?'

'Deal. And the taxi will convey us straight to a club, not back to Sandycove via Blackrock.'

'Certainly. You can choose whichever club you like, as long as it's not too noisy, too dark, too funky, too happening, too crowded or too hot.'

'Wonder which club is most popular with Dublin's Greek community,' puzzled Molly.

'Dublin doesn't have a Greek community. Now I'll wend my way back to the table while you set our fiendish plan in motion.'

The nightclub was predictably grim – 'face it, Moll, we're too ancient for clubbing'; 'speak for yourself, Sharkey' – but Helen enjoyed the sense of connection with the wider world that she experienced simply by being immersed in a communal mass of bodies. Sometimes she had the feeling she was too self-contained and an evening like this reminded her she wasn't an island. An isthmus existed, even if it tended to flood over.

Molly was right, there was nothing like a night on the tear. But in the aftermath Helen was jaded, spent both financially and physically. Her head was pounding – she couldn't consume alcohol at the rate Molly packed it away – and her system by the following lunchtime hankered for caffeine slightly more than it craved licence to lie on the sofa. Although both were imperatives. So Helen wandered out to the kitchen. As she pressed the button on the kettle, realisation slammed her with the jolt of a cattle prod. She hadn't thought of him once since 6.10 the previous evening. That totted up to eighteen hours in succession. Could this mean she was cured? Maybe the attraction was something she'd magnified out of proportion. Impossible to resist checking the answerphone, however.

She approached the phone, lifted it and the automated voice said: 'You have three new messages.' When she played them there was only static on the line – none of the callers had left a name. Except Helen knew there was only one caller and his identity was no mystery to her. A worm of unquiet niggled as she spooned granules into a mug patterned with an inverted comma – all right, it was a Celtic spiral although she tended to shy away from ostentatiously Irish objects. She made an exception in this case because it amused her to have a symbol representing infinity on an object with a lifespan as limited as a mug.

The phone rang: once, twice, three, four times. On the fifth peal she answered it.

'Helen, I've caught you in at last. Where were you last night? Never mind, you can tell me when we meet. I'm in Dublin, staying at the Fitzwilliam and I'm coming to see you. We need to talk. You must give me your answer. I'll order a taxi and be with you in half an hour or less.'

'No, wait. I'll meet you somewhere.'

'Where?' The man's accent was similar to hers, but with an English intonation overlaying the Kilkenny pronunciation.

'I'll collect you from your hotel; we can find a park to walk in.'

'See you in half an hour then. I'll be waiting in the foyer.'

'Patrick, I'm not even dressed yet. Make it an hour.'

Why oh why had she agreed? Why oh why had she stayed out so late last night? The hollows under her eyes would be sagging to her jawline. Why oh why hadn't she sprung up and taken a shower as she intended, instead of diving below the duvet for an extra snooze? Why oh why was she thinking in cliché-ridden why-oh-whys? But a final one – why oh why was she developing a spot slap-bang between her eyebrows? Still, she could take care of that in seconds; concealer was up there with the polio vaccination in terms of service to humankind as far as Helen was concerned.

She washed and dressed at warp speed, cramming herself into last night's moleskin rejects and adding a heavy woollen coat and velvet scarf. Her car keys went AWOL and she spent a frantic ten minutes turning her bag upside down and combing the pockets of all her jackets, until she found them in their usual place in the letter rack.

'Catch a grip, Sharkey,' she instructed the pallid face in the hall mirror. 'It's daylight, he's not going to pounce. And, above all, remember you have willpower. Use it.'

But as she jammed the gearstick into reverse instead of first she had a premonition it would take more than self-control to bring her home unscathed from this encounter. For he had a knack of dissolving any resolve she managed to muster.

CHAPTER 3

Patrick was standing on the steps of the Fitzwilliam Hotel scanning the traffic.

'You're late but I forgive you.' He jumped into the front passenger seat and skim-kissed her cheek.

She flinched, then tried to mask it by flicking her hair behind her ears.

'Will I find a parking space so we can go into the Green?' She gestured across the road towards St Stephen's Green, the city's oxygen lung.

'If you like. Or somewhere more private might be appropriate.' He took stock of her profile as she searched for a gap in the stream of cars sailing around the park

'Merrion then,' she agreed, and headed back the way she'd come.

He started speaking as soon as she'd parked her Golf. As she locked the car, still bending over it, words poured from him in a rehearsed cascade.

Helen touched his elbow. 'Wait until we're sitting down.'

But they didn't gravitate towards a bench; instead they paced the park's outer perimeter, past the gaudily painted statue of Oscar Wilde facing his home, looking as louche as any devotee of his work could hope for; past flowerbeds waiting for spring to resuscitate them; past the canvas backs of paintings attached to railings, artwork which tourists examined and sometimes bought. But only if it were sentimental or scenic and preferably both.

They returned to Wild Oscar's statue – another of Molly's nicknames – and paused to read some of his epigrams.

'I love his children's stories although I didn't discover them until childhood was a dim and distant memory,' said Helen. 'Especially "The Happy Prince"; I wept for days about the dead swallow.'

'How can a story called "The Happy Prince" leave readers sobbing? It's irrational,' Patrick objected.

'You've obviously never read it.'

'I'm more of a P. D. James man myself. That's when I find the time to read at all. It takes me weeks to plough through a paperback.' Patrick bent for a closer look at one of Wilde's witticisms on the plinth, immune to Helen's scandalised glance. 'How about this one, "We are all in the gutter but some of us are looking at the stars."'

'I keep hunting for my favourite one – his spin on the love–hate relationship between parents and children.' Helen followed the plinth around its four sides but couldn't locate it. 'I can never remember the exact wording but it's to do with children beginning by loving their parents, then judging them and rarely, if ever, forgiving them.'

Patrick zipped his flying jacket against the chill. 'Obviously too depressing for the tourists, that gem. Safer to stick with the ones that lend themselves to posters and T-shirts' He laid an arm casually across her shoulder; she sidestepped just as casually to widen the gap between them, and it dropped away.

Two Americans nearby were studying Oscar's statue.

'He made perfume, right?' The woman's voice was so penetrating it was impossible to ignore.

'No, honey, he was a writer.' Her male companion corrected her to Patrick's and Helen's relief. Otherwise they'd have felt obliged to set her right. National honour demanded it.

'One of his books was turned into a movie,' continued the knowledgeable American. 'It was called *A Picture of Dorian Black.*'

Patrick and Helen cringed in unison and turned their steps towards the centre of the park where there were no statues to attract sightseers. As they walked – it was too wintry for strolling – they spoke of his life in London, hers in Dublin, their shared experience growing up in Kilkenny, of jobs and homes and even the lighthouse tattoo he aspired to as a boy. It emerged that he'd actually visited a tattoo parlour, clutching the readies, during his first summer in England but reconsidered when he encountered the needles. Helen laughed aloud while he described his flight, still clinging to the patterns book, and again he spontaneously rested an arm on her shoulder. This time she allowed it to stay.

By and by she sighed. 'We should talk.'

'I thought that's what we were doing.'

'Chewing gum chatter.'

They ensconced themselves side by side on a park bench, isolated against the grumble of traffic a few yards away, not touching but acutely aware of each other, and he asked her to tell him what to do. She told him. He asked her again. Her answer didn't vary. Then he nodded in acknowledgement of her prudence and said he'd return to his hotel now. He was staying overnight, catching the Monday morning red-eye flight back to London.

Helen knew she should feel as though the iron bars encircling her chest had been yanked off; instead it was as if their diameter contracted and they tightened, a tourniquet on her diaphragm. But she realised it was impossible even to contemplate love with this man.

And so she prepared to walk away. Until a minuscule movement changed everything.

Patrick was waiting for Helen as she tugged at a glove lying in her lap, attempting to pull it back on, but her fingers couldn't find the openings. Her head bent forward, her hair shielding her face, a flimsy carapace against this world breeding bleakness now they were on the brink of taking their leave of one another. She struggled against a sense of loss, an emotion as bewildering as it was overwhelming, for how can you mourn the absence of something you've never had?

And yet she did keenly feel a void. She knew he couldn't be the one to fill it, although meeting him after three years had wrenched open the vacuum. So she heaved a rustling breath of resignation and nodded towards Patrick, signalling she was ready. Time to walk away from this windy park, where they huddled in scarves and coats, their bodies trembling in the winter chill but their minds impervious to it. Time to walk away from each other.

But the glove impeded her efforts at composure. Tears sprang in her eyes as she channelled her frustration at her and Patrick's self-imposed separation towards the glove. In a passion, she hurled it to the ground – an insignificant movement charged with import. The butterfly's wings that flapped up a hurricane. For he bent to pick it up and as he reached the leather to her, their eyes connected; it was as if her misery flowed and melded with his and he could not bear to acknowledge their imperative to separate. Patrick stretched his hand out and guided her head onto his shoulder and she nestled against it. They sat without speaking or moving, his hand splayed around her skull . . . there was such comfort in his touch.

In the aftermath, attempting to make sense of what followed, Helen thought there was an inevitability about their caress and the rollercoaster experience it precipitated. Did they really think they could put the brakes on something so powerful? Yet the human capacity for self-delusion is infinite. So she lay against Patrick with her head on his shoulder, his stubble bristling her forehead, and was suffused by exaltation. Nothing mattered beyond this moment ringfenced in time.

She had no way of knowing if they rested together for minutes or hours, leaching solace from their togetherness and content in the chrysalis of one another's embrace. After a while she became aware of children's voices as they ran along the path near the bench, arguing about the ownership of a comic. A woman's voice interjected, refereeing the dispute. Helen lifted her head in the direction of the sounds, hesitant about her and Patrick's public intimacy. Cities weren't truly anonymous, particularly not ones as village-proportioned as Dublin – above all when there was something to hide. The voices seemed to be receding. His hand on her hair urged Helen's head back to its perch. She needed no second bidding; it belonged there.

This time Patrick stroked her hair, winding its skeins around his hand and threading them through his fingers. Once she felt him incline and inhale their scent. Then his hand dropped to the area of her back between her shoulder blades and rhythmically he stroked in circles, easing away a misery she'd scarcely acknowledged existed. And still she kept her face turned from his, for she was loath to meet his eye. Reluctant and paradoxically drawn to it.

She felt Patrick's lips brush the top of her hair. It wasn't a kiss, more an unconscious gesture as he moved his head to incline it cheek down on top of her. She waited, accepting the weight of him, and then raised her face to his and they looked at one another. There was turmoil, a churning such as she'd known only with him. And without him. They gazed, grey eyes swimming into grey-green, then she found herself smiling and she could never recall whether he smiled first and she responded or if it was the other way around. But smiling they were, into one another's face, with an unfettered joy.

They had nothing to smile about. Even as he held her a recess of her subconscious warned she should drop this encounter into amber – store it up against future barrenness – and yet when she looked into the face of the man she loved she could not but register pleasure A memory of reading about Richard Burton gatecrashed her mind. He'd told once in an interview how he'd laughed aloud when he first met Elizabeth Taylor because she was so exquisite. Helen felt like laughing too, even as she studied the path Patrick's eyebrows cut across his face and the curve of his mouth – a mouth she knew already as well as if it grew on her own face.

A splattering of rain tiptoed across them, an apologetic reminder of a world beyond their cocoon, and Patrick stood, holding his hand out to her.

'Come on. I've already seen to it you're half frozen, I'm not going to have you drenched as well.'

His hand gripped hers, lacing fingers, and he pulled her to her feet. She'd gladly have sat on that bench until they seeped into the structure, matter fusing with matter, but she allowed herself to be drawn upwards, and walked towards the exit. Towards real life.

Near the gate a clump of snowdrops bowed their heads against the wind; Helen marvelled that no sound emanated from their bell-like heads – she always expected them to chime.

'There are snowdrops in the front garden of a house in the street behind mine,' she told him. 'I haven't been in my own house long enough to plant any. But whenever I'm melancholic I look at their snowdrops and my heart is lifted. I sometimes feel like knocking on the door and thanking the owners for planting them. I'd like them to know how much joy their froth of tiny blossoms have given me this winter.'

'Perhaps they do know.' His grey-green eyes softened. 'Perhaps they've been watching from the window, noticing how you pause to look. They probably say, "There goes the beautiful girl who likes our snowdrops."'

She felt bashfully enchanted by the compliment, hardly daring to believe that Patrick might find her beautiful.

They walked on and still his hand was woven through hers. But trepidation coursed through her once the park was behind them and they were on the pavement; other people appeared and she dropped his hand. She had to be sensible, even if he seemed impervious to others noticing them behave like sweethearts. Helen didn't realise that, whether they touched or not, the lover's mark was upon them. They were linked by that invisible chain binding those who love, a bond which others sense. And occasionally envy.

By her car she offered him a lift back to his hotel. Patrick demurred; he needed a brisk walk to stamp the refrigeration from his bones. Helen yearned for him to step inside the metal box with her, to breathe the same air, to be physically close again. Perversely, because she craved it so much, she knew she should deny herself.

'I suppose this is goodbye then.' She doodled her key fob across the moisture on the passenger window.

'I suppose.'

Vehemence laced her voice. 'How I hate that word.'

'Then let's not say goodbye yet,' said Patrick. 'Come for a coffee with me. Let's try the art gallery.'

She went. Virtue definitely wasn't its own reward and she was being pious enough without aspiring to martyrdom. Besides, they'd be safe in a public place. Consenting adults drinking coffee, what could be more innocent. To the onlooker.

'We have to admire one exhibit at least,' she stipulated. 'Maybe the Caravaggio. I'll show you where he painted Judas Iscariot's ear in the wrong place and had to blot it out and re-draw it. I like that – it shows genius takes effort as well as inspiration. More credible than being swept along by the muse.'

She was gabbling, Helen realised, but the way his eyes lingered on her mouth unnerved her.

She hurtled on. 'I can't be doing with people who only go into art galleries to drink coffee and buy greetings cards. Kevin Boylan, who's in my pod at work, meets all his pick-ups there. He thinks it portrays him as cultured, but he wouldn't know a Yeats from an O'Conor. He's the sort of culture you find inside the teapot after you've forgotten to wash out the dregs for a couple of weeks. My friend Molly, the journalist on the *Chronicle* – you should remember her, everyone does – has just signed on for a course of lectures here. I wanted to, but Thursday nights are impossible because –'

'Helen, we can look at the Caravaggio.' Patrick intercepted her torrent. 'We can look at as many Caravaggios as you like.'

'There is only the one,' she said. But she stopped prattling.

He fetched coffee while she pretended to read the gallery's February brochure. As he placed the cup and saucer in front of her he trailed his fingertips across her face. She started; the gesture was so tender, so instinctive, it sent delight coursing through her veins, but was he completely insane? Anyone could have observed them.

There was silence. When you want to speak of love, any other conversation is too trite to contemplate. Or maybe, she pondered, they were both struck dumb by their *coup de foudre*. It wasn't totally unexpected, it seemed to have been there always in her life, and yet . . . there's no way to prepare for meltdown.

'Do you believe in love at first sight?' she asked.

Patrick slanted a glance at her. 'How could I not believe?'

But love, she thought later, is supposed to exault you, to energise you. This love was packaged in wave after wave of misery. Being with him rendered her bleakly disconsolate and not being with him glazed her in yet more desolation. The joy was sporadic, the guilt permanent.

Some people, she reflected that night, lying in bed with her brain whirring, were able to make it work. They fell in love with people who reciprocated. They invented lives together – homes, children, pets, sun-and-sand holidays, Sunday lunches with other couples. Why not her? Why couldn't she fall in love with a man who was available – that would be a flying start. Start as you mean to go on, isn't that what they say? No wonder she was toppling over hurdles. But it was all a matter of luck, Helen concluded resentfully, and she'd been short-changed.

The theorising and labelling and deconstructing and attempting to make sense of something that defied definition came later, however. For now she was drinking latte, content to feel his shoulder against hers. Body heat – no comfort could match it. He brought her a scone and jam, she knew she'd never be able to eat it tidily and ignored it until he cajoled her to slice and nibble it.

'You don't eat enough,' he scolded. 'There isn't an ounce of flesh on you. You need someone to look after you.'

'There's no one to do that. I must be more trouble than I'm worth,' she shrugged, but her heart was singing.

'Do you remember when we all used to go on holidays to a leaky caravan in Tramore?' asked Patrick.

She rolled her eyes and giggled. Theirs was invariably the wettest fortnight of the summer, the first two weeks in July – decreed by Helen's mother from habit because her parents had always taken her away then. But her mother grew up in Belfast and Helen's grandparents had wanted to avoid the North's tribal tensions during the run-up to the Orange parades on the Twelfth; it was hardly relevant in Ballydoyle, a mote of a village in County Kilkenny.

'Who could forget Tramore: Aran cardigans over our swimsuits and goosebumps among the freckles – the epitome of the Irish summer?' said Helen.

'Do you ever go to Tramore at all now?' He tapped his spoon against the handle of his cup.

'Haven't been for years. The last time I was there we were on our way to the Burren – I know it was a convoluted route – and stopped off for chips. It looked seedy and peeling but it was out of season, and I've heard the place is buzzing now.'

'Shall we go? Will we jump in the car and head off?'

Helen looked at him in wonder. 'Tramore in late January – have you been so long in London you've forgotten what it's like, Patrick?'

'Come on, it's the best time. Think of the Atlantic breakers, the salt air, the strip-the-flesh-from-your-bones freshness of it all. We can go into the amusement arcade and shove coins into the claw machine, win you a cuddly toy instead of all the gobstoppers we ended up with as kids. I'll buy you an ice-cream cone with everything on top.'

His enthusiasm was infectious.

'Let's do it,' she concurred.

However, with her agreement, his get-up-and-go stood up and left. His excited expression evaporated, he clattered his cup against the sugar bowl. 'It's too late in the day.'

Did he mean literally or figuratively? she wondered.

'We'd never reach there before dark,' he added. 'We'll do it another time.'

'Sure,' she agreed, knowing there'd be no other time.

All they had was now. There was no future for them. Certainly not as lovers; she didn't think as friends – that required a mental somersault she was incapable of executing. And comradeship was unsafe. It offered intimacy and they needed distance.

She was word-perfect on the theory, no bother to her, it was this business of executing it that foxed her. So when they loitered on the pavement after their coffee, and instead of turning his steps in the direction of his hotel Patrick walked towards her car, she didn't object. Helen should have pointed out he was going the wrong way but she held her tongue.

Only five more minutes, she promised herself. That's not too much time to steal for ourselves; as remains of the day go, it's meagre enough.

At the car she paused and turned to him. 'Goodbye then. It's for the best. And for what it's worth, I truly think we're doing what's right.'

His bewildered stare implied the decision they'd jointly

made in the park was a revelation. Had he blacked out and forgotten? This was ridiculous – they *agreed* on a course of action. Mutually. She jingled her keys, stuttering something inane like 'Take it easy'.

'Can I come home with you? I'd like to see where you live. So I can imagine you there.'

'No!' Helen practically screeched the refusal. 'I mean,' she amended, 'the place is a tip. I'll invite you over sometime. Yourself and Miriam.' She said the woman's name deliberately as a reality fix.

He ignored it. 'Please.'

She compressed her resolve. One of the pair had to be strong and he was caving in like ice under sunshine.

'Patrick, don't ask me,' she supplicated.

'I am asking.'

He tilted her chin upwards so their eyes met and she felt like submitting because she didn't want to be firm any more. She didn't want to be virtuous or to worry about doing what was right. She wanted to love and be loved. And this compulsion was beginning to outweigh any other consideration.

'Another time.' Helen willed him to leave her alone, knowing if he pressed her again she'd yield. And a miracle happened – he retreated.

'I'll call you,' said Patrick.

He walked away without a backward glance. She watched him until he disappeared from sight and then she watched the empty space which his frame had filled. His tall, lean, rapidly moving shape.

She knew she should feel relief at averting something they'd both regret when the insanity passed. But she was conscious of desolation and the prescience that unfinished business dangled between them. As this certainty over

Helen she leaned against the car door to steady herself, for she suddenly felt unable to support her own weight.

Dear God, what were they letting themselves in for?

CHAPTER 4

Helen pulled over at a Centra to collect the Sunday papers on her way home. As she wandered along the aisles, lobbing into her basket purchases that she definitely didn't need and probably didn't want, the idea of surrounding herself with supplements and a conveyor belt of tea against a backdrop of easy listening music lacked its usual appeal. Molly's apartment wasn't much of a detour – she'd hive off there.

Molly was wearing glasses, which meant her hands were too unsteady to negotiate her contact lenses, although at least she was dressed. Sometimes she lasted all day Sunday without prising off her dressing gown.

'You're up and about early – it's only four o'clock,' said Helen.

By way of response, Molly extended the elastic on her joggers to show she was still wearing her pyjamas beneath. The polar bear ones. 'I like to keep them on during days when I might have to crawl back under the covers at a moment's notice. I suspected this might be one of those days,' she expanded.

Helen followed her through an archway into the kitchen, where unwashed dishes were stacked on work surfaces like mockeries of the tall food trend all the rage a few years previously.

47

'I don't have any milk,' said Molly, 'but I have lemon left over from the gin – I drank it all before I was halfway through the lemon. If I make tea you can slap in a slice.'

'I came prepared.' Helen brandished a plastic carrier. 'This deceptively humble container is a receptacle for milk, cinnamon bagels and Sunday newspapers.'

'Magnificent. If you remembered to buy proper coffee I could plunge us some. No? Never mind, saves me from overdosing and turning all jittery and thinking I need a cigarette, and if I could get through last night without buying, borrowing or mugging for them, I can get through the morning after.'

'So you saw some of the morning?' Helen was surprised.

'Negative. Technically I saw nothing of the morning, unless you count last night. But "the afternoon after the night before" doesn't have the same ring to it. Do the bagels have raisins?'

'Naturally, Molloy.'

Molly recoiled. 'Helen, I've begged you from the first day I met you never to use that name. It's meant to be a secret.'

'How can the fact that your name is Molly Molloy be a secret when it's splashed over the *Chronicle* on a daily basis?'

'I don't have a byline on a daily basis, only when I write a story – sometimes I only do a crossword puzzle and make personal calls. Anyway, when I'm not working I like to forget the tasteless joke of a name my parents saddled me with.'

'So you've changed it by deed poll, excised it from your passport, driver's licence, credit cards, electoral register . . .' Helen periodically trotted out the list to torment Molly.

Molly affected deafness, rustling through the carrier for bagels, which she jammed into the toaster – complaining when the raisins plopped out and joined charred bread crumbs on the floor of the gadget.

'Library cards, bank account, P60, health club membership . . .' Helen continued inexorably.

'You know I promised my mother I'd never change the name – it was Granny's.' Molly passed a couple of used mugs under running water, her concession to clean china. 'My only hope is to marry someone with a more acceptable name – let's face it anything else would do – and, hey presto, no more Molly Molloy. I could be Molly Dunphy or Molly McGinty or Molly Popadopolis.'

'Don't tell me that's Hercules' surname.'

'Haven't a notion. But it's bound to be something that defies spelling and pronunciation. And, you know what, it still has to be better than Molloy.'

'Only when it's teamed with Molly,' Helen objected. 'Although Malone wouldn't be an ideal partnership with Molly either. You'd never hear the end of that cockles and mussels song.'

Molly crunched on a bagel, spurting butter onto the worktop. 'I never hear the end of that as it is. Even last night's South Africans knew the words.' She wiped her fingers on her tracksuit bottoms – 'They're for the wash anyway' – and added: 'Greeks have a sweet tooth. Everything is drenched in sugar and deep-fried; I saw the tail end of a programme about Greek cuisine on the television while I was waiting for the *Fair City* omnibus. They eat honey balls and baklava and all sorts of cavity fodder.'

Helen struggled to follow Molly's thought process. 'So you've gone off him now because that svelte body is a blob waiting to erupt?'

'Absolutely not.' Molly was outraged. 'What sort of a flibbertigibbet do you take me for? Don't answer that. No,

I just thought it showed a human side. The next time I go to the offie I can look at Hercules, lounging there all remote and disdainful, and imagine him with honey dribbling down his chin.'

'Dangerous,' cautioned Helen. 'You'll find yourself wanting to lick if off him.'

Molly quivered, mimicking libidinous excess, and Helen set aside the *Sunday Tribune* headlines she was scanning. 'Tell me what else you learned about Greeks before you bring the ceiling crashing down on top of us.'

Molly sipped coffee and consulted a mental inventory. 'The men are philosophical and like to discuss Socrates. That reminds me, I meant to look him up, check out his spin on life: the distillation of Socrates' wit and wisdom in three sentences or less. Back in a second; I have to dig out the reference book.'

Despite the chaos Molly lived in she always knew where to lay her hands on a book. She returned and read: '"The celebrated Greek philosopher, died 399 BC, whose method of teaching was to ask his interlocutors simple questions, thereby exposing their ignorance."' She frowned. 'That's all very well but I need a bit more to dig my teeth into, did he sodomise boys, commit suicide, live in a barrel – no, that was Diogenes, now he was a dude. Alexander the Great offered him anything he wanted and he simply asked him to stop blocking his sunshine.' She tapped her teeth. 'What did Socrates believe in? Was life a vale of tears or is that Catholicism intercepting my brainwaves? Was he all for *carpe diem* or did he believe suffering maketh the man?'

'Check him out on the Internet at work. Now that the bagels are eaten shall we go to Blackrock market?' Helen required continuous distraction. Patrick's face kept superimposing itself on Molly's.

Molly's voice spoke from Patrick's mouth. 'All the stalls will be shutting up by now. Besides, I've no money.'

'Then don't buy anything.'

'Get thee behind me, Satan,' shuddered Molly. 'That's always the time you see hordes of possessions you can't live without. And apart from anything else —' she cast a critical eye around her cluttered flat — 'I need more chattels like I need liposuction. Correction, I *do* need liposuction, but that's another story. So that'll be enough temptation out of you, oh possessor of the face that launched a thousand guilt trips.'

'I thought you prided yourself on being perennially temptable.'

'No, it's becoming too predictable. People don't see me as a challenge any more. All the others in the office are coaxed when someone wants to drag them off to the pub or out to Bewley's for a cherry bun but they just assume I'm game, my coat is reached to me and off we head.'

'Will we take a walk, then?' suggested Helen. 'It can trickle past the off-licence if you like. You can check if the Geek is practising his profile angles?'

'Don't you mean the Greek?'

'Whatever. Anyway, I want a look at him. I have a theory he might be squinty-eyed if he keeps presenting his side view to customers. Doing a Padraig Pearse?'

Outrage emanated from Molly.

'Sharkey, I'm sorely inclined to frogmarch you straight to the shop so you can see for yourself how unsquinty his eyes are, how clear and intelligent and sensitive those compelling orbs are, but I look like a bag lady and my hair's a haystack. I can't go spoiling last night's lissom impression. Anyway, I suppose I should take a look at the Sundays in case any of

51

the stories have legs and I have to follow up the follow-ups in tomorrow's papers.'

She deposited her chin in her palms and started speed reading. Never was there a reporter less interested in news on her days off than Molly. Colleagues took trips to the jungle and still managed to devour papers; Molly couldn't so much as bring herself to turn on the TV headlines on a day off. It smacked of work.

Silence punctuated by rustling lasted half an hour while Molly digested the main stories and Helen read about how to achieve the minimalist style in your home. Interior decorator's suggestion: be ruthless. Helen's conclusion: be patient and the post-minimalist look, otherwise known as how real people lived, would be back in vogue. At least she kept her clutter tidy. She glanced around Molly's squalid kitchen and shuddered.

Molly slammed down the last of the newspapers. 'What about those rugged ruggers? We had a laugh with them. Why did we dump them again?'

Helen, who could restrain herself no longer, was binning some flowers so deceased they were virtually desiccated as they sagged from a Mexican pottery vase on Molly's windowsill. 'We had enough of them.'

'I hadn't. I was on the brink of having more of one of them.'

'Exactly. I rescued you in the nick of time. A simple thank you will suffice.'

'I'm not sure I feel gratitude,' complained Molly. 'I could be tucked up in bed with him in The Burlington, ordering room service and allowing him to give me a foot massage.'

'Or you could have your hand jammed to your forehead moaning, "How could I? Have I no self-respect?"'

'Now you're confusing me with yourself, Helen. My

52

self-respect would be one hundred per cent intact after a one-night stand with a South African too drunk to remember my name. Not everybody has taken your vow of chastity; some of us enjoy a straightforward lunge for the sheets.'

'Fair enough. But if you'd stayed with the tourists you'd never have gone clubbing and met Gabriel Byrne showing some Hollywood types around with a view to using Dublin as the setting for a film they're casting.'

Molly managed a passable imitation of someone whose jaw was about to sweep the floor, sand and polish it for good measure. She gathered it up and demanded, 'How could I have forgotten meeting Gabriel Byrne? It was the highlight of the evening. Didn't he kiss my cheek? He must have taken a shine to me.'

'It wasn't spontaneous, Molly, you commanded him to – the poor man was only following orders.'

'Ah, feck that, I gave him the opportunity for something he was panting to do all along. I'm a touch hazy on the details. He didn't ask for my phone number, I suppose?'

'Didn't get a chance to, you thrust it at him. In fact you attempted to write it on his arm but the pen wouldn't work.'

'Never mind that. So my phone could ring at any minute with Gabriel Byrne on the line pleading with me to go for a drink with him. The day is acquiring a completely different complexion, Helen.'

'If you say so.'

'You don't think there's a fractional sliver of a chance that Gabriel Byrne might be intending to use my phone number?'

'Not unless he has a photographic memory. I saw the drinks mat you scribbled it on lying under the table.'

Molly was stoical. 'Saves me jumping like a scalded cat every time the phone rings. Anyway, I prefer them taller.'

'Your Geek is about his height.'

'Greek. And these are exceptional circumstances. I always make allowances for men who can dance to bouzouki music. Now, will you watch *The Age of Innocence* with me or do you have to charge home and polish your brass?'

'I don't have any brass. But since I've seen *The Age of Innocence* eight billion times with you, give or take the odd million, I'll pass. So I'll adjourn to Sandycove and tackle the ironing, I feel the need for some repetitive action therapy.'

'We can lay that on for you here, easy-peasy, Helen. My fabled reluctance to handle an iron doesn't preclude me from allowing others to do so on my behalf.'

'Molly Molloy.' ('Eek!' squeaked Molly.) 'I brought you bagels, I brought you milk, I brought you newspapers, I brought light into your murky life, I reminded you about groupying Gabriel Byrne, which inexplicably thrills you, I gave you the strength to propose dragging yourself from the breakfast bench to the sofa to watch a video. Surely you can expect no more of me.'

'So you're off then,' said Molly. 'Fancy the pictures on Friday?'

'Suppose so, unless I have a better offer. Sick to death of Friday nights in the pub with the office crowd whingeing about the boss/how overworked they are/speculating on who's emailing who with a view to some hands-on networking.'

'Obviously if either of us gets a better offer all bets are off. So you can take it as read that if I'm waylaid by a Greek bearing gifts I'll stand you up. Similarly, if you decide you can no longer ignore the attractions of Kevin at work, despite bravely denying yourself the chance of a snog with him at every Christmas party since you started at J. J. Patterson's, I'll be munching popcorn on my own.'

'I thought we were never to trust Greeks bearing gifts.'

'No, that's Greeks cadging lifts. Gifts are fine, gifts are feckin' brilliant, especially when it isn't even Christmas or your birthday.'

'Molly, this conversation is too silly, even for you. I'm off.'

'Straight home now. No deviating for adventures without me.'

The streetlights were already on; God, for the arrival of spring and a stretch to the evening. Helen climbed into the Golf and pointed it homewards. Except she didn't want to go home. Without Patrick it wasn't a home, it was an empty house. And it would be cold because she'd forgotten to set the central heater timer.

Helen heard the radio chattering as she walked indoors; she'd exited the house in such a rush to meet Patrick she hadn't turned it off. No harm; it would have acted as a burglar deterrent. It was tuned to a play about a young couple with a baby and as she brushed and hung up her coat, Helen cocked an ear. The man and woman were arguing but their quarrel was intercepted by the baby's wails. The sound of its inarticulate protests catapulted her back in time almost three decades, to when she was a small girl woken by her infant brother.

The baby's squawks in the next room disturb Helen. She listens, marvelling at their ferocity, the howling blast of indignity issuing from such a diminutive form. She waits for her mother's step on the stairs and the murmur of pacifying words but there's no creak of floorboards. She nudges Geraldine beside her in the bed. She's a year, a month and a day older than Helen; it's up to her to halt the baby's tears. But Geraldine mumbles, and rolls over in her sleep.

Helen shuffles barefoot onto the landing and listens. The linoleum is freezing underfoot and she wriggles onto her tiptoes, hugging her hands around her body for warmth. She hears the familiar voices of her parents raised in argument, irascible sounds floating upwards from the kitchen.

The baby is still sobbing but it's a plaintive wail now, as though he no longer expects consolation. Helen tentatively pushes the partially opened door to her parents' room. There's an anticipatory shuffle in the cot and the baby turns his head towards the widening crack of light. He pauses mid-sob, as though considering his next move, then redoubles his efforts.

She skips towards the cot whispering, 'Hush, little man,' mimicking her mother right down to the pitch of her voice. His crying eases off and he regards her with bulging-eyed curiosity. Through the bars Helen tracks a path along his tear-damp face, breathing in his milky scent layered with the acrid tang of urine. She casts around for a way to reach into him, spies the pink padded dressing-table stool and drags it across. The baby watches her, frowning faintly, as she balances precariously on the stool and delves into the cot.

He's more awkward to hold than she expects, heavier than when Mammy sits her down and gives her the baby to mind. But she clutches him tightly, digging her fingers into fledging fat, and hoists him inexpertly over the wooden bars.

'Hush, little man,' she croons, slipping down onto the

stool and inserting her thumb into his fist. His fingers fasten atavistically and he gazes into her face, eyes luminous in their moistness.

She smiles at him and he smiles back. Mammy says babies can't do that, it's only wind, but Helen knows her brother is smiling at her. She listens to his snuffling breath and a sense of peace settles on her four-year-old frame.

'Helen, put that child down immediately. How dare you come in here and waken him?'

The rigidly disapproving outline of her mother obscures the doorway.

'I didn't do anything. He was awake and crying already,' Helen protests, but the woman grabs the child, setting him off wailing at his earlier decibel-defying pitch.

'Now see what you've done, miss,' shouts her mother, smacking Helen smartly on the backs of her legs. She deposits the baby in his cot, still bawling, and raises her voice above the din. 'Pat, can you come upstairs and help me sort out your children? Must I do everything myself in this house?'

Bringing her face down close to Helen she catches her by the arm, pinching her above the elbow, and hisses, 'You're in trouble, miss. Just wait and see the trouble you're in. Your father will take his belt off to you; I won't be able to stop him.'

The baby's howls are so anguished that Geraldine appears in her toothpaste-stained nightdress, rubbing her eyes.

'Geraldine, go downstairs at once and tell your father he's to teach Helen some discipline.'

Geraldine stares mutely and is skelped into action.

'At once, I said, or you'll have a taste of the same.'

Geraldine patters away while Helen waits, clinging to the cot bars, immobilised with fear.

She tenses at the tread of her father's boots mounting the stairs; his belt makes a slithering sound as it's uncoiled from around his waist, the buckle jangling against the door handle. The baby senses the tension in the room and his crying jerks into whistling half-sobs. It's as though he, too, is poised for what follows.

'Pull your nightie up and bend over.' Daddy's voice is conversational.

She whimpers, pushing her face so hard against the cot rails that two indentations etch themselves into her right cheek. The baby is mesmerised.

'I'm waiting.' The voice is still gentle.

She's incapable of obeying. Her puny body quivers, shuddering and subsiding with gulping breaths.

Her father's hands seize each shoulder, bruising the flesh, and haul her away from the cot. The nightdress is yanked over her head and a button pops and rolls dizzily like a spinning top. As her father propels her to the side of the bed, face pressed against the rosy candlewick cover, Helen's mother walks from the room, steering a gawping Geraldine ahead of her.

With the first blow of the strap, cracking against her bottom and thighs, the baby howls. The belt rises and falls to the baby's screaming and it saves Helen the bother of crying. Her body twitches as her brother sobs for her.

Later, when she's blubbering in bed with camomile lotion on her welts and the trace of her mother's kisses damp on her face, Geraldine slips something smooth and round into her hand. It's the pearl button from her nightdress.

'I crawled under the baby's cot and found it for you, Helen,' she whispers.

Helen's fingers close over the disc with the same reflexive action that the baby's fingers fastened on her thumb. It's still wedged in her hand when she awakens the next morning. She flushes it down the toilet and washes her hands afterwards like a good girl.

She returned to the present with a jolt, her nails jagging crescent moons into the palm of each hand.

'How can Patrick love me? I'm unlovable,' whispered Helen, awash with self-loathing.

CHAPTER 5

Molly knew if she didn't get up right now there'd be no lying in bed waking up gradually with a cup of coffee, no leisurely shower, no time to drink a second cup of coffee while she applied her makeup. She lay on ten more minutes: that meant slapping on the warpaint at the DART station again; another five minutes: she'd just traded in breakfast – what odds, the cereal was stale and the bread could probably crawl to the toaster of its own accord. She wrenched herself out of bed and made it to the bathroom, bouncing off walls, before she ran out of time to wash.

Minutes later she was at Blackrock station, waving a mascara wand, which could double as a threatening weapon, in the direction of her eyes, and debating whether to collect a chocolate chip muffin or a toasted cheese sandwich on her way into the office. She found herself ordering the sandwich; obviously the great nutritionist in the sky was on her case again. She even asked for a few slices of tomato to accompany the cheese as a nod to healthy eating.

It was quiet as she strode through the *Chronicle*'s newsroom, aiming for the seat furthest away from the newsdesk. Out of sight, out of mind. Hopefully it wouldn't be a busy day; maybe extra advertisements would be booked and they'd drop a few news pages. She was two months behind with her expenses and tomorrow was the deadline. The paper's expenses forms were demonic to fill out; if there wasn't money in it you'd never persist. She barely had time to slide the wrapper off her breakfast when a 127-page report from the Department of Justice into drug abuse in prisons landed on her desk. Stephen Horan, the news editor, delivered a crocodile smile along with the depressing information that the security correspondent, who'd normally tackle this tome, was on holiday. Frank Dillon could reel off the difference between hepatitis B and C without looking it up while Molly wasn't even sure how to spell it. Nevertheless she was stuck with making a page lead out of the report. May it be lashing with rain wherever Frank was. She hoped he'd spent a fortune jetting off in search of winter sunshine and wound up with freak monsoons. She studied the report's index, quivering with distaste as she imagined all those bruised and prominent veins locked up together.

If only someone had explained to the prison junkies how many KitKats they could buy for a fix before they started down that road. Molly was a great believer in chocolate as the ultimate high. Her life was devoted to reading the backs of chocolate bars to assess cocoa solid content. White Toblerone was her all-time favourite, especially the massive surfboard version, but she was forever keen to track down and taste new chocolate sensations. Her handbag always contained a part-nibbled bar of something. Today it was Cadbury's Bourneville. Sometimes she bought Wholenut for protein, but generally she believed the nuts used up valuable chocolate space.

'Good weekend, Molloy?' asked Barry Dalton, who tended to sit beside her when their shifts coincided and there was a free desk. News reporters worked four-day weeks, in varying shifts, and this system meant no one was in a position to claim a patch of Formica as their own. It was possible to go weeks without seeing some of your colleagues.

Molly hadn't borrowed pens off Barry in at least a fortnight, and she was delighted to see him. As he needed even more caffeine than she did to make it through the day, she could always rely on him for mercy dashes to the canteen or Café Aroma.

'Come for breakfast and tell me all about your endless hooleying since I saw you last,' suggested Barry, convinced single people enjoyed fascinating social lives.

'This is breakfast-a-go-go.' Molly indicated her toasted sandwich and polystyrene cup.

'Eat up and we'll head off so.' His sing-song Cork accent was as pronounced now as the day he'd first arrived in Dublin, hefting a portable typewriter for the novel he'd never finish and a miraculous medal from his mother, lost before it had a chance to work any miracles. Unless it was working them for whoever found it.

'Barry Dalton, what sort of a porker do you take me for? Don't answer that. But even I need a breather before tackling a second breakfast. You can bring me back another coffee if you're headed for the canteen, though.'

'I'll give it a few minutes. It'll be jammed with all the classified ads girlies shortly.'

'Shame on you, you're supposed to be a happily married man. Mind you, half the kerb crawlers in the city are happily married men.'

'Did I intimate I'd be doing anything other than salivating, Ms Moral Majority? Obviously I operate on the *noli me tangere* basis. Besides, looking isn't a crime. It only proves you're a normal healthy male.'

'And that, your honour, is the case for the defence.'

Molly fired her sandwich wrapper binwards and drained the coffee.

Barry passed her the serviette she was scrabbling for. 'Normal healthy males have normal healthy urges which they don't act on because, um, remind me why we ignore our normal healthy urges?'

'You're happily married. And because you'd have no chance with the classified girls anyway because you're twice their age, podgy around the love-handles zone and you don't wear your shirt outside your trousers like the lads they go out with.'

Barry rearranged his tie across his bulging midriff. 'So my wife is lying when she says there's more of me to love these days.'

Molly rolled her eyes. 'Kay's a martyr. Or the most deluded woman in the country. Did you do fatherly things with the girls at the weekend?'

He sighed theatrically. 'I'm surrounded by a monstrous regiment of women. It's petticoat power at every turn. I had to go shopping with Kay and the girls on Saturday afternoon. It was vicious – five-and-three-quarter hours of misery and only one coffee break. If I hadn't been browbeaten into that vasectomy I might have a son by now who'd back me up against them.'

'Vasectomies are reversible, Bar. Any time you find a young one who takes your fancy you can trot back to the doctor and go under the knife again. That's if Kay doesn't get to you first. Don't expect me to shield you. Of course,' mischief glittered from Molly's eyes, 'those nubile twenty-one-year-olds you're drooling over are mad keen shoppers. Friday nights may be paradise but it's purgatory all day Saturday as you lug carrier bags from shop to shop and debate the virtues of scoop necklines versus halter. Men with significantly younger wives don't look euphoric. Try downright drained. Those chicks lend their men a just-basted glow for a short time, then exhaustion sets in. Whereas a plumply rounded hen of your own vintage is like a roast dinner – familiar and satisfying.'

Barry's pointy face acquired a knife-edge aspect as he gazed into the future – and quaked. 'Must you make straight for the farmyard at this hour of the morning?' he objected.

'It's for your own good,' Molly said. '*La vida loca* isn't all it's cracked up to be, Barry.'

He nodded. 'Kay's sticking the times rightly,' he conceded. 'She can still fit into the same size beautician's uniform she wore when I first met her and there's not many forty-one-year-old women you could say that for.'

'She's a gorgeous woman and I don't know how you ever persuaded her to marry you. She obviously has an infinite capacity for pity. Now will I fetch the coffees or will you?'

Barry lurched to his feet, sending his chair clattering. 'I'll go. The girlies should be trooping out for their breaks around now. Expect me when you see me, Molloy. I may be some time.'

Molly returned to the Department of Justice report. Wouldn't you imagine, she fumed, they'd have included a hand-out indicating which pages had the meat on them? She phoned Damien in the press office to complain. He insisted there had been a press release included in the package couriered to the paper but he'd email another. Molly cast an eye in the direction of the newsdesk and spied her press release. Typical, the news editor was using the hand-out that could have made her life ineffably easier to eat toast from. She glared at Stephen, scattering dollops of marmalade on the Department of Justice's bullet points, and he winked.

'Hung over from all the strumpet city exploits you single girls get up to at the weekend?' he called down the room.

Another man convinced he'd voluntarily renounced Sodom and Gomorrah when he took the marriage path. To hear him now, you'd believe he'd been a heartbreaker. Instead of which he courted Clodagh from the age of eighteen and lived with his mammy until he'd saved enough for a deposit on their first house.

Molly surveyed the lack of talent in the office. Only four unmarried men in the entire pool of reporters, sub-editors and editors, while they had their choice of a bevy of stunning women. Four. Not that you'd actually want to go out with anyone from your floor – too close for comfort – but it would be pleasant to have somebody you could at least fancy from afar without having to listen to him describe the ecstasy of cutting his child's umbilical cord or shake his head over the criminal cost of school uniforms. And as for the four who were still on the market – three had been well and truly picked over and Molly was convinced the fourth was a twelve-year-old masquerading as a grown-up.

Most of the married men were up for a snog, or more, after a few drinks. Even the ones who never trotted out those 'I'm only with her for the sake of the children' lines that made you want to shake them had the capacity to surprise you at Christmas parties. They seemed to think they were allowed a night off from being married, an amnesty courtesy of Santa Claus. You could sit at the turkey dinner beside a mouse of a man who spent the year scuttling out of your way if you met him in the corridor, safe in the knowledge that at least *he* wouldn't make a pass. He'd be wearing a snowman tie to testify that he knew how to let his hair down and he'd show you the photos of his children he carried in his wallet. A few glasses of mulled wine later you'd be trying to extricate his tongue from your tonsils.

Sport was the only department with a concentration of single, reasonable-looking men. But then they'd only go and bore the ears off you talking about matches. Sporty types were obsessive. Molly dated a soccer writer briefly when she worked on the *Evening Standard* in London; she still hadn't forgotten the way he monopolised the remote control belonging to her – repeat, *her* – television set to check scores. And she was convinced he kept an eye on the league tables while they courted on the sofa; he always arranged it so he was facing the TV set.

So what you have here, considered Molly, ruling out the sports department arbitrarily as she waited for Damien's email, was a concentration of married men, some of whom may well be ill-matched with wives and biding their time until the children were grown up, but most of whom were bored, lying to themselves never mind the girls they eyed up, and ready for any bit of distraction they could lay their hands on. Especially the laying-on of hands part.

Barry returned in time to stop her sending out an abusive all-users message on the computer system telling her male colleagues precisely what she thought of them.

Molly twisted off the lid of her coffee and slurped. 'No sugar, Barry.'

'Couldn't remember if you were taking it or not – you're as changeable as the seasons, woman – so I brought some sachets.' He scattered half a dozen on the desk in front of her. 'I'm smitten. There's a new recruit in advertising, she has the face of an angel.'

'Admire her from afar, Bar. You don't want the mystique spoiled by hearing her Dub accent or by discovering that she's only a few years older than your daughters.'

Barry shrugged, then performed an exaggerated appraisal of his colleague. 'Your hair is lovely today, Molly. Have you done something different with it?'

'What's your game?'

He radiated injury. 'It's a sad state of affairs when a man can't pass an agreeable remark without it being misconstrued.'

'Once again for the hard of hearing, what's your game?'

'I need to trade weekend duty with you. The outlaws are encroaching from Monaghan.'

'But you're off this weekend.'

'Exactly. Be a pal and let me work Saturday and Sunday instead of you. I'll go nuts if I'm stuck with Kay's parents for forty-eight uninterrupted hours of close family living.'

Molly swapped – but not before she made him promise to do all the coffee runs that day.

She was debating whether there were any other concessions she could wrest from him when her phone rang. It was an old schoolfriend, Mary-P (to differentiate her from Mary-R and Mary-Mac in the classroom); excitement laced with triumph was sizzling down the phoneline. It could mean only one thing: another day out in an extravagant hat. Molly mentally added an extra lunch to her expenses claim to cheer herself up and prepared to sound delighted.

'You'll never guess what I'll be doing in nine weeks' time,' said Mary-P.

'Having a sex change,' speculated Molly. 'Paragliding over Uruguay. Forming a cult.'

'Molly, you have the strangest notions. I'll be saying "I do" in front of all our friends and family when Paul asks me to love, honour and cherish him all the days of our life. Even saying the words gives me butterflies.'

'So he asked you to take out a joint mortgage with him at last,' said Molly.

'We've had one of those for two years. He asked me to marry him.'

'And you told him you couldn't because you weren't a priest.'

There was a pause while Mary-P digested this and tinkled an uncertain laugh.

Meanwhile Molly decided she was being ungracious and launched into effusive congratulations.

'It was so unexpected,' burbled Mary-P, who worked as a physiotherapist in their home town of Derry. 'He must have been planning it for weeks. We were in Donegal and he brought me to a picture-postcard waterfall just outside Ardara. I thought we'd stumbled across it but Paul had gone on a reconnaissance mission the previous week when he claimed he was visiting his parents and he decided it would make an ideal backdrop to a marriage proposal. We turned the corner and there it was, tumbling amid the heather. We stepped out of the car for a closer look and then he asked me. I must have looked a sight, the wind was gale force and my hair was plastered to my head but I said yes straight off, not a second's hesitation, and then he told me he'd like us to be married as quickly as possible rather than linger with a protracted engagement and . . .'

Molly watched Barry send an email; she squinted to detect the identity of the recipient but drew a blank.

'. . . so he rang my father, who hasn't been asked his opinion in twenty years, never mind his permission, but Paul is so wonderfully correct, I adore an old-fashioned man . . .'

Just so long as she doesn't ask me to be bridesmaid. Molly mentally ransacked her wardrobe and pondered whether she'd need a new outfit or could she wear the primrose coat and dress bought for the last wedding she'd attended. Nine weeks' time was early April, perfect spring weather for the combination. Could she trot out the same clothes, though? It depended on whether there'd be a substantial number of guests common to both Mary-P's and those other nasty nuptials. All she seemed to remember was sitting on a slice of the strawberry meringue confection they'd substituted for a wedding cake and being obliged to keep the coat on all evening to cover the stain. She wondered if Paul had any unattached friends likely to be at the bash. Then again, Paul was an anorak so there was a fair-to-middling chance his friends were anoraks too. She wasn't that desperate.

'What do you think, Molly?'

What did she think about what? She improvised. 'It's a tricky one,' she hazarded.

'Don't I know it,' said Mary-P. 'But there must be some compromise. It's not that I expect to be able to exchange vows by the waterfall – I understand it has to be in a church – but if we could even pledge our love in a public manner there it would add immeasurably to the occasion. I feel such an affinity with that waterfall; it's our special place.'

Molly shelved the lemon outfit. Standing by a waterfall in the wilds of Donegal in April required thermals and waterproof clothing. Mary-P was back on her 'Paul caught me totally unawares' hobbyhorse. How unexpected could a marriage proposal be when she'd been courted by the man for eight years including living with him for two? Molly decided fifteen minutes of this blithe-spirit session were as much as anyone could be expected to endure – even if she did sit beside Mary-P for most of her secondary school days. Naturally she hoped she'd be ecstatically happy, of course she'd be at the wedding, now would she ever feck off and stop making her feel like a failure because nobody, not even a nerd such as Mary-P's Paul Sheerin, wanted her hand in marriage? Or any other body part.

Molly pushed the phone away and contemplated notching up her blonde curls from streaks to an all-over peroxide. Say, a corkscrew version of the Marilyn Monroe look – subtlety was wasted on men.

'Do you think I should go blonder?' she asked Barry.

'Will my answer alter your decision to swap weekend duty with me?' His hazel eyes behind their John Lennon spectacles flickered anxiously.

'No.'

'Lash ahead if you fancy it.'

'But will it have men swooning at my feet?'

'Sure they do that already. So we're definitely on for the weekend transfer then?'

'Barry, I feel bound to tell you that your objectivity is under the microscope and not standing up to scrutiny. Now stop annoying me, I have to push on with this jail report.'

She managed to work her way through to page twenty-seven before Barry spoke again.

'Call for you, Molly, on my line. Which extension are you on?'

'It's probably a reader.' Molly shrank into her seat. Readers had a tendency to keep you talking for ages, suggesting an exposé on whatever little unnewsworthy – they were always unnewsworthy – obsession they'd latched on to. 'You wouldn't take a message, Barry? I'll never wade through this tome before lunchtime if interruptions keep annoying me.'

'Fine by me but it sounds like a personal call. I formed the impression he knows you. He asked for Molly, not Molly Molloy.'

She brightened. 'He' and 'personal call'; the combination equalled promising.

'Four-six-three-seven please, Bar.'

It was a very personal call; Molly's pulse accelerated as soon as she heard his voice. It was Fionn McCullagh, her ex-almost-fiancé. Technically he'd never proposed but they'd lived together for a year and had gone out with each other for another year before that, and everyone had assumed they'd eventually marry. Molly knew it was only a matter of time, although Fionn had insisted from day one he didn't believe in marriage and failed to see how it enhanced a relationship. 'It brings nothing to the party' were the words he'd used. You were with someone because you wanted to be and not because a piece of paper decreed it, that's what he'd told her. She didn't mind too much so long as they were together. She hadn't started practising her wedding march at that stage.

Molly and Fionn had been a couple because they'd chosen to be. Because they'd been inseparable. Because everyone had said they were meant for one another. Because they'd laughed at the same jokes. Because they'd both liked Indian food. Because the weak Irish sunshine had warmed their backs when they'd felt it together. Because the rain mattered less when they'd shared an umbrella. Because they'd been in love.

Except a trial three-month separation (his idea) had intervened. And when they'd met again in the Westmoreland Street Bewley's, *à la An Affair to Remember*, he was married to someone else. Already. In the space of three months. Some men can't be trusted out of your sight. The fellow who told her marriage was an anachronism and the only vows he'd contemplate were mountaintop pledges in the presence of a druid – and even that would be only for the craic – had stood up in church and said 'I do'. Wearing a cravat.

Hypocrite. Even now she tasted bile when she thought of Fionn married to someone else. It had happened four years ago and Molly could still feel the shock, the outrage and, above all, the grief coil in the pit of her stomach as though it were yesterday. He had sat opposite her in a corner seat – it took her fourteen months to set foot in that branch of Bewley's – and she hadn't noticed his wedding band. The shiny yellow ring. He'd waited until she'd taken a bite of her almond slice before telling her; she couldn't smell almonds now, even in hand-cream, without her innards convulsing. Her eyes had been drawn to his left hand as he'd spoken and the proof had glinted at her. Molly had never seen a colder metal.

His wife was a Scandinavian-born American citizen and as far as Molly knew Fionn was living in Seattle, probably drinking better coffee than he'd been accustomed to in Ireland. Now he was obviously back on holiday and strapped for company, she decided, even as they meandered through the social niceties whereby former lovers pretend they're great friends when one or both of them would much prefer the other to slide off the face of the planet.

Fionn. Taller than average but otherwise your standard Irishman. Medium face, medium voice, medium frame, medium fellow – at first glance. To Molly he was anything but medium. She'd never been able to establish to her own satisfaction how or why it was he colonised her affections, and seemingly effortlessly. There were other men around with fairer hair and bluer eyes but none of them looked at her in quite the way Fionn did. He'd fractured her heart, although she'd patched it up eventually, because you never knew when you might need your heart again.

'So will we meet in Bewley's for old times' sake, Molly? I'll buy you an almond slice.'

That doused her in reality; the sense of betrayal writhed inside her again.

'Grand, tomorrow it is then. It's about time you introduced Helga to that staple Dublin tradition, coffee and cake in Bewley's.'

'*Olga* –' he emphasised the name – 'is in Seattle. I'm home on my own, Molly. For good.'

Which meant the whirlwind romance had blown itself out. Which meant Fionn was on the market again. Which meant her heart could be broken again . . . or maybe not. She was four years older, four years wiser, four years better armoured against Fionn McCullagh. Anyway, chances were he was only being friendly; she shouldn't read too much into coffee. It was hardly a declaration of passion. For all Molly knew he hadn't thought of her once during his blissful years in blissful Seattle.

'Molly.' Fionn's voice dipped to a whisper. 'You're my one regret in life.'

The connection was severed.

CHAPTER 6

Molly had contemplated (a) a day at one of those health farms where they guarantee chip-pans of fat reduction or, preferably, (b) a body transplant before meeting Fionn, but there wasn't time for either. Instead she bought a new shampoo – an inadequate substitute but then life can be an inadequate substitute, for that matter. She also purchased a breath freshener and had almost used up the spray before she walked into Bewley's, eyes searching for an ordinary-looking man of thirty-three who wouldn't stand out in a crowd. Not half.

As soon as he smiled at her everyone else evaporated into obscurity. She was pathetic; she'd swear someone was playing a violin. Snap out of it, it's not as though this is a date with Hercules. It's coffee with an ex. A former lover who's now exactly the right age to be crucified. Which he deserved to be for his treatment of her. Maybe that was extreme; a simple crowning with thorns might suffice.

After a few minutes in his company Fionn seemed maybe not her saviour but definitely not her tormentor. The familiarity was the deceptive part as they sat opposite one another, catching up on four years' worth of news. It lulled her into a false sense of security; she had to keep reminding herself this man had chipped at the corners of her heart. If that organ was lopsided now it was because of him.

But Molly was charmed, all the same, to discover they still shared the same sense of humour as they automatically began sparring with each other. There was also something intriguingly different about him. She assessed Fionn as he chatted: the trademark arrogance appeared dented, but he was changed in other ways too, she was uncertain specifically how.

Molly didn't mention his wife, waiting for him to bite the bullet, but he showed remarkably little interest in grasping nettles or seizing bulls by the horns or . . . For God's sake, woman, repeat after me: bullets, nettles and bulls' horns have nothing to do with this date. Meeting. Old friends meeting. It wasn't a date.

She decided she'd have to raise the subject of his wife herself. She'd do it discreetly, lend him the opportunity to disclose as much or as little of the marriage collapse as he chose.

'So, Fionn, Helga turned wise to your wicked ways and dumped you. Was it your pathological aversion to washing or did she read the psychiatric report?'

'I think it was the phone call from the Vatican telling her she was giving shelter to a defrocked priest that did the trick.'

'I didn't think you could defrock priests; I thought the Catholic Church was stuck with them for life,' objected Molly.

'You're right, I'm not a defrocked priest. I'm still entitled to practise all the sacraments including hearing confession. So if there's anything you feel the need to get off your chest, my child . . .'

'Your confession would be streets ahead of mine in terms

of audience ratings. However, if you're too ashamed to admit your life is a failure and the most important relationship you embarked on went belly up, who am I to compel you? Confession is only good for the soul if you have a soul. Obviously that rules you out, McCullagh.'

He laughed, caught her eye and reached out to cover her hand with his.

'You're wrong, you know.' Fionn pitched his voice so low she had to lean across the table to catch his words.

'You're claiming to have a soul after all?'

'No, Helga, I mean Olga, wasn't the most important relationship I had. That was the time I spent with you.'

It was one of those freeze-frame moments. Molly's hand curled around his, she opened her mouth to speak – and then she saw him. Hercules. Reflected in the mirror at a table just along from them. She turned her head, checked down the row for confirmation and sure enough, it was her Greek. Except he appeared to be someone else's Greek judging from the proprietorial way a sultry young woman was rearranging his jacket collar.

Fionn followed her line of vision. 'Someone you know?'

'Yes. No. Sort of.'

'That's as clear as mud. Would you like to join them?'

'No, they look fairly content in each other's company. I don't care to intrude.' Her eyes lingered on Hercules, engaged in such an intense conversation with the woman he appeared to carry the weight of the world on his shoulders. Of course that would make him Atlas, not Hercules.

'Penny for them.' Fionn interrupted her meandering brainwaves.

With an effort Molly refocused her attention, steeling herself not to watch Hercules in the mirror. 'You have been away a long time; a penny wouldn't buy you much.

Whereas in the days when you lived here you could have snapped up a house in Dublin 4 for that.'

'Even Cromwell couldn't have snapped up a house in D4 for a penny, Molly.'

'True. He'd have taken it for free. No point in being a conqueror if you turn all law-abiding afterwards.'

When Molly glanced again, Hercules was gone. But it was time for her to leave too. She was due into the office at 4.30 p.m., so she gathered up her belongings and prepared to make tracks.

'I never did recite my confession,' said Fionn. 'Can I see you again? I'm still working up to the great unburdening.'

'Must be a whopper. Of a lie or a confession.'

'Tonight?'

'Won't finish until twelve thirty – bit late in the day for gallivanting. But I'm off tomorrow.'

'I'll drop by your place in Portobello and whisk you away for a pub lunch,' he offered.

'You see, you've been gone for centuries, Fionn McCullagh. I'm out in Blackrock now. I submitted to the responsibilities of adulthood two years ago and bought an apartment. One of these days I may even manage to buy some decent furniture for it.'

'Blackrock with the indecent furniture it is then.'

'No!' She rejected his offer with sudden vehemence, then hastily amended her refusal. 'I mean, somewhere other than Blackrock would make a change.'

'How about if I borrow my father's car and we drive into the Dublin mountains? I missed those fellows in Seattle. We could call into Glendalough if you like,' Fionn suggested

'Fine. I'll meet you in front of the DART station at midday.'

'I can collect you from your apartment, Molly. I wouldn't

want you loitering around street corners in this weather.'

'The station would suit me better. It's only a few minutes' walk and I, um, I can drop off my dry-cleaning on the way. Besides, if you don't want me skulking on street corners there's simple enough solution – don't be late. See you tomorrow.'

For a moment Fionn looked as if he were about to kiss her but Molly stepped backwards so quickly he didn't have a chance. That was a kneejerk reaction too. What was wrong with her? A kiss wouldn't have triggered the end of the world. But her assiduously reconstructed universe wasn't ready for a peck on the cheek from Fionn McCullagh.

Just shy of midday, as she hacked at the tangles in her hair, Molly still wasn't lucid on why she'd circumvented his kiss. He seemed to be aiming at her cheek – there was no harm in that. Social kisses were simply sociable. She occasionally allowed men she couldn't bear the sight of to kiss her cheek (the tyranny of manners), never mind someone she once imagined spending her life with – growing old holding hands with him. Molly marvelled at elderly couples she saw ambling hand in hand along the street: was it habit, was it affection, was it affectionate habit? They couldn't all be foreigners; some of them had to be Irish. Imagine your arthritic hands clasping someone else's arthritic hands and the touch sustaining you. She wasn't inclined towards wallowing but when she indulged in the rare one, say if she were confined to bed with flu, she sniffled at the thought of being wrinkled and unloved. Heck, she was already wrinkled and unloved at thirty-two. She longed to believe there was someone out there who'd take her gnarled eighty-year-old hand and make her feel cherished. It wasn't going to be Fionn McCullagh, that much was cast in stone. Even with his melodramatic regrets. Second chances were so second-rate.

Her buzzer sounded as she laced on boots. Must be the postman with a package.

'Molly? I see you've grown no more punctual since I knew you before.'

Fionn was standing on her doorstep – specifically hers and twenty-three others – and she hadn't even applied her lipstick. Courtesy demanded that she buzz him up.

'Stay where you are, I'll be straight down,' she instructed him. Courtesy could take a running jump. And since when did ten minutes late count as being late? Anyway, it was his fault she wasn't there on time, confusing her by parachuting into her life again. She addressed a running commentary to the mirror. 'Where's my lickstick? Feck it, I can't even say it right – he has me all fingers and tongues.' She dropped the silver tube into the wash-hand basin.

'Thumbs, thumbs,' she screeched at her reflection. 'No tongues.'

Now, deep breaths and slick it on; Molly wasn't letting him see her without a painted pout. No point in giving him cause to believe he'd had a lucky escape from her. Despair at a life wasted because it wasn't spent in her embrace, that's what she'd prefer to inculcate in Fionn McCullagh. If she could just draw her Cupid's bow straight she could let those arrows fly.

Fionn was reading the notice board when she emerged from the stairwell. Something about the hot water being shut off for a day while electrical repairs were effected had him riveted. When he turned she was struck, as she had been yesterday, by the way his American tan turned his eyes to the colour of the ocean at Mullaghmore on a summer's day. His eyes had slid off hers on that Thursday evening when he'd told her he had a brand-new wife. Scarcely out of her packaging. So instead of reading the reason for his defection in his eyes she'd concentrated on his mouth as it opened and shut, the lips coiling around words she couldn't believe she was hearing. His mouth had betrayed his nervousness, the tongue flicking across to moisten it after each poisonous parcel of words plopped out. As he'd spoken she noticed a crumb clinging to the left side of the slit, not far from where a dimple would indent if he smiled. But he hadn't been smiling that day four years ago. Nor had she.

'Are you fit?' Fionn was smiling now.

Molly wasn't. He needn't imagine she'd be a pushover. 'Fit? Not yet but it's my New Year's resolution. I'm only a month late starting.'

'I meant are you ready – but feel at liberty to run through your New Year's resolutions, Molly.'

'Well, there's getting fit, solving global conflict, developing a machine that turns base metal into gold and repairing the hole in the ozone layer. I thought that might keep me occupied until summer and then I could reassess. How about yourself?'

'I didn't consciously make one but I suppose it would be to put my house in order.' Fionn looked sombre.

Molly panicked. It was too early for self-analysis – she'd like something in a glass to put hairs on her chest first, the depilatory cream could eradicate the damage later – so she started jabbering, 'Housework. Strangely enough I left that one off the list. Anyway, I thought we were supposed to meet at the station. I'm not that late. And how did you know my address? I don't remember giving it to you.'

'Spadework. You dropped clues about being a few minutes from the DART and passing a dry-cleaner's to reach it. So I continued driving past the station and this is the first apartment block I reached. Your name is above the bell.'

'You're wasted in architecture. You should have been a taxman,' she muttered sourly. 'Mustn't keep the great outdoors waiting; after you, super-sleuth.' And she held the door open for Fionn to wrongfoot him because he liked to be the one doling out gentlemanly gestures.

They parked near the entrance to Glendalough and managed a fifteen-minute stroll along a country lane before sleet sent them scurrying to the car.

'At least we've earned our hot whiskeys now.' Fionn drove the short distance down the mountain to a pub in Laragh. 'You didn't want to stay up there for a wander inside Glendalough, did you, admire a few ancient monuments, glory in our cultural heritage?'

'I wasn't tempted before the sleet came lashing and I'm even less disposed now. A hot whiskey sounds infinitely more promising. Anyway, we mustn't be purist about cultural heritage. Whiskey's just as much a part of it as monastic ruins.'

A coach party of Swiss senior citizens, a pile of sodden raincoats at their feet, were immersed in an alcohol-free lunch at two trestle tables towards the rear of the pub. But a cushion-jammed bench alongside the inglenook fireplace was vacant and Molly and Fionn commandeered it.

'Those monks had funny-peculiar attitudes anyway,' remarked Molly, apropos of nothing. 'Especially where women were concerned. Your medieval aesthetics viewed us as she-devils. Of course, that's just because they were scared witless of the other sex and in complete denial of their bodily urges.'

Fionn nodded. 'Denial of bodily urges is unhealthy – that's always been my credo.'

Molly frowned. 'On the other hand, gratifying all your inclinations is probably not advisable either. There has to be something to separate us from the beasts.' Fionn was excessively complacent. He needn't imagine a couple of hot whiskeys would generate any body heat from her. Just because their sex life had been sensational . . . Molly's hand flew to her mouth. Where had that sprung from? It was years since she'd allowed herself to dwell on their times in bed – and on the living-room rug and in the shower and on the beach at Mullaghmore that night when she'd admitted it had always been her ambition to make love beneath the stars. Only she'd anticipated a Caribbean sky rather than a low-lying Sligo one, but it had seemed churlish to mention it when he was co-operating so enthusiastically with making her wish come true.

'Be careful what you wish for,' Molly whispered.

'What did you say?' Fionn set down his glass and slid along the bench towards her.

Startled, because she hadn't realised she'd spoken aloud, Molly improvised. 'I was thinking about those monks. They were great ones for making rash vows and having to work around them, like St Columcille, who swore his feet would never touch Irish soil again after he stormed off to Iona. When he had to return he filled his boots with Scottish earth so they never did. Those fellows had plenty of mantras but they seemed not to extend to cleanliness is next to godliness.'

Molly noticed her fingernails weren't exactly pious using that criterion and sat on her hands in case Fionn spotted them too. She continued: 'But they were cunning enough to weasel their way out of definitive statements. Exactly like my first newspaper editor who wrote a provocative column and always concluded with: "If anyone proves me wrong I'll eat my Sunday bowler on the steps of the town hall." He had a supply of chocolate hats on standby in case anyone ever called his bluff.'

Fionn scratched the back of his neck and Molly noticed how the hair curled around the collar of his rugby shirt.

'Your conversations are deranged. Fascinating but demented,' he said. 'What have chocolate bowlers to do with medieval monks, or do all your stories feature chocolate? I haven't forgotten you're fixated on the stuff. Wasn't it myself who introduced you to white Toblerone?'

Molly smiled at him properly for the first time. 'I glimpsed Paradise, thanks to you,' she breathed. 'My gratitude is boundless. I'll buy you a drink to prove it.'

'That's another advantage to not being a monk,' said Fionn. 'You have licence to sip hot whiskeys with a divine creature on a weekday. And she buys her round.'

Molly vacillated between being flattered and indignant. But she felt obliged to put him straight on the monastic life as she riffled through her handbag for her purse.

'They didn't have it so spartan,' she said. 'St Benedict wrote that a pint of wine a day was ample per monk. I think I could manage very nicely on a similar allocation.'

'How come you're such an expert on the monastic life?'

'Newspapers make you instant experts on the oddest subjects. I wrote a feature last week on the history of winemaking for the drinks column. Lucky for you that you caught me while the information is still at the top of the pile in my brain. By next week it will have been evicted to make room for the mating habits of sea birds or a history of Jewish persecution.'

Waiting for the barman to boil the kettle, Molly tapped

her teeth with a mixture of vexation and attraction. There was a spark between herself and Fionn, she couldn't deny it. But sparks could cause blazes to burn houses down. He was still a married man. Just because he and Helga were on a lay-off didn't mean he could do his laying elsewhere. She was quite sure that wasn't what Helga had in mind. Then again, the Scandinavians had rampaged through Ireland fairly thoroughly in the first millennium – their American descendants didn't need to swoop down and scoop up all the available men in the third. That Helga sounded a right one. Although in fairness, admitted Molly, folding and unfolding a twenty-pound note, Fionn was biased. And not stupid. He'd make zero headway if he said: 'She cooked cabbage and bacon to titillate my tastebuds and bought camisoles to titillate my appetite, but it wasn't enough because I'm a self-centred animal.' She cast a glance back at Fionn. He hadn't even mentioned Helga; she might as well no longer exist for him. This buck took out of sight out of mind so literally his lady was in danger of being airbrushed out of existence. He'd pulled the same stunt on her.

On their second drink apiece, thawed by the combination of flames and whiskey, Fionn mentioned his wife.

'I can't believe how uncomplicated life is without Olga.'

Although crippled with curiosity and convinced he owed her at least a teaser in the gossip stakes, Molly found herself veering away from the subject. 'There'll be no more walking this day.' She indicated the hailstones bouncing off the nearest window. 'So much for today being the opener for spring.'

'Says who?'

'Says the calendar. It's the first of February, St Bridget's Day.'

'People must have been hardier in those days,' said Fionn.

'Most people date it from the March twenty-first equinox.'

'We've gone soft since St Bridget was around running craft workshops and showing the locals how to make rush crosses to sell to the tourists,' agreed Molly.

'Soft, now that's not a word you could apply to Olga.' Fionn looked woebegone.

Molly resigned herself to a deconstruction of the concept of marriage, as experienced by Fionn McCullagh. She preferred to believe in happily ever afters, even for people who swanned off to have their happily ever after with someone else instead of her. Four years ago she'd have climbed on a table and cheered if she could have gazed into a crystal ball and witnessed Fionn telling her his marriage was a mistake and she was the one he truly loved. But four years equals 48 months, equals more than 200 weeks equals – pause for calculation – nearly 1500 days. And she didn't want to hear a melancholy story on a storm-lashed day – or any other day for that matter.

Molly had experienced a surfeit of sorrow during the months following his rejection, when she closed down everything but the essential life-support system, and trailed vacantly from one day to the next. Helen had been predictably solid and Barry had been a rock too, cajoling her out for drinks and listening to her whine about being finished with love. Finished off by love. Even as she'd said it a spark of common sense had stirred within her and she'd realised she was talking nonsense. But she'd formed the words anyway and allowed Barry to pat her awkwardly, clearly horrified at being the recipient of so much naked emotion but determined to be supportive.

Now Molly only half-listened to Fionn's account of how two into one wouldn't go, swirling the honey-coloured liquid around in her glass. She inhaled: hot whiskeys always reminded her of being ill as a little girl, when her mother would add a teaspoonful of whiskey to sugar and warm milk to cosset her. 'Time to mollycoddle my girl,' she'd say. Suddenly she was suffused with an urge to ring her mother for a chat; she hadn't been home since Christmas and she missed her. No lover, no friend, was endowed with the capacity to envelop her in unconditional love the way her mother could. She'd go home to Derry at the weekend and take her to lunch somewhere smart where her mother would have the satisfaction of being scandalised by the prices.

Fionn was still talking, some drivel about Olga being so consumed by her job as an interior decorator that she sidelined their relationship, and Molly drained her glass. She must be wearing an appropriately sympathetic expression because he didn't falter as he unburdened himself of his saga; not much of a page turner but he was mesmerised by it – and he knew the ending already. All those years as a junior reporter sitting through council meetings without nodding off from the undiluted tedium were paying dividends; he hadn't spotted how deep into her zero-interest zone he was plodding.

'So we decided we'd take a three-month break from each other. I've come home to see if I can find work here and Olga is considering whether she could live in Dublin.'

Molly was so rattled she tore the menu she'd been covertly studying with a view to ordering lunch. That was more or less the same arrangement he'd made with her. The man was utterly devoid of tact.

'But I don't anticipate us ever being reunited, Molly. Now that I'm away from Olga I'm able to see what an ill-matched couple we were. We have nothing in common. Being with you reminds me what it's like to spend time in the company of someone you feel wholly at ease with. Sorry if I'm being precipitate here. I don't want to presume anything on your part, you haven't even told me if you're involved with someone else. But just being with you, Molly –' he allowed his eyes to mist over at this point. She thought about offering him a tissue for his snivelly cold but reluctantly vetoed the idea – 'allows me to recognise how sterile my life has become. And I've missed Dublin. She's grown up since I've been away and I want to check out all the adult bumps and curves the old girl has acquired.' He ran his fingers through his hair so that it stood up in spikes, a gesture she remembered, although he was wearing the hair shorter now and – could it be, yes – she did believe it was thinning at the crown. The sight of Fionn's scalp cheered her inordinately.

We should order something to eat, thought Molly, deciding it was a better idea to use her menu for that purpose rather than the one she'd been contemplating: slapping Fionn McCullagh on the back of his legs with it for vacating her life for four years, not so much as a postcard, then reappearing and assuming she was his for a brace of hot whiskeys.

'I'm ravenous. Shall we see if they can rustle up some food?' Her face was deliberately bland.

Fionn radiated disappointment at her studied non-reaction to his résumé of the marital minefield but he stepped up to the bar to order a spinach and blue cheese pasta and a shepherd's pie, with chips to share, the latter suggested by him.

Molly was reminded of Helen's joke: How do you know an Irishman fancies you? He offers to buy you chips. Helen would be so-o disapproving if she knew Molly were seeing Fionn again. She'd been a little too enthusiastic about wading into him when he and Molly split up. Make that split asunder, it conveyed a more accurate impression of their parting. Anyway, Helen always had reservations about Fionn's charms so she wasn't an honest broker. Molly lifted her empty glass. Closer inspection revealed that, yes, it was still empty.

Fionn, meanwhile, was trying to attract the barman's attention – easier said than done with a coachload of indecisive Swiss punters. Molly used the hiatus to contemplate what she'd learned about him. Fionn was single-ish, available and no less attractive or entertaining than he had been four years ago when she thought their destinies were interwoven. So why wasn't she twining her arms around him saying, 'You poor dear, how you've suffered,' and offering to soothe his woes away? Was it rancour because he'd once measured her, computed the statistics and discarded her? Or perhaps she'd outgrown him . . .

Molly regarded his rear view as he leaned on the counter, conversing with the barman, who'd discovered he wasn't among the Swiss party and all but fallen on his neck in gratitude. He was easy on the eye, easy on the ear too when he wasn't hammering on about Helga. Available men weren't that common; she shouldn't be profligate about discarding one until she was certain whether she wanted him or not. He gave every indication of wanting her, which was balm enough at the moment. If in doubt, hang on to a man – that seemed a sensible maxim.

When Fionn returned to their bench, the decision was taken. Molly treated him to a dazzling smile, gave her head a shake so the curls spiralled in every direction and allowed her leg to rest ever so slightly against his.

'Lunchtime's been and gone.' He was apologetic. 'All they have left are the day-long breakfasts so I ordered us two of those. You haven't turned vegetarian in the last couple of years, have you? I wondered if you might, on account of asking for pasta.'

'Only aspirationally,' she replied. 'I like the notion of it. All my veggie friends are shaped like carrot batons, even the ones fixated on chocolate, but I never have the willpower to reject a rasher when I see it nestling beside a fried egg on my plate. It seems so fastidious. I've never thought my body was a temple; I'd be more inclined to call it a supermarket if I had to put the name of a building to it. Crammed with an interesting mish-mash, nothing hallowed.'

'Helga, I mean Olga, was vegan,' said Fionn. 'She didn't like seeing me eat meat. She took all the good out of it. You'd have a nice pink lump of steak on your fork, poised to chew and savour, and she'd embark on a lecture about food additives.' He reached his arm around the back of the settle so it was draped behind Molly.

She was dubious. 'But the one time I saw Helga she struck me as your standard issue warrior queen, all huge and healthy and looking as though she gnawed raw meat for breakfast.'

'No, she ate muesli, not shop-bought but blended to her own specification. I had to have muesli too, to humour her.' Injury sluiced from Fionn.

Molly guffawed; his suffering demeanour intensified. 'I'm sorry,' she spluttered, 'it's just the thought of you spooning in the muesli, when the only cereals you'd allow into the flat when we lived together were Coco Pops, for the colour they turned the milk. It can only have been love.'

'Affection soon withers when it's reciprocated on a tough-love basis: "I'm doing this for your own good, hon." She wanted to take control of every aspect of my life: diet, wardrobe, hobbies, even my dental treatment. Can you believe this, Molly, she sent me to her orthodontist to have him service my teeth? She said they were a disgrace and she was ashamed to be seen in public with me.'

'They always looked fine to me,' said Molly.

'They *were* fine. By Irish standards. But American requirements are more exacting. So I was obliged to spend a fortune getting my overbite fixed –' he chomped enamel for the purposes of demonstration – 'and she still pleaded with me to smile without baring my teeth. I looked like a hirsute Mona Lisa. Without the frock, naturally.'

'Although you'd have been wearing one of those if Helga had decided trousers were symbolic of male superiority.' Mischief gleamed from Molly's face.

Fionn's eyebrows met and bristled. 'That woman had more testosterone than me. It's only now that I'm free of her I realise how controlling she was.' Even his eyelashes were bristling at this stage. 'And talk about law-abiding – if I so much as tried to jaywalk she threw a wobbler. Result: I'll only cross when the little red man flashes up now.'

How did we work our way back to the subject of Helga? wondered Molly. This was becoming monotonous. Someone should explain to the man that women turned restless when the subject was other women. Fortunately their mixed grills arrived so Fionn's substandard overbite was diverted into decimating Clonakilty black pudding.

On their way home, driving against the commuter traffic streaming out of Dublin, Molly considered asking him into her apartment. The day hadn't been a washout despite the weather and Fionn McCullagh still interested her. But as they passed the off-licence she found herself craning to check if Hercules was on duty. She could always parade in there with Fionn, demonstrate how other men wanted to spend time in her company even if he couldn't be bothered exchanging pleasantries, but she rejected the idea as petty.

Nevertheless Molly said goodbye to Fionn with considerably less regret than she felt at abandoning the possibility of showing Hercules she was a sought-after woman.

Fionn was disappointed she didn't invite him in. 'I promise not to outstay my welcome,' he wheedled.

Arrogant streak. One of his less alluring characteristics.

Molly planted a kiss on his ear. 'You can't do that if you aren't in the apartment to begin with. I have work to finish off tonight, Fionn. I'll call you in a few days.'

In fact she wanted to ring her mother and then flop on the floor cradling the TV remote control but she wasn't going to tell him that. He'd probably suggest they sit in together and watch *Coronation Street*. But he wasn't Tweedledee to her Tweedledum. Fionn McCullagh could play house with her when she chose and not a minute sooner. However she'd no intention of slinging out the baby with the bath water. Valentine's Day was on the horizon and she was looking into the maws of her first 14 February since the age of fifteen without a love token.

Molly wasn't about to scuttle her best chance of a bunch of roses and a soppy card. Let's be honest, her only chance.

CHAPTER 7

Helen willed her phone into life but it remained obstinately mute. She tried out some of the positive thinking technique she'd been reading about to see if that made a difference, visualising her number being dialled, fingers pressing the digits and herself answering. Still Patrick didn't call her. It was ironic, she grumped, preparing to channel excess nervous energy into vacuuming, she spent more than a week avoiding his calls and now she was pining for them. Maybe the phone was off the hook – she jiggled the receiver to ensure it was operating. In a fit of rage she dragged the vacuum cleaner out of the cupboard and plonked it in the middle of the living-room floor. She was disgusted at herself, behaving like a moonstruck teenager instead of a modern, capable woman.

The cleaner howled spitefully into life. But Helen had scarcely tackled the stairs before a realisation struck that made her switch off precipitately and return it to the cupboard: she wouldn't be able to hear the phone above its drone. Even as she humped the machine back to its hidey-hole she berated herself for waiting around for Patrick to call. If she was a modern, capable woman why couldn't she ring him herself? She ventured into the visualisation game again, this time with her taking the initiative, but when she reached the part where he said 'Hello' she caved in and admitted she couldn't manage it. Maybe her modernity was only skin deep. Or it could be that she didn't trust herself to make contact with him.

She was engulfed by a mental picture of his lips slithering along her neck, and panicked. What household chore could she embark on that would be both quiet and therapeutic? Perhaps polishing – she liked the lavender smell of the spray and the shapes you could draw with the foaming contents of the aerosol. Like a P for Patrick . . .

Her doorbell rang before she managed the first squirt. Still clutching the can she answered it – to be confronted by a ceramic pot of snowdrops on her doorstep with a luggage label attached and her name penned in violet ink. She hunted for a note but there wasn't one. As she stooped to grasp the pot, its concave centre encircled by a gauzy lilac ribbon, Patrick moved into her field of vision and spoke.

'Let me give you a hand with that. You look far too delicate to carry an ungainly weight.'

Helen dropped the aerosol.

'It's not that heavy, to be honest, but I'd still like to carry it in for you.' Patrick lifted both spray can and snowdrops, and stood aside to allow her precede him into the house.

'So, Helen.' He rested himself with such ease on one of her sofas he appeared to be a permanent fixture. She marvelled at the music his voice created, transforming a name she'd never particularly liked before. 'So, Helen, what have you been doing since our walk in the park?'

'Fretting.' She made no effort to disguise her agitation.

His face creased into worry lines. 'I'm sorry for being such a pest the other day. I don't know what came over me, practically demanding you invite me to your place. I just didn't want to let you go. I'm here to apologise.'

So his idea of a *mea culpa* was to turn up anyway. A novel approach. But she was too beguiled by the unexpected sight of him to voice an objection. Nonsense, of course she could protest; she took a deep breath and managed an approximation.

'Shouldn't you be in London planning a wedding with your fiancée?'

'You're right, I should. Treat me as a mirage.' Patrick pulled off his flying jacket and tossed it on the arm of the sofa. Helen noticed the zip was coming adrift at the bottom and smothered an impulse to sew it up for him – she wasn't his mother.

'I see neither hide nor hair of you for three years and now you're back twice in a matter of weeks. Miriam must think it strange.'

Patrick shrugged. 'A man's entitled to go home.'

'Dublin's not your home.'

It blazed out more jaggedly than she'd have chosen but the acerbity of her denial couldn't detract from its truth. Nevertheless she regretted it when rejection flared in his eyes. Then they clouded over and strayed around the room, ingesting its contents, lingering at a windowsill on a framed photograph of three children: two little girls in tartan skirts and buckled shoes with their smaller brother sandwiched between them, a pudgy hand clasped in each. His gaze seesawed from the younger of the two girls to Helen and back again.

'Ringlets,' he said.

'I wasn't consulted.' She flattened her bob with tremulous fingers; she could control her voice and expression but not her hands.

Helen hovered by the mantelpiece, irresolute where to sit. It struck her as singularly unsafe to join Patrick on the sofa, where she'd be close enough to detect the fabric conditioner smell from his clothes, to trace the indentations of a chicken pox scar on his forehead. Staying on her feet was the most sensible recourse.

'Come and sit next to me,' he invited. 'You're too far away.'

Helen threw caution to the winds and perched alongside him, simultaneously poised for flight and prepared to nestle against him.

Just as she remembered the obligations of hospitality and realised she should offer him something to eat or drink, he confessed: 'I'm not here to apologise at all.'

'I suspected as much, Patrick.'

'I'm here because I couldn't remember what your voice sounded like and that seemed quite literally sinful. I wished and wished that I could conjure it up but I couldn't. So I decided to do something about it.' Patrick folded his arms mock-aggressively across his chest and added: 'And before you tell me that I could have had a more straightforward reminder by lifting the telephone, you're absolutely right. But straightforward didn't appeal to me. Why be guileless when you can be circuitous?'

Helen chuckled but when the merriment died away she was equivocal about how to respond. Her head was telling her to tread carefully; her heart was waltzing. Finally, because she could not hold the words back, she murmured, 'Your face gladdens me, Patrick.'

They sat looking at one another for a few moments, both flooded with emotion. Then a gust of wind that sent a tree branch scratching against the patio doors fragmented the spell. She roused herself and bent to sniff the snowdrops.

'They're sublime. Did you have trouble finding them?'

'None at all. I knew exactly where to go. I prowled around

the park with my trowel and as soon as the light dimmed I was in like Flynn.'

'You didn't!'

'I didn't. The concierge at the hotel recommended a couple of flower shops. None of them had any snowdrops in pots for sale but I persuaded one enterprising member of staff to rustle up something for me. I can be very persuasive when I put my mind to it, Helen. In fact –' he leaned conspiratorially towards her – 'I'm a bit of an operator.'

'Don't I know it.' She lowered her nose to the miniature blooms again, floating above the foliage like froth on the sea. 'I've never seen anything so flawless in my life.'

'I have,' said Patrick.

The silence between them was charged with a thousand volts of electricity.

Finally he said: 'We have to talk.'

'That's what we did last time and look how we ended up. Canoodling on a park bench like a couple of youngsters, without even the sense to wait until the weather was fine.'

'True, but forewarned is forearmed. I'm prepared for the gravitational pull I feel when you're in my vicinity. I'm wearing my Superman vest under my shirt. So your wiles are useless against me unless you've Kryptonite secreted about the house.'

'I had a springclean and threw it all out,' she said. 'You've no idea what a dust collector that Kryptonite is. Will we do the talking now or would you like some coffee first?'

'Better make it now,' said Patrick. 'We have to knock this on the head as quickly as possible. We're in limbo at the minute.'

The day which had started so bleakly, with Helen spooning coffee granules into a mug and wondering how she was going to decimate time on her own, seemed rainbow-hued. Even if what they had to discuss was tinged with sepia.

'Limbo,' she reflected. 'I suppose that's about the height of it. Although technically it's been wiped from the theological map.'

'Since when?' asked Patrick.

'Years ago, the Church quietly dropped it. Limbo was never doctrine anyway, although that wasn't much consolation to all those generations of bereaved parents who were told their unbaptised babies would never go to heaven.'

'Helen,' said Patrick, with the determination of a man resolved to return the conversation to relevant matters, 'I'm in love with you. I don't want to marry Miriam – attractive, groomed, suitable, organised Miriam waiting for me in Camden Town. Waiting for me to set a wedding date with the same graceful patience she waited for me to propose. It took months to do it. I could trace the outline of her disappointment like you'd skim your hands around the contours of a bowl when another day passed and I couldn't eject the words. But ultimately I did it. I should never have asked her to be my wife. I thought it would exorcise my feelings for you, Helen, except it didn't. I can't ignore how moved I am by you, however inconvenient that might be. If I could press a button and eradicate it I would, believe me, but that's not an option.'

Dejection oozed from him and Helen had to suppress her instinct to reach out and stroke his hair. Instead she contented herself with watching the way it waved as it grew back from his forehead and in imagining herself running her fingertips along the sharply delineated outline of his widow's peak.

Patrick scattered her meandering thoughts with his next

words, dropped pebbles into a still pool spreading ripples with each sentence.

'I know I can't marry you, Helen, but I would like us to be together – somewhere people don't know us and can't be judgemental. Which rules out Ireland. But the world is a vast place. We could find a corner and claim it as our own.'

Her head reeled. He was articulating desires she'd suppressed for years – urges she thought were buried so deep they'd never surface. Wishes she could scarcely bring herself to formulate. But a few minutes in his company and they were basking in the open, clamouring for recognition. She allowed herself to luxuriate in the possibility of a lifetime with Patrick, tantalising her imagination as she rolled the scenario around in her mind's eye, then reality intervened and she clashed down the blinds.

'Is the world immense enough?' she asked. 'Truth will out whether you're in Ballydoyle or Borneo.'

He stroked the faint blue veins threading her wrist. 'I believe there's a crevice we could slide into, Helen.'

She reared back from the duplicity conveyed by his words. From the reptilian slant cast on their future behaviour if she decided they had a hereafter together. But the whispering touch continued against her inner wrist and its hypnotic repetition soothed her. She closed her eyes, excluding everything but the sensation. Until Miriam intruded.

'What about the woman you've promised to marry?'

Patrick's pupils expanded, black obscuring grey-green. 'I'll break it off. I'd never have become involved with her if I weren't homesick and lonely in England. Work kept me occupied most of the time but there was a chafing, inside and out, that begged for salve, and Miriam offered it. She

appeared when I was at my lowest ebb and made it apparent
she wanted to be with me on any terms I chose. At the time
that was enough for me.' Patrick shrugged and reached for
Helen but she moved and his hand fell in the gap between
cushions. It flapped, a stranded fish dangling from his shirt
sleeve. 'Before I knew where I was we were living together
and she was making plans that involved the two of us. I
went along with them, more from inertia than anything
else. I hadn't the heart to scupper her dreams. Until now.'

He looked appealingly at Helen but she didn't respond
because she could find no words within her. Patrick took
up his story again.

'The last time we were together, three years ago –' he
raised his voice to be heard above a flurry of agitated
protest from Helen – 'I know that's the time you keep
insisting we're never to talk about but I can't block out what
happened between us, even if you can. It was a validation.
But afterwards you were so insistent we must part for ever
that I couldn't allow myself to hope there'd be a reprieve.
You convinced me the feelings we had for each other would
eventually subside, so I waited for that. And waited. Life
without you was an amputation . . .' Patrick's voice trailed
off as he struggled with reconvened misery. 'Then Miriam
materialised and distracted me from the pain. She didn't
seem to mind that I was only there in silhouette for her.'

Helen shifted position so she was looking ahead, scrutinising
her china cabinet as though it had materialised overnight in
her living room. Each piece of ware behind the glass doors
needed cataloguing in her mental inventory. Count jugs and
sideplates and don't think about three years ago. What took
place had been a mistake, and if they buried it deep enough
they could pretend the error had never seen the light of
day. It was between the two of them alone – they made

it happen and they could unhappen it. They'd agreed it
was an aberration. So why was Patrick trying to exhume
it? A porcelain teapot blurred as Helen's eyes moistened;
unexpectedly she felt choked with a sense of betrayal at his
engagement to another woman.

'But you proposed marriage to her,' she accused. 'Nobody
forced you to say those words.'

Patrick cupped her chin, guiding it towards him. The cautious sun leaking through the French windows had taken
shelter behind a cloud and his face was in shadow, although
she could guess at its unflinching expression because his
tones were harsh. 'It's true I asked her to marry me and
she agreed. But I wanted to be normal, to have a home.
I thought Miriam and I could cobble together a reasonable
facsimile of a life, I truly did. You made me believe our love
had to be aborted, that it was warped and grotesque and
ultimately it would poison our lives.' The thumb holding
her chin, its pressure forcing her to meet his gaze, stroked
her skin. His voice melted. 'And then, Helen, we met again
a few weeks ago – not by design but because we were
meant to be together. What's unnatural is not how we
feel about one another but for the two of us to be apart,
denying our love. I recognised that the instant I looked
into your eyes again and something fundamental leaped
within me; it was as if there had been no parting, that
we'd been separated in body but not in spirit. I knew you
felt the same way. I know you do now, however much you
deny it.'

'I'm not going to repudiate it.' Helen's delivery was
sombre; she closed her eyes and fumbled for a path out
of the maze. Her brain was malfunctioning; Patrick had that
distracting effect on her. Love turned her critical processes
to slush.

Miriam's name – she couldn't even put a face to her – sliced through the silt. Helen had never met her but she felt a sense of responsibility towards the woman. After all, they were in love with the same man.

'Patrick, I long to believe in happily ever afters. I wish on every full moon and rainbow, on each coin I toss into a fountain, every black cat that crosses my path, and every candle I light there's one out there for you and me. But I can't convince myself. What's between us is intrinsically wrong. Nature, precedent, the force of history flows against it – we'd have no luck. And whatever else we renounce voluntarily, luck we can't forsake.'

She focused on his eyes, willing him towards comprehension, glimpsing a pair of tiny Helens in his pupils. They seemed to belong there. Oh God, to have this over with, to crawl back into bed and cancel out the world with its oppressive desires. Or to crawl back into bed and bring Patrick with her, to obliterate the world with him beside her, on top of her, inside her . . . Helen shuddered and, gathering together the tattered remnants of her self-control, she stood to distance herself from him.

'And as for yourself and Miriam, Patrick, it strikes me you're selling yourself short by planning to marry someone you don't love wholeheartedly, and you're selling her short too. She deserves better than a putative lover who's using her as emotional blotting paper.'

'But *you* urged me to go ahead and marry Miriam.' His black eyebrows were mutual rods of indignation. 'When we spoke in the park you insisted I was duty-bound to honour our engagement.'

'That was before I was aware of the circumstances. For all I knew you could have been in love with her and I was a spanner in the works. But if you're not utterly, unreservedly, passionately in love with someone you have no right to marry them.'

Her mental commotion had Helen pacing but she paused now and chewed a knuckle.

'I was being selfish too, telling you to forge ahead with the wedding. I thought if I knew you were married and completely beyond my reach, I might come to terms with the realisation we could never be together. Knowing you're out there somewhere thinking of me, just as I'm here longing for you, makes me feel plugged into the world in one sense – but in another it hinders me from moving on because I keep hoping, completely irrationally, there'll come a time for us. So if you and Miriam had a life together I'd know conclusively that you were going your way and I should plod mine.' She exhaled lingeringly. 'Does any of that add up? I know it's convoluted; I can hardly make sense of it myself.'

Patrick nodded slowly. 'If I take myself so irrevocably out of your life that there's no possibility of second thoughts, you believe you might be happy. You'd have a chance to meet someone yourself and have children, a normal life, everything you can't expect with me.'

Helen sat beside him and leaned her head against his upper arm – a gesture less of affection than of resignation.

'I won't ever marry and have children.' Her voice rustled so faintly he had to strain to catch the words.

'Yet you're telling me to do exactly that.'

'You're capable of it, Patrick. You showed that when you allowed yourself to imagine a life with Miriam. You may even have married her without discussing it with me if we hadn't met at the funeral the other week. But lives overlap for a reason. Auntie Maureen brought you back to me, on temporary loan, and I'm grateful to her

– she always was a romantic.' Helen's smile was subdued.

After a while she raised her head from his arm. 'Patrick, I've no expectations of finding a *doppelgänger* for you, possibly not even the pale imitation I realise is the best I can hope for. I'm not saying I'll never let another man touch me – distasteful though it seems now, I imagine one day I'll be lonely enough to agree to the usual trade-off. But I'll never exchange vows with someone because I've already pledged myself, in my heart, to you and there's no reneging on that. Apart or not, it makes no difference.'

His eyes had the sheen of unshed tears as he contemplated her.

'You're being unfair to me, Helen, the same offence you accused me of practising on Miriam. I'm supposed to vanish from your life and dismiss you from mine – but while I'm under instructions to go forth and multiply you're intent on living a sterile existence.'

Helen recognised they were both overwrought and needed some respite from the angst.

'I'm making tea.' Her tone was peremptory as she retreated to the kitchen. Patrick followed, unable to countenance losing her from sight.

'Would you bring these in?' She thrust mugs and a packet of Viennese whirls at him to keep him occupied. She could have found room for all of them on the tray but she was uncomfortable with the way he tailed her back and forth from sink to worktop.

As she poured, curiosity overcame Helen. 'What does Miriam look like?'

'Light brown hair, the sort that would have been fair when she was a child; slim; tans easily, unlike us; dark blue eyes. She's pretty. She has a way of cocking her head to the side when she's listening to someone speak that's endearing.'

'Is she at all like me?'

'No. She's very English. Miriam's a nurse; she has that aura of briskly compassionate competence that nurses perpetually convey. I always imagine you could hand her a screwdriver and tell her to rewire the house and she'd manage it. Whereas you, my love,' amused indulgence radiated from him, 'are a Luddite. I notice your microwave is still in its original wrapping.'

Helen reddened. She thought about lying and telling him she'd only just bought it, but stifled the notion stillborn. It was astonishing, she reflected, how one minute they could be threshing in an emotional whirlpool and the next they were placidly drinking tea.

'Even when she's off duty you can tell Miriam is a nurse,' continued Patrick, biting Viennese whirls into extinction. Helen had forgotten how rapidly he could decimate a plate of biscuits. 'You know how nuns have that convent air about them, even when they're in civvies? It's the same with nurses.'

Helen slid off her seat to fetch more biscuits; if she were truly performing her hostess duties she'd offer to cut him a sandwich but she lacked the energy. Emotional trauma was draining. This was like excavating a scab but she felt she needed to know more about Miriam.

'Does she realise you're back in Dublin so soon?'

'No, I told her I was going to Durham on business.'

She registered the lie, layering custard creams into a fan. Even to spare someone's feelings an untruth seemed shabby. Of course he could justify it as a kindness but she twitched uneasily until the need to interrogate goaded her to speak again.

'How did you meet?'

'We were introduced over pints of lager.' He was matter-of-fact. 'She's the sister of a colleague at work who was offered a new job and organised the usual leaving do in the pub on the corner. Miriam came along and Peter, that's her brother, asked me to keep an eye on her because she didn't know anybody.'

'From tiny acorns,' remarked Helen. Only a shade sourly.

She drank more tea, cogitating on how incurious men were. She could have had a string of lovers for all Patrick knew or cared. But it was of consequence to her to be able to imagine him in situ in London – which floor his flat was on, the way his furniture was arranged, how he travelled to work.

'Did you find it hard settling in England?' she asked.

'At first. Not because it was foreign – it was too familiar in some ways. I didn't want to vegetate in theme pubs distressed by interior designers with Micks distressed by alcohol, all of them wailing about how utopian the homeland was and how unfair life was to dispatch them into exile.'

'Then why on earth did you wind up in Camden Town – surely that's an Irish area?'

Patrick shook his head. 'Used to be. It's much more multi-ethnic now. You'll still hear Offaly and Wexford accents but they're in the minority. I didn't actively choose to live there. I was looking for a flat and someone at work was vacating theirs so I took over the lease. If they'd been quitting a place in Hammersmith I dare say I'd be living in West London.'

'And work – do you enjoy your job?' Helen probed. This was like extracting teeth – could the man volunteer no information?

He flicked at a snowdrop in its pot on the coffee table in front of him, setting its bell nodding mutely. 'Yes, there's potential for promotion. The firm's a reputable one, I do a little foreign travel, I like my colleagues. It's a fine life in the employment sense.'

'You're a souped-up accountant, right?'

Patrick pulled a face. 'I don't know if an actuary counts as souped-up anything. Anyway, how about you? Are you bathed in job satisfaction writing your computer programmes? You're obviously doing well if this house is anything to judge by. I leafed through the property section of one of the Dublin papers on the plane over and worked out I could only afford a place if someone advanced me a hundred-year mortgage. I rent my place. Miriam wants us to buy but we'll have to move out of town, we'll never be able to afford anything in Camden. She fancies Surbiton; there's a reliable train service.'

Helen regarded him over the rim of her mug. Men were another species. One minute it's 'You are my pulse, my heart beats only for you', the next they're casually telling you they'll probably buy a house in some commuter belt because the train timetable has passed inspection.

'You look cross. The job can't be that bad,' said Patrick.

'No, it's grand.' She rallied, clattering their mugs onto the tray and preparing to carry it out to the kitchen. 'I didn't realise it fully at the time I studied computers on a post-graduate course but it was a winning choice. There's always plenty of work around and your employers are more inclined to treat you well because it's temptingly easy to jump ship. There are all sorts of perks including shares. They've even installed a screen in the canteen so you can track their performance.'

He removed the tray from her hands. 'Allow me, Helen.'

He transfixed her with his lazy smile; with his fringe cascading into his eyes he reminded her of the gangly teenager she remembered with such affection – and more than affection.

As he turned the door handle he spoke with his back to her. 'If you're resolute on separation, I think you owe me something.'

A flicker in his tone activated her guard.

'What did you have in mind?'

Patrick faced her. He looked at Helen in a way that caught her heart between giant hands and mangled it. Then he spoke.

'One more night together. I know you're my sister but you're my lover too. Let me make love to you again. For the last time.'

CHAPTER 8

Molly was rushing to finish her court report so she could make it over to the National Gallery by 7 p.m. A session of lectures on Irish art was starting and, in a fit of self-improvement, she'd resolved to attend them. Experience had drummed it into her not to sign on for the complete term, a lesson she'd learned after paying up front for instruction in pottery, Spanish and bodhrán playing, and managing to miss more than half of each course. The bodhrán episode was particularly galling because she'd lashed out the money on a drum with a *Book of Kells* bird-beast undulating across it, convinced she'd be hammering away like a professional in no time. She'd nurtured visions of herself in a ceilidh band, giving it welly during an impromptu session in a little Donegal pub crammed to the rafters with an admiring entourage. That was before her debut lesson; she'd have borrowed a bodhrán if there'd been any hint she was going to handle it like a hen scratching – her instructor's description of her technique, an inelegant one although he couldn't be faulted for accuracy. Anyway the traditional music lessons had gone the way of good intentions. Never mind paving a road to hell, she could surface a motorway network. Although Irish motorways were few and far between, a particular handicap in a state where the roads tended to speak with forked tongue.

Still, she had hopes as high as Macgillacuddy's Reeks for the Irish art series. Based on nothing concrete admittedly. But she reasoned that even if she only managed five of the ten art lectures she'd be expanding her mind, instead of her stomach with alcohol and crisps in the pub.

Furthermore, thought Molly, muttering as her fingers flew over the keyboard – '. . . comma, close quotes, said Judge Justin Blanchard' – she couldn't be accused of going to these night classes because she was on the pull. She wasn't doing Essential Bodybuilding for Big Boys. There'd only be girlies at an art appreciation class. Molly giggled, struck by a recollection of one of Barry's previous assignments.

'Barry, remember the time you posed nude for a watercolours class?'

He quaked. 'Molloy, your memory is elephantine. I was young and suggestible. It was all the news editor's fault.'

'Wonder what happened to that photograph of you, newborn nude, goosebumps on sentry duty, not forgetting the essential prop of a rose between your teeth. And that toothy grin of yours – actually it wasn't so much a smile as a rictus. It was a classic. We had that pic pinned to the noticeboard for decades.' Molly tapped her teeth. 'Every time you annihilated it we had another copy printed up. It must be about time we rustled up the documentary evidence afresh.'

Complacency streamed from Barry. Molly spun a suspicious glance in his direction.

'You cornered the negative, didn't you? You bribed the photographer and ground the neg into infinitesimal atoms.'

Barry's smug aura intensified. He locked his drawer with

the self-congratulation of a man completing a solid day's work – every story passed to him by the newsdesk was knocked down into fillers – and announced, 'I'm for The Kip. Fancy a jar?'

The Kip was their local, a dive of a pub that lived up to its name by attracting gurriers and journalists – often interchangeable – in equal measure. It was actually called The Salmon's Leap but some wag had renamed it The Kipper's Free Fall and so it was universally known. It was a mystery why a city-centre pub was called The Salmon's Leap anyway – it didn't even sell prawn cocktail crisps.

Barry reached Molly her coat as though it were a foregone conclusion they'd spend an hour in The Kip whining about work and ducking the editor if this should be one of his evenings for fraternising with the staff.

'Sorry, you'll have to shred reputations without me tonight. I have other plans,' she said. With only an undertone of triumph.

Astonishment rampaged across Barry's narrow features as he watched her tug on her stone-coloured mac. 'It can't be a date. You haven't spent the past hour trooping up and down to the jacks to check on the size and hue of any spot you might be incubating. Nor have you legged it down to a cubicle and swapped your suit for something tight, teasing and singularly inappropriate unless you actively want to be molested. Are you paying a visit to an aged aunt?'

Molly raised her eyes heavenwards. 'Why do social plans always have to incorporate food or drink with you, Barry? I'm attending a lecture at the National Gallery, as it happens: *An Introduction to Irish Art*. We'll be examining the work of both Yeatses – that's John and Jack to a pleb like yourself – plus Lavery, Paul Henry and, um, I haven't read the syllabus all that thoroughly.'

Barry took a melodramatically enacted shuffle backwards. 'That's me stepping back in amazement. How long have you nurtured these leanings towards culture?'

'I've always been interested in it, except life in a newsroom tends to suffocate the tendencies.'

'First I've heard,' objected Barry. 'You never volunteer for the Wexford Opera Festival gig. You don't even write book reviews.'

Molly favoured him with a look that would have withered a rubber plant but which bounced off Barry.

He continued: 'And then there was the time Stephen sent us all a memo suggesting we do a Yossarian and eliminate adjectives and adverbs from our copy, sure you didn't even know who he was.'

Defensiveness distracted Molly so that she transmitted her story to the wrong basket. 'You never read *Catch 22* either; you only knew him from the film, so that makes you a culture crow rather than a culture vulture. If Sport ring down to say court copy has landed in their basket can you tell them to spike it? I've sent another version to the newsdesk. Now if you don't mind, Barry, I have paintings to appraise.'

As Molly headed for the door he called after her: 'I'll be in The Kip for however long it takes me to drink two scoops if you find art less soul-quenching than you expected.'

Molly bought her ticket in the gift shop and contemplated a rack of magnets. There was one of Ophelia drifting towards a watery grave but she decided it wouldn't sit easily on her fridge alongside her 'I Can Be Bribed – Try Chocolate' magnet.

She slid into her seat in the lecture theatre as the lights dimmed. Projected onto a slide screen at the front was a portrait of a well-fed man wearing an impressive wig which frolicked artlessly along the metal epaulettes on his armour. He was clean-shaven and had particularly moist and prominent lips. The purpose of displaying this lavishly coiffed warrior, she learned, was to demonstrate the artist's expertise with texture: the sheen of armour, the crisp linen of his lace collar, the soft tumble of hair. The lecturer didn't mention the dewy plumpness of his mouth. Then Molly caught herself short – imagine giving the eye to a fellow dead and buried these past three hundred years. Besides, he was probably five feet tall and riddled with syphilis.

Her attention wandered during an explanation of symbolism in *The Marriage of Strongbow and Aoife*, as portrayed being plighted on a battlefield. Historical authenticity obviously wasn't high on the painter's list of priorities. She registered the allegory about the broken harp strings and Strongbow's all-subjugating Norman foot straddling a Celtic cross but then her eyes wandered past a familiar outline two seats ahead of her, screeched to a halt and backtracked. Could it be? She was nearly positive it was.

'Turn sideways, turn sideways,' she hissed. The elderly woman in the seat next to her complied.

The broad shoulders were resolutely immobile, however, listening with a convincing air of attentiveness to the lecture.

Molly fidgeted for the remainder of the hour, fragments of the lecture penetrating her consciousness occasionally as the curator covered three centuries at a cracking pace. When the lights were raised the man two seats in front of her stretched and rose to his feet. Hercules was unveiled as an appreciator of art. Molly's heart swelled with pride: so she hadn't been guided purely – make that impurely – by cupidity in gravitating towards him. He wasn't just a he-babe, he was a cultivated man. Plus – a lifetime of stooping to pick up lucky pennies was finally paying off – he appeared to be on his own. The nymph who acted so proprietorial towards him in Bewley's was nowhere in view.

Surely now he'd have to speak to her instead of presenting that relentless, although still flawless, profile. She stood and looked directly at him as he ambled past; not a flicker of recognition. What was this, a farewell to his arms? Molly wasn't taking it stationary – she catapulted after him and fell into step alongside Hercules at the foot of the curveting staircase.

'You work in my off-licence, don't you?'

Not the most memorable of gambits but to the point and impossible to ignore. In the interests of future sales if not common courtesy.

Hercules' eyes flickered over her and retreated beneath their lids.

'Do you mean McDaid's?' He played for time – not in the guttural Greek accent she was expecting but the elongated tones of South Dublin. The limit of their previous conversations – that's £9.50, please – hadn't been enough to formulate an impression.

'The one and only. You've had a fortune from me over the years.' She beamed to conceal her nerves.

'Not me personally.' Definitely a South Dublin drawl, not a hint of anything foreign.

'Well, no, not you personally,' conceded Molly, 'unless you have shares in Rosemount wines, which is unlikely since they're Aussie. Mind you, there's a sizeable Greek community in Melbourne, so it's possible. I'm babbling, feel free to interrupt me.'

The Cadbury eyes slid towards her again; a gleam of something lambent within them. Molly was trying to decide if it was distaste or amusement when she missed her footing on a step and toppled chinwards towards the marble floor. Before she had time to feel mortification, let alone pain, a hand snaked out and grasped her none too gently by the elbow. She sneered at her flat brown and cream lace-up ankle boots – where's the benefit in being sensibly shod if you still risk falling face first?

She clung to the banister when his arm was removed, nails scratching along the polished wood. 'Thanks, I could see it if I were teetering around in stilettos but these shoes are verging on the maiden aunt. Which I am, incidentally – a maiden aunt, that is. Of course, it's not a term much in currency nowadays but I am unmarried and therefore a maiden of sorts, and I do have a niece back in Derry where I come from. That's more information than you need. I did advise you to take remedial action to halt my drivel. Obviously I'm incapable of something as taxing as simultaneously climbing stairs and chatting. I suppose I'm scarlet in the face now as well as limping along. You must be sorry you ever –'

'Come and have a coffee. The restaurant in here doesn't shut for another hour or so.'

His intervention silenced Molly. It was like turning a corner and catching sight of a rainbow straddling the skyline. One she needn't cross her fingers over because her wish had already been anticipated. Her Adonis was (a) on speaking terms with her, and (b) about to be on coffee-drinking terms with her. Plus he'd just saved her from making a complete fool of herself; well no, he hadn't quite pulled off that one but even gods had their limitations. She hobbled contentedly beside him, thinking: Fine, world, end any time you like now – life can become no more halcyon.

But it could. And it did. He settled her into one of the spillover tables in the glass atrium, sauntered off and returned, before she had a chance to pinch herself, with two cappuccinos and a muffin apiece – one topped with white chocolate, the other with chocolate orange.

'I like both types so choose whichever you prefer,' he invited.

Molly gasped. Not only was he a Greek god, not only was he interested in art, not only did he bring her buns unsolicited, not only was he waiting on her hand and food – stop, don't mention clumsy feet – but he had a taste for her favourite cake. In a burst of selflessness she indicated the chocolate orange muffin because it had less chocolate dribbled over it. She couldn't help noticing the hand that reached her the plate was coated in more hair than was strictly necessary in a member of a species evolved to the extent of inventing gloves for warmth but it seemed cavalier to quibble about feet of clay. Feck it, not feet again – would her brain ever give her a break? She knew she was a maladroit holy show, he knew she was a maladroit holy show, now could they draw a line under it.

'I'm Molly.' She took refuge in civilities.

'Georgie.' He extended the uncommonly hirsute hand and shook hers. She coated his palm with some extraneous muffin crumbs – she should have used the fork he'd provided – and decided Georgie was no substitute for Hercules.

'Georgie doesn't sound particularly Greek,' she remarked, apprehensive that she might have a coffee rim on her upper lip but not in a position to do anything about it short of rubbing off all her lipstick with the serviette or licking her mouth, which might send out the wrong signal. Or the right one too soon.

'What makes you imagine I'm Greek?' He folded his arms across his chest in a stereotypical defensive pose.

Molly noticed he had a groove on his chin, not quite a

dimple, and that his hair was completely straight, without a single kinking follicle.

'I thought someone told me you were. I didn't mean to offend you, I didn't realise it was an insult to suggest someone was Greek. Spartacus was Greek, wasn't he? And any number of philosophers, all of whose names temporarily escape me. Anthony Quinn was part-Greek, George Michael's London-Greek and that diva, Maria Don't-Be-Callous-To-Me-Ari, she was Greek too. I'm partial to vine leaves, the retsina I can take or leave. Am I rambling again? Perhaps my batteries should be taken out.'

He gazed at her obliquely. 'I don't know how to take you, Molly.'

Take me any way you like, she thought, but fortunately reined in the sentiment. Instead she laid down the spoon which she'd been on the brink of using to scoop up froth from her cup and smiled demurely.

'My parents are from Athens,' he said. 'But I was born in Glasthule. I prefer Guinness to retsina and my dolmades are legendary. The Georgie comes from Giorgios and the philosophers you mean probably include Plato and Aristotle. You prefer red wine, don't you? I notice you rarely buy white unless it's champagne.'

Molly recalled some crow's feet which had high-handedly emerged on the sides of her eyes that morning and shook her blonde fringe forward to obscure them. So he was familiar with her taste in wine – that was an encouraging sign.

'You have a very pretty friend,' he added. 'A slim, dark-haired gi- woman. I meant woman. Girl is pejorative, my sisters tell me.'

'Your sisters must be young,' said Molly. 'From where I'm placed girl sounds more than acceptable.' But her smile

117

was chiselled on and her spirits dwindled. He fancied Helen, chances were he was hoping to coax an introduction. No such thing as a free muffin.

'Does she live with you? You seem to be together often.' Georgie's revolting hairy hands, his unnaturally hairy hands, crumbled cake.

'Who?' asked Molly, perfectly well aware whom he meant.

'Your friend. The one with the disappointed eyes and the sweet smile.'

She contemplated telling him Helen lived with her professional wrestler husband and six children with a seventh on the way. Be gracious, Molly, she counselled herself, and ate a chocolate shaving for energy.

'You mean Helen – she's gorgeous, isn't she? Single too. We don't live together but she's only down the road in Sandycove. She discovered it after I bought my place in Blackrock and we started going for walks by the Forty Foot, obviously in the hope of spying on the naked male bathers there but they have so far eluded us. They must strip off very early in the morning to go swimming at the Forty Foot. Helen's none too keen on retsina either so now we all have something in common.'

Georgie looked dazed as he stroked his not-quite-a-dimple. Molly kept an eye on the jungle spouting from his hands by way of solace. He probably had acres of it clambering across his back too, and all over his shoulders and feet. If he were like that in his twenties heaven knows how simian he'd be by his thirties and forties. She recoiled. Then caught a whiff of fragrance and noticed he was wearing Fahrenheit, her favourite male scent. Sometimes for a fix of it she walked past the counter where it was sold in Arnotts, inhaling avidly. Imagine, disappointed eyes were what he was searching for in a mate. If she'd known that sooner she could have cultivated the disconsolate look.

Molly decided on heroism, since sour grapes were singularly indigestible, and proceeded to ferret out as much relevant information as possible about Hercules just in case Helen was interested in him. Which she seriously doubted. Even so, she should be encouraged to think in terms of having a crack at fun with the Glasthule Greek because she was too abstemious by half. And as far as Molly was concerned, sooner or later the body objected. Stashing money for a rainy day was a fool's enterprise let alone saving your body, in Molly's view. She suspected Helen's was already quibbling – why else would she turn all weepy on her the other night?

She discovered that:

- he was only twenty-five (black mark)
- he was single (gold star)
- he lived at home (pitch-black mark)
- he was writing a doctorate thesis on an obscure Armenian poet (borderline, but perhaps he should be awarded a gold star for originality)
- he worked part time at the off-licence to earn pocket money (neither a gold star nor a black mark)
- he had signed up for the art course at the National Gallery and fully intended to attend every lecture (gold star)
- the woman with whom he'd been immersed in conversation in Bewley's was one of his three sisters (gold star – men with sisters tended to have their act together).

She reviewed the situation as gallery staff called shutting-up time. More gold stars than black marks. On the one hand he was a moveable feast on the eyes plus he was bright. On the other hand he was a shade too young, subsisting on a grant and you couldn't really take a boyfriend seriously who lived with the mammy and daddy.

They separated on the corner of Pearse Street; he was steering towards Trinity College to collect some books and she was headed for the station.

'Thank you for the coffee. I'll buy next week if I manage to turn up for the lecture,' she said.

'But you must.' He waxed animated. 'It's about Harry Clarke, his stained-glass windows leave me awestruck. I have a book with some of his best examples – it highlights his love of detail, he was a great man for the finishing touches – but nothing compares with the vibrant colours of the originals. Apparently there's three corkers in a little church overlooking the sea in Castletownshend, commissioned by Edith Somerville who co-wrote *The Irish RM* books. One of the windows is a nativity scene. It's magnificent. Believe me, you can't miss the lecture.'

'I'll do my best.' Molly was nonplussed by his insistence. He obviously wanted to pump her about Helen. Good job she had Fionn McCullagh on the back burner or her ego would be seriously dented. And there was always Barry, who'd once pledged to donate sperm if her biological clock went into overdrive without another supplier on the horizon. Admittedly he wasn't stone-cold sober when she wrangled the offer from him – in fact it was unlikely he remembered making it – but she fully intended pinning him down and holding him to it if the ticking accelerated. Not that her biological clock would get a look-in while her wedding march neurosis was still festering.

Speaking of husbands – even other people's – she was supposed to be giving Fionn a ring to arrange another date. She should do that sooner rather than later. He was obviously in a highly vulnerable condition and apt to fall into the arms of someone else. She examined her emotions for telltale twinges of jealously and was reassured to encounter not so much as a pang. Still, at least he wanted her even if the Georgeous One didn't, which was essential oxygen to the deflated ego.

Molly felt a cramp in her twisted ankle as she walked and it nursed her sense of grievance. Whatever happened to blondes having more fun? Surely this couldn't be time for the brunette to bite back. Here she was, paying blood money to hairdressers and suffering hours of discomfort and tedium for that sunkissed California girl image, when she could have left well alone and mirrored Helen's dark mystery. Provided she also bought grey contact lenses. If there was a God, he was a prankster. Which meant he had to be a man and not a woman after all, despite having prompted someone to invent lipsticks with mirrors on the side of the tube for ease of application. Somewhat consoled by her deductions, Molly bought a ticket to Blackrock. And decided to ring Fionn before she went to bed.

Greek gods were all very well but if they were determined to occupy Mount Olympus then Irish architects would have to compensate.

CHAPTER 9

'I rang you last night to see if you fancied going to a film but your answerphone kept clicking on. I nearly invited it out instead.'

It wasn't Fionn returning her call – he hadn't been in when she tried reaching him with the impossibly exciting news that she was available for whisking off to dinner – but Helen on the phone to Molly at work.

'You should have left a message, Helen. I'd have called you back – I was at a lecture – I wasn't home particularly late.'

'Tried to but it kept cutting out. Anyway, I had an early night instead. Do you fancy doing something tonight?'

'Don't finish work until nine thirty or thereabouts so we probably won't make it in time for the opening credits of a film but we could split a bottle of wine in La Cave if you like, check out the foreign talent.'

La Cave was a winebar on South Anne Street which obviously featured in some travel guide or other, because the clientele was always peppered with tourists. The last time Molly and Helen were there they danced a merengue with two Basques between tables of diners, who held onto their glasses whenever the hip-swivelling became overly exuberant. Tipsy on too much Rioja and not enough pizza, the girls entertained themselves hugely by joking they'd nip home and change into their basques for the next set. They thought it was hilarious; the Basques' English didn't run to wordplay.

'Do you think La Cave is a good idea? We always have adventures when we go there and I fancied a quiet chat.' Helen was dubious.

'It's a Friday night, oh Helen of Athboy. You can have a quiet chat from Sunday through to Thursday but not tonight. When you're fifty you can go home and watch *The Late Late Show* on a Friday night but until then I regard it as my duty to ensure you receive your fair quotient of fun. I'll meet you in La Cave at nine thirty-one.'

'That's extraordinarily explicit timing, Molly. Remind me again, why Athboy?'

'Because it's dull. Like you're in danger of becoming, only fortunately I am your self-appointed guardian angel and I've made it my mission to save you from boring tendencies.'

'How about if we agree not to have more than one bottle and to catch the last DART home?' Helen essayed some negotiation.

'How about if we agree to wear knee-length cardigans and drink Ballygowans?' Molly declined to play ball.

'Fair enough. We probably have no chance of a couple of stools near the bar but I'll scout around if I get there before you.' Helen acknowledged there was no hope of meeting on middle ground and caved in. La Cave was designed for caving in.

'You'll enjoy yourself, I promise you,' Molly reassured her.

'I have no doubt. I'll also have a thumping headache and smoke-drenched clothes by tomorrow.'

'Small price to pay for a modicum of entertainment, Helen.'

Barry, eavesdropping shamelessly, pushed a coffee he'd brought from the canteen Molly's way.

'Going on the batter tonight?' There was more than a suspicion of envy in his voice.

'Just having a few drinks with Helen.' Molly grappled with the plastic lid, spilling frothing liquid on her notebook. 'Do you have a home number for anyone from the employers' group IBEC? I need a reaction to this shopworkers' strike story I'm writing.'

'I can manage a mobile for their press officer. Helen's the stern one with shoulder-length black hair, isn't she?' He told Molly the phone number. 'I met her at your flat-roasting party.'

'Sounds about right. What's the PR's name?'

'Sally Halligan. You'll have no bother with her, she's up to speed.' Barry sounded wistful. 'I wouldn't mind a night out myself. I'd love to go on the town with the two of you but Kay would never agree to it.'

'Voicemail.' Molly replaced the receiver. 'So have a night out with Kay. Any chance of a home number for Sally Hartigan?'

'Halligan.' Barry read it out and sighed. 'She'd never agree. We're supposed to be saving for a new kitchen although the old one hasn't a mark on it.'

Molly pulled a sympathetic face and made a mental note that the single life had its compensations.

La Cave was jammed. Molly, liberated from work earlier than expected thanks to the next day's paper being tight on space – hallelujah for active advertising staff – was paying for a bottle of house red when Helen arrived.

'Your little suede skirt, you must mean business.' Molly appraised her.

Helen tugged at the clotted-cream skirt without managing

to pull it any closer to her knees. 'May as well look the part if you're planning to have me dancing on tables with the tourists.'

'Around tables, angel face. The owner worries about the pock marks heels leave on his table tops.' Molly shuffled a few inches so that Helen could squeeze in beside her at the bar. 'Quick, empty a glass of this down your throat. Hundreds of grapes gave their life's blood so we could knock it straight back without bothering to taste it. You'll never guess who I saw at the lecture last night. Go on, guess.'

'I wanted to talk to you about something,' protested Helen, but Molly was so preoccupied with thoughts of Hercules that she didn't notice. Although not so distracted that she failed to spot she was being given the eye by a thirtysomething in the sort of stylish co-ordinates that marked him out instantly as European. Irishmen's idea of casual wear was inevitably crumpled.

She wrenched her attention back to Hercules with the heroic effort a Greek god deserved. 'He's an aesthete, Helen,' she announced.

Helen was bemused. 'Your man over there with the perma-tan leering at you?'

'Is he really leering? I must be looking happening tonight despite the work suit. No, Hercules. He materialised a couple of rows ahead of me at the National Gallery lecture, like Venus rising from the waves only fully clothed, of course, and male obviously.'

Helen smiled as she sipped at her wine despite Molly's injunction to wallop it into her. 'So this is one course of night classes where you'll manage to turn up for every lesson. Perhaps he's a plant, brought in by the gallery to encourage attendance.'

Molly laughed and attempted to refill Helen's near-brimming glass. 'We had a coffee together afterwards. It turns out he's from Glasthule, just around the corner from you, and I scarcely exist as far as he's concerned. but he's smitten by you. He called you my friend with the disappointed eyes. So he's on special offer to women with that thwarted look if you're available. By the way, his name's Georgie. Suits him. He has that look of a little boy who kissed the girls and made them cry.'

Helen was embarrassed and twirled the ends of her hair around her index finger. She knew how much Molly liked her Greek and was touched by her generosity in passing him on. Not that he was hers to dole out exactly. However, Helen wasn't the least bit interested in Georgie – those features could be carved from marble as far as she was concerned.

'He's all yours, Moll,' she said. 'Mediterranean types were never for me. I prefer pale, brooding individuals, even if their tortured expressions are due to hangovers as opposed to poetic angst.'

Molly was relieved. 'Felt I had to give you the option since you haven't paid much attention to men in several decades. God, this place is lethal, I may as well be back on twenty a day as sit in here.' She shot a baleful glance at a couple billowing smoke in their direction and was ignored.

'Stop behaving like a reformed smoker. If you fancied breathing clean air you should have opted for a stroll on the seafront.'

'True. Here's the plan: I am now going to undulate my way past that mahogany-skinned gentleman from foreign climes, flinging him my boldest come-hither glance. I don't actually propose to do anything with him if he does approach but it's essential to keep your weaponry in working order.'

'You're incorrigible, Molly,' said Helen.

'I know,' she replied complacently, and swayed her way towards the man in question and his friend, also a sun-worshipper from his complexion, tossing her curls as she manoeuvred by them.

Helen snatched the opportunity of her absence to order and dispatch a stealthy mineral water. Such a country they lived in, where drinking water was regarded as a social solecism.

Molly returned, lavishly lipsticked in babydoll pink, plonked her elbows on the bar and announced: 'So now we need to formulate a campaign which allows me to don a loin cloth and swing through the jungle ululating and snatching up my Elgin marbles mate who'll be trembling with desire and swooning in my arms.'

'On the other hand you could try throwing him one of those potent come-hither glances of yours and leave the athletics to the trapeze artists.'

'Also a possibility,' agreed Molly, 'but the way I see it –'

Insight into her perspective was delayed by the barman. He produced a bottle of Valpolicella, uncorked it and said, 'Compliments of the two gentlemen there.'

'You see, your come-hither glances are dynamite,' said Helen. Addressing the barman she added: 'Could you send it back, please? Tell them we only accept sweets from strangers. Unsolicited alcohol is too perverse by half.'

'Do nothing of the sort,' objected Molly. 'Splash a dollop in here and we'll toast their good health.'

She raised her glass to their admirers, hissing 'Smile' at Helen.

'I will not. We'll be tormented with them all night and I wanted to have a private chat with you.'

Helen had hoped to raise the subject of Patrick in a

128

roundabout 'I have a friend with a problem' sort of way. Molly wasn't having any of it.

'We can have a private chat any time. These lads will buy us drink all night and the craic will be mighty. It's our duty to drink wine or vineyards will go out of business – there are countries where the annual per capita consumption is only a teaspoon.'

'Which countries?' asked Helen.

'The entire Indian subcontinent for starters. Which nationality do you think they are? My money's on Italian. Here they come. Play nicely, Helen, for my sake. I fancy a flirt. You should try it yourself, sets the blood coursing.'

'Molly, we can buy our own drink. We're not penniless students any more.'

'I know but I like to relive the glory days.' To the tourists: 'Thank you for the wine. Would you like to share a glass with us?' My name's Nora and this is my friend Bridget, we're *ban-gardaí* here in Dublin. You don't know what *ban-gardaí* are? Female policemen. Yes, I know it's a contradiction but that's language for you. Don't look so worried, we're off duty. I promise this isn't an undercover assignment – would we admit we were in the police force if it were? Now tell us where you're from. Sicily, how fascinating. I tasted some of your Mount Etna firewater once. It left me all fired up – I suppose that was the intention.'

Helen raised her glass to her lips. The skirmishing was under way. She needed some ammunition and the bottled sort was at her elbow. Convenience had much to recommend it. She edged away from one of the Italians, who didn't recognise ground rules about personal space; if she were a *garda* she'd slap out her badge and intimidate him with it. Even amorous Italians had to back off from women with impressive police credentials.

Trailing her fingers down the stem of the glass, Helen smiled at her Italian without any particular zeal. Her mind was elsewhere. If only she'd been able to raise the subject of Patrick with Molly – her friend was unshockable. Sometimes Helen's brain seemed to constrict with the effort of clinging to her secret. It would be the sweetest relief to spill out the words, let them trickle into a sympathetic ear. She was at a crossroads – and undecided. What she could do and what she should do were vying for supremacy.

Helen hitched down her suede skirt, even as Molly deliberately inched her pinstriped skirt up her knees. She should have known better than to expect to introduce a subject as explosive as incest in La Cave on a Friday night when Molly was wired for frolics. But there was no appropriate time or place.

Incest. There, she'd said it. Rattled, Helen drained her glass and turned towards the man beside her, who immediately refilled it. She needed amnesia – concentrate on him and perhaps his voice would sound in her ears instead of Patrick's. Maybe she could dip a toe in brown eyes instead of drowning in grey-green. Helen's mouth pursed. Incest. The word reverberated through her skull with the persistence of a pneumatic drill. And it was equally impossible to ignore. She was drenched in self-repulsion. She drank again and felt herself grow light-headed.

'You find the wine good?' asked the Italian, bottle at the ready.

'I find it effective,' she replied, 'or at least I'm giving it the benefit of the doubt.' The corner of the bar counter bit into her back as she leaned away from him but she continued to smile. Distract me, she pleaded mentally. Incest was such a putrescent word.

At some stage of the evening – they'd lost track of time

– the girls, along with the other late drinkers, were ejected from La Cave and made their way to Lillie's Bordello where further drinking was assured in the nightclub's private members' bar; its attraction was that it scarcely felt as though you were in a nightclub at all. Around 2 a.m. Helen pulled off her usual trick of seizing Molly by the elbow and dragging her into the ladies, where she insisted they slope off and leave the Italians to their own devices.

'I know we're reputed to be a friendly race but we're not obliged by the laws of hospitality to sleep with tourists into the bargain,' she complained, rimming her lids with a wobbly line of black eye-pencil.

'I suppose not,' said Molly regretfully, nose a-glow from the killer combination of drinking and dancing.

'So what do you say we slip off for a coffee, just the two of us?' wheedled Helen. 'We could have some food – we forgot to eat in La Cave.'

She was tempted to evacuate on her own but conscience prevented her from leaving Molly to parry the Taormina Twins on her own. And an additional burst of puritanism hindered her from allowing Molly the freedom to decide against fending off one or other of the pair.

'We're out of here,' grinned Molly, with more alacrity than Helen had bargained for. Maybe her friend was learning restraint. Or perhaps the promise of food was the bait, as Molly added: 'I'm starving; I could eat the hand of God. You nip downstairs for the coats and I'll stand guard.' She paused and added, 'We're making a habit of this, sloping into the ladies as a prelude to abandoning men. If word leaks out we'll be banned from using toilets.'

Outdoors, giggling and insulated from the wind by the amount of alcohol pumping through their veins, they headed for an all-night café near Smithfield Market. By this stage Helen had lost interest in discussing her predicament with Patrick. All she wanted was something to eat – a cross between breakfast and supper. Perhaps poached eggs.

'So what was your Italian like?' asked Molly between bites of sausage as she devoured a cooked breakfast.

'He wasn't the worst. His name was Angelo and he was some sort of engineer. How about yours?'

'Paolo, also an engineer; they work together. This is their first time in Ireland. They usually go to France but they saw a behind-the-scenes TV programme about the Rose of Tralee competition and decided to establish whether the blooms compensated for the thorns.'

Helen lifted a triangle of buttered toast to her mouth. 'They talked excessively about food, that's what made me hungry. They think the food is abysmal but the craic compensates.'

'What's wrong with our food?' Molly was indignant.

'Pizza bases are too thick, pasta sauces aren't homemade.'

'You mean they're not even sampling Irish food, they're eating Italian nosh on their holliers?' Molly savaged a slice of fried tomato which splattered seeds on the plastic tablecloth. 'Of course it won't be as good as Mamma makes, stands to reason.'

'It's tricky for tourists to test-drive Irish food. There isn't any unless you count soda bread,' Helen pointed out.

'Can't they eat chips like the rest of us? They're made with Irish potatoes.'

'Most of the chippers are Italian.'

'So they are. Mine said,' Molly adopted an approximation of Robert De Niro's voice, '"You Irish girls are a handful, you like to laugh – I bet you like to love too."'

They convulsed in stereo.

'Of course,' amended Molly, 'he said it in an Italian

132

accent rather than a Bronx one. But you get the picture.'

'Remember the time,' reminisced Helen, 'we picked up the Germans at La Cave and made them drink Blue Nun all night to punish them for exporting it to us?'

'Tourists,' sighed Molly. 'What would we do with all that chunky crystal and those even chunkier sweaters if they didn't come here and buy them?'

'Here's to tourists.' Helen raised her orange juice and Molly clanked her tumbler against it.

Helen caught a glimpse of a man's back at the counter and stiffened for the space of two heartbeats as the set of his head led her to imagine it was Patrick, although the chances of him wandering around Smithfield at three o'clock on a Saturday morning seemed improbable. The expression that flitted across her face – a piquant combination of eager and wary – triggered in Molly the recollection that Helen seemed determined to talk to her earlier in the evening.

'So what's on your mind, Helen? Spill your guts to me, I'm a trained listener. Tape recorder's ready and running. I'm presuming you don't mind your secrets being splashed across the front page.'

But Helen, having longed to probe the intricacies of her situation – in a circumspect way, with someone whose judgement she trusted despite her wayward tendencies – was now defensively protective of her conundrum.

'Nothing that can't wait, Molly. We'll do the girlie chat another time.'

Molly studied her: purple blots were brushed beneath Helen's lashes; she was someone whose sleeping pattern had been disrupted. Molly was too weary and inebriated to tackle her now but instinct told her, at long last, that she should bend an ear to whatever was troubling Helen.

'We'll have to leave it until Sunday because I have a hot date tomorrow,' Molly mused aloud.

'Are your dates ever anything else?'

Molly cast her mind back over her last few encounters. 'They always start hot and grow progressively more luke-warm. But hope springs eternal. Give me a ring on the mobile about ten p.m. to be on the safe side. I can either claim you're a sick relative or tell you to push off, depending on the temperature.'

'Fair enough, but you have to promise to tell me all about it on Sunday. Especially if it's one of those dates where the poor fellow thinks you're saddled with a weak bladder because you keep bolting for the ladies to let your giggles erupt.'

'It's not my mission in life to accept gruesome dates to provide entertainment for my friends.' Molly pantomimed huffiness.

'No, but it's a useful bonus from my point of view,' said Helen. 'Do you want that phone call at ten o'clock or not?'

'Done deal, angel face,' agreed Molly. 'Why aren't you out on the pull tomorrow anyway? I presume you have something more pressing on the agenda, like rearranging the furniture.'

'Having an early night with my Filipino houseboy, if you must know. But I'll take a break and send him off for fresh supplies of baby oil around ten as a concession to friendship.'

Molly laughed and lightly punched her shoulder. 'Let's ring for a cab. And while we're waiting I'll remind you of some of the highlights of my dates from hell. You've no idea how I've suffered, Helen. And what's worse, I never learn because I plan to continue suffering.'

She contemplated admitting she was seeing Fionn the

following night but decided on discretion – not a virtue Molly was acquainted with but you were never too old to learn. Helen might try to talk her out of meeting Fionn. Her disapproval of his Stateside vanishing act had been comforting then but might incline towards the censorious now. Time enough to unveil Fionn to Helen if she chose to let him unveil himself to her first.

'Do I know who you're seeing tonight – it's not one of those seedy hacks you hang around with, is it?' asked Helen.

'I have my standards.' Molly looked virtuous. 'Low ones admittedly, but standards none the less. Hacks are out of the frame. It's a friend. I don't expect it will amount to anything; I'm really only taking pity on a sorrowful specimen tomorrow night, or rather tonight. He's been unlucky in love and is throwing shapes. Wounded warrior ones. I'm currently trying to decide whether to play doctors and nurses with him.'

'And there I was imagining it was true love with the Geek,' said Helen.

'Greek. And rule nothing out. Hercules is still up there among celestial clouds on Olympus but any time he fancies plunging earthwards, I'm his woman. In the meantime I need some distraction while waiting for him wake up to the fact I'm an über-babe. Which he will.' Molly clanged her knife and fork onto the plate and wiped her mouth with a paper serviette. 'The man hasn't a chance.'

'Fighting talk, Molly Molloy. Go get him.'

'On one condition.'

'Name it.'

'Never call me Molly Molloy in public again.'

CHAPTER 10

Helen was clamped in a vice. She wanted that night with Patrick, a night to store in her memory banks and carry with her as a bulwark against the bleakness threatening to engulf her. Yet she knew it could unravel a craving she might be impotent to curb. She'd just about managed to clamber out of the gully levered open three years ago. Survival had been achieved only by severance. She'd been steely for both of them. They had to be parallel lines from then on, she'd told him, all intimacy guillotined. That was when Patrick had moved to London. Unrelenting *in extremis*, she'd given him an ultimatum, virtually packed his bags and impelled him to the plane. If he didn't emigrate she would. It had been the correct action to take, they were unsafe together and Patrick had prospered in London while she had . . . coped.

Helen had never allowed herself to recreate that night three years ago, to sift through the sensations. Other vignettes, more innocent ones from their teenage years, often overwhelmed her, but this one had been painstakingly interred. Her sanity decreed it. But these recent meetings with Patrick had loosened the amnesiac straps she'd coiled around the memory and for the first time recollections of their encounter three years ago were unleashed. She parried the pictures swarming through her consciousness. Lava-like, they scorched her. And then she submitted to the imagery, wearied by the years of willing it into denial.

Her body is stirred as much by his sweet expression as by his sure touch caressing her. She is aroused beyond caring about the consequences. Tangled in each other's limbs on the cracked leather sofa of her flat in Kimmage, they're panting and semi-undressed – clothes scrabbled open in the compulsion for skin to connect with skin. His urgency is matched by hers. It's life-enhancing, a liberation, and she glories in it. Unexpectedly, at the moment of penetration, his frenzy abates; she hesitates momentarily until her body takes its cue from his. He smiles, she relaxes and a waft of honeyed leisure subsumes them at their joining together. 'We were born for this,' he whispers, hands alongside her head to steady her, shafting euphoria into her body. Closing her circle.

Afterwards he cradles her, lapping at her tears and promising the guilt will subside. She doesn't tell him she's not weeping from a sense of transgression but from the conviction they belong together. Later the guilt does float to the surface. But it does not drown out the desire.

'Dear Jesus, but I want him still,' she croaked.

Acknowledgement panicked her: three years of self-control were draining away; she was losing her grip inexorably. And that way lunacy beckoned. She shouldn't even be toying with the notion of agreeing to something so unnatural as a night in the arms of her brother. Or was it truly obscene?

It felt completely natural to love him, that was the crux of her problem.

Helen's head was reeling. She slumped at her computer screen with a blank expression and an even blanker productivity level, battling against the realisation she'd manage no work that day. She was supposed to be writing a new banking programme in C – a language which Molly joked could stand for cryptic as readily as code. But nothing was forthcoming. Perhaps if she allowed herself fifteen minutes to mull over Patrick's suggestion with a coffee for company it might eliminate the dilemma and concentration would be restored. What would Molly say? Helen half-smiled. She'd sing out: 'Duck, low-flying pigs overhead.' Nevertheless Helen groped by the side of her desk for her satchel and headed for the canteen, reconsidered when she saw how crammed it was, and stepped outside to José's sandwich bar opposite the sub-post office.

José, who preferred to be called Joe, personally delivered her latte to the corner table with its view of the street – a service reserved for regulars and women he fancied. He also brought a caramel slice which she hadn't ordered.

'On the house – you look like someone in need of cheering up.' He patted her seat back – Helen had an untouchable aura. 'My wife baked it only an hour ago.'

Although Joe gave a convincing impersonation of being a hulking thug he was a kind man, and while he liked to admire the pretty office workers who frequented his sandwich bar he never overstepped the mark.

Helen was grateful for the gesture and so, while she hadn't a sweet tooth, she perfunctorily forked some of the toffee-swathed biscuit base into her mouth. As she chewed she considered her life. Some would say she was blessed. She had her own home with a manageable mortgage; a two-year-old car with 14,000 miles on the clock; a job with excellent prospects which she enjoyed; a best friend who entertained her and could be relied on in an emergency; she was reasonably attractive and could still fit into the clothes she'd worn at eighteen, if she chose (which she didn't tend to because she'd outgrown unrelieved black as a lifestyle statement), she had no debts apart from her mortgage and seven more interest-free-credit instalments on a flat-screen television set described as sexy three times by the sales assistant in the space of a minute. Um, had she mentioned the career? That appeared to be it. Not such a disgraceful tally. There was no love interest but did she require a man in her life for fulfilment? Society seemed to believe so but she wasn't obliged to conform to its diktat.

The planned circumlocutory chat with Molly still hadn't happened because Molly had cried off on Sunday, laid low by a tummy bug after an Indian meal the previous night – although Helen reasoned that the culprit was the combination of a barrel-load of red wine in La Cave followed by her fry-up in Smithfield. Whatever the cause, the hot date morphed into a date from hell without passing through the lukewarm stage.

Instead of meeting Molly on Sunday afternoon Helen mooched around Blackrock market on her own. She inspected novelty clocks and stained-glass mirrors with even-handed indifference, almost bought a pair of candlesticks but reconsidered when she detected a flaw in one, and had a coffee and some quiche by way of lunch and dinner combined in a café. She phoned the invalid on Sunday night to check on her state of health and concluded she'd live, although she must truly be unwell because even a reference to what Molly should wear for her tryst with Hercules in the lecture theatre on Thursday night failed to spark interest.

Helen wished she could tread a path as uncomplicated as Molly's, for all her unrequited passions and recent fixation on a white wedding. But that would mean writing Patrick out of her life and, despite the turmoil, she wasn't ready to excise him just yet. She realised she had cut her caramel slice into eight tiny squares, the biscuit base crumbling around the plate, and scooped some up with a fork. A glance at her watch told her the fifteen minutes allotted by that mandatory timekeeper in her conscience had already elapsed and she was no nearer elucidation. There was a hole in her life, she admitted, but it wasn't a man-shaped void. It was a Patrick-shaped one. She didn't need him to transform her life but she knew he could enhance its monochrome, just as she could add colour to his. Helen pined to love and be loved in return . . . wasn't that what it was all about? Otherwise there was a pointlessness to this whole business of breathing and eating and going to work and dragging home.

Patrick had phoned twice yesterday while she'd wandered aimlessly around Blackrock market but she hadn't returned his calls. She had no answer to give him. Yes was impossible and no was equally unfeasible.

Helen sighed and made for the street, nodding at Joe on her way past.

He watched the pale woman with the fleeting smile that transformed her features walk, head bowed, in front of the plate-glass window and wondered how she could look so care-ridden. As far as Joe was concerned, beautiful girls had no serious problems.

If only, thought Helen, back at her desk again, she could sleep round the clock she'd have the energy to devote to this. She was so tired, energy sapped from insectile beating against the window of her brain. She'd make an appointment with her doctor, concoct an excuse for why she needed a prescription for sleeping pills. Telling him she was exhausted from pondering the implications of sleeping with her brother wouldn't pass muster – he'd be quicker to refer her to a shrink than dole out some little white tablets. She'd fabricate something – say, stress from overwork. Helen caught her boss, Tony's, eye resting on her and hastily clicked her mouse onto an icon.

The doctor, tweed-suited among ferns and spider plants on his desk and on the window ledges like some Victorian botanist, gave her a lecture about Mogadon – it had a half-life the following day, which meant she wouldn't be firing on all cylinders – and then prescribed some. The packet specified one to two and Helen dithered on quantity before deciding to try two with a milky drink later. But she couldn't settle – even ironing failed to soothe her as it usually did with its mechanical precision – so she conceded defeat and unplugged the phone at eight o'clock, then squeezed a couple of pills from their foil container onto the palm of her hand. She swallowed them with a glass of pear-flavoured water.

Helen slept heavily, although not tranquilly, until shortly after midnight, when she awoke lathered in sweat and with the tongue sticking to the roof of her mouth.

Must've taken only one after all, otherwise I'd still be asleep, she thought thickly, barking her shin as she stumbled to the bathroom. She knocked over a bottle of conditioner, groping for the pills, the orange liquid glooping out in pools, but fastidiousness declined to assert itself and she left it to coagulate on the floorboards. She staggered to the kitchen, located the pills by the sink and downed another. She was virtually comatose by the top of the stairs.

Next morning Helen awoke with a Red Bull and vodka hangover. She lay for a few minutes, watching the light glance off her framed print of waterlilies, in a state of some bewilderment. She eased her neck sideways – it appeared to be cast from concrete – and studied her alarm clock. There must be some mistake – it read 12.10 p.m. Panicked, she leaped from bed, thudding clumsily, and snatched up her watch. It was in on the 12.10 p.m. conspiracy, which meant she had slept through the alarm. She was never taking those pills again.

She slumped back on the bed, legs dangling over the side, exhausted by her adrenaline rush, and cradled a pillow. She knew she should ring work and tell them she'd been delayed but she hadn't the energy. She nodded off again and woke at 2.25 p.m., gasping for water. Exigency coerced her lethargic legs downstairs and into the kitchen, where she gulped two glasses in succession from the tap and a third more slowly. There was no point in going into work at this stage; she'd ring and tell them there was a family emergency and she hadn't had an opportunity to reach a phone until now. Helen never skived off; she was confident her boss would be understanding.

She filled the kettle and made a cafetiere of strong coffee, drinking it black as she leaned on the worktop. She must never, not ever, take three Mogadon again. One was her limit and even then it would have to be dire straits before she'd consider it. And after she'd taken the pill she'd lock the rest away where she'd never find them. Helen massaged her aching temples. The coffee seemed to be stripping away the cotton wool layers that cushioned her and allowing pain to trickle in.

She swallowed more coffee, then realised she might as well sit down to drink it, and crossed to the living room. En route she spotted a couple of envelopes on the mat by the front door and diverted to retrieve them. She assimilated her haul on the sofa: an Eircom bill and a postcard from her sister, Geraldine, already back in Galway a fortnight – Helen had declined to accompany her on that trip to Turkey; she and Geraldine always bickered on holiday. The third missive had no stamp and she recognised the handwriting with an accelerated pulse. It was from Patrick.

Helen opened it, ripping the single sheet of paper inside in her haste. Beneath a hotel letterhead it read:

> Dear Helen,
> I keep getting your answerphone or the engaged tone when I ring you. So I dropped by tonight – yes, I'm in Dublin again, Ryanair are making a fortune out of me – on the off chance you'd be at home. Maybe you've gone away for a few days to think over our last conversation. I'd appreciate hearing from you as soon as possible. I know this is probably turning your life upside down but it's not exactly lending serenity to mine either. Please ring me at the hotel. Soon.
> Yours, Patrick.

Afterwards Helen wondered, with the benefit of hindsight, whether the sleeping pills had warped her judgement; but she was acting on a visceral propulsion as she dialled the number and asked for his room.

Patrick wasted no time on civilities. 'Where are you, can we meet?'

'At home. I have a day off.'

'Please let me come over, I'll be there in half an hour.'

'Yes,' she agreed, without pausing to consider she was unwashed, undressed and unpresentable.

The doorbell rang as she emerged, dripping, from the shower. She pulled on leggings and a loose shirt, left waiting on her Lloyd Loom bathroom stool, and was still rubbing at her hair with a towel as she opened the door. Without speaking, he took her in his arms, kicking the door shut behind him. When she surfaced from his embrace Helen found the damp towel draped on their feet where she'd let it slip from her hand.

Patrick stepped back to scan her face anxiously. 'Are you ill? You sounded blurry on the phone, as though you were coming down with a cold.'

Helen told him about the sleeping tablets and his horrified reaction disconcerted her. He tried to dragoon her into promising never to touch them again and virtually demanded she reach them over so he could flush them away, which rendered her mutinously determined to hold on to them and she all but sprinted upstairs to secrete them into her bedside cabinet. But even after a shower she hadn't the energy to break into a trot. And she still wasn't hungry either, which made it nearly twenty hours since she'd last eaten. Better not tell Molly or she'd be chewing Mogadon as a diet supplement.

Patrick realised Helen was tense and spoke more moderately.

'Listen, don't feel I'm overreacting, it's just that I'm concerned about you. I couldn't live with myself if I thought the pressure I was exerting on you was the reason you started cramming pills into your system. It would be insupportable and –'

'Three sleeping tablets won't turn me into a junkie,' interrupted Helen. 'Come on, Patrick, you know I rarely take so much as paracetamol for a headache. I'm more inclined to walk it off or rustle up some herbal tea. Now could we drop this? My system is clamouring for more coffee. And don't start implying that makes me a caffeine addict.'

Helen turned on her heel and headed for the kitchen, expecting Patrick to follow. When he didn't she stuck her head out of the door and called to him. He was standing where she'd left him, uncertainty personified, and she saw again her brother as a teenager, cycling home from school, with his sheepdog, Prince, pounding along by his mudguards.

'Patrick,' her voice mellowed from its previous indignant pitch, 'Patrick, won't you come in and sit down?'

Relief flooded his face and he was almost immediately sprawled at her kitchen table. As she placed the cafetiere on a marble-effect placemat, Patrick produced a beribboned package from his breast pocket. He placed it wordlessly in front of her.

'Is that for me?' Nonplussed, she fingered the mole on her jawline just south of an ear.

He nodded.

'Shall I open it?'

'No, you can just sit there and admire the shiny paper.'

Helen laughed and lifted it, shook it and unpicked the knot in the mint-green bow.

'There's no need to bring me gifts, Patrick. You turned up with snowdrops the last time you called.'

'It's not about need. It's about inclination.'

Beneath the embossed green paper was a bronze oval box a few inches in diameter and when she raised the lid, a silver apple brooch gleamed from its cushioned interior. Helen lifted it out, her mouth curved in an O of exclamation.

Watching her, Patrick quoted softly. '"And pluck till time and times are done/The silver apples of the moon,/The golden apples of the sun."'

'You remembered,' she whispered, tears welling in her eyes.

'I was so proud of you that day.' He stretched out a hand and covered hers.

'But you can't have been more than six,' objected Helen.

'Sometimes incidents which happen at that age gleam more luminously in your memory than what comes later.' His fingers were stroking the back of her hand now, moving across the knuckles, forward and back.

By one of those curious lateral leaps the mind sometimes takes, she thought of Paris and the golden apple he gave Aphrodite to win Helen of Troy. She'd always taken an interest in the *Iliad* because of her name; perhaps if she'd been called Joan it would have been Maid of Orléans stories that moved her. She recalled how Paris and Helen paid a price for love which neither could have envisaged. And a premonition gripped her so that she fumbled as she fastened her silver apple to her white linen shirt, just above the heart.

Patrick lifted a fold of material and finished the job, inadvertently brushing against her left breast. The nipple made an indentation against the cloth and she was acutely conscious of him looking at it.

She caught his eye and, to disguise the moment, he said: 'Do you remember the poem?'

'Swathes of it. It's been a while since I took a stroll through "The Song of Wandering Aengus" but what you learn at nine stays with you.'

He dragged his chair closer and, one arm around her shoulder and the other clasping her waist, leaned his jaw against her temple and closed his eyes. Helen allowed her eyelids to drift downwards too, and her mind floated backwards to the local feis when she'd won a silver cup for her recitation of the Yeats poem and repeated her triumph at the winners' grand finale.

Her father had bought tickets for the family and she remembered standing in the wings, shivering with anticipation at the knowledge that Geraldine, Patrick and her parents were in the belly of the auditorium, waiting to applaud her performance. It had been a gilded moment, one of those rare occasions when you experience happiness and realise it simultaneously instead of in retrospect. To celebrate, her father had brought them out for a meal afterwards and, stiff with solemnity, opened his wallet and placed a note in front of Helen's place. She'd never owned more than coins before.

Helen is afraid to touch the money – wary of it being snatched back. It looks such a lot. Maybe it would be enough to buy her a baby doll that can cry and wet herself. Mammy says nine-year-olds are too grown-up for Tiny Tears dolls but Helen longs for one.

The note's dog-eared dilapidation in no way diminishes its lustre for her. She plaits her hands under the table to stop herself reaching for it until she's certain it's allowed. The other children are equally fascinated by the money.

'Pick it up, girl,' says her father. 'You've shown people around here the Sharkeys can amount to something.' He scrapes his soup spoon along the bowl, unfamiliar in his good grey suit – and in the benign expression twinkling from his eyes. Helen checks her mother's face; the woman nods her approval.

'Can I spend it on anything I like, anything at all?' she breathes, not daring to mention a baby doll. Doubt assails her. 'Or must I put it in my piggy bank?'

Her mother purses her lips. 'Of course it's your money and you've earned it but I think you should save at least something.'

'No.' Her father's tone is peremptory and his contradiction is delivered so swiftly that disappointment has no chance to pinch in Helen. It's the first time that she can remember him speaking up for her. 'Let the girl enjoy her money. Spend it however you please.'

Helen risks a glance at her mother, whose lips are folded over her teeth to stifle an incipient objection. Patrick diverts the woman, grabbing Helen's bill and trailing it through his soup. She slaps him while her husband eats, unruffled.

Helen feels she might burst apart because so much joy is building up inside her. Everything would be different from now on. She's made her father proud of her and she could do it again.

'I deserve something too', objects Geraldine. 'I spent all my spare time coaching Helen – she'd never have won without me.'

'Of course she wouldn't, princess, you're the star of the family.' Pat Sharkey clinks his spoon into the empty bowl and reaches across a fistful of loose change to his eldest daughter, fingers closing over hers.

Helen's heart withers within her.

Instead of a doll she'd bought a silver apple brooch from Roches Stores with the money. The trinket had tarnished after a few months and the marcasite stem of the apple lost its stones and blackened, but she'd worn it on the lapel of her Sunday coat until it disintegrated.

'He loved me that day, I know he did,' she murmured now against Patrick's chest. His mouth brushed the top of her hair. But when he felt the splash of a tear on his hand he opened his eyes in alarm. Patrick lowered his face, seeking to press his cheek against hers and mop up the tears like a sponge, but she clung to him as to driftwood in a current. He lifted her onto his lap, wrapping his arms around her so fiercely that he imagined he might snap her in two with the slightest additional pressure. Her face burrowed into his neck. If she and Patrick never had another moment together she could not complain, for this was rapture unvitiated by another intruding emotion. She strained to prevent herself from moving, from breathing even – loath to break the spell woven around them.

Then of its own accord her body moulded against his and her lips sought his out. Thinking only to comfort, he was unprepared for the turbulence of her passion – or it could have been despair. He pushed away the fleeting analysis. But the pace of his ardour outstripped hers as, rough now in his heated state, he prised himself from her lips and pushed up her shirt. Helen stiffened as he fastened his mouth on a nipple, wrenched herself from his arms and retreated to the furthest corner of the room.

'Come here, Helen, I'm not going to molest you,' he beseeched.

She ignored the entreaty in his voice.

'Go away,' she intoned over and over, as though repetition could make it happen.

And it did. Anger and rejection jostled across his features, he snatched up his jacket and pulled the front door closed behind him.

Even when the coast was clear Helen remained where she was, wedged alongside the cooker, at a loss to know what had halted her headlong pelt into the oblivion of connecting her body with his. She'd been incapable of rational thought during those minutes in his arms, she realised that. But

150

something had stopped her – a flicker of self-preservation, perhaps . . .

Helen needed help, she knew that incontrovertibly. Patrick was intruding on her life with the finesse of a wrecking ball. And she was crumbling before him.

'I'm teetering on an abyss,' she murmured, desolate. The apple brooch stabbed her breast, its pin unhooked, and physical pain reclaimed her to reality. She unclasped the trinket and held it in her hand, oblivious to the spot of blood that stained the material of her shirt.

'I wish I were dead,' said Helen. And meant it.

CHAPTER 11

Valentine's night in Ricardo's of Kildare Street where passion meets pasta – or so the squiggle across the cover of
their menus alleged. There may have been something in it,
for Molly was eyeing Fionn across the table with a *frisson*
approaching desire. She knew she was a pushover if a man
made all the right moves – and when it came to romancing
a woman he had nothing to learn. He was off to a flying
start when he insisted on collecting her from her apartment
instead of meeting her in town; he'd be hurling his overcoat
onto puddles for her to step across next. Fionn arrived on
her doorstep brandishing a bouquet of roses bulked out with
a proliferation of fern. When closer inspection revealed just
five crimson blooms, Molly decided florists must be cutting
corners (perish the thought it could be her suitor taking
shortcuts). There was also a heart-shaped box of chocolates.
Tacky under normal circumstances but tacky was allowed
on 14 February. It might possibly be obligatory.

She planned to wear a dress he used to love, a silver
lurex affair she called her tightrope act. Not alone owing
to its circus gaudiness but because it took a fair amount
of balancing to keep her cleavage inside. However it no
longer fitted her across the hips so she brought on the
substitute. Fanfare, please, for a scallop-hemmed fuchsia

dress that flirted around her kneecaps and threatened to do a *Seven Year Itch* at the slightest draught of air. She wanted to look her best for Fionn, both to show him what he'd been missing all these years – all right, to rub his nose in it – and in gratitude for the Valentine's card that had flopped through her letterbox. It tinkled the initial bars of Love Me Tender when she opened it – Molly had an inexplicable passion for Elvis, whether jailhouse punk or Graceland slob, and was gratified that Fionn remembered. She hadn't bought him a card; she was unversed in the etiquette of Valentine's declarations towards former lovers who were barely separated from their wives.

The meal was progressing reasonably well considering the distracting proximity of banks of tables-for-two occupied by lovers drooling at one another across candles. It was a wonder some of them didn't splutter and extinguish, there was so much saliva dripping in the vicinity. Even more wince-worthy were the smirking waiters, who tiptoed up to herself and Fionn as though fearful of interrupting some Buzz Lightyear-style declaration of love to infinity and beyond. Still, cringing as it was to find herself trapped inside a Barbara Cartland novel, she'd be a sight more touchy if her Valentine's night revolved around a Dunnes' microwave dinner for one.

'There's no pleasing you,' Barry at work had told her as she whined about going out to dinner on Valentine's night with an ex when the world was bulging with new conquests if she could only get around to conquering them. She wondered who Hercules was romancing for Valentine's Day. He hadn't turned up for this week's art lecture, although she'd been there early in new earrings for enhanced confidence. Everyone knew ear lobes did it for the thinking man; they galvanised him into action man. That's what she'd

told Barry anyhow; he'd looked dubious. He felt towering stilettos took a giant step in that direction and then
had wobbled off at a tangent about fishnet stockings and
push-up bras – the latter worked best for the people who
didn't need them, Molly had pointed out – but she'd been
wasting her breath because by this stage a glazed expression
had permeated his features. However, for belt and braces
Molly had nipped out and bought a pair of tapering heels
in addition to the new earrings. Hercules expressing an
interest in Helen didn't mean he was a lost cause, she'd
reasoned, as she'd crossed her legs first one way and then
the other to gauge maximum impact. Except Hercules'
no-show had meant her Chrysler Building-proportioned
heels were squandered on the lecture crowd. Of course,
new shoes were never completely wasted; as far as Molly
was concerned they were among life's essentials, up there
with milk in the fridge and bread on the table. But she'd
have preferred to unleash them on her Greek than on a
classroom of art aficionados. Who didn't look inclined to
rate a Russell & Bromley's exhibit alongside a Leech.

Right up until that morning Molly had toyed with the idea
of sliding a card through McDaid's letterbox for Hercules but
decided she was too old to send an unsigned Valentine and
too proud to send a signed one. Chercher Le Ram was easier
said than done, even for a thoroughly modern ewe.

Barry knew she was seeing Fionn again, unlike Helen.
Molly judged it as well to spare herself a lecture and was
resolved to neglect mentioning she was back in his arms
until she was literally back in his arms. Molly wasn't overlooking how loyally Helen had operated a tissues conveyor
belt, passing dry supplies to her and binning soggy ones during the gloomy months following Fionn's defection; nor was
she forgetting Helen's altogether too-enthusiastic trashing

of his behaviour, his morals and even his fire-engine-red sportscar. 'Sportscars should never, repeat, never, be red,' claimed Helen. 'It's gilding the lily.' Anyway he'd sold it when he emigrated. He was now driving his father's borrowed Toyota Corolla. Colour: dark blue. No danger of ostentation there.

Meanwhile Barry – who thought sportscars should come only in scarlet, and fantasised about waking up one birthday to discover Kay had traded in their pension plan for a Lamborghini – reckoned Molly should accept Fionn's re-entry into her life with gratitude as a chance to settle old scores. By which he meant she should shag him and then dump him from a great height. Say, the distance from bed to floor. Molly was not impervious to the attractions of this plan but felt Barry didn't realise how few men there were out there. He imagined she could pick and choose. Which she probably could if prepared to make her selection from nineteen-year-old wide boys and forty-year-old mammy's boys.

'How is there no pleasing me?' she'd demanded of Barry, with her hand over the phone mouthpiece as she'd waited for a Fine Gael deputy to take her call. 'Aren't I permanently on tenterhooks to be pleased? There's nothing I enjoy better than being pleased.'

Barry had carried on typing. 'Ireland is choking with women who rely on Valentine's Day as the one time of year when they might be reached a few flowers or a box of chocolates, even if they were bought from the garage on the corner and cost as much thought as choosing a packet of cigarettes. And here you are whingeing about going out for dinner with a fellow whose ambition it is to stuff you with expensive food and drink and then kiss you until your mouth drops off. Or your underwear.'

'A married man,' Molly had pointed out.

'You're quibbling.'

'And you're just standing up for him because you're married too. Anyway, if I'm not choosy for myself nobody's going to do it for me.'

Her politician's voice on the line had ended the exchange, but later Molly returned to it.

'And is wining and dining and snogging the living daylights out of Kay on the agenda tonight?'

Barry had been aghast. 'Jayz, no, the restaurants will be jammed, overcharging for their Valentine specials and emotionally blackmailing you to buy hyper-frothing fizz at inflated prices. But,' he'd added virtuously, 'I won't expect Kay to cook. We'll have a Chinese takeaway and a rather saucy little wine I selected from the supermarket at lunchtime. If she behaves herself I may allow her to run my bath before bed.'

'Will she share it with you?'

'Steady, Molloy. That sort of disgusting behaviour may be acceptable in Derry where families of eight probably pile into the bath *en masse* but it's not what we'd be accustomed to at all in my patch. I'm not averse to sharing my body although I draw the line at my bath. Kay can perch on the edge and admire my manly physique, maybe scrub my back before we adjourn to the nuptial chamber.'

'Oh, to die and be reborn as Kay Dalton.'

Barry had flicked a paperclip at her.

A long drink and a short shower later – no time for a bath – Molly was sitting opposite Fionn as he flashed gum and tooth enamel profligately and entertained her with a rant about a corkscrew called the Socrates he had spotted in a shop that day. She made a mental note to buy Helen one.

'I wouldn't mind if Socrates were particularly associated with wine,' chafed Fionn. 'There was an English duke sentenced to death who chose to be drowned in a vat of wine – they could name a corkscrew after him with my blessing. But a Greek philosopher? They'll be selling us Albert Camus tin openers next.'

Molly was sorry he'd mentioned Greek philosophers, it reminded her of Hercules, but she mentally chanted 'furry fingers' until the distraction faded. Even supposing Hercules had a rush of blood to the head and invited her out on a Valentine date, it would probably have been a few glasses of retsina in The Acropolis on Lower Leeson Street. This was much more agreeable, she instructed her doubts, clinking glasses of the widow Clicquot in Ricardo's with the mad keen Fionn McCullagh. And Fionn was easy on the eye. Life would be most harmonious if it could be played out in restaurants with subdued lighting and attentive waiters. Familiarity was supposed to breed contempt but Molly needed convincing that she'd ever want to swap an ice-bucket with champagne for a mug of tea.

She didn't envy Kay Dalton her cheeky bottle of wine and Chinese takeaway. And she certainly didn't covet the apogee of Kay's evening, as plotted by Barry – the chance to work herself into a lather soaping his shoulder blades. Whereas Fionn was looking distinctly appetising tonight – and dripping wet, he'd present even more of an *amuse bouche*. Which reminded her, it had been about twenty-three hours since lunch; Molly felt a hunger pang and popped a length of breadstick in her mouth.

She watched Fionn as he examined the menu and compared him with Barry of the thinning hair and thickening waist. Barry was a pet but he was also fairly representative of the fellows she met, and Molly was resigned to the fact that Irishmen tended not to resemble Pierce Brosnan. Not unless they had a head and body transplant. Some days Barry's face looked like it had worn out a couple of bodies. The twelve-year-old masquerading as a reporter was from Navan; it seemed inconceivable the same town could produce both himself and Pierce Brosnan. Molly's next-door neighbour Elizabeth was always threatening to move there to hunt out a posse of Brosnan cousins who might bear a passing congruence to Navan's best-packaged product.

'Is the champagne chilled enough?'

Fionn's voice recalled Molly to Ricardo's. Whoops, she'd taken her eye off the ball. A man in the hand is worth any number in the bush, especially when he's buying bubbles.

'Ambrosial,' she smiled, observing her companion with an ever-more appreciative eye.

Fionn, it must be conceded, had a certain something, and living abroad had accentuated it. Exposure to foreign situations tempered Irishmen; it should be compulsory, like inoculations. Whereas Barry, whose exotic experience amounted to a couple of weeks a year in Spain or Portugal, was as cosmopolitan as a sack of potatoes. He was a mate, great company in The Kip and he'd borrow your last tenner to buy someone a drink, but he wasn't in the same league as Fionn McCullagh, who effortlessly caught waiters' eyes and hailed taxis. Barry had trouble persuading bus drivers to slow down, let alone halt cabs. And Fionn had ordered champagne without consulting her as soon as they were shown to their table – exactly the sort of assertiveness she liked in a man. Molly preferred consultation on everything else but her preference for champagne was a foregone conclusion.

'Any word on the job situation?' she asked, a ploy to terminate their silent monitoring of one another.

'I start back with my old firm on Monday.' He squirmed in his seat. 'It's not exactly a retrograde step. They've expanded and moved into other areas. They think the expertise I acquired in high-rise office developments in Seattle will be a boon.'

'Hey, so that's what we're celebrating.' Molly clinked her flute against his.

'That's not what I'm celebrating.' Fionn watched her over the rim. 'Celebrating may be premature, anyhow. Call it marking the occasion in an appropriate way.'

'What occasion would that be?' Molly was having difficulty keeping her heart inside its fuchsia satin wrapper.

Fionn glanced away and then back at her, too sturdily built to play coy and yet giving it a lash anyway. 'A second chance. If you'll have me, Molly.'

The waiter arrived with their starters. Even on Valentine's Day they have a sixth sense for the verbal equivalent of *coitus interruptus*. But Molly welcomed the distraction of salmon and ginger parcels to slice through – Fionn was spreading his cards on the table while she was still wondering if it was time to break the seal on the deck. She felt he was rushing her. She wanted him to rush her. She was muddled. She needed more champagne.

Aware of his scrutiny, she allowed her eyes to circum-navigate the restaurant with only a faint blush betraying her confusion. There was nobody she knew in the room, a rare occurrence, for Molly had a wide circle of acquaintances. Maybe they were all disguised as attentive lovers – you wouldn't recognise your own father if he were wearing an expression as maudlin as some of the samples on the faces surrounding her. A battery of waiters hovered a discreet distance from the diners. What about their Valentine's Day? wondered Molly. Did they defer it until the restaurant closed? Did they pull down shutters and lock doors and then relight the candle stubs, pop their own corks and recreate the let's pretend magic for their partners?

'I'm curious,' said Fionn.

'Curioser and curioser,' said Molly.

'About why you didn't answer me.'

'I didn't realise you asked a question,' hedged Molly.

'Questions aren't always in the interrogative.'

'Neither they are.' She dipped her chin so that her hair streamed forward to hide her face.

Fionn reached under her mask of curls to stroke her cheek. 'Have I told you yet how bewitching you look in that dress?'

'The drink is obviously hitting home. You said no more than that I looked very well in it when I took off my coat.'

'That was a gross understatement. Try fabulous, try stunning, try divine.'

'No more adjectives,' surrendered Molly. 'You're leaving me breathless.'

'Try spellbinding, try riveting, try mouth-watering enough to eat.'

'I draw the line there, Fionn McCullagh. That's cannibalism.'

Over Irish coffees he returned to the subject of second chances. In a more acerbic frame of mind, Molly might have said second chances were for second-rate chancers. But she was mellowed – as much by the bubbles of admiration lapping her all evening as by the champagne – and Fionn seemed less like a villain who'd misappropriated her heart and more like a suitor who'd taken it away and treasured it.

'I could never track down a decent Irish coffee in Seattle.' He swirled the liquid in his glass. 'They always used the spray-on cream that disintegrates and they drew shamrocks on top, a ghastly affectation. You make lethal Irish coffees, don't you?'

'Everyone should have one talent,' replied Molly.

Fionn transfixed her with a gaze so solemn she almost sniggered.

'You have more than one talent, Molly, you have dozens. And I took you for granted; I can never forgive myself for that. But I swear I'll never take you for granted again if you'll let me back into your life.'

That was enough to set a woman swooning. So why wasn't she? It had to be the fault of the irritatingly unromantic voice in her skull, the one prevaricating that making assumptions was exactly what he was about here: assuming she'd be ready to serve him drinks in the second-chance saloon as soon as he'd abased himself. Just a little. He was fond of the more-sinned-against-than-sinning scenario. There came the unromantic voice again, the one which didn't realise it was Valentine's Day and it was talking out of season; it suggested she tell Fionn he'd staked his money on the wrong filly. He'd backed a loser and there was no point in crying to the bookies that he wanted to switch horses mid-race. But Molly wasn't sure she wanted to be left alone with the unromantic voice for company, especially if it kept relying on gambling analogies.

Neither did she want to pass over her heart to Fionn McCullagh for safekeeping. He mislaid it once, he could do it again. Still, it wasn't a case of all or nothing; she could adopt the middle ground. Barry's advice had to be worth something. He was a man, wasn't he? That put him on the inside track. There was nothing to stop her cherry-picking where Fionn was concerned, gorging on the fruit and pushing the stones to one side. Their love life had been the most satisfying she'd ever experienced, even allowing for that wanton summer in a kibbutz the first year she went on the pill. But only, she claimed to a disapproving Mary-P, for the purpose of regulating her periods.

So Molly captured and licked a trail of cream snaking down the outside of her glass and looked at him from under the eyelashes she'd meticulously separated with an instrument of torture known as an eyelash pin. The 'buy me' pitch on the front of the box promised it would be worth the effort and judging from the puppy dog gaze Fionn was training on her the blurb hadn't exaggerated.

'I've missed you, Fionn,' she murmured.

He read the green light and put his foot on the accelerator. Grasping both her hands in his, he responded. 'I've missed you too, Molly. I've been an idiot. Let me make it up to you.'

She was about to acquiesce – to any suggestion that ensued – when he added melodramatically, 'I've never known peace since the day I left you.'

Oh no, there was that wayward giggle threatening to erupt again. It had to be the fault of the fellow with the unromantic voice skulking in her brain. If Fionn didn't quit giving her brooding looks and heaving Byronic sighs she'd be teetering home on her own. With indigestion. There was something faintly ridiculous about a thirty-three-year-old man playing the heavy breather over love's labours lost. Especially when love's labours were waiting to be regained if he'd only show some initiative like shedding the Heathcliff act and whisking her off somewhere intimate, like a borrowed penthouse in Manhattan. Or whichever sophisticated capital was the handiest, really. Dublin at a push.

A visit to the ladies seemed in order while she reconsidered

163

her position and allowed him a breather to do likewise. There was a scrum around the mirror as women slathered on vamp-it-up lipstick. They studied their lip lines with as much reverence as if they held the answer to the Third Secret of Fatima. And sure hadn't the Vatican revealed it anyway, in the Holy Mother of all anti-climaxes? Molly waited her turn to layer on more of the Barbie pink which matched her dress, bought in Grafton Street that lunchtime (probably around the same time as Barry had been selecting his wine) on the basis that every scarlet woman deserved a flaming lipstick. Even if the smouldering date subsided at least the lipstick would carry on throbbing. It had attracted her attention immediately she'd spied the tester in the shop. It looked downright trashy on the mouth and Molly brought it straight to the cashier without checking the price.

The girl on the till had a diamanté nose stud and an interest in lipsticks that coincided with Molly's.

'I have this one too.' She'd pressed the bar code on the packaging against her till. 'It's called "Pretty In Pink" but I think "Trollopy In Pink" is nearer the mark. It's a winner. If you like this you want to check out "Puce Abuse" in the same range.'

Molly had made a mental note of the name; there wasn't time to ferret through any more makeup right then.

'Thanks for that,' she'd said. 'I don't suppose you've tried out the new lipsticks with traces of St John's Wort that are meant to combat depression?'

'Haven't come across them. They sound like a fad.' She winked. 'Sure there's built-in anti-depression in anything that makes you feel like a siren.' As the shop assistant had counted out Molly's change she'd noticed an indignant circle of skin around the nose ring; recently pierced from the look of it. A certain restlessness emanating from the queue behind suggested it was time to move off. Molly had felt buoyant as she'd retraced her steps to the office: you could always rely on the assistants at the Mac makeup counter to lob some pop psychology in with your receipt.

Her turn at the Ricardo's mirror arrived and she layered and glossed, then sashayed as provocatively as she knew how back to Fionn. And she was no slouch in that department.

'I hope you don't mind but I've been rather masterful,' he stuttered, her provocative wiggle obviously hitting a bull's-eye.

'You've ordered more champagne?'

'No, but I can collect a bottle from an off-licence if you like. I've ordered something else in the meantime – a taxi to take us to your flat. Or wherever else you'd like to go, it's your choice. Just so long as we can be alone together.'

Molly started to tap her teeth but had second thoughts – it wasn't the most alluring habit and it might smear her lipstick. Inviting himself home with her wasn't masterful – try arrogant, a word she continually tripped over in Fionn McCullagh's company. But she was kitted out in underwear that deserved an audience, she did have a taste for more champagne and, what the heck, she fancied some company. Specifically she fancied Fionn. He might not be as heroic as his namesake and she certainly doubted his ability to follow the first Fionn's lead and strew a few rocks around to create another Giant's Causeway. But why would she need a rockery in a second-floor apartment?

Furthermore, tomorrow was Saturday so there was no work. She could sit up half the night drinking and flirting if she chose. Alternatively she could cut to the chase. Allowing him to think he was the one doing the chasing, naturally. Choices were wonderful commodities. Molly was so enchanted with herself she forgot to suggest they stop off at McDaid's off-licence to buy the champagne, thereby establishing whether Hercules was on a Valentine's date and if not – please God not – showing him she was.

Halfway down the bottle opened in her living room, they decided to finish it in bed. Except they forgot to empty it. Fionn had brought an excessive number of condoms with him – another sign of his conceit but Molly was too grateful for his forward planning to feel resentful. They never did reach bottoms up with the bubbly, even later, after fumble-unclasp-slither-plunge gave way to floating cheek to shoulder in one another's arms. Just as she caught sight of the discarded bottle and contemplated jiggling it to measure the contents, Fionn distracted her by behaving as though the condoms' use-by date was looming. Later, towards dawn, swimming between sleep and a languorous consciousness, he seemed inclined to repeat the exercise a third time.

'You must be wrecked,' said Molly.

'Certainly I'm erect,' he flashed back, and she tittered herself awake.

Subsiding, she felt an irrational spasm of irritation. Who was this man to play fast and loose with her heart and then imagine he could make up for it with bedroom games? Anyway she was tired. She felt like telling him tomorrow was another day, except she thought he was overconfident enough, without suggesting they'd be doing this again in the future. He probably imagined they were an item again just because her hair was tangled through his on a pillow.

Molly twisted her neck and studied the face grinning so hard there was a danger its ears might plop off. It was impossible to resist smiling back. Fionn propped his arms under his head, eyes roving the room.

'I recognise him.' He gesticulated towards Nelson, snout down on the floor. 'It's Napoleon.'

'Nelson.' She rescued him and positioned the teddy on sentry duty at the foot of the bed. Belated sentry duty since he'd already let one intruder in . . . unless Fionn knew the password.

'And I remember those too.' Now he was indicating a set of wind chimes in the shape of shooting stars.

She followed his eyeline. He'd bought her the trinket during a holiday in Morocco. There was a lot to be said for never retracing your steps where boyfriends were concerned: you weren't blasted with a history lesson.

'I'm wide awake, fancy some herbal tea to help us sleep?' she asked.

'I'll make it.' Before the words evacuated his lips he was out of bed and groping for boxer shorts. At least Helga hadn't switched him to Y-fronts. Molly debated whether or not to follow him to the kitchen because he wouldn't know where to find the camomile tea or mugs. Feck it, let him wait on her hand and foot if he insisted – he'd just have to fling open cupboard doors until happenstance intervened.

Fionn returned with a china mug in each hand. Both had heart-shaped handles: one mug was adorned with a Cupid whose bottom was particularly flabby, the other featured a cross-eyed Cupid fitting an arrow to his bow. He would choose them.

'Remember the day you bought these?'

'No,' Molly lied.

Fionn looked wounded.

'Oh, all right, it was the day you first told me you loved me and I said I loved you back,' she grumped.

Fionn beamed. 'You said you wanted something to remind you of our special day. Naturally that required a shopping expedition. We trailed around every store in Dublin until you settled for these mugs. You joked we were turning into a his 'n' hers couple and we'd be wearing matching sweaters next.'

Molly's post-orgasmic glow was fading by the nanosecond. If Fionn were determined to prove he'd once been a linchpin in her life he was going the right way about it. But he was also reminding her that he'd been a linchpin which was removed – and the edifice had come within a hair's-breadth of tumbling down.

She contemplated sending him back to the kitchen for the Valentine's chocolates stashed in her fridge but couldn't stomach another caper down memory lane if he imagined he recognised a pint of milk. So Molly drank tea while Fionn made a nest for her against his chest and she wondered how to dismiss a lover politely once he'd done the business and you hadn't much use for him. You could learn a lot from men. They preferred jiggery pokery in the woman's bed and it wasn't only because her sheets were cleaner. Departure time was your decision and it was infinitely less complicated to dress and slope home afterwards. Molly abandoned her tea and slid off Fionn's chest and into the pillow. All that lovemaking had sobered her up – but if she didn't manage a few hours' sleep she'd have an exhaustion hangover instead of a champagne one.

CHAPTER 12

Next morning Fionn seemed inclined to play cosy couples and devise plans for the day. Molly couldn't manage to make toast, let alone a plan, until after a coffee. It had been enough of a struggle to dig out a dressing gown in view of the fact she had company. She was obliged, in the interests of self-respect, to produce a rust-coloured Chinese silk affair instead of her usual motley bathrobe, its colour so faded she couldn't remember the original shade. As she tugged it on Fionn retrieved her cream lace pants from the floor where he'd sent them sailing last night and inserted his finger in the label.

'This reads "Secrets, size 14,"' he remarked. 'But they don't look big enough to hold any size of a secret.'

Molly's mouth twisted sourly. She wished he'd take his wit and post it special delivery to Seattle, where Helga might appreciate it. She staggered kitchenwards to service caffeine requirements without answering.

He followed, unfazed by her trademark morning surliness, and sprawled at the kitchen table while she sleepwalked through the process of filling mugs with coffee. After several gulps she noticed he was lolling in his boxer shorts and last night's dark blue shirt, which he hadn't bothered to button. Probably because he knew how well it looked against his tan.

The coffee revived her sufficiently to contemplate checking for mascara smears under her eyes but not enough to remind her to offer Fionn anything more substantial than a share in her liquid intake for breakfast.

'If I had to choose between coffee and alcohol I'd be sorely tempted to turn teetotal,' she remarked, trying and failing to assess the state of her appearance in the chrome kettle on the worktop. Of course, she hadn't mustered enough energy to put her contact lens in yet, so even if the kettle were polished her vision would still be blurred. She abandoned squinting and returned to coffee. 'Especially if I could drink nothing but Jamaican Blue Mountain,' she added.

'Since when did you become a coffee connoisseur?' Fionn tipped backwards on his chair, resting his bare feet on the table supports. 'When I knew you, as long as it was hot you'd no complaints.'

'You don't know me any more.' Her tone was more glacial than she'd intended. His expression registered hurt and she felt obliged to add, 'No more than I know you. Four years can bring a lot of changes.'

He nodded.

She continued, 'Barry tells me –'

'Who's Barry? Is he your boyfriend?'

'No.' Molly was gratified he'd jumped to this conclusion although the idea of Barry as her boyfriend was anything but gratifying. Still, no point in letting Fionn off the hook too readily.

'Barry's a close friend of mine. I'm very attached to him. He's as devoted to coffee as myself although he tried to persuade me once that I wasn't drinking it for the narcotic high, I was drinking it to reverse the sluggishness prompted by my previous cup of coffee. Caffeine isn't a pick-you-up, he maintains, it simply reverses the fatigue-inducing symptoms of previous caffeine intake. Barry reads science magazines; he's always spouting theories.'

'Is he married?' Fionn ignored the theories and homed straight to practicalities.

Molly felt positively benign: a man hadn't bristled with jealousy over her in centuries and it was a most rewarding sensation.

'Barry doesn't believe in marriage. He says it can't possibly add anything to a relationship.' She relished Fionn's wince as his own words were rehashed, diced and served up to him. 'But he has a long-standing girlfriend,' she added, in case she was too heavy-handed with the cattle prod.

'How about,' said Fionn, changing the subject with the delicacy of a JCB operator, 'we have a lightning wash apiece and I buy you brunch in that café near the DART station? Maybe we could take in a walk on Dun Laoghaire pier afterwards. I saw a seal there once. It looked directly at me, a mesmerising sensation.'

Molly had nothing better to do and Fionn hadn't out-stayed his welcome yet – despite borderline oscillations – so she allowed him first turn at the bathroom while she ferried used condoms and torn purple wrappers from the bedroom floor to the kitchen bin. Surely etiquette demanded the man dispose of his detritus, or did the person who owned the bed also take charge of the mop-up operation? Ground rules should be formulated and adhered to; it was as crucial as knowing what time to arrive at a party and when to decorate your Christmas tree.

The phone rang as Fionn emerged from the bathroom wrapped in a towel.

'Let the answerphone pick it up,' he said.

It sounded more like a command than a suggestion. She'd been intending to do just that but his tone caused affront.

'Might be work.' She reached for the receiver, although Saturday was the one day the newsdesk never bothered her because the Sunday paper was a separate operation.

It was Barry, who had last phoned her at home several centuries ago to ask her to swap shifts and had promptly rung off once she'd agreed. He didn't believe in social chitchat on the telephone. His voice sounded frail today, like someone dealing with bereavement.

'I need to see you, Molly. It's an emergency. Kay's thrown me out. I spent last night walking on Dollymount Strand and then I slept for an hour or so in the car – I didn't know where to go; I hadn't the sense to check into a hotel. Can we meet? I must talk to someone. I'm at my wits' end.'

'Do you still have my address?' Molly didn't waste time trying to elicit details on the phone. Time enough for that when Barry was upon her with a face that matched his voice. 'It's the block of flats right beside Blackrock DART station. I'm number sixteen, on the second floor. Come straight over.'

Molly experienced a backwash of relief that she'd been offered a bona fide excuse for cancelling quality time ambling around the neighbourhood with Fionn. Quality time was all very well, but she preferred it in the bedroom rather than on the pier. She didn't want to be catapulted into coupledom with Fionn – before she knew it they'd be pricing three-piece suites together in Meadows and Byrne. And while she had no objection to that in principle, especially if she and her co-shopper also looked at iced brilliance in the form of engagement rings, it would be a waste of energy doing it with Fionn because he was married already and in no position to become imminently unshackled.

So it was with considerable difficulty that she restrained her satisfaction as she told Fionn she had a friend with an emergency arriving at any moment, helped him into his coat and suggested a couple of coffee shops where he could count on a superb all-day breakfast. To be eaten alone.

'Perhaps I could ring you later and see if you're free to take in a film? Your friend's Mayday can't last indefinitely,' he suggested.

'Impossible to predict.' Molly's tone was brisk. 'I make it a rule never to prophesy, especially about the future.'

Barry looked utterly wretched as he slumped on her doorstep half an hour later. It had given Molly enough time to shower, change the sheets, load her washing machine, steep her dishes and deposit the third-full bottle of (probably flat) champagne in the fridge with a teaspoon in its neck in case there were any bubbles left to keep in detention. Which was as much housework as she felt willing to pencil into her schedule this weekend.

She ushered him into the kitchen, where a full pot of coffee was waiting to be plunged. She lifted the heart-handled china from the draining rack, reconsidered in view of Barry's domestic situation and replaced them with an orange spotted mug and an equally virulent yellow and green checked one.

'Drink this.' She pushed coffee into his hand and he cupped it automatically but didn't bend his lips to it. Nor did he speak. He gazed at the framed print of a higgledy-piggledy wooden dresser, complete with hen roosting, on the wall behind Molly, with the concentration of a man who'd shortly be ordered at gunpoint to describe every detail of the picture.

Molly saw the plump brown hen reflected in his spectacles as she sipped her coffee in silence. There was no rush, he could confide in her when he was ready. In the meantime his face was grey with exhaustion and she debated suggesting he lie down for a few hours.

Barry pre-empted her by lurching forward to gulp coffee like a drowning man swallowing sea water; he spilled it down his navy polo shirt and disgorged words with equal dispatch.

'She said I repulsed her. She said she faked every orgasm she'd had with me. She said I'd be bald by fifty. She said living with me was purgatory and she didn't hold with suffering now to be happy in a hereafter because she didn't believe there was one. She said if I were footwear I'd be carpet slippers and if I were trousers I'd be fawn slacks. She said I was nondescript. She said she wanted a divorce.'

Molly cringed at the unguarded misery in his hazel eyes, murky needle-points behind their oval windows. Barry had a rash on his neck which his hand kept agitating towards. She waited. But he was waiting too.

'Barry, this is a row – couples have them all the time, then they kiss and make up. Kay's probably beside herself with worry. Have you spoken to her since last night? You haven't? Ring from here and tell her you're safe and sound.'

He shook his head. 'This wasn't a row, it was Armageddon. She was spitting with rage. She despises me and it was written all over her. Vitriol banked up for years bubbled to the surface – and I was just as cruel. I said shamefully wounding things, Molly. I told her she was middle-aged before her time, that there was more to life than shopping for kitchen worktops which didn't even need replacing and that not everyone washed down their front doors on a nightly basis before bed. Some people didn't care what the postman thought of the state of their doors, I suggested. We were completely off the leash, it was obscene. My only consolation is that at least the girls were staying overnight with friends and didn't have to witness their parents savaging one another.'

Molly tried and failed to imagine trim, petite Kay Dalton with her helmet of hairsprayed chestnut hair and her too-carefully made-up baby blue eyes savaging Barry. She'd been to their home once, a 1930s semi that acted as a backdrop to their collections of Belleek china and Waterford glass. There were display cases everywhere. Molly was convinced Barry eyed up the classified dollies because work was the only fun in his life – days off were spent dusting vases.

'She said she couldn't bear to be in the same room as me any more because I'm dull and predictable.' Barry's voice was shuttling towards incoherence. Molly decided remedial action was required to stave off tears.

'Of course she isn't planning to divorce you, Barry. Dull and predictable aren't an adequate basis. Grounds for dumping a boyfriend, yes; grounds for exiting a fifteen-year marriage, absolutely not. If that were the case there'd scarcely be a solid marriage the length and breadth of the country.'

Barry was advancing ever more maudlin. 'She's the best wife a man could hope for and I'm a brute who doesn't deserve her. I know I ogle the advertising girlies occasionally but it's only for fun. I'd never actually do anything to risk my marriage. It's the most important part of my life.'

He subsided into his coffee, Molly braced herself for a soggy interlude, but he rallied as he studied her for the first time since arriving.

'Don't often see you in specs – they make you look almost prudish.'

Molly fingered the legs of her glasses self-consciously.

'Couldn't be bothered fiddling with the contacts: too much to drink last night.'

Barry lost interest again, consumed by his plight. 'Kay's right, I will be bald by fifty, while she doesn't look a day older than when I first met her at the Four Seasons in Monaghan. She was there with her sister Breda and I was staying for the weekend with my friend Michael Lemass from Castleblayney and we all turned up at the hotel for a Big Tom dance. She was an eyecatcher then and she's still an eyecatcher.'

Molly wondered about furtively popping her head into the fridge and glugging flat champagne. This was turning into The Long Bad Saturday. And it wasn't anywhere near three p.m. yet.

By now self-pity had a quicksand grip on Barry. His head capsized onto his hands and he howled about spending the rest of his life in a bedsit, with his daughters crossing the street to avoid him because they blamed him for leaving home. He'd lose his job, wind up as a petrol pump attendant and be crucified with colds every winter because of being stuck out in the elements with his bald head.

'You could always apologise,' suggested Molly.

'What for? I don't know what I did wrong,' he moaned.

'That's irrelevant,' said Molly.

'Tell me what to apologise for.' The torment of the damned had nothing on Barry's wail.

'Anything. Everything. Apologise for the Famine, the sinking of the *Titanic*, the Hiroshima bomb, the Cuban blockade, Cork beating Monaghan in the All-Ireland hurling semi-final, falling off your bicycle and ripping your First Holy Communion trousers when you were seven, being born a week premature and spoiling your father's plans to go fishing. Just grovel – the details are unimportant. Women like an apology. It assuages them.'

Barry brightened. 'Could it work?'

'Absolutely.' A thought struck her. 'Barry, did this tongue-lashing from your mild little Kay have anything to do with Valentine's Day? – because if it did you're in more serious trouble than I suspected.'

Barry wriggled. 'It might have done. Kay was in a strop when I arrived home with the Chinese takeaway and Chianti. She said all the other beauticians in her salon were being chauffeured to expensive restaurants or having gourmet meals cooked for them while they sipped Krug with their feet up.'

'The Krug was probably a flight of fancy on Kay's part, but she had a point. You weren't exactly fanning the embers of passion with a takeaway and some red wine – a drink, by the way, which you like better than she does. A woman needs pampering occasionally, Barry Dalton. Haven't you worked that one out by now?'

'I thought I *was* spoiling her,' he lamented.

'It's not too late. Go straight home, shave and make yourself presentable, and book dinner somewhere grandiose. Better still, check into one of those country house hotels while you're at it. Try Tinakilly House – Wicklow's about the right distance to drive. When you reach it stick rigorously to this plan: a cocktail at the bar; dinner with no cheapskate remarks about their prices; something bubbly to accompany the meal, although not necessarily Krug; retire to the four-poster where you give her a foot massage and you can wing it from there. And remember to order breakfast in bed the next morning. Possibly incorporating a pitcher of Bucks Fizz if you have the energy to play the don again.'

'Don Corleone?'

'Don Juan, you sap.' Molly resisted the inclination to shake him – but only just. 'If you follow my instructions without deviating she'll be putty in your hands for another fifteen years. I'll waive my consultancy fee but feel free to keep me in coffee supplies until Hallowe'en.'

'So that's how you pamper a woman.' Barry sounded exhausted at the prospect. 'They have lofty standards, don't they?'

'If they had any kind of standards they'd never take up with men. Now run along and rescue your marriage.' Molly decided she'd held Barry's hand long enough.

Left to her own devices, she contemplated calling over to Helen's to replay the details of her deeply satisfying Valentine's Night. But Helen had probably sat in on her own watching *Frasier* last night so it seemed unfair to crow about Fionn. Especially as Helen might tackle her about becoming involved with him again. She believed everyone should share her aptitude for chastity.

Alternatively she could ring Fionn and see a late afternoon film with him as he'd somewhat plaintively suggested. But if he were disposed to make assumptions about her already on the strength of one set of twisted sheets, meeting up with him again so soon would only copperfasten his hyper-confidence. Molly considered. What she really wanted was to see her mother. It was a hike without a car but if she caught the four o'clock bus she could be in Derry by dinnertime, spend the night and return to Dublin on Sunday evening. A lengthy round trip for less than twenty-four hours, but what the heck, she was young and fit. Or young and fat, depending on her time of the month, which tended to distend her stomach. Had to be menstrual, couldn't possibly be her fondness for chocolate.

Her mother had an immune deficiency in that sphere too. It was obviously a familial disposition and beyond Molly's control, she reasoned, throwing Fionn's heart-shaped tin in her bag for a mother–daughter bacchanal.

Molly carried her overnight bag to the front door, debating whether she should also arrange a Sunday lunchtime drink with Mary-P. Ah sure, why not? She could trowel on a smile for an hour while her old schoolfriend from Thornhill burbled about wedding plans. It would also give her the opportunity to probe whether there was the remotest possibility of someone unattached and uncertified on the guest list. Male too, obviously. No point in getting all excited about a sane, available female. The phone rang but she decided against taking the call, waiting while the answerphone screened it. Fionn's voice sounded over the speaker. She noticed for the first time that he'd acquired a slight American twang. After only four years there. Shame on him.

Fionn was hoping she'd be free later, he'd love to see her. He had a sensational time with her last night, it stripped away the years. (Molly chortled like a skittish schoolgirl at his choice of verb.) If she were busy tonight maybe they could meet tomorrow – there was still that walk on Dun Laoghaire pier outstanding.

Someone should explain to Fionn the principles of playing hard to get, reflected Molly, climbing into a taxi at the rank. Although maybe not. Hadn't he been there, done that and bought the playground? Swanning off to America for four years showed he knew all about hard-to-get. Molly was grinding her teeth as they drove towards Bus Aras for her express coach – a contradiction in terms but no mileage in quibbling with Bus Eireann. She pushed tooth against tooth until her jaw ached and reminded herself she had the whip hand now. And she wasn't about to throw open her arms, her legs *and* her heart to Fionn McCullagh just because he'd said sorry and had bought her dinner. He'd have to content himself with the first two and then only on her terms. The advice she doled out to Barry applied equally to Fionn. Groveling was on the agenda. She needed some breast-beating from him. Particularly if he left his shirt open while he did it because she'd always liked that smooth, virtually hair-free chest of his.

So yes, she concluded in the back of the taxi, wrestling with her seat belt; yes, she'd play with Fionn, although it might not be the game he had in mind. That didn't mean she'd be playing hard to get, however, for Molly had a theory about people indulging in those stratagems.

Play hard to get and you could get left behind.

CHAPTER 13

Molly arrived into work on Monday on tenterhooks to see Barry. She half expected a pot of caviar – not that she liked the taste of it – on her desk by way of exuberant thanks for resuscitating his marriage. Or a gift voucher to spend at the Powerscourt Townhouse. Or an air ticket to Bermuda. Or, better still, the unexpurgated version of Barry and Kay's reunion. She felt she'd earned her stripes as agony aunt par excellence. However, Barry didn't materialise, although she checked the roster and saw he was marked for an 11 a.m. shift, the same as herself. Perhaps his passion pitstop in Tinakilly had stretched to a three-day event. If there was a minibar in the room they might never have left it. You could develop a taste for foreplay in a four-poster provided there were brandy miniatures on hand for reviving flagging energy levels – at least Molly suspected she could. And Barry was so panicked for paradise regained with Kay he'd be willing to acquire a penchant for anything.

Molly tapped her teeth, wondering how to distract herself until either Barry arrived to appease her curiosity or the newsdesk lobbed a story in her direction – she wasn't daft enough to volunteer for one. Of course she could generate her own stories. The *Chronicle*'s advertisements for reporters were always insisting they only employed self-starters (which made the old lags chortle), but she'd go off-diary later in the week and drum up something exclusive. In the meantime she had personal matters to deal with. First she should call Helen, who'd been trying to reach her since yesterday evening. She rang her work number but was fobbed off by voicemail. When someone compiled the top ten *bêtes noires* of the decade, Molly was convinced voicemail would loom large: 'To hold until the cows come home, press 1; to hold until rigor mortis sets in, press 2; to hold until the Last Trumpet sounds, press 3.'

She was sorry she hadn't phoned Helen last night. She'd torn off to Derry in such a flurry that she'd left her mobile plugged into the charger on her dressing table and had found messages on both her land line and mobile when she'd arrived back after midnight. However, she hadn't liked to disturb Helen so late – she tended to be at her desk by 8 a.m. – although postponement had left her unsettled because Helen sounded desperate. Molly would have been home hours earlier if she'd caught the bus, but she'd been given a lift and that allowed her to stay on later in Derry. Swallowing the bitter pill of someone else's bridal hire, florist and catering arrangements *ad nauseam* had produced a sugar coating – Mary-P's conversationally challenged younger brother, Aidan, was driving to Dublin that night and would be glad of the company.

It provided Molly not just with door-to-door transportation but the opportunity to browse through and mentally ridicule someone else's collection of in-car music. It didn't produce any stimulating exchanges to pass the journey because Aidan's notion of banter was 'How's about you, any craic?' at twenty-minute intervals. Derry boys; that must be why she'd transferred her attentions further south. Hang on a minute, was she being unfair on Aidan? She'd just unearthed an Undertones tape in his car.

'Feargal Sharkey was my first fantasy figure, even before Elvis,' she confided. 'I wept when he moved away to London. It meant we'd never have teenage kicks together. Although I was a decade too young to have teenage kicks with him anyway.'

'Feargal who?' Aidan overtook a lorry outside Carrickmacross with a recklessness verging on criminal.

Molly glanced right, aghast at his ignorance. 'Isn't this your Undertones tape?'

'Nah, think it's Paul's. How's about you, any craic?'

Now she wandered over to check her pigeonhole for post and a reader's letter lay there: the spidery handwriting signalled nutter. Molly ripped it open. She was an instrument of destruction and would meet with appropriately agonising perpetual punishment on the far side of the grave. What story had sparked this? Her eyes skimmed the page. Not last week's innocuous piece about the abortion referendum, surely? She'd been straight down the middle with that article. Some people had no sense of perspective, especially children of God. Time to try to circumvent Helen's voicemail again.

The arrival of Barry diverted her. If he'd looked exhausted on Saturday, it was exhaustion with extra whipped cream on top today – like a Munch scream without the cavernous mouth because he hadn't the energy to open it. He slid into the only spare seat, a few desks away from Molly, so she was unable to whisper to him. She sent him a message on his computer screen instead.

'Meet me for coffee in the canteen in five minutes. Must know everything.'

'Can't vanish off. Already half hour late for work,' he tapped back.

Her fingers bickered. 'Need to know situation. Will throw in Danish with coffee. You'll get no work done until caffeine streams down your neck and I won't let you have any peace until confession is recited. Agent's orders.'

He surrendered. 'Need extra-strong coffee. Accept nothing unless you can stand a spoon in it.'

She hoisted her bag over her shoulder.

Molly was waiting with the coffees and an apricot Danish at a corner table when he arrived. She propelled a mug and plate towards Barry as he eased himself into the bench opposite with the gingery care of a man who'd slept a handful of hours in as many days. For all the right reasons, Molly trusted.

'You could trot a mouse on that coffee,' she encouraged him.

'Aren't you having a bun?'

'Too bloated. The mammy was fattening me up like a spring lamb at the weekend. She believes I'll never find a husband unless I'm all rump and chest like a prize heifer. Unfortunately I'm doing very nicely on my own without her help.' Molly regarded her curvaceous form ruefully. 'Now that's enough sidetracking, supply the gory details. Leave nothing out, it may be germane. Or titillating at the very least. Was Tinakilly a honey trap? Are you cooing at one another like newlyweds?'

'Didn't go.' Barry aside the Danish and concentrated on his coffee.

'Booked out?' Molly's eyebrows played hide and seek in her blonde curls.

'Kay refused to go away with me. She confiscated the car and the girls and went to her sister Breda's in Monaghan

184

instead. And she must have been desperate to escape from me because she hates driving further than the shopping centre. She's convinced the N2 is thick with sociopaths in company cars.'

'So it is. But sure you loathe it when she drags you up to the home town. You insist your brother-in-law's addiction to power tools makes you nervous.'

'Under the circumstances I was more agitated about being left on my own. I'm convinced she and her coven of sisters made a wax doll of me and filled it with pins. I'm a walking mass of aches and pains. And I can't stop scratching.'

The rash on his neck had spread like a choker. Molly tried not to stare as she reached across and broke off a corner of the discarded Danish.

'Didn't you try apologising? Didn't you describe the four-poster beds at Tinakilly House, the unabashed opulence, the prurient pleasure of spying on Hollywood stars up close and personal?'

Barry removed his glasses, polished them against an ancient egg stain on his tie and replaced them. His hazel eyes were tram-lined with red and without their spectacles they disappeared into bruised sockets.

'Didn't have a chance. As soon as I started apologising she lambasted into me again. She appears to have compiled and memorised a list of every transgression I've committed in the past fifteen years. There was the time I declined to drive her to Breda's for some tedious family get-together involving a barbecue and holiday slide show, and my excuse that I was working wasn't palatable. It's true I could have changed shifts but it was a last-minute invitation and I didn't want to go.' He added more milk to his coffee, slopping it over the rim. 'There was the Christmas I bought her a pair of size six shoes when if I'd really loved her I'd have known she wore a five. There was the time I wilfully and maliciously added tea towels to a white load and turned the wash pink. And there was the honeymoon débâcle.'

By now Molly had commandeered the Danish and was on her penultimate mouthful. 'I didn't know your honeymoon was a débâcle, Barry. Where did you go?'

'Minorca. And it wasn't a débâcle, it was fabulous. In fact I was contemplating bringing her back there for a second honeymoon for our twentieth wedding anniversary a few years down the line. But Kay claims the place is tinged with unfortunate memories for her. She has some notion she left me alone for a couple of hours one afternoon while she had a nap in the hotel bedroom and I attached myself like a limpet to a German woman.' Barry eyed his coffee mournfully. 'I don't recollect ever meeting a German woman, never mind attaching myself like a limpet to one on my honeymoon. It's the sort of incident a man would remember.'

'So is Kay tippling? Inhaling the cosmetics in her salon? Sliding into a midlife crisis? Growing magic mushrooms in her vegetable patch and sprinkling them on her pizza?'

'Ssh.' Animation flitted across Barry's morose features. Molly's suggestions were uttered loudly enough to attract the attention of a couple of business journalists at the next table and Barry didn't want his personal life to become office gossip. Other people's personal lives should fulfil that function.

'Your guess is as good as mine,' he sighed. 'But it transpires she's been nursing a grievance about this imaginary woman for a decade and a half.'

Molly insisted: 'There must be some substance to the accusation. I've seen the way you drool over the classified girls, Barry.'

'I'd been married less than a week.' He was indignant. 'Anyway, I never salivate, I simply admire in a theoretical way. But a foreign woman did ask me to read the news headlines to her one afternoon when the sun was too powerful for Kay and she left me alone at the poolside while she had a snooze in the hotel. She may have been from Germany; she may have been from Pluto for all I know.'

'Venus.'

'Sorry?'

'You know, women are from Venus. Never mind, what about your poolside pick-up?' prompted Molly.

'She was hardly that. I can't remember what the woman looked like but Kay even described her swimming costume.'

'Scanty,' guessed Molly.

'An orange bikini with a white trim. Apparently. She was on the sun lounger next to me, she noticed I was reading a newspaper and asked me to check it for election results in whichever country she was from.' Barry's fingers fiddled with his rash and he undid his shirt top button to relieve pressure on the inflammation. 'I could see it if Kay returned to find me sharing a lounger and whispering sweet nothings, but I was calling out exit poll predictions.'

'There's no reasoning with a woman when she decides she's been wronged, especially if she's harboured the grudge for years. Accept it, pal, you're for the divorce courts.' Molly clattered her chair as she stood up.

Alarmed, Barry caught her by the arm. 'Tell me you're joking.'

Molly sat down again. 'I'm joking. But decisive action is imperative. There's no one else involved, right?'

'Of course not.' Barry looked affronted. 'Kay is a lady.'

'I meant you, actually. Have you been messing around and did she catch you?'

Barry was doubly affronted. 'I never mess around.'

'Thought crimes, Bar. Fortunately, Kay doesn't seem to share my gift for reading your murky little mind. And I wouldn't wish a man homeless, childless and penniless for imaginary transgressions. Otherwise half the married men in Ireland would be sleeping under railway arches.' Molly tapped the opening bars of Suspicious Minds on her front tooth. 'I need to ponder this situation. I'll report back to you later in the day when inspiration strikes. Are you owed any holiday time? Excellent, you may need to take a few days. Leave it with me. Problem-busting is my forté.'

Outside the canteen door Barry touched her elbow. 'I really do love her, Molly. Promise me it will be all right.'

'I'm not one of the Sibyls,' replied Molly, 'but neither am I Cassandra. Everything will be fine.'

He was a pitiful sight, she thought. It was a good job Kay couldn't see him now. He wouldn't stand the ghost of a chance with her. Unless she liked her men to ooze pathetic hopelessness. Few women did.

Helen still wasn't picking up her phone calls; she must be in a meeting. Molly left another message on her voicemail and considered Barry's situation. Fortunately, Stephen, the news editor, gave her piddling stories to chase so her brain wasn't overly taxed with work. She was able to chip away at Barry's difficulty while phoning and typing. A gesture was in order: something monumental but not toe-curling, sentimental but not mawkish. A public declaration perhaps, such as dedicating a novel to her – except it would take too long to have the book written and published. She twiddled her malachite beads for inspiration but they provided questionable stimulus.

Lunchtime came and went and Molly was no nearer a solution to Barry's conundrum. The newspaper wasn't getting its money's worth from either of them that day. He seemed to spend most of it staring anxiously at her. She had to pull a rabbit out of the hat, if only to stop those doleful eyes haunting her. Barry was transmutating into an incubus. Think, woman. Molly longed for a cigarette but substituted a pen for the forbidden object and chewed savagely until the plastic cracked. This was driving her demented. She never had the nicotine jitters unless there was a drink in her hand but Barry was pushing her over the edge.

In desperation she scrolled through her brain for the most romantic gesture she'd ever experienced. There was the time Fionn had met her at the airport with a banner reading I Fancy Molly; there was another boyfriend, Niall, who sent her a white rose every day for a fortnight until his bank manager intervened; there was the fellow who turned up on her doorstep with a naggin of whiskey, half a dozen oranges and a packet of Lemsip – all avenues covered – when a cold forced her to cancel their date. He said he was there to pamper her and he made a reasonable fist of it. Shame she couldn't drum up his name but she had a suspicion it began with an L. Anything else? She drew a blank. Feck it all, was that the sum total of her tender moments? Wait, that Niall lad had also taken her photograph on her thirtieth birthday, she wallowing in misery because she was an old hag on the slippery slope to forty, and stuck it in a double frame with another photograph of herself at twenty-nine. He'd written on the back: 'No difference; as drop-dead gorgeous at 30 as at 29.' That wasn't half bad – why had their relationship petered out? She could've jumped aboard the bridal merry-go-round with him. No, wait he had Blue Shirt tendencies. She could never have brought someone so unsound on the national question home to Derry.

Helen rang, rescuing her from the need to wade back any further through discarded boyfriends in search of the ultimate sentimental gesture.

'Quick, Helen, I need to help Barry Dalton inject some romance into his banjaxed marriage. Supply me with your knee-trembler to outstrip all knee-tremblers.'

'Someone bought me a silver apple brooch,' replied Helen.

'You've led a sheltered life, angel face. Come on, someone must've launched a thousand ships to chase you or bribed the odd goddess to wheedle their way into your good books. Focus. My peace of mind and Barry's eternal happiness are depending on you.'

'Does holding your hand during the multiple pecking scene in *The Birds* count?' (Patrick had done that in the vespertine womb of the cinema one Sunday evening in Kilkenny.)

'It certainly doesn't. We need to make Kay Dalton feel like Tippi Hedren *before* she's attacked. The full Hitchcock treatment will leave her ravished instead of ravishing.'

'Molly, you've had tonnes more relationships than me – what about some of those English lads you courted while you worked on the *Evening Standard*? Didn't they know how to give a girl the wobbles?'

Molly cast her mind back. They certainly went in for filling a girl full of drink to make her wobbly but that wasn't quite the knee-trembler she was searching for in Barry's case.

'I did have one who serenaded me with a song he wrote

himself but it wasn't up there with Heartbreak Hotel. He rhymed "Molly" with every "olly" sound he could find, so it had inane lines about my sweet Molly, she's so jolly, not spiky like holly or pointed as a brolly, she's as loyal as a collie – I'll spare you the rest.'

'Enthralling,' said Helen. 'Listen, I have work to do even if you're a layabout. When can we meet? I need some advice. Since you're in Wonderwoman mode you may as well cast an eye over my entanglements as well.'

'Everything all right, Helen?' Molly's tone was concerned. 'I thought you sounded a bit stressed from the messages you left on my machine.'

'I could use some company. Can you come over tonight?'

'I'll arrive bearing fish and chips. You can supply the mayonnaise so we look whimsically European while we nosh up.'

As the day was ending Molly reconnoitred with Barry at the back of the news library.

'What song did you dance to at your wedding reception, Bar?'

'Love Is All Around.'

Surprisingly tasteful. She'd have put money on some Tammy Wynette saccharine overdose – Kay was a country fan.

'The Troggs or the Wet Wet Wet version? Oh, fair enough, the Jerry and the Jittery JCBs interpretation – I forgot they still go in for showbands in Monaghan. Now, do you know the words? Prepare to learn them. You're to walk through Kay's salon singing about feeling it in your fingers and feeling it in your toes and feeling it in your kneecaps if that's what it takes.'

Barry quaked. 'This has to be a wind-up. I could never make such a show of myself. And even if I were able to psyche myself up it would be counterproductive. My voice croaks like a frog's.'

Molly, leaning on the photocopier, was inexorable. 'You have to transform yourself into a prince for Kay, even if it's a frog prince. This is a racing certainty to be an enchanted moment, Bar. She'll be transported back to her wedding day and she'll see you again, aged twenty-eight and with all your own teeth and hair. It can't fail.'

'But what about tonight? I can't go through another one like last night. Kay arrived back from Monaghan, liberated a bottle of vermouth from the drinks trolley and adjourned to the bedroom where she locked the door ostentatiously. I had to sleep in the spare room and it doesn't have an electric blanket. It was freezing last night.'

Molly checked her watch: going home time had a prior claim over Barry's domestic arrangements.

'Not as cold as sleeping in your car. At least you're still under one roof. Now stop moaning and start rehearsing. You're on a day off tomorrow – that'll give you a chance to be word-perfect by the afternoon and ready to catch Kay unawares before she embarks on the final manicure of the day. Try and manage a night's sleep – you may be called upon to stay awake all tomorrow night surrendering yourself to an insatiable woman.'

'I'll have you know that's my wife you're talking about,' objected Barry.

Molly rolled her eyes and flicked the photocopier light from A4 to A3 for absolutely no reason and returned to the newsroom with the air of a woman for whom splitting the atom held no challenges.

She left the building with a distinctly reluctant Barry, who showed an inclination to deviate into The Kip rather than go home. Molly steered him towards his bus stop and then made her way to Tara Street station via the Abbey Theatre (she really ought to take in a play one of these days; she was vegetating towards philistine status). Waiting for a Bray-bound train, she realised she hadn't returned Fionn's call from Saturday afternoon because Barry had monopolised all her attention. About to rectify this via her mobile, Molly was distracted by her promise to arrive at Helen's bearing fish and chips, which meant staying on the line as far as Sandycove. Food made sense; woman cannot live by good works alone. Instead of Fionn she called up Helen to tell her she'd be with her in 40 minutes or so depending on the chip shop queue.

'The day I've had,' she announced, depositing a leaking bundle on Helen's kitchen worktop.

'Busy in the office?'

'Not especially, just worn out rescuing Barry. Don't even think about using plates, we're eating these straight from the wrapper.'

Helen produced her latest gadget, a rubbery yellow sunflower that folded around the lid of the mayonnaise jar allowing her to grip and open it. Before Molly could object that she was being finicky *and* creating unnecessary washing up, she decanted some creamy blobs into a ramekin.

While they munched Molly updated Helen on Barry's connubial trials – casting Barry in the role of relatively innocent casualty.

'I have to redeem him in Kay's eyes,' she explained. 'He's my friend and he buys me coffee. Plus if women went around binning men because they made eejits of themselves under the affluence of incohol there'd be no relationships left.'

Helen shrugged. 'Sounds as if, whatever his sins of commission or omission, he's being punished enough with your master scheme to make a pop star out of him. Or a laughing stock. Want the rest of my chips? I can't manage any more.'

She'd decided to wait until after they'd eaten before broaching the subject of Patrick. It was deferral, she knew, but she needed to choose her moment. Helen gathered chip wrappers and sent Molly into the living room to put her feet up on the furniture. As Helen binned the debris, congratulating herself on her foresight in buying scented liners, Molly's voice roared at her. Helen popped her head around the living-room door to witness Molly brandishing her new goose girl figurine as though it were exhibit one in the case for the prosecution.

'Shopping without me?' Molly challenged.

'Guilty as charged. I went for a walk on Killiney beach yesterday and ended up in Dalkey so I had a wander along the main street and this little knick-knack shop was open which I took as a sign.'

'That you should spend money?' Molly was encouraging.

'Naturally. Anyway, I thought I could always return her if I didn't find anywhere appropriate to display the goose girl – especially as I paid by credit card so it's toytown money. At least until the statement arrives.'

'You never go overdrawn,' objected Molly. 'It's unnatural.'

Helen ignored her. 'She's porcelain, French-made, and dating from the 1850s, according to the owner. She suits my mantelpiece, I don't believe I will return her.' Helen turned away. 'Anyway, she earned her keep yesterday, which was to keep the miseries at bay.'

'Hey.' Molly laid aside the figurine and wrapped an arm around Helen's slight frame. She always made Molly feel like a giant although there were only a few inches' difference in their heights. 'I'm thinking of applying for a job as agony aunt on the evening paper; let me practise on you. What's the matter, angel face?'

Helen's answering sigh would have extinguished the candles on a sixtieth birthday cake.

Molly checked the mantelpiece: no Valentine's card, no red roses about the house either. Poor Helen, she was obviously suffering the pangs of neglect.

'It's not the end of the world if no one sends you a Valentine,' Molly consoled her. 'You could be up to your oxters in them, should you choose, but if you will insist on living like a nun you can't expect suitors. Convents have rules about that class of carry-on.'

Fury welled from Helen. 'Molly, why do you insist on trivialising everything? You're as shallow as a saucer of tap water and there's no talking to you.'

Even before finishing Helen was regretting her outburst. She wanted to confide in her friend – she'd been thinking about little else all day – and yet here was Molly making cracks about convents and dragging up Valentine's Day, as though she cared what date it was. February 14 was all about sugary love and Helen knew the version she'd blundered into was anything but sweet. It was as tart as fresh sweat, dangerous and exhilarating and ultimately terrifying, and she'd wanted to confess this to Molly but her flippancy had spoiled the moment. She'd never manage to tell her about Patrick at this rate. Already the opportunity was past.

Molly's arm dropped from round Helen's shoulder, and she looked uncertainly at her; Helen never showed flashes of temper. Either she was hugging her tetchy duplicate or Helen's stress levels were out of control.

'Tell me what's troubling you.'

Helen shook her head. She looked weary now rather than irate. 'I feel blurry,' she mumbled. 'I haven't been sleeping too well – maybe an early night will clear my brain. We'll talk another time. I'm sure you'd like to head home.'

Molly hovered, reluctant to leave and yet uneasy about staying when Helen made it so apparent she'd prefer to be alone.

'Shall I fix you a hot-water bottle and lock up while you brush your teeth?' she suggested.

Helen shook her head again. 'Don't fuss, Molly, I'll be fine by tomorrow.' A knife-edge of rancour crept back into her voice. 'In the meantime, the last thing I need is you crowing about your Valentine conquests or condescending to me about the way I choose to live my life. I wish everyone would leave me alone.'

Molly backed off. A caustic retort was on the tip of her tongue but she clamped it – she could see Helen was at the end of her tether. Perhaps she shouldn't have chattered about Barry but she thought it might amuse Helen. This was the closest they'd come to an argument in years and it disconcerted her. Having Helen turn on you with that scornful light in her eyes was as unlikely and unwelcome as being savaged by her teddy bear, Nelson. What would she have been like if Molly had mentioned Fionn McCullagh?

Emotions churning, Molly collected her belongings and left, and for the first time Helen didn't stand on the step to wave her off.

Indoors, Helen hovered irresolutely. She wanted to follow Molly, who looked so concerned as she edged away, but her legs seemed averse to carrying her. She leaned against the mantelpiece for support, almost knocking over her goose girl. The diversion of the purchase had kept her sane. But what could she use for a distraction tomorrow? And the day after that and all the days whorling remorselessly ahead of her? Were they all to churn as bleakly as yesterday . . . Helen cringed at the prospect. Virtue was a poor substitute for a lover's arms.

To prevent herself from phoning Patrick she'd spent most of Sunday walking – on the beach, on the winding headland stretching from Killiney to Dalkey, on the streets of the small town. She hadn't noticed the seafront houses others paused to admire or heard the seagulls swooping overhead or smelt the salt air. Her senses had been suspended. Once, she'd continued to walk as a BMW had backed from its driveway onto the pavement, and the elderly man behind the wheel had quivered, too distressed by his near-miss to blare the horn. Her aimless perambulation had led her to a café where she'd surrounded herself with a fortress of complimentary newspapers whose pages she would never turn – but their conversation-deterring presence had comforted her. She'd lingered over a coffee that cooled, untasted, at her elbow, and immersed herself in a make-believe world in which a letter was produced by the director of an orphanage to reveal that Patrick wasn't her brother at all but had been adopted. So their love wasn't abnormal and she wasn't obliged to choke it. Cue pulsating score and credits.

Compelled outside again by a restless urge, she'd mooched around the shops and bought the six-inch-high figure. The goose girl had a look of Patrick as a small boy, she'd thought, cradling the porcelain in her hand. Here lay irony: she was doing anything to avoid going home, to evade Patrick's reach, and yet she saw him everywhere. Even in the face of a porcelain ornament. And then she'd remembered Molly, with her rational approach and her light-hearted company, and her friend had seemed to offer an antidote. But Helen's phone calls hadn't reached Molly so her inner wrangles had continued. She was disintegrating under the weight of arguments raging in her head. No wonder a headache had pounded, even in the fresh air. Helen had walked until her soles and calves ached but still they plodded forward because her brain told it. If only hearts were as biddable as legs.

The children are woken shortly after midnight by the electric light flashed on in their rooms. Bleary and confused, still in their pyjamas, they are shepherded downstairs by their silent mother. Their father is waiting in the kitchen. His belt is already in his hands and he fondles it almost absentmindedly. The children are immediately apprehensive at the sight of the cracked leather strap.

He smiles in a parody of an affectionate welcome. 'Come in, don't huddle by the door. I'm wanting a word with you fine characters. One of you might be in a position to help out with some information.' He reaches for his whiskey glass and the smile has faded by the time he finishes swallowing. 'Your mother's engagement ring has gone missing. If there's one thing I won't tolerate in this family it's a thief. So I'm proposing to punish all three of you, one after the other, unless the culprit confesses.'

Geraldine whimpers. 'Not me too, Daddy. I did nothing wrong.'

'All three of you, one after the other,' he repeats, while his wife folds her arms and prepares to watch.

'Now, who will I take the strap to first?'

His gaze fastens on Helen and she's petrified. At fourteen her dread of corporal punishment has not diminished; familiarity has not accustomed her either to the pain or humiliation, although she cringes almost as much in anticipation of the blows as at the reality of belt slicing through air and exploding onto flesh.

Helen panics as he beckons to her: he'll make her count each whack aloud and she knows she won't be able to control her quivering voice. Automaton-like, she moves towards him, noticing his boots are unlaced, wishing he'd trip and break his neck. Wishing for any kind of intervention. Please, God, please.

'I took it.' Patrick halts Pat Sharkey as the man reaches for his daughter.

'What did you say, sir?'

'I think you heard me.' Equal measures of bravado and trepidation permeate the boy's voice.

'I'm waiting for an explanation.'

'It was lying on the draining board. I borrowed it to tie on my fishing rod, I thought the trout might be attracted by something shiny. It must have slipped off.' Patrick takes a step towards his father. 'You can let Helen go and hit me instead.'

Helen creeps into her eleven-year-old brother's bed later that night with a bar of chocolate. She finds him bruised but phlegmatic. 'You must have been mental to think that you could get away with using Mammy's engagement ring as bait,' she whispers. He tries to smile, but is in too much pain, and shares the chocolate with her.

A few days later the ring is discovered inside a saucepan under the sink. Patrick invented his fishing rod expedition to spare Helen a beating.

Sunday had given way to Monday, and Helen was still hoping to exorcise her demons by talking about them.

She knew Molly would be shocked but she was counting on friendship to outweigh distaste. And she'd been trying to repress her feelings for Patrick – surely that counted for something? The delirium of potential unloading had possessed her all day. But she'd dismissed Molly and her chance. Now here she was, alone again. And the burden was still pressing on her. Oppressing her.

Helen buried her face in her hands and her legs crumpled under her so that she sank onto the floorboards. She hugged the sofa cushion as wave upon wave of darkness teemed over her. First Patrick, now Molly. She seemed intent on pushing away everyone who loved her.

CHAPTER 14

Molly phoned Fionn on arrival home from Helen's, still shaky from their contretemps – if you can call it such when only one person is slinging insults. Fionn would apply the salve, she reasoned, and he did – with a generous hand that soothed her brittle spirits. His delight when he recognised her voice almost humbled her. He missed her, he'd been thinking about her constantly, he was ready to meet her as soon as she chose. Right now if necessary. Too late? Then tomorrow for definite.

His enthusiasm was a warm bath and Molly slipped into it with relief. Being found irresistible was irresistible. He even imagined she was ringing to enquire about his first day in the new job, which she'd temporarily forgotten about, so she trailed clouds of glory for being considerate. They arranged to see a film together the following day. Molly had philandered with the notion of a night in – it went against the grain but she was thirty-two, for heaven's sake, she had to ease off sooner or later – but she was easily enticed to ice-pack the slowing down process until later in the week. Or later in the decade. Fionn sounded eager to meet and she preferred her men keen. It made her feel sought after.

Stephen, the news editor, spotted she was in date mode as he stood close, closer, closest to check her storylines for the 4 p.m. editorial conference, when a news list for the next day's paper would be produced, scoffed at and revamped.

'Either you're drenched in perfume or I'm hallucinating,' he remarked.

'You're in a permanent state of hallucination. Do you like it? It's called Contradiction.'

'It's certainly not called Contraception,' Stephen smirked, delighted with his wit.

Molly affected deafness. 'It has an ylang-ylang base with jasmine top notes. It's supposed to unleash the woman in me while subtly defining the child.'

'Nothing subtle about it but I can vouch for its potential to unleash. I hope you don't intend to wear that while sitting in an enclosed space with a man. He won't be responsible for his actions.' Stephen pretended to slaver, which didn't require thespian mastery because he was all but dribbling as he leaned over Molly.

'Does the cinema count as an enclosed space?' She shifted slightly so he couldn't see down her shirt.

'Too right it does, Molloy. Prepare to be jumped.'

Molly smiled mock-appreciatively at the boss, thinking: I can sidestep lechers with one hand tied behind my back. It's all the practice I get in this place.

He ambled back to his seat thinking: I could have that woman at the crook of a finger. Good job I'm pumped full of moral fibre.

After the film Fionn suggested adjourning to a pub. But by then it was already close to last orders. Molly considered her options:

- she could have a drink and go to bed with Fionn
- she could skip the drink and go to bed with Fionn

- she could have the drink and skip going to bed with Fionn.

If she had alcohol she'd want to sleep with him, that was how it affected her system. Two glasses of lager would be enough. If in doubt, avoid decisions, was her motto. She decided to skip the drink *and* the sex and catch the last train home. It was nearly her time of the month and that always fatigued her.

'Spoken to Helga recently?' she asked as Fionn walked her along the quays to Tara Street.

'No. We weren't planning to be in contact during the three-month cooling-off period.'

'So she doesn't know you're seeing someone else?'

'God, no, there'd be war.' Fionn instinctively glanced over his shoulder to check his wife wasn't shadowing him.

Illuminating, thought Molly. He has a bird in the hand and one in the bush. And he was still managing to play the forlorn lover. This man should give lessons; he'd earn a fortune.

'I wish you'd let me see you home,' he said at the station barrier.

'Blackrock isn't on your way to Rathfarnham.' She mentioned where he lived deliberately, to rub salt in the wound of being a thirty-three-year-old under his parents' roof and therefore unable to invite the girlfriend home.

'I won't be in Rathfarnham for much longer. I'm hoping to rent a room in a house belonging to one of the architects in the firm. He has a place in Leopardstown – couldn't be handier for Blackrock. This fellow's often up the country on business because he's overseeing a development in Dundalk so it'll almost be like having my own space.'

Molly brightened; that was a distinct improvement. He

could invite her over and cook meals for her – she missed Fionn's chicken paprika. He even chopped his own onions to make French onion soup from scratch. Perhaps he'd perfected some new recipes in Seattle – she was always willing to let chefs experiment on her.

'Last train,' intoned the guard, as the bridge rattled overhead. Molly landed a kiss on Fionn's mouth and legged it for the escalator.

The message light on her answerphone was winking when she reached home but Molly was so exhausted she didn't notice.

Shuffling her post next morning she listened to Helen's voice telling her she'd be going away for a few days. She planned to jump into her car and drive in whichever direction the fancy took her. Molly rang Sandycove, hoping to catch her before she left, but Helen had already gone.

'I wish she'd buy a mobile like everyone else,' frowned Molly, searching for something that didn't need ironing to wear to work. 'Why do I form the distinct impression Helen's running away from something?'

Helen's green Golf was travelling west. Irresolute about her destination, she came to a halt in Sligo town and booked into a hotel overlooking the river. The only certainty she could cleave to was the knowledge that she wouldn't return to Dublin until she'd reached a decision about herself and Patrick.

Her boss, Tony, had been understanding when she'd turned up at work, looked him in the eye and claimed there were family problems in the Kilkenny outback. She'd been aware of his curiosity but he hadn't pried. Helen never mentioned her family, unlike most of the staff, who chattered freely about feckless brothers and uncommonly talented nephews. Her department head had a hazily formed notion Helen was an only child whose parents were dead. Tony had the impression she always spent Christmas in Dublin – certainly she never objected, as the others did, to being rostered to work on Christmas Eve or St Stephen's Day. As they'd spoken his electronic diary had beeped to remind him he was due at a meeting with J. J. Patterson, the founder of their computerised feast, so he'd told Helen to take as long as she needed and promptly forgot about her. His brain had been grappling already with how to sidestep a christening invitation so he and his wife could fly to Barcelona for the weekend for a virtuoso flamenco display he'd read about in that morning's newspaper. Tony's misfortune was to live for dancing but not dance for a living. He lacked that extra sliver of talent: he had the trifle but not the cherry.

Helen crouched on the window seat in her hotel bedroom and watched the river. It was brackish, which meant it had flooded recently. Her mind mirrored its eddies; it swirled around the subject of Patrick, skirting but not addressing it. Perhaps that was for the best, she thought, shifting position in acknowledgement of protests from her knotted back. It could be that the only way to tackle such an explosive topic was by skirmishing as opposed to full-scale engagement.

Patrick didn't know where she'd gone or even *that* she'd gone. She was guessing he'd be obliged to return to England. After all, Miriam thought they were due to be married. He hadn't agreed to a wedding date but she must imagine it would happen sooner rather than later.

Helen wondered if Miriam wore Patrick's ring and, if so, what it might be like. Had he surprised her with it or had they chosen it together? She considered the woman Patrick was engaged to marry, possibly sitting at home in the apartment they shared in Camden Town at this very moment, admiring his solitaire – or it could be a cluster – and counting the days until his return. Patrick said she was pretty and iced cakes like a professional. Had she surprised him with a shamrock-shaped one last St Patrick's Day, somewhat to his embarrassment, or had Helen imagined this detail of their life together? She could scarcely distinguish any more between real and fake. For no apparent reason it became critical to know if Patrick had bought Miriam a ring and whether he had pledged himself in diamonds or sapphires. Not pearls, she trusted, for they signalled tears.

Helen continued to watch the river. A dark rectangle floated towards her – it was almost past before she identified it as a tree branch. For her eighteenth birthday her sister, Geraldine, had given her a scaled-down silver tree to dangle rings from. She still had it in a drawer that housed the flotsam of earlier years. She should hunt it out. Except Helen knew an engagement ring would never hang from it. She'd never be given one of those; her hands were ringless and they'd remain that way. She pressed them together into prayer peaks and thought of Molly, who couldn't see an engagement ring without borrowing it to make a wish, twisting it three times heartwards. 'Not allowed to wish for a man or money – doesn't leave much else,' she'd invariably quip. Helen never asked to fit on other women's rings and always demurred when the offer was presented. She'd plenty of wishes but there were full moons and shooting stars on which to float them into the ether.

Geraldine had inherited their mother's engagement ring,

a clump of pinprick diamonds neither valuable nor attractive. Geraldine suggested Helen take it and she'd have the eternity and wedding bands but Helen had wanted none of them. Particularly not the engagement ring. Geraldine didn't coerce her – she could see Helen writhe – instead she wore all three layered one above the other on the ring finger of her right hand. Her sister wasn't wed either. Helen suspected the Sharkeys weren't marriage material, despite Patrick's stab at it.

No point in driving all this way to sit in a bedroom. She'd walk by the river instead of just looking at it. Helen dragged her arms through the sleeves of a wine-dark reefer jacket, buttoned it up to the neck and dropped her plastic key card off at reception. She strolled in the direction the river was running, hands bundled into her pockets, thinking about Geraldine. Did she know about herself and Patrick? She was their only other sibling – surely she must have suspected the affinity between the two younger ones. Or maybe, reflected Helen, as the wind whipped her hair into a Gorgon's head, Geraldine shied away from a truth she'd regard as too degenerate to acknowledge.

If only she and her sister were more compatible Helen could confide in her. She could have gone to Geraldine's house in Galway and sweated through this temptation with her for company instead of kneeling alone in a Sligo Garden of Gethsemane. The fault was as much hers as her sister's, Helen was aware, for she'd developed a carapace to tide her through the years in that bleak County Kilkenny house at the end of the laneway, at the end of the village – at the end of the world. And if the fortifications excluded her sister, that was the price she'd been prepared to pay. Geraldine had never attempted to scale her rampart; perhaps she detected some hint of the chaos on the other side.

Helen had paid for being the less pretty, less clever, less well-behaved daughter. The less-loved daughter. Only Geraldine's Holy Communion and confirmation photographs had been framed and hung in the living room. Only Geraldine had been invited to stand out and recite a poem or sing a come-all-ye for visitors, even after Helen's feis triumph. Only Geraldine had been important enough to warrant a family car excursion to Dublin to settle her into digs when she started at college – Helen made the same journey, the following year on the bus, weighed down by bags.

But for all the favouritism it was possible Geraldine had to make a settlement to the inexorable tallymaster too. Their parents' hopes had rested on her, and expectations and disappointments were inseparable.

Helen shivered. She was floundering in self-pity; she should find a café and another outlet for her melancholic thoughts. There was a kettle and sachets of Nescafé and Lyons teabags in her room, but she was aware she should avoid her inclination towards solitude. Even if she kept her own company the reality of other lives around her was a healthier alternative.

She pressed a hand against her breastbone as her steps turned away from the river and into the town. Through the heavy woollen jacket she could feel the outline of a silver apple pinned to her sweater.

Dusk mantled the utilitarian concrete hotel frontage in an unearned glamour as Helen returned to her room after dawdling over a pot of tea in a café. It doubled as a craft shop and she'd cast a desultory eye over painted plates and mugs, sipping a beverage that purported to convey the aroma of peat smoke – which, on reflection, wasn't a taste she particularly wanted to experience. Tea and decorated ware with price tags had been discarded alike, and she'd trudged back towards the riverfront and her hotel. She switched on a metal-stemmed lamp to illuminate the room with a single pool and fiddled with the radio knob until she found Lyric FM. Boots off she lay back on the double bed, feeling vaguely discontented above and beyond the mental tumult caused by her feelings for Patrick. Staying alone in hotels was a forlorn pastime; she imagined how different an aspect the room would acquire if it were shared with a friend. Or a lover. Another pair of shoes beneath the bed, another coat draped over the chair back, perhaps the shower running in the bathroom and someone's voice calling: 'Will we eat in the hotel or do you fancy exploring the town for a restaurant to take our fancy?'

Helen could bear the isolation no longer. She extracted an address book with a Monet print on the cover from her handbag, flicked to Geraldine's number and dialled Galway. It was only down the coastline from Sligo; there was nothing to stop the sisters meeting. Geraldine had missed Auntie Maureen's funeral a few weeks ago. There had been no way for the family to contact her on her winter sun holiday because no one had known which hotel or even which resort in Turkey she'd been staying in. Geraldine had phoned Helen to complain about being overlooked on her return and their conversation had been terse, each deflected into roles they thought had been abandoned with childhood: Geraldine had played the heavy-handed older sister and Helen the recalcitrant younger one.

However, it didn't need to be that way. Perhaps Helen should swing down the coastline tomorrow to visit her sister, seize this opportunity to mend fences with her. She could volunteer to run through the details of the funeral service and list everyone who attended and how they comported themselves – Geraldine enjoyed the minutiae of family events. Helen could tell her about Patrick flying in from London for the funeral and about his fiancée. About how successful Patrick had become and how disappointed he was to miss her. The addendum was untrue but Geraldine wouldn't suspect it. Patrick found their sister as overbearing as Helen did and made no effort to see her.

Geraldine didn't immediately recognise her sister's voice and it saddened Helen when she recalled this later. Sisters should know one another's cadences. Did seventeen years of sharing a bed count for nothing?

'Patrick's been looking for you,' said Geraldine abruptly. No civilities. No chatting.

Helen felt a twinge of alarm. Might he be driving towards her now, on the brink of occupying the strip of carpeted corridor outside her hotel room? It was irrational, for he couldn't know where she was staying, yet she had to subdue an urge to step across to the door and flick down the lock.

She forced herself to affect nonchalance. 'Did Patrick say what he wanted?'

'Just to tell you to contact him if you rang. I said I wasn't expecting to hear from you since you don't exactly make an effort to keep in touch with me, I'm only your sister.'

Helen suppressed the irritation which Geraldine's habitual complaint aroused. She banked down too her usual retort that Geraldine was at liberty to contact her if she chose. Instead she selected an all-purpose agreeable note and injected it into her voice.

'I suppose you know Patrick took time off work for Auntie Maureen's funeral, Geraldine? He stayed on a while afterwards to conduct some research for his firm. They're thinking of opening a branch in Dublin.'

'I only learned it when he rang, and he only phoned looking for your whereabouts.' Tetchiness sharpened Geraldine's voice. 'He hasn't improved any. He doesn't remember my number except when he wants something.'

'He'll have to want then.' Helen was dismissive. 'I'm on business in Sligo but I could slip away tomorrow and come and see you, if you like.' She waited for a response but the line crackled. 'Would you like me to drop by, Geraldine? We could meet for lunch.'

'School teachers don't have the luxury of a lunch break long enough to pay restaurant visits,' snapped her sister. 'I'm in no position to drop everything on a weekday and gallivant with you.'

Don't allow her to rile you. Big breaths, Helen advised herself. The hackneyed *Carry On* joke, 'Yeth, and I'm only thickthteen', sprang to mind. A chuckle bubbled out and the giddy burst of euphoria that lacquered it empowered her to handle her prickly sister.

'So how about if I meet you when school's out, say four o'clock? We can have afternoon tea somewhere. Lady Grey tea – is that still your favourite? Lady Grey tea and scones with cream. Sounds an idyllic way to spend a Thursday afternoon to me.'

It struck a chord with Geraldine too, who sniffed but issued precise directions about where to park and which table to choose in the Carleton if Helen arrived there ahead of her. Helen had every intention of doing precisely that because Geraldine became rigid with hostility if she were kept waiting. And there was no sense in driving to Galway to rekindle a relationship with a sister whose antagonism was stoked by the time she arrived.

Helen decided to skip dinner. Her energy levels were drooping; all she craved now was to crawl between the starched white sheets already turned down by a hotel employee, and sleep until it was time to drive again. She was too tired to find a nightdress and slid under the duvet in her pants. Her brain switched to oblivion as soon she was horizontal but shortly after 1 a.m. something woke her. It may have been the sound of the people in the room next door, knocking over furniture as they fumbled for the light. Or it could have been the dream that left her tingling with desire so insistent she was propelled back into consciousness. She lay there, acutely attuned to her body, and the dream bloated her senses.

Patrick tracks her down to Sligo after all; he arrives at the hotel and persuades the receptionist he's her husband. He is supplied with a key and lets himself into the room. Then, without disturbing her, eases himself into bed beside her.

When Helen awoke the sensation of his mouth trailing kisses from instep to calf was vivid. As was the wasteland within her when she realised she was alone in the bed. A thread of sweat trickled between her breasts, needlepoint raw on her bare skin. Helen threw off the duvet and snatched a T-shirt from her overnight bag to cover herself. Then she lifted the book on her bedside locker, the Nora Barnacle biography Molly had given her for Christmas. Dawn was breaking before her eyelids slanted downwards again.

Helen sat in the Carleton within view of the entrance. Geraldine's face as she swooped through the swinging door tangled with a spot in Helen's diaphragm and winded her, just as it always did. It was their father's face turned feminine. Same Slavic cheekbones, same thin nose with flaring nostrils, same high forehead, same scantily defined

212

eyebrows above the palest of blue eyes, same shoulder blades that sloped too steeply away from the elongated neck. Smaller versions, granted, a simulacrum none the less. Patrick and Helen resembled their mother – both darker-haired than Geraldine, with creamy skin that didn't take readily to the sun, unlike her tanned complexion.

The sisters kissed awkwardly, bumping chins.

'Mademoiselle Sharkey,' said Helen. She sometimes called Geraldine that since she qualified as a French teacher – an attempt at an affectionate nickname. 'I brought you these.' She pushed a beribboned package towards Geraldine containing crystal stud earrings which reflected rainbows of light. She'd bought them that morning on a final stroll around Sligo.

'It's not my birthday,' countered Geraldine.

'I know. I liked them, I hoped you might too.'

Geraldine lifted one of the glass studs from its box and held it against her left ear. 'What's the verdict?'

'Dazzling. They show off your Turkish tan. Did you have a good holiday?'

'No such thing as a bad one. Not compared with the alternative.'

The waitress arrived and Geraldine looked enquiringly at Helen.

'I haven't ordered yet, I was waiting for you,' said Helen. 'Why don't you choose for both of us?'

This pleased Geraldine, who liked to take charge. She fired off a volley of instructions to the waitress and then deposited her new earrings in her handbag. It was a Prada; Geraldine was partial to logos.

They chatted about her job in an all-girls' school, about Auntie Maureen's funeral, about Geraldine's plans to do Italy thoroughly from boot toe to knee during her summer holiday, about the criminal house prices in Dublin, and sure Galway wasn't much better. Geraldine set the agenda. Helen tuned in and out until a remark from her sister poached her full attention.

'His lordship was flying back to London today. He couldn't manage to squeeze me in before he left despite being home for days on end. Family means nothing to that fellow.'

'Do you mean Patrick?'

'Certainly I mean Patrick.' Geraldine dabbed at the corners of her mouth with a canary-yellow serviette. 'I intimated I might be willing to take a run up to Dublin this weekend. I could have called by the Alliance Française and met up with him afterwards but he wasn't having any of it. Pleaded some excuse about this Miriam woman leaning on him and the work piling up. What do you know about Miriam, anyway? You'd imagine he'd make some effort to introduce her to his sisters.'

Helen shrugged. 'She's a nurse, they live together, he met her through a former work colleague who's her brother – that's the height of it.'

Geraldine sniffed. 'Little enough. Is she Irish?'

'Not a drop of Irish blood in her veins to the best of my knowledge.'

Geraldine sniffed again; Helen contemplated offering her a tissue but decided that would be construed as provocative.

'Rare enough in London,' said Geraldine. 'Is she Catholic at least?'

'Geraldine, I couldn't care less if she's Hindu and neither, I suspect, could Patrick.' Helen allowed irritation to streak her voice but the other woman was unconcerned.

'These things acquire an importance where children are involved.'

Helen crushed and frayed her serviette, tussling with her exasperation. 'Not in London they don't, nor in Dublin, for that matter. I doubt if it makes a blind bit of difference in Galway. This isn't Fethard on Sea, you know, and Fethard on Sea probably isn't Fethard on Sea any more either. And don't even think about using a ridiculous expression such as "mixed marriages". Patrick and his fiancée –' Helen stumbled over the word – 'are planning to live in London and for all I know they may not be intending to have children. In any event, it's hardly relevant at the moment. They haven't even set a date.'

'It's a pity Mammy and Daddy aren't here to see him wed,' said Geraldine. 'Although they'd have preferred it to take place in Kilkenny instead of England. Still, I suppose it's traditional to go to the bride's home.'

Their parents were both dead. Their apoplectic father had keeled over with a heart attack five years previously. Their mother had found him slumped face down on a slice of toast and honey, a wasp gorging alongside his left nostril, when she returned to the kitchen from pegging out washing. Shortly afterwards she was diagnosed with breast cancer. She'd touched the contours of a lump some years previously but hadn't liked to make a fuss and no one was told until the disease had a noosehold; she'd simply withered away. The family home had been sold, with the proceeds split three ways. Helen had used the money as a deposit on an apartment, which she'd later sold to buy her house. She suspected Geraldine had bought property also from an incautious reference to a flat she rented out to students to supplement her income – how else could she afford so many foreign holidays? But Helen didn't choose to pry and Geraldine was tightfisted with personal information, particularly of a financial nature. As for Patrick, he'd splashed out on a Corvette Stingray and driven it into the ground.

Helen, always circumspect around Geraldine, became cautious with the subject of Patrick's wedding. She'd exhorted him to marry but now that it was being discussed as common currency she felt overwhelmed by the prospect of losing him. Once his life was inextricably enmeshed with another woman's, Helen's place in his universe would shrivel. Of course that was healthy and positive . . . but it stung.

Geraldine perked up. 'How about if we take a trip to London for Easter and meet this mysterious Miriam whose surname no one seems to know?'

Helen was aghast. She preferred Miriam insubstantial. And she certainly didn't want to see her with Patrick – touching his arm, proprietary, calling him darling in that confident English way. Would you freshen my drink, darling; could you answer the doorbell, darling; can we ram our coupledom down a few more throats, darling? Only English people talked about freshening drinks; it always made Helen think of someone squirting an air purifier into the glass.

'I don't think they have a spare bedroom,' she objected. 'Patrick was complaining about how small their flat is.'

'We can find a bed and breakfast. It'll only be for a night or two.' Geraldine was not to be deterred.

'Besides I'm not due any more holiday time – it's all used up,' continued Helen.

'There's a four-day weekend at Easter, you won't need to dip into your holiday time. I feel we owe it to Mammy and Daddy to do this. Patrick may be an important London actuary but he's still the baby of the family. Imagine if he's taken up with someone totally unsuitable – we can't exactly shout halt as she approaches the altar rails.'

'We can't exactly shout halt now. He's a grown man; he doesn't need our seal of approval. Anyway, if she's good enough for Patrick she's fine by me. I'm simply astonished he feels able to commit to marriage – that he thinks he's found one woman who'll supply all his emotional, physical and intellectual needs and that she'll go on doing it for the next fifty years.' Astringency crept into Helen's voice and she made no effort to mask it. 'It's a leap of faith I could never make. The entire business seems woefully unfeasible.'

Helen knew she was being inconsistent – hadn't she urged Patrick to marriage? – but she couldn't stem the feelings of betrayal. He was back in Miriam's arms right now and she was making small talk with Geraldine, who'd end up as shrivelled and unloved as herself.

Geraldine was nonplussed. She'd never heard that acidic note in the determinedly serene Helen's voice before. She checked herself; actually she had, but it had been many years ago when they were both children, perhaps thirteen and fourteen – when she'd pledged to escape from under their parents' roof and never return after one of her father's . . . Geraldine hesitated over the word beatings. That was too strong. Chastisements. Sometimes he disciplined Helen for her own good because she was headstrong and needed to be checked.

Geraldine couldn't imagine why Patrick's marriage was touching an exposed nerve in Helen. She examined the face a few feet away. People occasionally told her it was lovely but she couldn't make a judgement call, for it was almost as familiar as her own. But now she noticed purple-grey shadows under the eyes and the collarbone protruding at a more prominent angle, suggesting weight loss. Perhaps Helen was overworked and spent physically – that could be what was denting her composure. In which case, surmised Geraldine, a weekend break in London was the perfect tonic.

Ignoring Helen's remonstrations as blithely as she disregarded the chorus of 'Oh, miss' when she announced an exam to one of her classes, Geraldine deliberated aloud.

'If we book now we can probably swing cheap seats – maybe one of those two-for-the-price-of-one deals. We'd certainly need to get moving and confirm times and dates because Easter is always manic for flights. Do you prefer flying into Stansted or Gatwick? I'll come up to Dublin the night before and stay with you, then we can share a taxi to the airport. Or better still, catch the airport bus. Those Dublin taxi-drivers must imagine people are made of money.'

Helen considered pouring the dregs in her teacup over her sister but drank them instead. They were cold and trailed sourly in her mouth. She had two options: she could lose her temper or she could conserve it. She forced herself to speak evenly. 'Geraldine, go to London if you like but count me out. I have other plans for Easter.'

'What sort of plans?'

Helen improvised. 'I promised Molly I'd go to Derry with her. Her mother's expecting us. She's forever inviting me, I've run out of excuses. Anyway, I've never walked the city walls. I'm told there's a bird's-eye view of the Bogside murals: Bernadette Devlin in her student days, all long-haired and fiery, and ready to topple the Establishment single-handed, with the other civil rights protesters ranged behind her. I'm ashamed of myself, Geraldine. I'll gladly rattle over unapproved roads and tramp through fields to examine megalithic rock art if the guide book recommends it, but I've never troubled myself to look at a wall daubed with living history a couple of hundred miles up the road.'

Actually she'd seen the murals already with Molly as her personal guide, but Geraldine didn't know that. As for Easter in Derry . . . she could always claim that Mrs Molloy cancelled nearer the time.

'I might still go to London on my own.' Geraldine exuded scratchiness. She resented it when her plans were thwarted.

'Grand.' Helen stroked the tumescent body of the teapot.

'Some people might put family first.'

'Molly *is* family to me.'

Geraldine slumped moodily. Helen knew she wouldn't risk a visit to Patrick alone, she'd be too uncertain of her welcome. Geraldine and Patrick were never intimate as children, for she resented his preferential treatment as the only son and he bucked against her imperious elder sister stance. Nowadays they behaved towards each other with polite reserve – and Geraldine continued to use Helen as a conduit to Patrick, much as she had when they were children.

Geraldine fidgeted, poking her nails beneath the logo on her bag. Helen warmed to her in her discomfort. It was pointless driving to Galway especially to see Geraldine and then making her miserable. Say something to change the subject.

'What age groups are you teaching this year?'

'Thirteen to sixteen.' Geraldine – she was never Ger or Gerry – continued to fuss with her bag.

Helen signalled for fresh tea and watched Geraldine for evidence of a thaw. 'Difficult age, all those free-floating hormones. I was a demon myself at that stage. I suppose they give the teachers lip, don't take to discipline at all – there's none in the home so they react like little madams when they come up short against it in school.'

Geraldine abandoned her logo. 'You've no idea.' Animation warmed her tapered features. 'They all have mobile phones and boyfriends and they're let gallivant the country at weekends. The sixteen-year-olds believe oral sex is no big deal. When I was their age I thought oral sex meant talking about it.' Helen laughed dutifully. 'They've nothing to learn, these girls. The only way I can keep a check on them is by confiscating their phones – that's the one punishment to hit them where it hurts.'

The teapot arrived and Geraldine paused in her assessment of thirteen-to-sixteen-year-olds to request clean cups, insinuating the optimum amount of arsenic into her tone to prompt the harassed waitress to break into a trot. 'Something happens to them when they hit their teens, I'm convinced of it,' she went on. 'You can have the prettiest, most obliging little twelve-year-old in your class and wham! she turns thirteen and you may as well write her off for the next four years.'

'So they revert to sweetpeas around seventeen?' suggested Helen.

Geraldine reluctantly admitted something of an improvement and stacked the discarded cups and saucers.

Helen racked her brain to give Geraldine another opportunity for a rant to restore her equanimity. Inspiration dallied but then made a belated appearance.

'Are you still involved with amateur dramatics?'

Geraldine, it transpired, was virtually single-handedly staging a production of *Philadelphia, Here I Come*. About the only role she wasn't taking on was an acting one but everything else from costumes to sponsorship was her responsibility. She had contemplated updating the play but her cohorts prohibited her from writing to Brian Friel for permission to send Gar to Hong Kong instead of Philadelphia, plus a few other liberties she had in mind. Such as recasting him as a banker so that she could approach the Allied Irish Bank for a donation. Helen shuddered but Geraldine was too engrossed to notice.

Public Gar and Private Gar were both wooing her, she confided in Helen, but she was irresolute about which to bestow her favours on. Public Gar was witty but sported a dodgy bandito moustache; Private Gar had a boat he could take her sailing in and beguiling dimples when he grinned but he only reached up to her chin.

'Which would you choose, Helen?'

'The one with the biggest mickey.' Helen's hand flew over her mouth as the words escaped. She'd never said anything like it to her sister before and expected a prudish response. 'That wasn't me, that was my evil twin,' she gasped, but Geraldine was already in knots of laughter and suggesting a certain amount of auditioning might be required. They indulged in badinage along the lines of go for it and I'll keep you posted and a letter would take too long, email me instead – and all the time Helen marvelled that she could have a Molly conversation with her own sister; it must be a first.

After they'd exhausted the two Gars' possibilities and contemplated the director as an outside contender should the others prove disappointing, Geraldine returned to Auntie Maureen's funeral. Their aunt was their mother's sister and had no children of her own so she'd always been particularly attentive to the three Sharkeys. Geraldine considered she hadn't dissected her penultimate pain-drenched weeks or the funeral arrangements in adequate detail and Helen humoured her. It was ironic, commented Geraldine, that their childless aunt died from ovarian cancer. Helen was taken aback by her sister's lateral viewpoint but conceded there was a certain paradox inherent in the situation.

The waitress sweeping up around them alerted the sisters

to closing time. Geraldine insisted on settling the bill in acknowledgement of the gift Helen brought her.

'You'll come home with me and spend the night.' Along with her purse she produced a crocheted skullcap from her bag and settled it on her head. It was a statement, not an invitation.

Helen had tossed the idea around already in anticipation, but decided she'd prefer to push back to Dublin since the danger of Patrick confronting her had receded. The most alarming weapon he had in his arsenal now was to telephone her. She could be back in her own home this evening and return to work tomorrow. Time to clutch at normality until the semblance became the reality.

Their farewell was as gauche as their greeting, dry kisses that clanked against cheekbones, but a hesitant warmth marked this second embrace that had been missing formerly.

'Come and stay some weekend,' said Helen on impulse as they separated in the car park.

'My weekends are tied up with the drama society. It's very time-consuming mounting plays – I doubt if the public realises a fraction of the unpaid work that goes into it.' Geraldine shook her head sorrowfully. 'But I might take you up on the invitation later in the year if it's still on the table.'

'It's an open invitation,' said Helen. '*Mia casa, tua casa* as they say in Mafia films.'

Geraldine opened her mouth to protest she had little time to be watching Mafia films between the drama society and exam papers to correct but, unusually for her, reconsidered. Generally Geraldine believed if a thought occurred you expressed it and never mind the consequences. But she held back, contenting herself with telling Helen to ring her some time and went off to the next level in search of her own car.

Helen created a tranquillising vacuum around herself in the Golf, slipping in her *Phantom of the Opera* tape, and pointed the car towards the N4. It was already dark, she'd make inching progress, but the idea of being back in her own bed tonight appealed; she was always drawn towards familiarity. Others preferred the excitement of the unknown but she was never attracted to the strange. Where was the comfort in it?

The music failed to pacify her, however. She grew progressively more unsettled as she drove and eventually pulled off the road and into a small hotel for a little-needed coffee and a much-needed break. What was bothering her, she realised, was Geraldine's resemblance to their father. And Geraldine had acquired a speech tic of his. She'd only used it once during their conversation in the Carleton but it was enough to agitate Helen. 'As quick as God'll allow you,' she'd said, describing how she'd sent a pouting teenager who'd declined to switch off her mobile phone in class to the headmaster. Immediately the expression pitchforked Helen back to their house in Ballydoyle, with her father saying, 'Get up those stairs as quick as God'll allow you' and Helen and Geraldine scrambling for bed before he'd translate the threat underlying his words into something more concrete. She frowned into her coffee; how could a sentence containing the word God be so intimidatory? She tried to corral it but her mind went slipsliding back.

All the others are at church for the Easter Sunday service, even Patrick, whom she believed would support her. But

223

he's only a kid, thirteen to her sixteen – what does she expect? Their local church is called the Church of the Holy Martyrs. Helen has taken to referring to it as the Church of the Wholly Bored Martyrs because she's spent so many tedious hours in there she feels martyred herself. She does some mental arithmetic. If she's been to church for an hour every Sunday of her life – well, say since the age of three – plus all those holy days of obligation, how many are there, let's be cautious and estimate half a dozen a year that don't fall on Sundays although there are probably more she's overlooking, then there are the years she was browbeaten into daily Mass attendance for Lent to take into account, that adds up to – she lays aside the potato peeler to use her fingers for the calculations. Good God above, that works out at more than nine hundred hours. Even allowing for the therapeutic daydreaming she was able to indulge in while her lips automatically mouthed the responses, it strikes her as an appalling waste of time. You could pick up Kiswahili with that stockpile of hours, knit a Dr Who scarf to circumnavigate the globe, become a champion set dancer, learn how to mix the perfect cocktail and acquire all the showy baton-twirling gestures to accompany it. Nine hundred hours. Her mind reels with the enormity of the figure. It's months of a person's life.

Now *that's* sinful – she addresses the potato peeler as she returns to preparing the vegetables – digging her heels in over Sunday Mass attendance isn't in the same league. Her mother, caught unawares, can't devise a punishment for her when she declines to go to church that morning and orders Helen to make a start on the lunch.

'You needn't think you can loll about painting your nails,' she says. 'And don't imagine you're going to get away with this regularly. Your father and I didn't scrimp and save to rear heathens. You'd never pull a stunt like this if he were here instead of down below in the hospital in Cork waiting for an operation. And on Easter Sunday above all days to decide you aren't going to Mass – it's only the holiest day in the Church calendar.'

True, concedes Helen, dropping the last potato into a saucepan of cold water and turning her attention to the beans. She wouldn't have the nerve to face down her father.

'Get out that door to Mass as quick as God'll allow you,' he'd tell her and, sixteen or six, she'd do as commanded. But insurrection has to start somewhere and her father's gallstones-induced absence is a heaven-sent opportunity. She giggles as she realises that heaven-sent might not be the most appropriate adjective and hums while she tops and tails.

Patrick is first home, his long legs carrying him in ahead of the others.

'Geraldine's collecting the *Sunday Independent*. Mammy stopped to talk to Father Hogan,' he responds to the question in her eyes. 'You couldn't have picked a better day to stay away from church. The sermon meandered for hours. If old Hog Nose Hogan had a point it escaped me.' Patrick grabs a handful of beans and crunches. 'You're in trouble,' he continues. 'Mammy's invited Father Hogan around after the Sunday dinner to deliver your own personal sermon. Theme: How People Who Miss Sunday Mass Wind Up Sleeping Rough And Covered In Warts. She told the neighbours you were holed up in bed with stomach problems before any of them had a chance to enquire where you were. That's assuming they would have noticed your absence, although Mammy made sure all of them did by drawing attention to it.'

It's nearly a relief when Father Hogan arrives, radiating bonhomie, after the dishes are washed and the Easter eggs opened. Cell by cell Helen is being worn down by her mother's reproachful expression and accusatory silence. She's not convinced she can weather another Sunday like this. It might be easier to suffer the hour at Mass than the subsequent hours of recrimination. As soon as tea is brewed Helen finds herself alone with the priest, Patrick and Geraldine ushered outside on a pretext.

'What I don't understand, Helen, is why a grand girl like yourself is intent on causing her parents so much grief,' he mumbles between bites of her mother's trademark walnut cake.

'I'm not doing it to deliberately wound them, I just don't believe any more,' she explains.

He sighs and leaves aside the cake; this is shaping up to be more difficult than anticipated.

'What about going to Mass while you explore your faith?' he suggests. 'This is a small community; your parents are bound to feel compromised in the eyes of their peers.'

'I don't see how.' She's mulish.

'Of course you do, an intelligent girl like yourself. And you know you're setting a bad example to Patrick and Geraldine. Carry on with Mass for now and you and I can have a few chats about whatever it is that's troubling you, answer some of the questions you have.'

Wouldn't you imagine, thinks Helen, the Church would have more to do than bandy words with a teenager? Has Father Hogan no sick calls to make, no deserving poor to feed, no GAA teams to coach, no First Holy Communion classes to take? Apparently not. He has no more pressing calls on his time than to wolf her mother's cake, spill crumbs on his trousers and adopt a placatory tone with herself. She could understand it if she were the leading light in the Legion of Mary and then decided to abandon the Mass-going, that might be a disappointment. But she was never a player: she didn't sing in the choir, count the collection proceeds or read bidding prayers. Her presence or absence wasn't worth a penny candle. If he asked her did she ever get urges she'd shove those walnut slices in his face. Ram them up against his cake-hole.

Unaware of the internal monologue, and with no notion at all of quizzing young girls on their urges – they might tell him and then where would he be? – Father Hogan reads her silence as a chink in the armour. He pats her hand encouragingly: 'Grand girl, so I can count on you next week?'

She nods reluctantly.

The priest reaches for another slice of cake and settles himself more comfortably in his chair. 'Excellent, I knew you'd see sense. I told your mother we'd sort you out in jig-speed time. The last thing we want is worrying reports going down to your father in hospital. He needs to concentrate on making a full recovery.'

Helen's chair clatters and tips onto its back as she stands up. 'If I thought staying away from Mass would hamper my father's recovery I'd never set foot inside a church again.' Her voice drips corrosion onto the bottle-green lino; a slice of walnut cake with Father Hogan's teeth-mark ends up there too.

Patrick taps on the door of her bedroom half an hour later.

'Hog Nose has left. I saved you the last chunk of cake before he annihilated every morsel.'

'Thanks, I'm not hungry,' mumbles Helen. Her temples are throbbing; she wants to slip downstairs and flee outdoors but is wary of bumping into her mother or the priest.

Patrick stops rearranging the bottles on her dressing table and directs a level look at her, not the sort a thirteen-year-old boy generally has in his armoury. It's awash with a combination of knowingness and commiseration.

'Do you need a hug, Helen?'

It's been more than a year since she crawled into his bed in search of comfort after another of her father's rages.

She doesn't hesitate; she nods mutely and he folds her into his arms.

Helen paid for her coffee and made her way back to the car, remembering the tantrum her father had thrown after being discharged from hospital, when he'd threatened her with everything from being cut off without a penny – as though she cared about his money, miserable few pounds that it was – to taking her out of school and putting her to work. The household had gone to pot in his absence, he fumed, incandescent that Helen could no longer be cajoled or browbeaten into setting foot in church again. Barring weddings, christenings and funerals, she never had. She'd hesitated at the blackmail about being forced to leave school but called his bluff, gambling that he wouldn't want to lose face by passing up the chance of a second daughter at college. Geraldine was due to start at St Pat's in Drumcondra as a trainee teacher that autumn and Helen's school was confident she'd be offered a place at University College, Dublin. The dice rolled in her favour; her father left her in school. The one inducement he had at his disposal was taking off his belt to her, for Helen had never lost her dread of physical pain, but the man hadn't the nerve to beat his daughter any more once she reached sixteen.

The signpost told her it was another seventy kilometres to Dublin and an older one on a pole alongside translated the distance into miles. Helen focused on the journey's end to encourage herself: she drew pictures of her Golf pulling up on the street outside the house, of turning the key in the lock, stooping to collect mail, switching off the burglar alarm. Retreating to a safe haven where no bogeyman could follow her.

She shivered, adjusting her car heater to maximum: who'd have suspected that the bogeyman would turn out not to be her father but her baby brother?

CHAPTER 15

Molly walked along Merrion Square to the art gallery, telling herself she didn't care if Hercules was there or not. She deliberately didn't check her appearance as she left the office. He'd made it abundantly clear he wasn't interested in her. She didn't need to read it in Morse code as well for the message to sink in. He wouldn't notice if she arrived for class in a nun's habit, unusual in itself because even nuns didn't appear to wear nun's habits any more. Then she chastised herself for being extremist. What if she had ink stains or newsprint smudges all over her forehead and looked completely ridiculous? There were more people in the class than a Greek boy who hadn't the sense to appreciate her. So she paused and peered at her reflection in a parked car's wing mirror to check nothing was too far awry.

She saw him instantly, of course. He was flicking through greetings cards in the giftshop when she walked in to buy her ticket. She could even distinguish which card he held: Sir John Lavery's study of his second wife, the epitome of bohemian chic in a feathered hat, with her daughter seated alongside and his daughter leaning slightly apart. Molly knew the painting well; it occupied an entire wall. She liked to look at Hazel Lavery and speculate on whether or not

231

she'd been Michael Collins' lover. Muse to both painter and rebel, the one offering her immortality, the other blistering with immediacy, saturated in the adrenaline of danger. The society hostess bedded by the guerrilla leader.

Molly thought not, on balance. Still, she must have been tempted. Even with the mammy's boy haircut parted at the side and brushed straight across, Collins cut a handsome figure, especially in his Sam Browne belt. And the charisma of the man – it must have been leaching from him with the network of people he was able to establish, all of them risking their lives to pass information to him. You don't do that for Mother Ireland if her firstborn's an eejit or a yob.

'Hello there.'

Hercules hauled her back from contemplation of past affairs to a present one that held all the promise of a soggy teabag because he was no more taken by her than by the mysteries of pattern-cutting.

'Tonight's about nationalist allegory in depictions of the landscape. It should be fascinating. You look flushed, Molly – was it a rush getting here?'

Flushed nothing, she was blushing. Molly mentally shook herself and struggled to keep the warble in her voice to a minimum. What was it about this man? He only had to look at her and she was a quivering wreck. And the chain reaction principle meant she daren't so much as meet his eye in case the crimson spread from her face to her neck and travelled along her wrists to her ankles. If Molly weren't so distracted she'd be formulating choice swear words. She was too old to behave like a teenager.

Having her Greek elbow to elbow all through the lecture was distracting: Molly didn't register a word of it. Not so much as a syllable. Yet despite the concentration vacuum her sense of smell seemed heightened. She could detect his Fahrenheit aftershave, and an underlying muskiness that had to be his body scent drifted across to her. She risked a peek at his hands: the hair curling finely down to the knuckles didn't seem so repulsive, sure it was only natural. The lecture theatre was dimly lit and he was angled slightly away from her so she was unable to tell if he had a pool of hair spouting from the shirt opening at his neck but she suspected it was so. Now why didn't she mind that? Normally she preferred her men as smooth-skinned as Fionn.

Molly felt a sense of shame ooze up inside her as she remembered Fionn. She'd slept with him only the previous evening – although he was chased home afterwards because she had work the next day and wasn't up for a marathon session – and yet here she was allowing her eyes to linger on another man's hands. To imagine them touching her. Stroking her. Travelling across her body in a pleasure-giving odyssey.

She had no reason to feel abashed, she reminded herself. No vows were pledged to Fionn McCullagh. Their lovemaking wasn't that of marionettes; it was given and received in the spirit of no strings. At least that was her understanding; it might do no harm to check his interpretation. Did his reading of the small print differ? Stop that, Molloy. They'd signed no contracts.

The lights were raised and Hercules turned, brushing against her upper arm. 'I must take a look at that *Men of the South* painting in Cork Museum we saw in the slide,' he said.

'Mmm,' agreed Molly, realising she was in trouble if he insisted on deconstructing the lecture. Sorry, Hercules, so fascinated by the way your hair carpets the back of your hands I haven't a notion what was happening on the podium. Flattering, yes. Too flattering, definitely yes. Unflattering to her, feck it yes. She'd come across as a solid-gold sap.

They filed out, collecting their coats from the rack by the door. She noticed her eyes were on a level with his nose. And yes, there was an excess of hair tumbling from those nostrils. Nasal hair wasn't bestial, it was nature's filter system.

'Fancy a coffee?' enquired Hercules.

If he'd asked her did she fancy rat poison she'd have agreed.

'Love some, it's my turn to buy. You bags a table and I'll queue-jump. Hey, I'm only joking about the queue-jumping,' she added, perceiving his alarm.

So he was law-abiding – it matched that manly profile. He probably never skipped paying for his DART ticket, even when there were no staff on duty in the station.

Setback: no chocolate muffins. Solution: carrot cake.

'The good news is I come bearing cake,' she told him.

'What's the bad news?'

'It's healthy cake, if you overlook the butter cream topping.'

He examined the plates with interest. 'Carrot cake is the business, healthy or not. Are these lattes or cappuccinos?'

'One of each, I was feeling indecisive. Still pining for my friend Helen?' she asked, having practised sounding casual at least a dozen times in her mind before saying the words.

'Pining might be an exaggeration.'

'Supply the verb of your choice,' invited Molly.

'Noticing her is a possibility.'

'When do you see her to notice her? You work in my off-licence, not hers.'

'I think she must live near me. I've seen her in downtown Glasthule a couple of times.'

'Trundling around The Tool – that makes sense,' admitted Molly. 'I seem to remember some salerooms she mentioned wanting to visit there in search of furniture. She's only round the corner from you in Sandycove.'

'Whereabouts?'

The question rang in Molly's ears with studied nonchalance. 'I don't know if it's safe to divulge that information. You could be a stalker. Or a Scientologist. Or a travelling salesman who won't rest until she buys a complete set of plastic bowls for the freezer.'

'You don't have a firm grasp on sanity, do you?' remarked Hercules, a globule of butter frosting clinging to his lower lip.

She had trouble thinking of him as Georgie. Nearly as much trouble as she had stopping herself from retrieving the icing and depositing it inside his mouth. Or hers.

'Sorry, what was that?' She needed to carry a cold water spray in her bag at this rate.

'You aren't one hundred per cent sane.'

'Wouldn't want to be. Are you?'

He appeared to consider the query seriously. 'Near enough, ninety-eight or -nine per cent, which is probably top-of-the range. I don't imagine anyone has perfect sanity.'

Such certainty, marvelled Molly. It was begging to be teased. 'They say mad people believe they're the full shilling and everyone else is a lunatic.'

He considered it, chin on hand, while Molly stared; who *was* this man, Rodin's model? Think less, react more.

'If I were a lunatic I would have gauged my sanity

at one hundred per cent,' he pointed out. 'It's common sense.'

True. But Molly still didn't feel like giving him the location of Helen's house, not even the street name. It was probably jealousy, although she could gloss over such an unattractive response by calling it instinct.

'Common sense isn't all that common,' she said, meanwhile plotting a 180 degree-angled change of subject. 'Do you cook, Herc– Georgie?'

He was confounded; she saw the yellow flecks in his eyes glowing as he tried to take the measure of her. 'Naturally I cook, why?'

'I always associate you Mediterranean men with stirring vast bubbling cauldrons of pasta sauce, while the record player (never a CD player) blasts out a song about someone's tiny hand being frozen.'

'I'm Greek, not Italian.'

'So you're not going to lecture me on buying the best quality olive oil I can afford, explain how to skin tomatoes or produce a bottle of bellissimo vino from your father's vineyard?'

'No.'

'Well, how about if you put me straight on the best way to stuff dolmades, pit olives and avoid retsina?'

Hercules rubbed his chin and took stock of her. It was a square chin with a cleft; Molly ordered her trembles to get a grip before they became visible.

'Are you always like this?' His air was faintly admiring. It wasn't outright appreciation but there was a certain element of the partisan.

It had a narcotic effect on Molly – she was illuminated.

'Afraid so. I've been this way since I could talk. Which I started doing at the age of fifteen months and I haven't shut up since. Look, it's time for me to lay my cards on the table – I worship people who cook for me. It's the ultimate sensual experience. The idea of their hands chopping and stirring and ladling out food for my delectation is ecstasy. I adore eating, but as for shopping for food, forget it. Your brain hurts making shopping lists and I always overlook something crucial like the lamb for the lamb balti or the cauliflower for the cauliflower cheese. Some people can improvise – I bet you'd find yourself out of cauliflower so you'd rustle up a broccoli instead and have everyone say they were only going to eat broccoli cheese from now on. So tell me what you like to cook. Name your seduction speciality.'

Hercules didn't hesitate. 'Caesar salad followed by seafood risotto and then fresh fruit salad soaked in Cointreau.'

'Served with Greek yoghurt?' asked Molly. Mischievously, of course.

'Extra thick cream. I whip sugar into it for added energy.' His eyes were catlike.

Ooh, thought Molly, he was finally being bold. 'Added energy for . . . ?'

'Tackling the dishes.'

She laughed; a touch of one-upmanship never harmed anyone. 'Love makes cooks of men, you know.' She was conscious that she might be prolonging a conversational volley – but then he was returning her serve with as much zest.

'How did you work that one out?' asked Hercules.

'It's that primitive hunter instinct. They aren't out there tracking down herds of bison-type creatures into extinction any more to show their cavegirls what top-of-the-range caveboys they are, so they rely on cooking lumps of meat instead of slaughtering them. Prowling butchers' shops fulfils their tracking instincts, ditto deciphering recipes, and then when the meal is served up they move in for the kill.'

'The anthropological imperative,' Hercules said approvingly. 'So it's not lust at all. I've been ashamed of it needlessly all these years. I wonder if that would work as a chat-up line: fancy pandering to my biological impulses?'

For one unhinged moment Molly imagined he was genuinely posing the question. But Hercules was already on his feet and helping her into her coat; it was one of those rhetorical questions. Those literary devices should be arraigned for misleading people. As he shrugged on his black donkey jacket she noticed a patch of silky blonde hairs on the lapel and had to fold her arms to resist the inclination to pull them off – she'd be damping down wayward tufts of hair next. His eyes followed hers to the hairs.

'The cat,' he smiled, 'she tries to nest in this coat.'

I don't know why I'm feeling so relieved, thought Molly. Which was a huge fat lie because she knew exactly why.

She reached for her umbrella at the street door. Raindrops dribbled, although in no great hurry, but as for the night sky – not a star in sight. Even the moon was hidden behind a bank of cloud. Where were the props when you needed them? Last night with Fionn there'd been a perfect yellow sphere suspended in the sky. If she'd known the romantic accoutrements were going to be in short supply she'd have sent back yesterday's moon to the manufacturer and asked for a replacement by today.

'Where are you headed?' she enquired.

'Pearse Street.'

'Me too. I'll share my brolly with you as an act of

supreme sacrifice because these yokes are incapable of keeping two people dry.'

He ducked his head under the somewhat battered umbrella, avoiding an exposed spike, and she felt his hand on her elbow. Such a nice feeling. She knew nice was an anodyne word but there was no other way of describing it. It felt nice walking in the rain under an umbrella with Hercules.

'Just to tether our twin themes this evening onto one pole,' she said, hoping for delays on the southbound DART line. Say of two or three weeks.

'What twin themes would they be?'

'Insanity and love.' Molly shook out the raindrops from her umbrella by the station escalator. 'They go hand in hand, you know.' (She should be hand in hand with Hercules.) 'Writers were always ranting about how they'd sooner someone took a whip to them than that they'd fall in love. That must be why the rose is the symbol of love – the thorns are handy for flagellation.'

He smiled and by a passing van beam she saw a raindrop cling, as though fitted with a magnet, to the tip of his nose. On Hercules, make that Georgie, it looked appealing.

I'm talking way too much, Molly reminded herself as they caught their train. So she wired her mouth shut and they sat in companionable silence watching the diadem of lights blink around Dublin Bay. He had four stops further to travel than she and as the train pulled into Blackrock Molly hoped he'd suggest another meeting. They sparked off each other, that had to count for something. Hercules simply said, 'Be seeing you,' which was hardly up there with the great one-liners. Now if he'd told her, 'I know a bank whereon the wild thyme blows' she'd have been ready to go cavort on it, even in a biblical deluge. A bed of dandelions would do just as well.

Instead of which she had a drizzly walk back to her flat, a lightning chat with Elizabeth, her neighbour, who was dressed to kill, thrill, fulfil and anything else she chose in a ruffled señorita dress which ended so close to her waist it was a wonder she bothered with a bottom half at all.

'That's quite something you're almost wearing. Expecting a heatwave?'

Elizabeth winked. 'Ask and you shall receive, seek and you shall find.' Her hair was dyed a shade of magenta that exactly matched the almost-frock.

'You must have the constitution of an ox,' said Molly. 'I'd be sneezing before I was halfway down the street in that number. No shortage of volunteers to take your temperature, however, I imagine. Remind me to buy one exactly like it.'

Her answerphone had two messages: one dull, the other potentially exciting. The boring one was from Fionn. He wanted to let her know what a wonderful time he had last night. Ho-hum, he was behaving like a big girl's blouse. Whatever happened to hump-'em-and-dump-'em men? He wasn't giving her a single sleepless night. If this was love it had lost its edge.

The other message was from Barry, who'd been off work since Monday and wanted to meet her. But under no circumstances was she to ring him at home. Molly wiped Fionn's message and replayed Barry's to assess whether there was defeat or victory in his voice. She couldn't gauge. And how was she supposed to ring him back if contacting him at home was embargoed. Unfathomable. Or just plain dense. She stomped into the kitchen to scrutinise the contents of the fridge, although she had a suspicion they'd be uninspiring because she hadn't darkened a shop in at least a week, but was saved from a fruitless errand by the phone jangling. She snatched up the receiver. Barry was on the line in autocratic mode.

'Caught you in, you gallivanter. Stay where you are – I'm on my way over,' he all but bullied.

CHAPTER 16

Nothing to do while she waited but eat. Nothing to eat but bread. Molly couldn't locate any jam or honey so she spread it with treacle, a sloppy operation. It was all that discussion of seduction theme meals with Hercules – her body was stirred up and she craved something sweet. Treacle dripped onto her fingers and she licked them; the sugar rush shimmered in her eyes as she opened the door to Barry.

Something utterly unexpected happened. She'd have been less surprised if the moon had emerged from behind a cloud and Barry had metamorphosed into a werewolf, a haunted-looking Lon Chaney Junior with a lilting Cork accent in her hall. It was verging on the lupine all the same. Barry seized her in his arms and planted a prolonged kiss on her goldfish gaping mouth.

Her initial reaction was: this is sizzling, he's quite an operator. Swiftly followed by the realisation it was Barry kissing her and it had to stop. Swiftly followed by the realisation it must simply be gratitude for her efforts in activating the matrimonial lifeboat patrol. Swiftly followed by the realisation it was nothing of the sort as she felt his tongue probing to separate her lips.

She prised him off. 'Barry, are you insane?' (There was

dementia in the air tonight, a full moon had to be lurking behind that cloud cover.)

'No, I had a moment of epiphany. I realised it was a waste of time attempting a reconciliation with Kay when I've loved you all along. Kay taxed me with it during yet another argument – strictly speaking, it was a conflagration; arguments are too tame for the thrashing we give one another – and it was as if cataracts fell from my eyes. She said, "You've always had a massive crush on Molly Molloy, whose parents should be shot for saddling her with that name, but you're too stupid to see it." And suddenly everything made sense.'

Barry's eyes had acquired the deeply disturbing glint of the zealot. He reached for Molly again but she stepped back in the nick of time. His hands groped space.

'I knew beyond a shadow of doubt this was it, The Big One. I've been treading water but not any more. You're my love, Molly. Kay was an aberration.'

'Barry, aberrations don't last fifteen years and produce two beautiful daughters.' Molly was hoping mention of his children would deliver a slap-in-the-face reality check.

Barry paused and wrinkled his forehead, more like a man temporarily pulled up short by the referee's end-of-round whistle than someone flattened by an upper cut.

Meanwhile, Molly was dismayed. This development wasn't going to win her an Agony Aunt of the Year award. Some fancy jetés were *de rigueur*, if only to take her sailing out of his reach, as opposed to leaping like a scalded cat if he made another lunge for her. Life was a nuisance. She'd just left a monk who wouldn't dream of touching her and here she was with Rasputin, convinced he'd only to snog her and she'd say: 'Move all your worldly goods into my flat. And half-inch a couple of those cute Fabergé eggs from the Tsarina's dressing table while you're about it.'

Could that be it? Was Barry latching on to someone with a nest before he was given his eviction notice from the house of straw on the other side of town? Molly retreated to the living room and crossed to the window, peering down at his silver Vauxhall Astra in a futile effort to see if it was crammed with possessions. Too dark to tell. Barry followed her to the window and insinuated his arm around her waist.

'Barry, would you ever stop handling me?' Molly twisted round, exasperated. 'Assuming for a moment – and this is a major assumption – that you actually do love me, it's self-conceit to convince yourself it's reciprocated. Have I ever given you the slightest encouragement? You needn't answer that because I haven't. Sure don't you know full well I'm seeing Fionn again? That's seeing as in sharing a bed with. Didn't you tell me yourself to shag him and ditch him, if I remember your choice of words correctly?'

Barry interjected, 'I was in denial then. I didn't realise how I felt about you. It took my wife to highlight it, and then it was blindingly obvious.'

'Detour off the road to Damascus, Dalton. Now repeat after me: I love Kay.'

'I love Molly.' Barry's features had an obstinate cast.

'You love Kay, you love your daughters, you love your home, you love those hybrid tulips you grow, you love your mile-high collection of science periodicals. Not me. No. N. O. I drive you crackers demanding you do coffee runs and carping about my men problems.'

Barry snatched at the last observation. 'But the reason

you have men problems is because you haven't met the right one yet. Except you have and he's been under your nose all along.'

'Men aren't supposed to read bodice rippers. You stick to detective novels, Barry Dalton.'

'Even gumshoes notice dames,' muttered Barry.

Molly was at her wits' end – there was no reasoning with him.

A knock on her front door was a gift from the gods; exactly the diversion she'd wish for, if she had the presence of mind to formulate a wish. She wrenched the door open to expose Fionn, hair plastered to his head and darkened to the colour of weathered beech from a downpour. Oh no, oh no, oh no. The scriptwriter handling her life was too attached to farce.

'Sorry I didn't ring the buzzer. One of your neighbours was on their way out and let me in.'

Molly was aware that frying pans and fires were featuring in this particular plot twist but bundled Fionn indoors anyhow.

'Let's get you out of these wet clothes,' she said loudly for Barry's benefit.

Fionn was patently gratified. He dripped along the hall-way towards the bathroom without noticing Barry's even more patent chagrin. Molly bustled in after Fionn with dry towels adopting the role of Concerned Girlfriend with all the underplaying of a silent screen star. Maybe when she emerged Barry would have taken the hint and shuffled off. Maybe she should develop a stoop to avoid all those flying pigs.

'I'll fetch you my bathrobe,' she told Fionn, whose delight was ratcheting upwards by the nanosecond as Molly smoth-ered him with solicitude

'The boyfriend,' she hissed at Barry on her way down the corridor.

'Looking forward to meeting him.' His face was vanilla cone bland.

She could have told him to push off. A woman of more volatile temper and less Christian forbearance (Christians needn't think they had the monopoly on forbearance) would certainly have enjoined him to sling his hook and the whole feckin' fishing rod. Instead of which she rolled her eyes and left her bathrobe outside the door for Fionn, then put the kettle on for tea. Hot whiskeys weren't in the script. A sober Barry was more than she could manage, let alone an inebriated one.

Fionn balanced on the saddleboard, a distinctly unalluring figure in a faded bathrobe that showed more calf than a man with skinny legs might desire if he had any sense for his girlfriend's need to display him at his best. Now what was she doing referring to herself as his girlfriend? Her head was all in a muddle.

'I'm Molly's boyfriend, Fionn.' He extended his hand to Barry.

'I'm her workmate, Barry.' Palms were gripped with a degree of force not a million miles removed from the impact of a rugby tackle. Fionn's radar must have intercepted some unworkmate-like signals from Barry.

They'd met at a Christmas party once but neither now showed a flicker of recognition. The men set about exchanging some basic information and found, despite their initial horn-locking, they occupied common ground. Manchester United players were living deities, setting foot in a balti house was on a par with entering an orgasmatron, Nick Hornby was a literary genius. Molly wet the tea while they sized one another up.

'A tea party,' said Fionn as she lugged a laden tray through to the coffee table.

'Thanks, gallant of you to notice how heavy it is, but I can manage,' she snapped. There'd been an incipient sneer in his voice and she wasn't having it. Barry snatched his moment to shine by ripping the tray from her hand, jeopardising an unremarkable blue-and-white teapot she was devoted to, and carrying it the remaining eight inches.

Humiliation: she had no biscuits. Molly was incapable of serving up unaccompanied tea, even when her guests were gatecrashers. She was obliged to open her box of real fruit jellies, sugar-drenched globules approximating in shape but not taste to the fruit they were intended to represent. She was saving them for a rainy day, which is what she had now, except she envisaged storm clouds plus a roaring fire (metaphorical, she was not equipped with a fireplace), a glossy magazine and, pivotal to the success of the operation, no one to share the jellies with. They had actual fruit juice in them, she needed the vitamins.

'I should have some Toffeypops behind one of those "in case of emergency break glass" windows,' she announced to a bemused audience. 'If anyone takes sugar in their tea they'll have to go to the all-night garage two streets away because the jar's empty. Or –' she ripped the packaging off her jellies, spewing stray granules of sugar underfoot – 'they could always tap a spoonful out of the bottom of this box.'

'A spoonful of sugar helps the medicine go down, in the most delinquent way,' warbled Barry, sounding more like Mary McAleese than Mary Poppins.

Even he seemed to realise he'd lost ground and subsided onto the sofa. Fionn took up position on the other sofa and both visitors waited expectantly to see whom she'd sit beside. Molly spurned both and kneeled by the table, geisha fashion, to pour tea.

'Nobody's allowed the purple jellies,' she instructed, handing the box round. They each treated it as a joke and selected a blackcurrant-flavoured blob apiece.

When Barry was in the bathroom, and he'd put his bladder under serious pressure with an attenuated ignoring of its exigencies because he didn't want to leave the other two alone, Fionn mumbled at Molly: 'Lose the gooseberry.'

She resented his squatters' rights manner. 'The only gooseberries are the green sweets in my box and I notice everybody's left them until last.'

'But I want us to spend time on our own,' he protested.

'Barry's a friend.' She erased from her memory banks his bid to significantly alter the relationship; pragmatic measures held infinite appeal for Molly.

'And what am I?'

'The jury's out. We know what you used to be, we know what you'd like to be, we still haven't decided what you are.'

'But we made love last night.' Fionn's hair, by now dry, was flicking into 'stroke me' waves.

Molly averted her eyes. 'And your point is?'

The silence was throttling.

'I'll get dressed then,' said Fionn. He passed Barry at the door.

'Couldn't help overhearing,' smirked Barry. He helped himself to another jelly, not a green one, and added: 'Glad to see you're taking my dumping advice.'

'Says who? I just don't want him slapping a sold sticker on my front. Sleeping with someone doesn't mean you have to move in together and become a couple. There can be sex followed by more sex with no commitment. And no ditching either.'

'Courtship has changed since I tried my hand at it,' muttered Barry.

'And nobody calls it courtship any more; it smacks of honourable intentions. Personally I've always preferred the dishonourable variety.'

Molly airbrushed out her hankering for a white wedding. Or any colour of a wedding.

'I can see you're overwrought,' said Barry. 'I'll head off now and catch up with you tomorrow. When your man's been dropped from a great height. I'd recommend Liberty Hall.'

'I'm on a day off tomorrow. And I'd sooner sign up for a frontal lobotomy than darken the newsroom door on a day off. Stephen would lasso me and have me covering some nondescript story or other. "I'm not rostered to work today" does not compute with him.'

Fionn, who had spent so long dressing himself Molly started to wonder if he needed someone to tie his shoelaces, stalked out of the bathroom just as Barry had his coat on.

'Can I give you a lift? Are you headed northside or southside?' Barry was breezy.

'I have my own car, thanks.' Fionn was equally breezy.

Molly didn't elaborate it was actually his father's. No point in kicking a man when he was down unless you actively wanted to commit grievous bodily harm. Now that both were leaving she felt kindly disposed towards them. She patted Barry's shoulder, steeling herself not to cringe from his lips as he kissed her cheek, then she kissed Fionn's cheek – noticing he seemed to be cringing from her lips.

Alone at last. Bliss. Molly ran a bath and switched her mobile off. The landline rang as she slipped on the bathrobe so recently vacated by Fionn it encased her in his body heat. Would she or wouldn't she answer it? She counted seven rings and then lifted the receiver. It was Helen.

'Just letting you know I'm back in the heaving metropolis.'

'It should be heaving even more right about now because I've just hoisted a right pair back out into it,' replied Molly. She wasn't going to mention Helen's tantrum on Monday night if her friend insisted on playing the speak-no-evil monkey.

'Any reprobates I know?'

'Fionn McCullagh and Barry Dalton. Don't ask.'

'Fionn McCullagh? Rewind there, Molly, the last I heard he was married and living in Seattle. So how come he's in your apartment – have you been holding out on me?'

'It's complicated.' Even Molly realised she sounded evasive but she needed a rebuke like she needed a parking ticket. Barry had just given her his 'make the beast with two backs and then back off' credo; she couldn't face Helen's polar opposite mantra. 'I'll explain when I see you, Helen.'

Helen was not so readily fobbed off. 'Fionn McCullagh – you must have taken leave of your wits and your memory if he's back on the scene. No wonder I can never catch up with you when I ring, the pair of you used to be permanently horizontal.' Her voice, already deprecatory, adopted a yet more hostile note. 'Before he left you high – although not dry. I seem to recall an ocean of tears.'

Molly slumped on the sofa, switched her brain to neutral and allowed Helen the prolonged reprimand to which, she conceded, her friend was entitled. When Helen wound down she grasped the opportunity to change the subject and discovered she'd been to Galway to visit her sister.

'And how is the gorgeous Geraldine?' enquired Molly. (No more talk of Fionn please.)

Helen was wrongfooted. 'Is she gorgeous? I've never noticed. She seems to have a couple of boyfriends on the horizon, an inadequate marker but a marker none the less.'

'All you Sharkeys are gorgeous, especially the fleeting glimpse I had of your brother at that funeral a few weeks back. But you hustled him away from me in a most possessive fashion.'

'I didn't.' Helen was defensive. 'I barely had a chance to talk to him myself that day. There were second cousins and uncles by marriage and assorted relatives everywhere you turned. Anyway, he lives in London; he's not exactly on the doorstep.'

'There's a walloping big key in your back which is far too easy to wind up,' said Molly. 'Besides he's way too old for me. I've decided I like my men *very* young and *very* grateful.'

'How young?' Helen was relieved to be off the hook so painlessly. 'Are we talking Mrs Robinson?'

'Dustin Hoffman's age in *The Graduate* is probably bang on, although I'll have you know I'm no Anne Bancroft yet.'

'Patrick's twenty-nine so he's off limits on the grounds of decrepitude, is that it?'

'Well . . .' Molly pretended to ponder. 'I might give him houseroom for a one-night stand but nothing more because he wouldn't have the stamina for me. Borderline thirty, he's on the turn. I've decided my cut-off from here in should be twenty-five, maximising gratitude and prowess in one fell swoop. Stop cackling, Helen. Mockery ill becomes you. I've given this subject extensive consideration. I could manage a dissertation on it – or anyway a one-thousand-word feature in the lifestyle section – and this is the optimum melding of my needs and his.'

'Do you have a particular his in mind? I hope it's not Fionn McCullagh.'

'That old fogey. I'll have you know there are other, considerably younger males in my circle of admirers. Discretion prevents me from revealing identities.'

'It's not like you to be demure.' Helen was laughing so much the exhaustion from her drive home from Galway had started to ebb.

'Demure! Now I'm insulted. It's Hercules, if you must know.'

'And would I be correct in deducing that he sneaks into the aged twenty-five cut-off zone.'

'By the skin of his teeth. Helen, we had another coffee-drinking session and I'm truly smitten. Cupid feck off, your work is done.'

'Excellent.'

'Not excellent at all.' Molly was rueful. 'He fits the age profile but not the appreciation-for-services-rendered one. He's manifesting a disconcerting tendency to treat me like one of his sisters.'

'Show him the error of his ways.'

'I wish I could, Helen. You've no idea how much I wish it.' Molly recollected herself. 'My bath's going to be sub-zero by now. Unlike my blood, which is revved up with all this talk of Greek stallions.'

'Bulls.'

'Sorry?'

'The Greeks went in for bulls – remember the Minotaur?' said Helen. 'Think athletic Cretan damsels and lads playing leapfrog across bulls' horns. Think primitive world potency symbol.'

'Now I'm getting even more het up. I need a cold shower and not a bath at all. I'll give you a shout in a day or two, bring you up to speed on the Fionn, Barry and Hercules situation.'

'So many men, so little time.'

The glow that one of their jocular conversations always induced in Helen stayed with her while she pottered about watering plants and leaving out her binbag for the next day's collection. But, later in bed, agitatedly anticipating sleep, she wished she could be more like Molly: regard life as a vehicle for fun instead of visualising tragedy on every corner. Talk about what was on her mind, as Molly did with Hercules, instead of dip it in quick-setting concrete and then roll the ungainly ball into a corner of the back yard.

'Molly's not the only one making wishes,' she addressed the alarm clock. 'I could use a lamp in need of a shine and a genie to emerge from it too. I wouldn't even need three wishes. One would do.'

CHAPTER 17

The early hours of Wednesday morning and it looked like she was condemned to yet another sleepless night. Helen had had a surfeit of them since returning from Sligo last week. Her days had passed in a blur of lapsed concentration at work, with a few phone conversations with Molly at night her only respite from anxiety. Geraldine had rung once, to Helen's surprise, but she'd missed the call and lacked the energy to return it. Still, it was some comfort to know lines of communication were opening more easily between the sisters. From Patrick she'd heard nothing. And yet he was continually in her thoughts – a harpoon dragging Helen after him.

This was exhausting – she should get up rather than lie in bed swamped by the contradictions of her feelings for Patrick.

Divert yourself, that's what the manuals advised. She retreated downstairs and filled a mug with milk. While she was waiting for the microwave to ping she wandered out to the bookcase in the living room and her eye landed on the dark blue hardback outline of her *Philip's Modern School Atlas*. Inside the cover was a pair of photographs taken by NASA: the land block of the Indian peninsula, and Sinai peninsula with the Jordanian desert to one side and the

Egyptian coast to the other. The world looked messily drawn from space, as though the creator's artistic skills leaned towards the slapdash. The Sinai peninsula picture always reminded her of a lump of burned fish, probably skate.

As ever the atlas fell open at pages 98 and 99: South America. Ecuador was on page 98, she found it immediately – a strip of purple which meant it was extremely high above sea level according to the colour chart on the side. Helen read the place names aloud, her tongue easily tickling the awkward words by dint of practice. Guayaquil, Chimborazo, Cotopaxi, Cuenca. So many k sounds. Her eyes travelled southwards to Bolivia and she thought of Che Guevara's last days in the jungle; they veered north to Venezuela and she chuckled to see Caracas, for ever fixed in her memory as a place where women outnumbered men by a massive differential. Or so two lascivious schoolboys claimed in *Gregory's Girl*.

She was drawn back to Ecuador. As a teenager her feet steered her automatically towards Eason's whenever she was in the bright lights of Kilkenny – Ballydoyle was too insignificant for its own branch. She'd head straight for the travel guides section and read up on Ecuador. She knew it was acceptable to spit in public but not to burp there and that the unit of currency was sucre, which, disappointingly, had nothing to do with sugar-cubes doubling as cash. She knew that adventurous travellers could go on hair-raising bus journeys through the mountains, sharing a seat with an Indian peasant who'd have a basket of live chickens at his feet. She knew the Galapagos were within reach of Quito where tourists could swim with giant turtles and stroll on the beach sidestepping puffins and iguanas which hadn't learned to fear humans.

That was the part of the guide she liked best: *which*

hadn't learned to fear humans. No fear. Helen quaked at the liberation of it. And then one day it dawned on her that fear and *fear* were spelled the same: the English word for heart-hammering cold sweats and the Irish word for man. If she believed in patterns in the universe she might devise a theory to rationalise that coincidence. But she told herself that not everything could be explained. Nor should it be.

'If wishes were horses then beggars would ride.' Her mother was fond of quoting that at Helen to slap her down when she expressed an ambitious wish. And where is the use in tame ones? asked the adult Helen. Why wish for an ice-cream cone when you could wish for the moon? But the unformed Helen was more readily subdued by her mother.

Ecuador was where Helen longed to run away to; in her early teens she'd thought it might be just about far enough. At thirty-two she wasn't convinced but she remained captivated by its associations: a country which was an oasis in her teenage years could never be downgraded to arid desert. She'd contemplated visiting it for a holiday when money became more plentiful after graduation but something always deterred her. The year she'd flown to Singapore instead of Quito she'd finally realised why she was so reluctant: Shangrila shouldn't be taken out of its bubblewrap. She might start popping the bubbles. And while that was cheaper than therapy, in what protective covering would she then sheathe her land of milk and honey?

Speaking of which, Helen remembered the milk. She turned back to the kitchen and discovered the milk had frothed a lace pattern over the glass floor of the microwave. It was only a notion anyway; she didn't fancy hot milk. A tot of sherry would be considerably more effective. It might chase her dragons away. Her dragon. She only had the one.

Safely back in London, though it made no difference: out of sight out of mind didn't apply in her circumstances. At least he was beyond turning up on her doorstep and rocketing all her resolutions into orbit.

Helen scrubbed at the congealed milk stain, incapable of leaving it until morning, and debated taking the sherry bottle as well as a glass to bed but decided that constituted a slope so slippery she'd need skis to negotiate it. She poured herself a couple of inches and tucked the atlas under her arm. If alcohol didn't lull her to sleep maybe maps would.

Buttering toast later that morning she heard the post bellyflop on the doormat. She sucked at a patch of butter on her thumb and lifted the sole item of mail, a postcard showing Gustav Klimt's lovers kissing. She flipped it over without so much as a premonition but her stomach churned as she read: 'Helen, I'm booked on to the first flight from Stansted to Dublin on Saturday morning. If this ends it has to be by mutual consent, not because one of us bolts. Patrick.'

Helen was exasperated: he was flying backwards and for-wards so often her head was spinning. Behind the irritation lay trepidation: she could procrastinate no longer. Molly's advice was indispensable, and the days of 'I have a friend with a problem' were long past. She had to be completely honest even if she emerged as a freak. Perhaps if she wrote to Molly . . .

As she collected her briefcase from the foot of the stairs and abandoned her toast uneaten, her eye fell on a trinket Molly had bought her. It was a snowglobe showing two laughing girls playing ring-a-rosy. 'I never liked that game – everyone falls down,' Helen had remarked. 'But they help each other to their feet again,' Molly had countered.

Helen lifted the snowglobe and shook it, watching the

children sway amid the vortex of flakes. By the time they settled, she'd reached a decision: she'd speak to Molly face-to-face. Worst case scenario: she'd lose a friend. Best case scenario: she'd lose a problem.

Helen activated her burglar alarm and walked towards the DART station with a lighter heart than she could have believed possible. The taciturn man in the ticket office who once accused her of littering (a tissue had blown out of her bag while she'd ransacked it for coins) stared after her, wondering why he'd never noticed before what a winsome smile she had.

Meanwhile, Molly lay in bed with her brain on a work-to-rule and a cafetiere of coffee on the bedside table. Today was a day off. Ostensibly she was re-reading *Anne Frank's Diary* but it was less than congenial charting the cabin fever rampaging through the attic inmates' hidey-hole. Instead she counted the buds on the tree outside her window. Spring was about to be sprung, in another month or so she'd be woken by sunlight streaming through the window. Touch wood. Perhaps she should pick up some travel brochures and plan a holiday – the dangling carrot of a fortnight in May somewhere exotic might encourage the rising sap to the surface. She'd cajole Helen into joining her; she seemed in dire need of a break judging by her performance the other Monday. It might cure her moods – nothing like sun on the back for defrosting someone. Apart from valium, of course. A suntan would sort Helen Sharkey out in record time. Whereas Barry was a trickier proposition altogether although he could do with chilling out too, he was way too libidinous. Luckily Molly's shifts hadn't coincided with his at work since last week. She tapped her teeth as her coffee cooled. She was supposed to be treating herself with Jamaican Blue Mountain, which meant it deserved to be consumed black, but she'd added a splash of milk. However, cold coffee was cold coffee even if it cost twice as much as her usual brand. Molly absentmindedly took a sip and wrinkled her nose. A trip to the microwave was in order.

Only one way of defusing Barry, she decided, back in bed with heat-zapped coffee and the Irish Film Centre bulletin, which she'd found lying on top of the microwave. It was out of date but she could scan it and mourn all the films she'd missed. Barry needed his eye redirecting to the ball, namely Kay. If he were reunited with his wife he wouldn't have time to imagine he was in love with Molly. So now all she had to do was unleash the brainstorming potency of Jamaican Blue Mountain on her febrile imagination and she'd be inundated with solutions.

Just a minute . . . Molly held the coffee in her mouth, swishing it from cheek to cheek, as she remembered the genius of her serenading idea. How had Barry been received when he arrived at Kay's salon word-perfect in Love Is All Around? It should have been the clincher but it augured inauspiciously that he'd pitched up at Molly's and pounced on her; Kay was the woman he should be pouncing on. Despite her reservations about Stephen's grasp of the concept of days off if there were stories to write and no staff to write them, Molly decided to drop by the office. Self-respect demanded she quiz Barry on his singsong; there was no point in wasting her inspiration on people if they didn't enact her brainwaves. She'd have a shower, collar Barry and sort him out, hive off to Café Davide for a well-deserved plate of blueberry pancakes and she'd ask for extra maple syrup this time because they never trickled enough into those minuscule pots they provided. Then she could check out the swimsuits in Arnotts – if she were going to balmy climes she'd need a new costume. Her current one must have shrunk in the wash because it didn't fit her any more.

Barry gave her a dazzle-you-in-the-next-county grin when she appeared in the newsroom, sidling past Stephen, who was engrossed in the racing pages.

'Couldn't stay away, Molly?' beamed Barry.

'You've got me bang to rights, guv.'

'Glad to see those two years in London weren't just wasted on journalism and you took diction lessons from cabbies too.'

'Nope, did a week's worth of shifts on the *Currant Bun*. Even filled in for their Page Three girl one day when she went on a bender with some sports reporters the night before and missed her 10 a.m. photo-shoot.'

Barry brightened still more. 'Back issues will be ordered. Don't think you can suppress this pic with the success I've achieved in quelling copies of my own, er, somewhat under-clothed pose. And where were you when there was drinking and steam being let off and sundry high-jinks with sports journalists? How come you missed the roistering?'

Molly tossed her hair so boisterously the blonde curls pirouetted and all but took a bow. 'For starters I wouldn't want to suppress the shot, my body looked exceptionally luscious in the *Soaraway Sun*, if I say so myself. Must have been the Vaseline smeared on the camera lens. I was approached by a lingerie catalogue on the strength of it. Just because your weedy art-class pose did nothing to promote confidence in your physique, don't imagine others are ashamed of their forays into the world of glamour modelling. Secondly, who do you imagine organised the knees-up with the sports department and invited along Jenny Jivebunny, 44–24–34, a girl with her brain cells stored inside mammaries, whose grooming for stardom did not include advice on declining the occasional drink when a dozen men on testosterone overload are including you in their round. She told me the next time we met up she thought testosterone came with a conscience. Now that,' Molly paused for ultimate impact, 'counts as truly dim.'

Barry ignored the jibe about his art-class photograph, concentrating on the infinitely more tantalising information about a lingerie catalogue. 'So there's photos of you in flimsy undies too?' The needle on his excitometer threatened to spin off the scale.

Molly took pity on him. 'Of course not, Barry, nor is there a Page Three spread featuring my unclad bosoms, but I did manage a week of reporting shifts on the *Sun*. Bought a CD player with the proceeds.'

'At least tell me Jenny 44–24–34 Jivebunny exists,' pleaded Barry.

'There is no Easter bunny and no Jenny Jivebunny either.' Molly steadied him with a hand on his shoulder before recalling that she was meant to be discouraging the man, not pressing flesh. Or in Barry's case, bony ridges.

'Molly, the very woman. We're short-handed at the Four Courts. Can you zip straight down and cover a rentboy trial in court number two? The accused is the justice minister's son. This is a stonker.' Stephen was standing behind Molly, emanating too much of something squirty from a can that must have been bought in a Pound Shop.

'No, I'm on a day off and I've appointments to keep. Dentist's and a facial.'

'Your teeth are perfect, so is your face. It's going to be a sensational trial. The word is the prosecution intend to subpoena a circuit court judge alleged to be one of his regulars. His mother is expected to be in court offering family solidarity. You must know Sheila Mulvey – she's on the board of at least three charities and never out of the social columns. If the copy is spicy enough they'll run a front page write-off and a story inside.'

Molly wavered. It sounded like a cracker. And she had a weakness for seeing her byline on the front page.

Stephen scented blood and moved in for the kill. 'It might even be a picture byline on the inside copy. Come on, this has everything: rentboys soliciting around the papal cross in the Phoenix Park, a kinky judge and pillar-of-the-community parents struggling to understand their deviant son.'

Molly plucked a notebook from her drawer and spun on her heel. 'I expect a Sunday off for this the next time the roster has me marked for weekend duty, Stephen. And Barry, I'll be back here late afternoon when the court rises. We're going for coffee.'

Barry and Stephen wore identical triumphant grins as she stalked out.

'Is a circuit court judge really implicated in the rentboy scandal?' asked Barry.

'Negative, just lobbed that into the mix to sell it to Molloy – she has a weakness for stories about deviant legal eagles. She maintains people who wear wigs and aren't country singers are fair game.'

'You mean you lied to persuade her to cover the story?' Barry was impressed. Stephen shrugged modestly. 'Creative use of the truth, no more. For all I know there could be a bent judge on his client list.'

*　　*　　*

Back at base in the late afternoon, Molly flung off her coat and started pounding the computer keyboard.

'What about our coffee?' asked Barry.

'It'll have to be a pint in The Kip. This story is The Business. The judge fined the defendant for contempt of court over an outburst. I thought the old boy was going to shout "Off with his head!" he was so unhinged. But he'd obviously left his Queen of Hearts outfit at home.'

'What sort of outburst?' Barry was passing time. He'd finished all his own stories but was avoiding sending them to the newsdesk in case he were given more to do.

'Magnificent. He leaped to his feet in the middle of the arresting officer's testimony and yelled that at least he earned his money honestly by performing sexual favours, he didn't snatch handbags or mug old ladies. I nearly burst out cheering. It's set to run for another day. I'll be back in court number two tomorrow listening to details of these same sexual favours. A detective told me the kid's policy seemed to be that no request was too extreme if the readies were lavish enough.'

'Why's the expensively educated son of a government minister selling his body in the Phoenix Park?' Incredulity radiated from Barry.

'Drugs. Rebellion. Intoxication of the illicit. I'll fill you in later but I want to wrap this up. The sooner the subs have their hands on it the better my chances of a decent show in the paper. Apparently his clients tended to be happily married men who didn't want to admit they were gay or bisexual.'

'There aren't any Irish bisexuals. Just men who like women as well as drink,' said Barry.

Molly laughed. 'Stop distracting me, I've just spelled

"soliciting" wrong. By the way, the judge is antediluvian. I keep expecting him to ask, "What is a rentboy, anyhow?" Although I imagine he understands the concept, if not the terminology.'

The chief sub passed Molly's computer terminal en route to the water cooler and called over his shoulder: 'I presume Stephen's told you we want eight inches for the front to go with a photograph of the rentboy.'

'Working on it now,' Molly nodded.

'I could crack a rude joke about column inches and rentboys,' remarked Barry.

'Quit while you're ahead,' advised Molly.

A couple of hours later, in The Kip, Molly and Barry were walloping into their drinks. There were too many people from the office within earshot for Molly to enquire about the efficacy of her plan for a yodelling Barry to woo Kay at work. On the other hand, she'd need to intimate her intentions were the strictly supportive variety sooner rather than later because he appeared to think they were on some class of date. She scooped the lemon slice out of her gin and sucked it. Barry and herself had been drinking together in The Kip for years – why was he suddenly going off the rails on her? If he had to have a crush on someone he should have chosen Natasha, the education correspondent. She bought her entire wardrobe from Louise Kennedy. Or that new sub, Aileen O'-something, who was a ringer for Enya.

'Fancy a curry later?' asked Barry.

She shook her head. 'You should be making tracks home to your nearest and dearest – the salmon en croute will be crisping in the oven.'

'It's meatballs in tomato and basil sauce on Wednesdays,' Barry corrected her. He lowered his tone: 'And I've told Kay not to cook for me any more.'

'That's a bit extreme. I understood you were as wedded to her culinary prowess as to the woman.'

'Habit, Molly, but habits can be broken. Is that a new blouse? Green suits you.'

'Hold it right there, Dalton. Point (a) you've seen this shirt dozens of times, and point (b) the couple who slurp meatballs together stay together.' Oblivious to the consequences Molly raised her voice. 'You'll never patch up the marriage at this rate, Bar. Now tell me how the salon serenade passed off.'

'Sssh,' Barry hissed. 'It didn't. I couldn't get the chorus memorised and I took it as a divine red card telling me I wasn't to do it. Anyway, I don't want to patch up a clapped-out marriage; I want to rent a flat, turn over a new leaf and start seeing you. I'm mad about you, Molly.'

Alarm propelled Molly towards brutal honesty. 'You're mad, full stop. And why on earth would you imagine that with diverse conflicts and famines and megalomaniac dictators to contend with, whoever's handling the divine end of things has time to zap your memory banks to hamper you from learning a couple of bars of mush?'

Barry pushed the drinks to one side and lurched through the air towards Molly, his face inches from hers and closing fast. 'I'm wild about you. I think about you all the time when I'm conscious and dream about you when I'm not.'

Dismay was overtaken by full-scale panic. She cast around desperately for an alibi as to why she was unavailable to entertain his advances. 'I don't fancy you' seemed too brutal – although she wasn't ruling it out as a last resort.

'Barry, be honest, have I ever done anything to encourage you? I thought we were supposed to be mates. This isn't how friends behave. Besides, you know I'm seeing Fionn. I never truly got over him; I think this time it's for keeps.'

She gulped her gin, hoping he wouldn't notice the fingers on both her hands were crossed.

Barry slumped. 'You don't fancy me, do you? I'm middle-aged and stodgy, just as Kay said. No woman in her right mind would take me on.'

Molly noticed a couple of feature writers casting curious glances in their direction and one of the copytakers was eavesdropping openly. She hustled Barry into his coat and outdoors. She must have been deranged imagining they could have a private conversation in the office drinking den. She marched him into Supermac's and ordered them both cheeseburgers and chips; he'd feel better on a full stomach. And if he didn't she sure as heck would.

They ate in companionable silence. For a man whose hopes had been blighted a few minutes earlier Barry regained his appetite with suspicious alacrity. When the meal was finished he remarked, 'I never thought we'd be all that compatible anyhow after the sex appeal had burned itself out.'

Molly choked on her strawberry milkshake, recovered and considered leaving him to his own devices – he could make a banjax of his life for all she cared – but decided to be magnanimous. Obviously he was pining for her; the comment about having nothing in common after the jiggery pokery lost its edge could be attributed to pique. Besides, did she really want Barry believing they were kindred spirits? She didn't even care for his allegations of sexual compatibility.

Molly resumed slurping. 'Listen carefully, Barry, I have an artful plan.'

'Don't you mean a cunning plan?'

'No, this is too devious to be relegated to mere cunning. Here's how you lure Kay back: make her jealous.'

'She's already jealous. Of you. Fancy some ice cream, Molloy?'

'No. And don't attempt to move until after I've outlined my artful plan. Picture it: your place, Saturday night, eight o'clock. Kay's driven into a jealous frenzy of spring-cleaning overload while you ponce around putting the finishing touches to your *Night Fever* attire, ready for a session with your new love.'

'Which is you?' Barry looked hopeful.

'Which is not me.' Molly looked adamant.

'Who then?'

'Helen.'

Barry was crestfallen. 'I'm nervous of her; she's too forbidding. How do you propose persuading her to become my new girlfriend?'

'Aye, there's the rub,' said Molly. 'I suppose we could always throw ourselves on her good nature.'

Barry was visibly intimidated.

Molly decided to play it reassuring. 'Leave the Helen end of this triangle to me. I'll have her primed to drape herself all over you somewhere v. public. You'll be making out like teenagers, and as soon as Kay realises you're a desirable object she'll stake her prior claim. Cue reconciliation, cue a long hot summer of love. Now, Barry, go home, be cheerful, don't let Kay imagine you're devastated by the impending split, and my bet is she won't like this transformation that has you resigned and no longer pleading with her to change her mind. She'll start worrying this was your idea instead of hers and before you know it she'll be beckoning you from the bedroom door in a diaphanous négligé.'

'A what?'

'A see-through nightie. Now let's go home, my brain is

tired and I need to rest it before tackling the problem of the elixir of youth.'

Back at the apartment Molly decided the best way to lure Helen on board was to cut a deal with her. If Helen play-acted smitten with Barry, she'd give her a Get Out of Jail Free card. That meant she could call in a favour any time; they'd operated this system since college.

She phoned Helen with the proposition.

'Molly, you're meddling.' Helen sounded less than enthusiastic.

'Someone has to, man's as precarious as three-legged stool with only two legs. If I don't take a hand he'll forfeit his home, his family and his grasp on reality.'

'Reality's overrated,' said Helen. She made no effort to curb her bitterness.

'The alternative's not a viable option,' insisted Molly, disturbed by Helen's grim assessment. 'Fantasy isn't for grown-ups, not long term.'

'But adulthood's overrated too,' said Helen.

Molly held the receiver away from her ear and looked at it. Who'd confiscated Helen's toys? 'You need a holiday, Helen. How about calling over to me tomorrow evening after work? I'll collect a stack of brochures in my lunchbreak and we can pore over superlatives. I'll even rustle us up a couple of mojitos to capture that sensation of lolling in a hammock with the crickets chirping. We can also negotiate on the Barry front, a get out of jail free card has to be worth a little discomfort lending him a hand in his hour of need.'

'I'll expect you to lay down strict ground rules with him if I agree to this, Molly.' Helen realised she was eyeball to eyeball with her best chance of talking candidly about Patrick. 'I'm not saying yes yet, mind you, but I'll consider it. And scoop up a couple of brochures on Ecuador while you're in the travel agent's.'

'Consider it done.'

Molly was all but chortling as she replaced the handset. 'I can be beamed back to the mother planet any day now. My work among earthlings is done. And I've had enough of this inter-species dating.'

A jarring note spoiled her self-congratulatory high. Specifically two. Fionn and Hercules. One was all over her and the other was nowhere near her. Longing flattened her.

'I wish to God Fionn would vanish and Hercules would move in next door. No, that's a waste of a wish. I wish Fionn would vanish and Hercules would move in with me.'

Molly spoke with such conviction she unnerved herself. She waited for something spooky to happen, like the electricity flickering or a rap on the ceiling. Normality reigned. She decided to give herself a rest from men, even Hercules, which meant no art appreciation lecture the following day but she felt she could handle the sacrifice. Take to your bed with a book instead of a body, Molly advised herself and searched for something diverting. She hadn't the energy for Anne Frank tonight either. What a relief the diarist didn't become a journalist as she projected; she was so promising at fourteen she'd make the rest of them look inadequate. Molly extracted a book at random from a precarious heap behind the sofa and glanced at the cover. It was *The Mill on the Floss* by – good God, by George Eliot. Was this fate's not-so-cryptic intimation that Georgie her Greek was ready to flood her life – just as she was veering towards the conclusion that men were almost – almost – more trouble than they were worth? Or was she delusional now, to cap it all? She clambered into bed without brushing her teeth, was nagged by guilt and trotted off to the bathroom to repair the omission.

Flossing vigorously – always suggestible, she had been reminded by *The Mill on the Floss* of weeks of neglect – she made a resolution. Fionn was toast, even if nothing sparked with Hercules. There was no point in keeping to a man until something better happened along. It was energy-sapping and she needed all her stamina for directing Barry's life, deciding whether she had the stamina to pursue Hercules and ferreting out whatever was wrong with Helen. Molly had a suspicion Barry wasn't the only one ricocheting off track; Helen was showing evidence of someone out of kilter too.

Molly accidentally soaked her pyjamas at the washbasin as she tossed around possibilities to explain Helen's prickliness of late. Early onset of the menopause: doubtful. Sexual frustration: possible. Midlife crisis: too soon. Money worries: improbable, she had share options. Sexual frustration was the clear favourite. There now, that left her with a moral dilemma. Maybe she should hand Hercules over to Helen on a dish as the *plat du jour*. He'd already expressed an interest in her. Just because Helen was currently indifferent didn't mean she'd stay that way. She could be persuaded to reconsider if the suitor was ardent enough, although he'd have to be inordinately persistent – if the original Helen had Helen Sharkey's temperament there'd have been no Trojan War because Paris would never have enticed her to run away with him. But Hercules could win an Olympic medal for being coaxing, Molly was convinced. And his Greek lineage lent a certain symmetry to the possibility of his pairing off with Helen. Sure didn't he have the weight of history on his side.

She trailed off to bed somewhat forlornly. It was a desperate pity Helen and Fionn didn't hit it off. Sacrificing him to Helen would be no tribulation. But Hercules . . . now passing him on was genuine hardship. However, Fionn was a non-starter because Helen would never contemplate one of Molly's rejects, which only left the Greek god. Oh God. Why couldn't he be cloned? Medical science should get a move on and solve her dilemma with Identikit versions of the same man, one for Molly and one for Helen. Of course she'd never agree to it.

'She'd never let herself be palmed off with Hercules or Fionn, for that matter. She'd regard it as incestuous,' Molly explained to Nelson as she relegated him from the pillow to the foot of the bed. 'Such a shame about her lofty moral standards.'

CHAPTER 18

Molly opened the door of her flat to Helen and nodded at Elizabeth, clinging like a precarious Bambi to the wall by the lift in transparent sandals with heels at once so towering and so narrow they tricked the eye into believing she was walking on tiptoe.

'Fetching shoes. You need to be fetched in them. Those heels shouldn't be allowed anywhere near pavements or stairs,' said Molly, as Helen stepped past her into the hallway.

Elizabeth tottered but rallied. 'Style over balance is the plan for tonight.'

'Does your neighbour ever spend a night in?' asked Helen when the front door was closed.

Molly reflected. 'I have no evidence that she does. I haven't bored a peephole into the wall yet so I can't confirm this but my gut reaction is that Elizabeth last spent a night at home eight years ago. The experience must have been so harrowing she vowed never to repeat it. Hey presto, party girl.'

'What's her other name? I've only heard her called Elizabeth.'

'Carroll or O'Carroll, I forget which.'

'A Kerry name,' remarked Helen.

'It's far from Kerry that specimen was reared. Now, prepare to be dazzled. I bought you a present.'

'I hope this isn't intended to soften me up for a pivotal role in your masterplan to tamper with Barry's relationship.'

'Naturally it is,' replied Molly. 'Here you are, it's called a Socrates because it's such a clever corkscrew.'

Helen was enchanted. 'A new corkscrew, I can't wait to try it out. It is foolproof?'

Molly was dubious; it might be foolproof but it would take a genius of a gadget to be Helen-proof. 'I think it works on the lazy fish principle but it seemed churlish to buy someone a gift and use it before they did so I couldn't say for definite. You can experiment in the privacy of your own home, Dr Frankenstein, and publish the results in the appropriate scientific manual. Barry should be able to recommend one. It'll give you a talking point.'

Helen grimaced, removing her hip-length raincoat and crossing the corridor to hang it over Molly's shower rail although it was barely damp.

'Come out of there, Helen. I can't trust you not to start checking if I've scrubbed down the bath recently. Now, the mojitos are blended, all that remains is the fresh mint I trust you remembered to pluck from your herbal window box – splendid, reach it here. Strew yourself wantonly across the kitchen table. It'll save you the bother of collapsing presently when you taste how potent these lads are.'

They tasted, decided simultaneously to abandon sipping and savouring and proceeded to swig. On the second mojito apiece Molly took the initative.

'About Barry and you . . .'

'Eek!' squealed Helen. 'I don't like the way you coupled his name with mine.'

'Uncoupling can be arranged as soon as we have mission

274

accomplished. Kay doesn't look like a woman of iron to me, she –'

'Doesn't drink enough red wine,' interjected Helen.

Molly eyed her suspiciously. 'Have you been imbibing?'

'I cannot tell a lie. I have a mojito in my hand even as I speak. My senses tell me it contains alcohol. My sense of sight, to wit the bottle of gin beside your microwave, my sense of smell,' she inhaled with some enthusiasm, 'and my sense of taste. And that, Molly, is the best part.' At which Helen tipped up her glass and glugged.

Molly shrugged. If she didn't know Helen better she'd conclude she'd been tippling before her arrival. But Helen had a horror of solitary drinking on account of watching her father stagger home from the pub and wallop into the Jameson's night after night. She used to explain to Molly it left her terrorised she'd become too fond of the booze on the genetic legacy principle. Molly decided Helen had a puritan-ical streak and this was one more way of denying herself the bare necessities. But it wasn't worth arguing the toss.

Helen had indeed uncharacteristically fortified herself with a nip of sherry before catching the DART to Blackrock; she wanted to be relaxed enough to broach the subject of Patrick early in the evening rather than blurt it out in some befuddled state in the wee small hours.

'So have we a deal?' asked Molly.

Helen twiddled her empty glass. 'Tell me exactly what I have to do.'

'Keep phoning his house until his wife answers. Act guilty and hesitate and then ask for him. If that doesn't arouse her suspicions she isn't human.'

Helen was relieved – it didn't sound too difficult. 'Game on,' she acquiesced.

'Wait, suspicions must be compounded by proof. Kay has

to see the pair of you out together, yourself exceptionally glamorous and besotted with Barry, and him looking like the cat that's licking the cream.'

'How besotted?'

Molly pursed her lips. 'Gazing intently into his eyes, collecting stray hairs from his collar, proprietorial gestures.'

'But no real physical contact?' asked Helen.

'Trust me, angel face, Barry's more nervous of you than you are of him. He says you're a ringer for a teacher who was always slapping him into detention.'

Helen curled her legs up under her on the chair. 'Remind me again why I'm doing this.'

'To save a faltering marriage, as a favour to me and for a get out of jail free card. Now, time to pore over those holiday brochures. I have two on Ecuador, plus purple prose hawking Mexico, Venezuela and Cuba.'

'Pour me another mojito,' said Helen. 'I need to talk to you about something else first. Something personal. I'm calling in my get out of jail free card in advance.'

Molly regarded her friend. She saw eyes which were fever bright, and a fidgety quality in her mien quite unlike the serene Helen. Molly opened her mouth and then thought better of speaking. She'd whip up a new batch of mojitos first. Helen rasped her Socratic corkscrew with what remained of her fingernails while bartending duties were carried out, Molly shimmying and singing, 'I-I-I-I-I like you verr-ay much' in an accent more Hibernian than Hispanic.

Two brimming glasses were next to them before she addressed Helen. 'Ready when you are. Yourself and this pale green concoction have my undivided attention. Or to rephrase it, you're sharing my attention but it's with a cocktail which won't be around as long as you.'

'It's going to shock you.' Helen reached for her drink.

'Sounds promising.'

'A lot.'

'Don't you have a get out of jail free card? Lash away,' invited Molly. 'Let me guess. You had a rush of blood to the head and a one-night stand with someone unsuitable, unknown, unpalatable, ungovernable, delete as appropriate.'

'Worse than that.'

'The mind boggles. Have you been forging fifty-pound notes, throwing away the gas bill unpaid, converting to Breatharianism and trying to subsist on oxygen instead of food?'

'Molly, this is serious,' said Helen. 'It's about –' she faltered, inhaled and rallied – 'it's about Patrick.' And with that she dried up.

Molly waited patiently, then impatiently, as Helen trailed her index finger around the rim of the glass. The urge to consume alcohol had abandoned Helen as precipitately as it had struck her.

'It's about Patrick and what? Or who?' prompted Molly.

'Patrick and me.' The 'me' fluttered from Helen.

Molly continued to wait. 'Are you having problems?' she ventured. This was like extracting teeth.

Helen nodded.

'Helen, I can't help you if I'm not told what the trouble is. Now, I've known you fourteen years. Nothing you could say is going to make me recoil. So if you'd like to confide in me I'm ready, and if it's too painful for you to discuss intimate family matters I understand.'

Helen twisted an earring so that the gold crescent moon shape ended face down in a topsy turvy smile that was no smile at all. She struggled for words and tripped over a torrent, all of them delivered with her eyes on the table. She shrank from Molly's gaze for fear of reading censure in it.

'Patrick and I are in love. I don't love him, I'm *in* love with him. Not like brother and sister but like man and woman. He's engaged to be married and wants to end it and go away somewhere with me, live with me as husband and wife. I've told him the world isn't wide enough but he disagrees. When I'm with him he almost convinces me because it seems eminently reasonable that two people who love each other should be together. And when we're apart I'm repulsed by what he's proposing.' She glanced at Molly to see how she was digesting the information and was heartened by the fact her face wasn't registering revulsion. Indeed, it looked sympathetic, if somewhat dazed, so she continued. 'It's the classic scenario of can't live with him and can't live without him. I'm crazy about him, Molly. I've loved him since I was a little girl. He's the reason no boyfriend lasts the distance with me. I measure them all against Patrick and they fall flat on their faces . . .' Her voice trailed off.

Molly, more shell-shocked than she appeared, collared her straying senses and essayed a question. 'Have you . . . have you been together, I mean like a man and woman?' She sounded hollow, even to her own ears.

Helen continued to explore the lip of her glass with a fierce concentration. 'Sex? Is that what you mean? Incest? Yes, three years ago. It put the fear of God in me. Patrick moved to London afterwards and we didn't see each other until my aunt's funeral a few weeks back. I imagined it would be safe by that stage but it wasn't. I don't think we'll ever be safe together, Patrick and I.' Her mouth twisted as though she were tasting vinegar.

Molly's head was reeling. Patrick was a handsome man

– she'd be the first to acknowledge that – but your own brother, for heaven's sake. It made her flesh crawl. Her brother, Timothy, was stolid and reliable, he ran a small grocery shop a few streets from where they grew up and Molly would sooner have considered sleeping with Barry or the news editor Stephen, or even the twelve-year-old at work masquerading as a reporter, as with Timothy. On second thoughts she'd simply take a vow of chastity: all the men at work *and* Timothy were equally unappealing.

But Helen was her friend. She loved Helen; she shouldn't be judgemental. And just look at the woman, she was in ribbons. She wasn't doing this for kicks. Molly swallowed an excess of saliva, which seemed to be cluttering up her mouth. Don't go all tongue-tied now, Helen needs to talk about this. Encourage her to open out. But what on earth could she say? Molly grappled for comprehension. Meet Helen's eyes, don't look away, don't let her think you're repelled.

'Most people have a lever inside that flicks to "not interested" when it comes to a sibling, Helen – what happened to yours?'

Helen chewed her lip savagely. 'Defective model; I was born minus that lever. Some of us have to be, just as some are born colour-blind or diabetic. And if your brother or sister is also born without the lever you're in trouble. You see,' she frowned, willing Molly to understand, 'I don't regard Patrick as a brother in the same way as I look upon Geraldine as my sister. I've always understood that my feelings for him were special, that they went beyond affection or loyalty or comradeship or however brothers and sisters are supposed to feel for one another. And I always knew it was reciprocal, that's why such an enduring bond formed between us. He went to England to escape

279

the connection but there's no eluding it.' The sorrow that laced Helen's voice attempting to explain the inexplicable subsided beneath a swelling of elation as she added: 'Yet it gladdens me to realise there's no reprieve for him from his feelings, that he can't obliterate them, even while it creates tortuous complications. Amidst all the turmoil, there's a pea-sized part of me that's delirious with rapture that he can no more forget me than I can forget him.' Helen subsided, caught in a maze of half-formed imaginings.

Molly drank, refilled her glass and drank again and felt more sober than ever before in her life. She supposed it was possible for a brother and sister to love one another but not if they'd grown up together surely? She could only imagine it if they were reared separately. Her eyes flickered across to Helen, a stranger to her; she thought of a swan, graceful on the surface yet pedalling furiously below the water line. And then she remembered that swans started life as ugly ducklings – the ugly duckling was still inside the swan somewhere.

The silence was protracted. Molly grappled with Helen's – what? confession? revelation? disclosure? – and wanted to say or do something that would show Helen she wasn't alone in her quagmire, that she'd continue to be her friend come what may. Although Molly shuddered to imagine what might transpire. She groped for words but could find none.

Finally, when both women thought they could toler-ate the hush no longer, Molly spoke. 'What do you plan to do?'

'I don't know.'

The stillness extended again until Helen picked up the thread of her concentration.

'I know what I should do, I know what I'll probably end

up doing, I know it'll be for the best. It's just . . .' her voice quavered, 'Christ, Molly, I'm so tempted. I want him so much and I know we could make each other happy. We're all going to be dead in fifty or sixty years anyway, as you're forever reminding me. Why shouldn't we eke what joy we can from life?'

Molly could think of a dozen reasons off the top of her head but kept her counsel. Helen, she realised, wasn't looking to her for a solution – she was easing the misery by acknowledging it. I'm not going to condemn her, Molly reminded herself, it's not my place. Helen and she had been through too much together to falter now. Nevertheless she was frozen. This went so far beyond confessions about teenage abortions or cameo roles in porno flicks it was torpedoed into another stratosphere. Be supportive, she screamed at herself.

'When did you first know?' she asked Helen.

'I always knew on one level. And then there was an incident that cemented it for me. I suppose I was pro-active then, more so than Patrick, but you have to remember he's three years younger than me. I was twenty, home from college for the summer break, and he was studying for his Leaving Cert. I knew there'd only be the two of us in the house. Geraldine was working in Munich as a chambermaid in a hotel, and Mammy and Daddy had gone to Tramore for a week. So help me God I came close to seducing him, Molly. I can remember the searing sensation of his flesh against mine as if it were yesterday . . .' Helen's voice trailed off and she stared into middle distance. Molly could see she was travelling back through time.

And Helen was remembering the sensation of his lips coalescing with hers; the network of hairs on the back of her neck sprang to attention as she inhaled the lemon peel scent of his breath. She wanted to recall every detail. Even for the sake of peace of mind she'd never annihilate the memory of their moments together. As though she had a choice – it was indelible. Yet she welcomed it, the aching and the euphoria.

It's one of those idyllic June days that happen all too rarely in Ireland. The heat is already palpable when Helen awakens and it mounts as the hours progress. The knowledge that she and Patrick are on their own in the house stokes her excitement as myriad-eyed midday sinks towards the privacy of evening; by then anticipation is heightened to almost unbearable levels. The day is eternal as it winds down and her sense of expectation ascends with pressure cooker inevitability, even as she carries out mundane chores: washing the kitchen floor, changing the bedding. There's a sensation in the pit of her stomach that bites with the insistence of cramp and she hasn't been able to eat since a nibbled slice of toast at breakfast.

As twilight filters indoors she moves from kitchen to living room, so fluttery with anticipation a draught of air would waft her skywards. It's a room they rarely use and mildew assails her senses. She draws the curtains, lighting the electric fire so that it glows invitingly, carrying the heavy old-fashioned radio – their father still refers to it as the wireless – through from its home on the kitchen dresser and settling it on the sideboard. Finally she steps outside and by the light of the kitchen window cuts a jugful of cream roses. Their heady scent alongside the radio helps to veil the room's mustiness.

Helen glides into her bedroom, treading lightly so as not

to disturb Patrick, studying next door, and slips out of her jeans and T-shirt before stroking on some of Geraldine's Chanel No 5 – on her wrists, at the hollow of her neck and finally, furtively, between her breasts. She catches sight of her naked upper body in the mirror, hesitates and examines it. Black hair coils onto white skin. She looks like someone else. Someone desirable. A hint of a smile flits across her face at the realisation. She pads downstairs, moves rapidly about the kitchen and returns to the hallway.

'Patrick,' she calls, 'I've made some tea and sandwiches. You've been worrying at the books all day – too late now to cram for your exams.'

He appears at his bedroom door and lopes down, grinning.

'Revision gives me an insatiable appetite, Helen. What sort of sandwiches have you made?'

'Ham, your favourite.'

He heads for the kitchen but she calls him back and gestures to the living room, where a tray rests on the rug before the triple-bar fire.

'I thought it might make a change to have them in here. We never use this room. It's a waste.'

Patrick looks surprised but nods. 'It's dark in here. You can hardly see your hand in front of your face. I'll put the light on, Helen.'

'Ah, let's leave it a while, it's cosy. You've been swotting all day. It'll do you good to rest your eyes. Come and sit beside me on the rug.'

He lifts a sandwich and regards the fire with consternation: 'It's been a scorcher, have you lost the head entirely?'

'Don't worry, we won't overheat. None of the bars of the fire are on, only the light that passes for flames. Besides, Patrick, it's pretty.'

He wolfs another sandwich.

She leans against an armchair and sips a cup of tea while he eats, observing him from a sliver of sight under lowered eyelids. He's a foot away and oblivious to her.

Or is he? He rotates a half-circle away but not before she notices him taking in the strip of uncovered stomach between her jeans and T-shirt.

'Aren't you having any sandwiches, Helen?'

She shakes her head.

'I should take exams more often, you're spoiling me.' He hesitates and adds. 'You look different tonight.'

'Different good or different bad?' She digs her hands into her pocket and the hollow of her navel, with its mole duplicating his, is exposed.

'Different different.' A troubled expression clouds his face.

She crosses to the radio and trawls through stations until Dusty Springfield joins them in the room singing about being loved by the son of a preacher man.

'Dance with me, Patrick.' She extends her arms.

He rolls his eyes, joking that she's using him as target practice for the next foray to The Gap ballroom, but joins her obligingly on the lino beyond the paisley-patterned rug.

Only seventeen and he's already more than a head taller than she. She moves her body in time to the music and after a few bars' hesitation Patrick slips into the rhythm, humming along with Dusty. One hand is around her waist, the other loosely clasps hers. There's a few inches of distance between their bodies and she's angled to see over his shoulder instead of into his face.

Helen steps sideways so that both her feet are inside Patrick's and now she looks directly ahead, eyes level with his throat. His Adam's apple bobs – is he nervous? Is he becoming attentive to her body as she is to his? She leans forward slightly so that her hair brushes his chin. At once he steps back, as though exposed to an electric shock, but recovers his balance and closes the distance between them.

The song dies away and Helen tilts her head to watch him. His eyes slide away but the hand that's holding hers is damp with perspiration. Both of them hover, straining for the next song. Make it another slow record, she wishes, and Nat King Cole's cinnamon toast voice replaces Dusty's. She relaxes into the melody and her body continues moving. Patrick follows her lead.

It's now or never, Helen thinks, and rests her face against his shoulder. His cheek dips immediately onto the top of her head. She smells him against her, at once familiar and unfamiliar. The scent of the little boy she bathed and played with is mingled with an adult male fragrance that's new to her. Her lips brush against the collar of his shirt and she smiles, thinking it fortunate she isn't wearing lipstick. She wonders if he can detect her perfume. Helen stumbles and her thigh brushes against his, a whisper of contact that causes him to release her abruptly and slap silent the radio controls.

'Better get back to the books.' His tone is as curt as his expression.

Helen watches him stalk from the room. His back radiates anger, she fancies. A door slams upstairs, she sighs and clears away the crockery.

'You miscalculated there,' she admonishes herself, as she sits at the kitchen table smoking cigarette after cigarette. She's usually no more than an occasional smoker but tonight she's desperate for the nicotine's narcotic boost.

It's after midnight before she heads upstairs to bed. In the dim of the landing, lit by skylight, a lifeline of electric beam seeps from Patrick's room. She cannot bring herself to grasp it and enter, rejection seems inevitable. Instead Helen takes advantage of Geraldine's absence and lies in bed smoking, using the lid of an empty moisturiser pot as an ashtray. The glow at the tip of her fingers comforts her as much as the smoke flooding her lungs.

She hears a click as Patrick's light is extinguished and imagines him climbing into bed. There's no way to put this right. She made a clumsy pass at her brother and he rebuffed her. It will always rear, an unspoken reproach between them.

When the packet is empty Helen slides the overflowing lid under the bed. The only sound in the darkness is her breathing as she lies and waits for sleep. But smoke tingles in her mouth still, she runs her tongue along her teeth, grimaces and swings her legs out of bed and pads along to the bathroom.

In darkness she brushes her teeth, looking at the moon. Another day and it will be full. As a girl she used to wish on the full moon: for Maggie Buckley at school to be her friend because she was the most popular girl in school; for her breasts to grow; for Geraldine to lend her the oatmeal-coloured swing coat she bought for a cousin's wedding. Helen wipes her mouth with a towel and opens the bathroom door. A mass of darkness leaning against the banisters detaches itself from the gloom: it's Patrick. Her heart lunges while he closes the gap between them. She expects him to speak but the strained-looking white face with black pools for eyes doesn't move, except to come so near to her that it blurs. His hands cradle her face, their noses bump and his lips land on hers, moist and surprisingly soft. A host of firecraker sensations burst through her as, scarcely daring to breathe, she feels his mouth move against hers. Her heart hammers in her eardrums and then he moves his head away to break the embrace. Patrick's face is again visible, his breathing appears to be as laboured as her own. The expression in his eyes is questioning as his thumbs sweep her cheekbones.

She moves her head so that his hands drop away, then twines her fingers in his and leads him into her bedroom. It smells smoky but neither notices as they sit on the edge of the bed and swivel towards one another. They sink onto the pillows, face to face, swimming in kisses. Patrick rolls on top of her and now there's an edge to their embrace, an insistence in the way his mouth fuses with hers. His hand travels along her body, lingering on the curve of her breast before descending to her stomach.

Only the persistent jangling of a telephone stopped them that night, the intrusion propelling them apart in a welter of guilt and fear and drumming pulse points. But there had been no timely interruption three years ago, when Patrick and Helen took their irrevocable step . . .

'I think it's time I made us some supper.' Molly's voice reached down the years and yanked Helen back to the present.

The vacancy in Helen's eyes unclouded and she nodded.

'Have you spoken about any of this to Geraldine?' Molly filled the kettle with her back to Helen.

'God no. I don't find her particularly approachable, I never have. She suspects nothing and I'll be doing everything in my power to keep it that way.'

'Going to be tricky if you and Patrick vanish off the face of the planet to an Amazon rainforest or wherever you plan to construct your love nest.' Molly was striving to keep her voice deliberately light as she persuaded the freezer to part with a couple of slices of bread and laid them under the grill.

'That's not on the agenda,' insisted Helen.

By unspoken mutual consent they abandoned the subject while they ate toasted sandwiches. Molly made a desultory attempt at conversation but Helen was monotone.

'I think I'll catch the last DART home,' she told Molly as soon as was decently possible.

Molly inclined her head. She'd welcome a breather herself; this would take some absorbing. Helen oozed exhaustion and Molly knew exactly how she felt.

'Listen, we'll talk about this again,' she promised Helen, dimly conscious they hadn't so much tackled a problem as let a few gasps of air into it. Helen didn't respond; Molly thought she was withdrawing into a defensive remoteness, already regretting the confidence, but she was wrong – Helen's brain was swirling with images of Patrick.

'There's something about all this I can't understand,' Molly said to Helen by the lift.

Helen turned to her.

'Patrick's your double. The pair of you are obviously brother and sister. It's more difficult to see the attraction when you're mirror images of one another.'

Helen stuck her foot in the lift door to force the mechanism to wait. 'That's not so unusual. You often see couples who're alike – as though they feel validated by a lookalike partner.'

'True,' conceded Molly. 'Is that how it works for you, the ratification experience?'

Helen stepped into the lift. 'I've never audited the attraction, it's simply there. He's just the man I love. Who happens to be my brother.'

The door closed on a tormented face. The face of a woman in love.

Molly found herself shaking. If that was how a woman in love looked she'd settle for lust any day.

CHAPTER 19

Next morning Molly was ashamed of herself. She should have said or done something to remind Helen that she wasn't alone, instead of which she'd sat there like a lump of wax waiting to be moulded into the appropriate shape. It was ludicrous expecting Helen to play her puerile game with Barry under the circumstances. She'd ring her at work and scrap that plan.

'It was a ridiculous scheme anyway.' Molly chattered aloud, padding about the apartment, tidying up after the previous night's session. 'I must think I'm God Almighty to interfere in people's lives. I'm not even sure I was doing it for the right reason. It was as much to unhook Barry from the limpet-like position he's adopted on my back as to save a friend's marriage.'

She stacked glasses and mugs in the sink, briefly considered washing them and jettisoned the notion as a waste of morning-fresh bursting energy banks. Dishwashing was a tail-end-of-the-evening task when the brain cells weren't powering on all cylinders. Admittedly you were more likely to break something then but who wants a mug to last a lifetime anyway? She spotted a pile of holiday brochures on the worktop and sighed. Presumably her wizard wheeze to take a trip away with Helen was off the agenda.

Molly felt a list demanded compilation. She adjourned to the sofa with one of her employer's spiral notepads, chewed the top of her pen and decided the crux of everyone's problems was they were in love with the wrong people. Including herself.

- Helen: monumentally in love with the wrong man. And that was an understatement, scribbled Molly.
- Barry: in a state of emotional chaos but still in love with Kay despite it all.
- Fionn: imagined he was in love with Molly, possibly in love with the uncomplicated relationship they had four years previously. Marriage obviously not devoid of complexities, she might need to reconsider appetite for day out in white frock.
- Herself: fancied she was in love with her Greek, may well be in love with him, but he was a lost cause unless she could dream up a wooden horse stratagem to storm his citadel. And was all that effort really worth it for a twenty-five-year-old student with a minor crush on her seriously deranged friend?

Molly re-read her list, enchanted with her perspicuity if a little less captivated by the negative conclusions she was drawing. A church clock nearby chimed to remind the faithful it was time for ten o'clock Mass – and she was supposed to be in the law courts at ten thirty for the next instalment of the rentboy episode. No more lingering over lists – she'd have to dash for a train. And if she wanted another coffee she'd need to drink it on the Howth-bound DART because judges were odd about people carrying polystyrene cups into their courtrooms. They seemed to regard it as offensive to the majesty of the law. Although there wasn't supposed to be any majesty in Ireland, it being a republic, try telling that to people who wore wigs and gowns dating back to colonial days.

Sidling into court number two fractionally after the judge's arrival, Molly nodded at the detective who'd filled her in on some background yesterday and borrowed a pen from the RTE reporter. She switched her mobile off, checked out what the rentboy was wearing – a navy suit, as decorous as a choirboy; someone had done a makeover job on him – and listened to the senior counsel for the prosecution.

There were two messages on the mobile when she turned it on at lunchtime, one from Barry suggesting another drink in The Kip after work (he really doesn't want to go home at night, deduced Molly) and the other from Fionn on an insistent rather than conciliatory note, stipulating a meeting either tonight or tomorrow. He didn't expect to hear back from her because she didn't have the manners to return calls (ouch) but he'd be in Kehoe's from seven until eight on both evenings. No word from someone you'd really like a message from, such as Hercules or, er, Hercules. Molly chewed glumly on a prawn salad sandwich from the Epicurean Centre.

Hammering out the court copy later, Molly was aware of Barry watching her. He was nudging her off stride with those beseeching eyes. Now she couldn't remember if it was Judge Kelly or Melly presiding; the sooner she sorted Barry out the better. But that meant contacting Helen, and she needed a breather before she could stomach more tribulations. Fionn was her best alternative – she'd allow him to buy her a drink and worship her for a couple of hours this evening. They might even go for something to eat since it was a Friday night. There was a new restaurant on Wicklow Street the food critic had been raving about in the office yesterday. Once the review appeared she'd have no chance of booking a table so she might as well put her inside knowledge to some use. A self-satisfied smile played around Molly's lips as she typed.

'You look pleased with yourself – did the rentboy go down?' Stephen asked Molly.

Barry smirked.

She favoured them both with an old-fashioned look. 'A fine plus suspended sentence in view of the fact he comes from a worthy family, et cetera. Kelly was a Fianna Fáil appointment so someone in the minister's department obviously leaned on the judge. My bet is he'll be back turning tricks at the papal cross by tomorrow night if either of you fancy the look of him.'

Both reacted as though their flesh were crawling.

'Bestial,' spat out Stephen.

'Depraved,' hissed Barry.

'Business was brisk so not everyone shares your sanctified responses,' remarked Molly. 'Now stop distracting me, I have a hot date.'

Tepid was nearer the mark but Fionn might know how to operate the thermostat.

She spotted him immediately as she entered the crowded pub; he'd monopolised a corner, thrown his overcoat on a spare stool and was nursing his pint of Guinness over the *Chronicle*'s crossword puzzle. Molly felt a tingle of anticipation when she saw him.

'What's a lovely boy like you doing in a gurrier's dive like this?' she asked.

'This isn't a dive.' He checked it out, surprised.

'Must've muddled it, so. What's a gurrier like you doing in a lovely place like this?'

'I preferred it the first way,' said Fionn. 'Wine, beer, gin, all three?'

'Think I'll have a Pimms and white in honour of the blink of sunshine I detected between rain showers today. But don't make the barman feel inadequate if he lacks cucumber slices to garnish it.'

'Your chances of cucumber slices are about equal with your chances of sunburn from that scintilla of sunshine earlier today.'

Molly affected distaste. 'Standards just keep on slipping. They'll be serving the drink in plastic beakers next.' She dampened her forefinger and wiped at an ink blot on Fionn's chin. 'Tell me some of the clues you can't work out, McCullagh. We used to be a winning combination on the crossword front.'

'What blows hot one day and cold the next?' asked Fionn, catching the barman's eye. 'Pimms and white, please. With ice.'

'Haven't a notion.' Molly removed her coat and draped it over her stool. 'Wait until I wind my fingers around a drink, it always helps my powers of concentration. Here's to the weekend.'

She clinked glasses with Fionn and drank deeply. 'Looking promising already. What blows hot one day and cold the next? It must be some kind of wind, a mistral or whatever you call them. How many letters?'

'Five. Begins with M, ends in Y.' Fionn was looking decidedly attractive in a pale grey suit and shirt so white it blinded the eye. Did this indicate she was now such a boring grown-up that men in smart suits appealed to her?

She drank again and laid her glass on the bar counter. 'Of course, you mean me.'

Fionn folded up the newspaper.

Molly waited for him to make a pitch but he finished his Guinness.

'I'll order you another,' she offered.

'I only wanted the one here. I have plans,' he said. 'I'm meeting some of the lads from the office in The Norseman shortly. We'll have a few jars and find somewhere to eat. No shortage of restaurants in Temple Bar.'

'I thought you and I could have a meal, Fionn. We should talk.'

'Actions speak louder than words and you've made your feelings plain enough. It was foolish of me to imagine I could stoke up four-year-old embers anyway. So I wanted to buy you a drink and say goodbye. I've bought the drink, only the goodbye remains.' And he kissed her on the cheek, lifted his coat and walked away.

Molly was dazed. She cast tentative eyes right and left to assess how much of the farewell scene had been overheard, finished her Pimms and rattled the ice cubes. Typical. Fionn McCullagh's looking his most ravishing on the night he heaves her overboard. Was she going to sink without a trace? Was she heck. Fionn and she were finished when she decided and not before. Molly slapped her glass onto the counter, sent her curls somersaulting with a high-tempered toss of the head and followed in Fionn's footsteps to The Norseman. If she picked up her pace she might head him off at the pass.

His stride was longer than hers, and he was ensconsed at a table with three other men and a quartet of Guinnesses when she caught up with him. Molly decided to be brazen and approached the foursome.

'Fionn? Fionn McCullagh? I thought I recognised you. When did you arrive back from the States? It's ages since we met up. Can I lure you away from your mates for one quick drink? You don't mind, do you, lads?' She exposed them to a megawatt smile. 'Come and join me at the bar, just for ten minutes.'

Fionn looked at her as though she were deranged; he seemed on the brink of refusing but the man sitting next to him said, 'Head on, McCullagh. I wouldn't say no to a drink with a girl like that,' and he lurched to his feet and followed her with ill grace.

'What's all this about?' he demanded as soon as they were alone. For a moment she doubted her wisdom in giving chase: here was the stern-faced Fionn McCullagh who'd left her, citing the love of another woman, not the eager-to-please lover she'd been treating as a sexual convenience store.

'I owe you an apology,' said Molly. 'I wasn't convinced if I wanted you or not so I kept you dangling while I debated the pros and cons. A pleasant position for me to be in but not so snug in your shoes. I wouldn't care for anyone to treat me that way and I'm not proud of doing it myself. In my defence, I can only offer the following: you knocked the breath, the hope and the heart out of me when you left and when you reappeared I went spinning off at a tangent.'

Fionn's demeanour, which had been Siberian, thawed.

Molly continued, 'Then you seemed to make the same arrangement with your wife as you had with me: three months to loiter backstage followed by either curtains or show time. How do you think that made me feel, Fionn? For all I knew you could be dallying with me and planning to return to your Viking muesli-muncher at the end of your sabbatical.'

Self-pity engulfed Molly at this point, although it was more the remembrance of tears shed four years ago than the prospect of streaming cheeks a few hours down the line that motivated the surge of emotion. Moisture glistened in her eyes; she sniffed audibly.

Fionn leaned forward and dabbed tenderly at her eye sockets with both thumbs, although the tears never materialised so he was rubbing dry skin. He didn't notice, for his fingers were ensnared in her hair now, winding fistfuls around his fingers.

'Silly girl,' he whispered. 'Why didn't you tell me this from the start instead of leading me a merry dance? I'm footsore from sidestepping you.'

'I wasn't thinking straight,' admitted Molly.

'Come away with me.' He leaned forward and brushed her lips with his own. 'I know exactly what you and I need – some quality time together.'

Not quality time, groaned Molly inwardly. Quality time always ruined everything.

'That would be perfect,' she agreed.

They gazed at one another for a minute. Molly was somewhat surprised to realise she didn't need to fake the dewiness.

'And now,' she announced, rising to her feet, 'I'm going to send you back to your friends and have an early night for a change, read a novel in the bath with a glass of wine at my elbow.'

Fionn grinned. 'Is there room in that bath for two?'

'Another time. You'll appreciate me all the more after an evening among the stag and hen parties in Temple Bar.'

'I thought they weren't encouraging that sort of trade any more,' said Fionn.

'There's a difference between principle and practice, my dear Fionn. Just as there's a difference between an early night with a paperback and an early night with your boyfriend. Give me a ring.' Molly deposited a kiss on his nose and vacated The Norseman. Game, set and match. Unless he favoured a rematch.

She didn't have long to wait for his serve – and it was an ace. Once indoors Molly abandoned the bath – she'd only mentioned it so that Fionn would have an immediate mental picture of her damp and naked – slammed a chicken curry in the microwave and ate it standing up scanning the television page in the newspaper for a Channel Four sitcom. Excellent, a *Cheers* rerun was on in ten minutes. Just time to change into her bath robe, wipe off her makeup and select a bottle of wine that would blend with the taste of Devonshire cream toffees because she had a huge bag of them in the press begging to be decimated. Something cheap on the wine front, she decided – no point in wasting her Chablis on toffee-flavoured tastebuds. Cut-price Chardonnay would serve the purpose.

If she had willpower she'd save the toffees until the opening titles, she ruminated, chomping on one as she threw her work suit in a heap and retrieved her bathrobe from the overflowing laundry basket.

Five minutes into *Cheers* the buzzer sounded. Molly ignored it. It drilled into her eardrums a second time. It was probably Elizabeth minus her keys again. Although it was too early for her, by at least four hours. Molly vacated the sofa with the utmost reluctance and pressed the speaking mechanism.

'Molly? It's Fionn, may I come up?'

She'd just cleaned off her makeup and a cream toffee was lodged in her cheek. No way, José, said her brain. 'Could you give me a moment, Fionn?' said her voice.

Land-speed records were broken sprinting to the bathroom, mascara combed on at a similar pace, teeth brushed simultaneously, leading to mascara blotches around her eyes, bathrobe kicked under the bed and a velvet dress, chosen solely on the basis of its pull-over-the-head merits, prised from its hanger.

Molly galloped back to the intercom and pressed the admit-all-comers button. She'd just have time to hide the toffees and bin her curry carton before he made his way up. Opening the door of her apartment to put the lock on snib, she encountered Fionn lounging in the doorway with a smile on his face and a tissue-wrapped bottle in his hand.

'Hope I didn't catch you at an inconvenient time.'

Molly ushered him in, noticing the bottle was champagne-shaped, and fulminating silently against residents who allowed strangers into the block, where was the point in intercoms if neighbours allowed in burglars and boyfriends willy-nilly? Nevertheless, champagne went a long way towards soothing a savage beast. Much less hit and miss than music.

'Are we celebrating?' she asked as he reached her the bottle.

'I hope so.' He ferreted out her champagne flutes.

Cheers was consigned to oblivion, she sank onto the sofa alongside him and he stroked her instep while she sipped liquid rapture. So what if he weren't Greek? At least he knew where her Achilles heel was on the alcohol front. Not to mention – oops, he was kissing her toes now – her Achilles tendon.

Helen was edgy. Her fingers itched to phone Molly for a second opinion on what she should do – but what if Molly told her and she didn't like what she heard? Nevertheless she was desperate for advice, better still a miracle, except this wasn't Knock, and you needed faith for miracles to happen. But miracles were like wishes that came true and why shouldn't hers? Somebody's must. Helen massaged her throbbing temples, her brain whirring. Nothing could change the fact that tomorrow was Saturday and Patrick was arriving off a plane from London. She could choose not to be at home all day but that would only suspend confrontation for both of them. Confrontation – is that what this had to be about? Helen lit a cigarette from the butt of her smouldering one and paced the living room. Her first cigarettes in twelve years. This is what he's driven me to, she raged, even as she inhaled avidly. I'll die screaming and retching, riddled with lung cancer because of him. When had Patrick become so dogged, so obdurate, so unlike the loping teenager with the ready grin?

Helen was disappointed Molly hadn't phoned – maybe she no longer wanted to be her friend. She was probably nauseated by Helen's disclosure. She stubbed out her cigarette half-smoked and immediately lit up another – anything to deflect the agitation in her hands.

She needed a diversion. Helen thought of Barry, wavered, then shrugged.

'Why not?' She spoke aloud in the empty room, aware for the first time that it was dark and she hadn't turned on the light. 'Molly asked me to do it for her; specifically she pleaded with me.'

She took out a telephone directory from the drawer beneath the phone, frowned as she concentrated on remembering his name and experimented with various combinations. 'Barry Skelton, Barry Dunne, Barry Dwyer.' Inspiration struck – she had a copy of the newspaper under the coffee table; his byline might be there. She paused at Molly's piece on the rentboy – his photograph caught her attention; outworn eyes in an unworn face – before flicking onwards. There it was, under a headline that read 'Boy Band Go Bananas and Buy Shares in Chiquita', a story about the latest teenage sensations with so much dosh to invest they'd hired a consultant, who'd advised them to trade in the banana market. ' "I'll only be drinking banana milkshakes and eating banana yoghurts from now on," pledged lead singer Darren (17).' Barry Dalton's name was affixed to the story. For his sins.

So here's the deal, Helen addressed her conscience. He lives northside somewhere, not too far out of town. If I find his name in the book I'll ring him and if I don't there'll be no call.

There was a Barry Dalton at 11 Eden Terrace, Glasnevin. That had to be the right one. Helen dialled and a man's voice answered.

'Barry? It's Helen Sharkey here, Molly's friend. Molly's dreamed up this flimsy idea that I should appear to make a play for you . . . Oh, she's told you about it, right. Well, look, I'll ring back in ten minutes and maybe you could make sure your wife takes the call. Are you definite about wanting to do this? I feel foolish; grand, if you're determined on it. So I'll sound wrong-footed and claim I've dialled a wrong number, then I'll ring a few minutes later – your wife has to answer it again – and this time I'll stumble but ask for you. Then you can recite "Baa Baa Black Sheep" down the line as far as I'm concerned because I'll have hung up. It's over to you to leave your wife with whatever impression you choose from the conversation.'

It happened as Helen specified; she felt a twinge perceiving the leaping jealousy in the other woman's voice when she asked for Barry on the second phone call. She sounded agreeable; from somewhere near the border, judging by her accent. It seemed unfair to play games with her.

'Helen,' said Barry, shady rather than loverlike.

Janey Mac, she meant to warn him not to use her name.

'I'm hanging up now,' she announced. 'Why don't you buy your wife flowers and treat her properly for a change?'

The phone shrilled three-quarters-of-an-hour and eight cigarettes later. Helen still hadn't eaten, nicotine had eroded her appetite, lacklustre at the best of times, but she was considering tea when the bell propelled her from the kitchen to the living room. It might be Patrick cancelling his flight. Or Molly telling her she wasn't a degraded person because she was attracted to her brother. It was Barry. He must have found her number in the directory too.

'Kay's stormed out. This is working a treat,' he virtually sang down the line.

'Don't even think about ringing me again. I'm not your partner in crime and I'm having serious reservations about the stunt you're pulling on your wife. I've a good mind to call her up and enlighten her.'

'Don't do that.' Barry's courage, scrunched up to ring her because he needed to talk to someone, didn't so much take flight as disintegrate.

Helen relented – she was probably walloping down on him like a ton of bricks because of her own frustrations.

'All right, I won't, but why are you ringing me up? I've played my part.'

'Magnificently,' he quavered. 'I thought you might like to know it worked. I told Kay you were my new girlfriend, she lost the head completely, stormed out of the house to her friend's shrieking she'd be on to the solicitor at the crack of dawn tomorrow.'

303

Helen was puzzled. 'But you want to save your leaky marriage. A solicitor will transform a tear into a gigantic hole.'

Barry had to be beaming from the vowel sounds travelling down the phone line. 'Tomorrow's Saturday, it will be two days at the earliest before she can initiate legal action, by which time we'll be inseparable, or so Molly assures me.'

'Have you been speaking to Molly?' Helen felt excluded that Molly could have spared time to talk to Barry but she hadn't checked up on her.

'Couldn't reach her. Home phone and mobile are both on electronic voice mode.'

'So my part in this charade is over now. You're on the brink of wallpapering over all cracks and whisking your wife out to dinner. As soon as she's on speaking terms with you, naturally.'

'Hopefully we're home and dry. Thanks a million. You'll have to let me buy you a drink for your trouble.'

'No thank you. And a word to the wise, Barry: it's never too late to become the person you might have been.'

He was at a loss as to how to take that. 'Fine,' he managed, hanging up. Was she needling him or being nice to him? He'd never get to grips with the female psyche even if he came back in his next life as a woman *and* a shrink.

Helen replaced the receiver and decided on bed. There was one certainty facing her tomorrow, a meeting with Patrick. And whatever came of it a night's sleep was essential. She'd have to take another tablet, it was the only way she could be guaranteed a few hours of oblivion. Just one pill, she bargained with herself as she heated milk to consume with it. And she'd set her alarm clock and book a telephone alarm so there'd be masses of time to shake off the effects of the tablet before Patrick arrived. She should have phoned Dublin airport to check what time the first Stansted flight landed. It couldn't be before nine o'clock at the absolute earliest; it was a Saturday, after all. Ten o'clock was likelier. And then he'd need to grab a taxi and reach Sandycove, say another forty-five minutes. He shouldn't be with her before about eleven. This was ridiculous, guessing; she might still catch up with someone on the information desk at the airport. No joy there, the phone chirruped unanswered, so she fiddled with her alarm clock and programmed it to go off at eight thirty because there was no way that Patrick Sharkey was going to catch her on the hop; she'd be professional, unflinchingly in control and ready for him. Should it take a box of sleeping pills, followed by a succession of alarm calls and an intravenous injection of caffeine.

CHAPTER 20

Stomach cramps awoke Molly. She lay there, trying to work out where the pain was located, followed by its source. Hunger was her first impression – she was always ravenous in the morning and astounded at people who didn't bother with breakfast. Then she realised her period was due and tumbled out of bed, reaching for her dressing gown. The Feminax and tampons were in the bathroom cabinet, which seemed to be located halfway across town at this precise moment. Perhaps she should consider rehousing them in her bedside locker. As Molly groped towards consciousness she noticed a male foot protruding from underneath the duvet and deduced that it belonged to Fionn. His face wasn't visible due to his habit of tunnelling nose-first into the pillow.

I'm a slut, she thought. I had him all but dumped and then I decided to keep him after all. I can't even remember if it was because he was good in bed or good in parts. Where's the point in going to the bother of making your mind up if you turn around and change it again?

She stumbled out, swallowed down a couple of Feminax with a glass of water – smiling at the discarded Lanson bottle – and returned to bed. Instead of bringing a hot-water bottle with her for the spasms in her stomach she curled her body around Fionn's roasting frame; may as well put a man to use when he turned up in her bed.

Fionn mumbled sleepily, rolled towards her and burrowed against her neck. The nuzzle turned into a clamber as first his leg and then his torso landed on her.

'Permission to board, skipper?' he murmured sleepily.

The man was insatiable – she couldn't recall him being so amorous before he married the Scandinavian creature. Perhaps their cavorting was thin on the ground. She suspected yoghurt was definitely for eating with muesli in that household, not for smearing on bodies and licking off, which is what they'd ending up doing last night. She checked the sheets; yes, there was a definite Fruits of the Forest trail.

Meanwhile Fionn took her lack of response as acquiescence and was steaming ahead.

'Steady, shipmate,' said Molly. 'My body's still suffering sleep deprivation. Can we leave the heave-ho till the sun's further up the yardarm?'

Fionn good-naturedly rolled off her while Molly mentally scolded herself for being too squeamish to admit she was menstrual.

'You're having sex with him, you're even sleeping the night through with him, which is more intimate again, so why can't you tell it like it is?' went her interior dialogue.

After all he'd encountered periods before; in their previous life he thought nothing of buying her tampons occasionally.

'That was different, we were in a relationship. I planned to marry him, for heaven's sake,' the internal sideshow continued.

Unconvincing, she knew. But she wasn't obliged to tell him if she didn't want to.

'I just don't feel like it,' Molly burst out.

'Hey, nobody's forcing you,' Fionn placated her. 'Put your head on my shoulder and go back to sleep.'

Molly couldn't settle. She rolled out of Fionn's encircling arm to check the alarm clock: ten o'clock. Was it too early to ring Helen? She meant to call her last night to talk to her further but Fionn had proved something of a distraction. Ten o'clock would be unacceptable to most people on a Saturday morning but Helen's unpredictability meant she wasn't like most people – she'd be either dead to the world or dressed and on her second cup of coffee, having scanned the newspaper and compiled her plans for the day. Molly decided she'd let the phone ring just a few times and if it wasn't answered she'd leave Helen in peace. She eased out of bed again, moving slowly so as not to disturb Fionn, who was snuffling into the pillow. She cast a backward glance at him. It wasn't safe for that man to bed down alone. His *modus operandi* in the sleeping compartment meant he was in serious danger of suffocating.

Helen's voice sounded muffled when she answered the phone.

'No, it's not your wake-up call, it's Molly,' she repeated twice before Helen grasped her meaning. And panicked.

'It can't be after ten,' Helen wailed. 'I've overslept. But I don't see how I did. I set the alarm clock and ordered a phone call – maybe I overlooked it. That blasted tablet, when I took it I forgot about everything I was supposed to do. Molly, I can't talk, I have to spring into action. Patrick's flying in; for all I know he could be in a taxi and on his way here this minute.'

'Helen, tell me you're not taking sleeping tablets.'

'I just took the one. I knew I'd never sleep otherwise,' fretted Helen.

'I can't believe you'd be so stupid. You know you react badly to aspirin, let alone sleeping pills.'

'That's priceless coming from someone who sat their final exams on a chemically induced high,' snapped Helen. 'Look, I haven't time for this. I don't want to be in a flap when Patrick arrives. I was supposed to be stripped for action an hour and a half ago.'

'Do you really mean stripped?' Molly chipped at her toenail polish.

'No, yes, go away, Molly. No don't, wait.' Desperation left Helen dithering. 'I really appreciate your call – I'll get back to you, all right?'

Molly felt reluctant to hang up; she sensed that Helen's internal compass was spinning out of control.

'Don't do anything reckless,' she cautioned. 'Ring me as soon as you can, preferably not from Bolivia as a runaway bride.'

'I haven't a notion what I'm going to do.' Helen's voice was sombre. 'Except to try and survive.'

The connection severed and Molly slouched out to the kitchen to make coffee, shrouded in anxiety and some free-floating guilt, although she wasn't precisely sure what there was to feel culpable about. Had she been derelict in her duty as a friend? She turned on the central heating and tried to assuage her agitation. She should have made time to see Helen yesterday evening before her meeting with Patrick. She'd shied away from an unseemly subject. The truth was that a date with Fionn appealed to her infinitely more than addressing the gargantuan issue of Helen's predilection towards her brother.

Molly reflected on what she remembered of Patrick as she sipped instant coffee, which she wasn't overly fond of but she judged it unwise to subject her cramping stomach to the real McCoy.

Gorgeous: check

Charming: check

Intelligent: check

Well, he'd passed her evaluation with flying colours. Lived in London, was a couple or so years younger than Helen, worked in some financial field or other – did Helen say he was living with someone or had she simply assumed that on the basis someone so ornamental to a woman's arm had to be snapped up? English girls weren't stupid.

There was something mysterious about him all the same. Of course, now she knew what it was; he didn't fit the mould. None of the Sharkey family did. In the cold light of day Molly was inclined to airbrush Helen's version of events and decided she couldn't actually mean she and her brother wanted a physical relationship. They must be extremely attached to one another to the extent of wanting to live together like, well, brother and sister.

Molly fed the Dualit with a couple of slices of bread and contemplated phoning Barry to brew up an alternative to the Make His Wife Jealous arrangement but hadn't the heart for it; periods left her drained.

'Periods leave me drained,' she told the marmalade pot.

'I take it this is your time of the month. Presumably you don't normally have conversations with Golden Shred.' Fionn rubbed his eyes blearily under the kitchen archway.

'Um,' said Molly, the best response she could dredge up.

He removed the toast from her hand, spread the butter to the corners instead of allowing it to blob in the middle, and returned it to her. 'Well then, we'll have to treat you like a queen, my Molly. Since it's too late for breakfast in bed how about I take you shopping for a new pair of shoes?'

Molly gasped. 'I thought I heard you volunteer to accompany me on a shopping expedition. I must need my ears syringed.'

311

'I did.' Complacency emanated from him. He scratched his head and rubbed butter into his hair.

'What's your ulterior motive?' Hands on hips, she pretended to survey him suspiciously.

'I'm wheedling my way into your good books so you can't live without me and you invite me to move in,' Fionn responded.

Out of the mouths of babes and pushy boyfriends, thought Molly. He was presenting it as a joke but that's exactly what his strategy was. Still, forewarned was forearmed. And she fancied a shopping trip. A pair of mules patterned with a bamboo tree had caught her eye in the window of Don't Walk On By in Wicklow Street the other day. She was fairly sure she'd end up with them but she'd need to try on at least a dozen other pairs first. In the interests of market research.

Molly invested a mainbeam smile in Fionn. 'I'm going to dive into the shower. I'll be washed and dressed in six-and-a-half minutes,' she promised. 'And that includes my coat on, ready to leave.'

Patrick felt edgy as he approached Helen's doorbell. For all he knew she might not be in; she might have decided to bolt again. He fingered the spot where he'd cut himself shaving at seven o'clock. Miriam had insisted on rising with him to make his coffee before he'd set off; she'd thought it strange he was returning to Dublin so soon but he'd told her as one of the executors of his aunt's will he was obliged to liaise with the others.

'Will you come back tonight if you finish your business sooner than expected?' Her face had been wistful.

'Absolutely,' he'd lied, smudging the tip of her nose with his thumb. 'Go back to bed, honey-bunny. It's too early to be pottering about on a Saturday.'

But Miriam had wound her arms round his neck and raised her mouth for the kiss he'd wanted to avoid giving her. 'Perhaps you'll take me to Ireland with you one day, Patrick.' Her brown eyes had been pleading.

'You can count on it, honey-bunny.' His kiss had been cursory and he'd been unable to maintain eye contact. What in the name of God was he doing with this decent woman? He knew he should love her but he didn't. Should and love don't sit easily together.

The cut on his chin had opened up again. Patrick dabbed at it with a tissue and cursed beneath his breath. He tried to assess if Helen were at home but couldn't decide. Only one way to find out: he stuffed the tissue into his pocket, ran a hand through his nearly black hair and leaned his finger briefly on the doorbell. Helen opened it almost immediately. He smiled instinctively when he saw her and she returned the smile tentatively. Relief coursed through him, even as trepidation inched its way down to the pit of her stomach.

'I didn't hear the taxi pull up.' She stepped back to let him pass into the living room.

'I jumped out a street or two away and walked. I needed to shake off some excess energy.' Catching hold of her hand he curved towards her. 'It's wonderful to see you again,' he whispered.

Helen forced herself to pull away. 'I'm sure you're ready for a coffee. I've just ground some beans. I only do it at weekends because I'm always in such a pre-work rush in the mornings.'

'You look like you swish through life on castors, I can't imagine you dashing.' Patrick followed her through the living room and into the kitchen. 'Although you left town in quite a hurry last week without saying goodbye. I formed an impression the departure was unplanned.'

Helen gazed levelly at him. 'It was flight, as simple as that. For the purpose of survival. Body, soul and sanity.'

Patrick stroked a strand of hair out of her eyes. 'I only want the best for you, Helen. You make me sound like a malign influence.'

'Please stop touching me,' she entreated.

He stepped back, stung.

Patrick watched Helen's slim figure move from fridge to kettle to table. Aware of his observation she felt clumsy, fingers plucking nervously at the lint on her clothes.

They pretended to drink coffee while he wondered how to play persuader – how to convince her to give living a chance instead of just existing. Patrick saw nothing wrong with their going away together; there was no shutdown switch inside him to suggest Helen was off limits. He saw her as a woman he loved, a woman he was physically attracted to, a woman who'd been part of his existence as far back as he could remember and whose life was inextricably bound up in his own. To Patrick, Helen wasn't his sister; there was no duality in their relationship in his eyes. Geraldine was his sister: repugnance would set in instantly at the suggestion he should sleep with her. He'd never even considered it – in her case he was equipped with the default mechanism to veto it. But not in Helen's. Quite simply he didn't regard the two women in the same light.

Where Helen was concerned he had no moral qualms because to Patrick it wasn't a moral issue. It was a question of love. In so far as he had considered it, love transcended good and evil. True, there had been a convulsion of shock the first time he and Helen had kissed; it had been in the woods, he remembered, when she'd tried to comfort him after a blazing row with his father that left him strung out and close to retching, although he couldn't for the life of him bring to mind now what their argument had been about. However, the shock had been overtaken by certainty, an overwhelming conviction that he and Helen were meant to be together.

The intensity of his feelings on seeing her at their aunt's funeral after a three-year absence was a revelation. It was as harrowing and as euphoric as falling in love for the first time, and he realised their strategy of distance was preordained to failure. He could be in London or Laos and Helen's face would be with him. His fingertips knew the outline of her jaw and the sleek texture of hair that was the identical shade to his own. As for Miriam, he must have been deranged to imagine he could carve out a life with her. Patrick assumed he'd been sleepwalking these past three years but he wasn't ready to become a zombie again; he was determined to convince Helen to be with him. He knew he could make her happy because she felt the same way about him as he did about her. That much was indisputable. She could articulate as many denials as her sense of propriety deemed fit but he read the truth in her eyes. Helen loved him as intensely as he loved her.

All this was passing through Patrick's mind as he drank coffee facing her in the terracotta kitchen. It was an overcast morning – they needed the light on but neither moved to alleviate the gloom. Patrick could see the edge of his over-night bag where he'd dropped it in the living room. Miriam had packed it for him; she enjoyed such gestures although he imagined other women would find them demeaning. He wondered idly why he felt no guilt when he remembered Miriam and whether this made him a callous person. And then he drank some more coffee because it seemed to be what Helen wanted them to do.

Helen didn't know what she wanted. But she was clear on what she didn't want. She didn't want to be sitting here stealing glances at this familiar stranger, she didn't want to be churning with emotion while she did it; she didn't want the ordered stability of her life splintering into chaos. She wanted Patrick but not the ensuing maelstrom.

'I'm here because I love you.'

Patrick covered the hand that clung to a mug with his own larger one and then moved it away before she could flinch from his touch. He waited for Helen to marshal her thoughts. He'd drink coffee beside her from now until New Year's Eve if that's what was required. He'd wait for the coffee beans to grow, ripen and be picked. But he also knew Helen well enough to realise it was a balancing act between giving her space to still her vacillations and not allowing her so much time she'd dither their chances away.

Helen was incapable of seizing the wayward thoughts that sheered off from her brain and cannoned away in a multiplicity of directions. Fragments strayed into her mind: a memory of Patrick aged seven, kicking a football into the stream near their home and risking drowning as he dangled from a branch to retrieve it. A memory of Christmas morning with Patrick in a cowboy outfit shooting herself and Geraldine, and the acrid smell of the caps he discharged. A memory of Patrick, just a head shorter than their father at thirteen, standing up from the kitchen table and challenging the older man when he told Helen she wasn't too grown up to feel the back of his hand.

'She *is* too old,' Patrick contradicted him. 'And you're too old to do it.'

His father slammed down his mug so hard a crack spidered

out from top to bottom and their mother wailed that money didn't grow on trees but that was the last time Helen's father threatened her with physical violence.

Helen tilted her head, pushing back the hair, and Patrick noticed the narrow scar below her ear from a collision with a tree when she'd taken him riding on the bar of her bicycle, experimenting to see how well she could manage with her eyes shut. She'd sheltered Patrick with her body and taken the force of the impact on her shoulder and the side of her head. Her blood had trickled warmly onto his arm. Patrick felt a wave of belonging to Helen engulf him. And at that he arbitrarily jettisoned his intention to allow her time to consider the permutations and summon up all the reasons why they shouldn't clutch at happiness and to hell with the consequences; he hadn't come here to shake hands with defeat.

'Helen, let's go away. I don't mean rush off to Ecuador – that's an irrevocable step and I can see you're not ready for that. But we should spend some time together. It's been so long since we've mooched around enjoying each other's company. Remember what great friends we were as kids? I miss you, Helen; I miss your companionship.'

She was infinitely touched by his plea and incapable of denying him. His spontaneity seized her. 'I'd love to do it. But can we manage it without burning bridges?'

'Of course, my love. We'll go away just for a weekend. We can do it this weekend if you like.'

Helen recoiled. 'That's too soon. We need to get right away from here. We need to think about someplace to go where memories or acquaintances won't intrude. Next weekend – we'll leave it until then.'

Patrick laughed, willing to allow her latitude in the wake of her concession. 'Whatever you like. And now I'm taking you out to lunch with a map, if you have one, so that we can plan where we go.'

'A map of Ireland or of the world?'

'Both. Let's keep all options open.'

'The worldwide options for a weekend away are self-limitation,' Helen pointed out.

Patrick shrugged into his flying jacket that he'd draped over the back of the chair. 'Repeat after me, Helen: self-limitation is a concept we reject.'

She smiled as she fetched maps and a coat. 'There's a fish restaurant just around the corner – you tend to need a reservation but I'm feeling lucky today. Let's chance it.'

They were both fortunate and unfortunate: a cancellation at Caviston's allowed them to lunch on fish pie and salad, conversing as companionably as they had in former times. Helen described her visit to Geraldine, and Patrick mentioned Miriam was always cajoling him to meet his sisters because she had none and longed to share his. Helen shifted on her wooden seat, ill at ease with Miriam's name cropping up so naturally, but then decided it was better if Patrick felt able to refer to her; her name shouldn't be a graveyard to cross the road to avoid.

They spoke of their weekend together. Patrick was anxious they should have two nights away and volunteered to take a half-day from work on Friday afternoon. Helen thought she'd manage that too, even though she'd had time off only last week. They debated flying to Paris or Amsterdam and meeting one another there but Helen said she was too busy to arrange a flight and currency, so Ireland was agreed on and they decided to visit Westport.

The arrival of a neighbour in the narrow restaurant intruded on their intimacy and crippled Helen's enjoyment of what could possibly be construed as a date. It was the woman who had snowdrops in her garden, although their season was finished now, and hybrid tulips nodded in their place. She approached Helen with a smile and glanced expectantly at Patrick. Helen began to make the introductions obediently.

'This is my –' she began, then paused. Her what? Her brother, lover, friend? 'Agnes, this is Patrick,' she managed lamely.

'He has to be a connection of yours,' said the country-woman, button eyes twitching from one to the other. 'Isn't he the spit from your mouth? You must be brother and sister.'

The room rang in Helen's ears. She heard snatches of conversations alongside her – 'So she said to him, "You're not the man I married twenty-five years ago"' – and the neighbour's stocky shape swayed before her. She wondered if she were about to faint. Then she felt Patrick's hand on hers and the haze cleared.

'We're cousins, quite distant ones,' he responded. 'It's lovely to meet you, Agnes. I'll ask for the bill, Helen. Remember I have a plane to catch.'

On the street he slid his arm around her waist to steady her; she was whey-faced, grey eyes smeared to black.

'I don't know why I'm reacting in this way,' Helen apologised. 'It's so foolish. I hardly know the woman. But I feel like a criminal.'

'You're not a criminal,' he assured her. 'What's between us is natural.'

'It's not natural.' Her voice was low; she struggled to put one foot in front of the other.

He brooked no argument. 'It is to us.'

Back at Helen's house, Patrick chafed her hands while she huddled by a radiator, chilled to the core.

'*Do* you have a flight to catch?' Helen asked.

'No, I have an open ticket. I don't need to be in London until nine a.m. on Monday. Would you like me to spend the rest of today with you?' His face as it bent towards her was bathed in love.

She fed off it momentarily, then said: 'No, Patrick, go back to London.'

'But I'll see you next weekend, right?'

She gazed at him blankly.

'Right?' he repeated. There was an urgency within him that she swam towards.

'Right,' she agreed. And felt elated.

As he prepared to leave Helen made a half-hearted offer to drive him to the airport.

'DART and airport bus from Bus Aras are just as handy,' he countered. 'I can pick up a couple of papers to pass the journey – does Carlos Murphy still do his restaurant reviews on a Saturday?'

She laughed: why on earth would Patrick care about reading a restaurant review for a city that was not his home?

He shrugged. 'I'm as likely to eat out here as I am in London, maybe more so because Miriam thinks we shouldn't waste money in restaurants when we ought to be saving up for the wedding of the decade. Besides, I like Carlos's critiques. He'll do everywhere from his local chipper to a four-star shrine to affectation. I'm convinced I even read a McDonald's review by him once.'

'Thumbs up or down?'

'Curate's egg. He quite liked one of the burgers but gave out yards about the plastic bucket seats. He could see why kids were charmed by the place, though. And now, my love, I'm going to catch the big silver bird that wings across the sky. But I'm going to tell you something truly miraculous about big silver birds: they come back as well as go away.'

His kiss on her forehead was as chaste as a parent's. Helen lifted her face towards him and smiled into eyes that smiled back at her with the self-same expression. Her earlier misgivings in Caviston's were atomised: she loved and was loved. Helen wrapped her exhilaration around her like an embrace and was warmed by it.

Much later she touched her face and discovered she was still smiling. But Helen's nature did not allow for unclouded joy.

'Hope,' she whispered. 'I can have faith and I can hope but I needn't expect charity. That particular part of the triumvirate won't extend to Patrick or me.'

Her brain worried at the deficit for a time and then she straightened her shoulders: so be it; she'd take faith and hope. Unless they were a mirage; unless you could only have the whole triumvirate or none of the components at all . . .

CHAPTER 21

During the week Helen had second thoughts. Third and fourth thoughts. She was continually on the brink of phoning Patrick to cancel their weekend. If she could have contacted him at work she'd have pressed stop and rewind but Helen only had his home number and was reluctant to risk encountering Miriam. The idea of making polite conversation with Patrick's fiancée was more than she could stomach. There was always email, of course – she had his address – but presumably if Patrick and Miriam shared a computer they shared access to each other's electronic messages. She couldn't write to him in code. She cudgelled her brains for the name of the firm where he worked but drew a blank. Helen wavered from day to day about the Westport trip and by Wednesday was so unsettled her boss collared her and brought her to the canteen for coffee.

Tony Dooley, a well-meaning company man in his early forties, whose stripey shirts were always ringed with under-arm sweat stains by mid-afternoon, dreaded the encounter as much as Helen did but felt obliged to make the effort. He'd recently been sent on a management course which recommended taking an interest in staff's personal lives. It dissuaded them from feeling like microserfs and lent the illusion of belonging to a user-friendly organisation, the evangelical trainer had insisted. Tony was dubious about the benefits of user-friendliness in the workplace. His preference was for doing the job and skedaddling home.

However, the managing director, J. J. Patterson, was a Californian by instinct (although a Clonmel man by birth) and smitten with the notion of work and home lives merging. The concept's appeal lay, to some extent, in the managing director's realisation that he could expect a fair amount of unpaid overtime from staff if they felt at home by their work stations. For this reason he encouraged employees to scatter ornaments and pot plants on their desks. Snapshots of partners and children were not encouraged, although there was no formal veto, because he had a theory that a photo-framed, pigtailed daughter might galvanise a parent into signing off at the terminal to see the image made corporeal.

'Ask your team about their hobbies, remember the names of their partners and take an interest in their holiday plans,' exhorted the trainer during the weekend conference at which Tony had fretted about the rumba steps he could be perfecting instead of enjoying the luxury of the country house retreat paid for by J. J. Patterson. Probably as a tax write-off, Tony had grumped. His subordinates giggled at mental visions of Tony, representing Ireland on the international amateur ballroom dancing circuit, in cummerbunds and frilly shirts, and speculated about whether he slapped on fake tan for the spotlights. Molly met him once when Helen had invited her to a staff party, and had remarked on the dancer's patent shoes that encased his ridiculously small feet.

Now Tony sat opposite Helen in the canteen, size sixes tapping on the tiled floor, and struggled to download any personal information he had retained about her. There were no plants or trinkets on her desk to signpost clues. All he knew was that she was one of his most reliable and thorough programmers and she'd scarcely managed a stroke of work in the past fortnight. Should he ask about her health? He cringed at the prospect: the last time he'd formulated an enquiry along those lines a female employee had bombarded him with details about her fallopian tubes.

What about her romantic life? Tony pondered Helen as she twirled an amber drop in her earlobe and affected equilibrium; she wasn't helping him out in his task as chief redcoat to a team of happy campers. An eyecatcher like her must have a partner, he thought. Not that she was his type, Tony amended hastily; he preferred his women a little less shatter-proof. Helen's fragility alarmed rather than attracted him. He couldn't remember her bringing anyone to the last office party – alternatively, he might not have noticed. All he could call to mind about last Christmas's enforced merriment was his wife remarking how few young women took the trouble to accessorise nowadays. They'd buy the dress and slingbacks but not the matching earrings, tights and nailpolish, she criticised. Helen had been singled out for censure as particularly under-accessorised; but was she matched with a man?

Tony oscillated about raising the subject of male friends as he plaited stilted conversational threads with Helen about a forthcoming salsa competition in Edinburgh, downhearted that she remembered his obsession and encouraged him to talk about it while he could call to mind nothing about her. Just a minute, she'd taken a few days off the other week on family business. Tony's sweat circles emerged earlier in the day than usual as he loosened his tie and longed to be anywhere else but here, charged with probing into whatever was bothering this self-contained young woman.

Still, family business might be less messy to deal with than blocked tubes.

Best foot forward, he advised himself. It's what he always said when his name was called out to step onto the dancefloor. Not original but appropriate. Best foot forward.

He dusted off his competition smile; it struck an inappropriate note. 'Helen, you've seemed a little distracted lately. Is there anything we can help you with?' (The trainer at the country house session always advised talking in the plural to convey an impression of benevolence.)

Helen was startled. She knew her work had been patchy but convinced herself she was adept enough to disguise it in the short term. Heaven forfend she was in line for a 'how do you like to spend your free time' chat with Tony.

Oh God, he seemed to require a reply. She ought to cobble together something.

'Thank you,' she murmured. Lame-brain, she scolded herself.

'Don't thank me, I mean us, until we've sorted something out for you.' Tony flashed that disconcerting spangled smile again. He waited.

Helen harried her braincells into action. They ignored her.

'Are you still having family difficulties?' he prompted her.

Gratitude was instantaneous. 'Yes. Family difficulties.' Would that do? She peered sideways to see if she was off the hook, trying to ignore a disconcerting picture that sneaked into her mind of Tony in an angler's hat and herself coated with silver scales. He seemed to want an elaboration. Her heart plummeted.

'There are . . . difficulties,' she managed.

He inclined his head in what he believed to be a gesture of encouragement.

'It's tricky to explain. We're not a close family and when problems arise the, um, difficulties take more effort to sort out.'

Please let that be adequate. Sufficient unto the day. Helen found herself crossing the fingers on both hands the way she used to as a small girl.

To hell with J. J. Patterson and his user-friendliness, Tony decided. That was as much touchy-feely palaver as he was prepared to expose himself to; Helen Sharkey was an adult perfectly capable of conducting her own business. He didn't have any more time to play nursemaid to programmers, he had an interview panel to sit on this afternoon. And he was not, oh boy was he not, intending to ask applicants how they spent their weekends.

'We value your contribution.' He rose to his feet.

He had double buckles on his patent shoes, noticed Helen. Even Michael Flatley would balk at them. She subdued a hysterical giggle.

'If you feel you need more time out to arrange something at home . . . ?' Tony looked down at Helen, who was still seated.

She denied this would be necessary, to his manifest relief. There was already someone in her section on maternity leave who hadn't yet been replaced. It was becoming increasingly impossible to find and hold on to programmers. Tony suspected the day wasn't far off when he'd be stocking up their fridges and collecting their dry-cleaning, simply to keep them on side. The circumference of each sweat patch expanded by an inch.

'You haven't forgotten I'm taking a half-day on Friday. I arranged to work an afternoon on Saturday week instead.' Helen intruded on his nightmare.

Tony agreed, anxious to be gone. Friday afternoons

were never particularly productive anyhow. Staff tended to extend their lunch breaks and evacuate to the pub as soon as was decently possible in the late afternoon. He sidled away. 'Remember, my door is always open.'

In fact he hadn't so much as a screen around his desk in J. J. Patterson's vision of the optimum office environment but Helen nodded vigorously. They were even Stevens now on the embarrassment front, if they only knew it.

Back at her desk she attacked a job she'd been stockpiling and worked steadily through her lunch break and into the afternoon before slowing down. By four o'clock she had a tranche of computer code rewritten, and allowed herself to idle for a few moments, her weekend away with Patrick monopolising her attention. Realistically, Helen reasoned, she couldn't call a halt at this late stage. She was due to meet Patrick at 1.30 p.m. on Friday, less than forty-eight hours' time, and he'd have booked his time off, his flight, and devised a story for Miriam by now. The arrangement was that she'd collect him from the airport and they'd boot straight for Westport, stopping en route for a meal although not until they'd put an hour or two between themselves and the streets of Dublin.

Helen doodled 'Mayo' on a notepad. She hadn't been there in years, not since she'd set off from college with a group of friends who'd planned to join the annual expedition of pilgrims, many barefoot, climbing Croagh Patrick. They decided against it when the weather turned foggy, and adjourned to a pub near the village instead for pints of Guinness – apart from Helen, who could never manage more than a glass at a time despite experimenting with blackcurrant to sweeten it. One of the innumerable benefits of forfeiting student status was no longer being obliged to drink Guinness.

Perhaps it was incalculably foolhardy of her to accede to this time away with Patrick. She was no Daniel to venture into the lion's den. Not that their relationship would stray into a physical one, on that she was resolved. When Patrick had told her he'd book a hotel he'd also mentioned two rooms. Helen remembered it clearly because she had been chagrined to find herself overtaken by a mottled blush that swept from forehead to chest. Wouldn't you think at the age of thirty-two she could discuss sleeping arrangements with a man without behaving like a vestal virgin?

Helen glanced at her scribbles and saw that in addition to doodling 'Mayo' and 'airport' she'd looped a rosary of hearts along the page. Disgusted, she crumpled the page into her wastepaper bin and slopped in the dregs of a coffee she'd been nursing.

Doubts clamoured as profuse as dust motes now. She couldn't go through with the trip, she shouldn't go through with it, it wasn't sensible. But she'd been prudent most of her life – she wished she could throw caution to the winds for a change. Backwards and forwards her brain whirred as she frittered time. It was a mercy Tony was off interviewing graduates who thought the world was their oyster when it was really a lobster tank with glass-walled limitations.

And then clarity intervened. Molly would steer her through this. Helen dialled the *Chronicle* and was elated to discover her friend had a day off. Which meant she could meet her to thrash out whether or not to go ahead with the weekend plans. But both Molly's home number and mobile were switched to answerphone. Helen left forlorn messages on each; Molly could be incommunicado for the rest of the day. However, her friend rang back within ten minutes, declaring herself free to meet Helen after work.

'I'll call for you at the back door of the building, if you

like,' she volunteered. 'Sorry I've been a bit evasive this week. It's been . . .'

'Difficult?' suggested Helen.

'Difficult,' Molly agreed. 'For a swarming horde of reasons, I'll fill you in later. But I'm delighted you left those messages, Helen. I've been meaning to have a proper chat with you.'

Relief at catching up with Molly sent a shaft of giddiness through Helen. 'That's a coincidence because I've been meaning to have an improper chat with you,' she responded.

Another confessional session was looming and she welcomed it. Even if Molly couldn't give her absolution she could manage guidance.

'An improper chat? Sounds promising. See you at five.' Molly kept her tone deliberately carefree, although she suspected Patrick was on the agenda. But it wasn't her place to moralise to Helen, just see to it that she didn't end up like Humpty Dumpty.

'Don't let go of the wall,' she advised

Helen was disconcerted. 'Which wall would that be?'

'You'll know yourself.'

Molly prided herself on being unshockable but as she loitered for Helen at the back door of her office block on Upper Baggot Street she thought about the brother-and-sister scenario. And her flesh crawled. It didn't make sense to her, with a city full of men. Molly conveniently overlooked her own rants about the dearth of sane, solvent, single men to choose from. Not necessarily in that order.

'It's a toss-up between twelve-year-olds and Norman

Bates clones,' she'd grizzled to Stephen only the other day in The Kip. Stephen had blossomed as he'd listened to Molly's tirade. 'I'm neither a twelve-year-old nor a psychotic murderer,' he'd pointed out.

'Nor are you single.'

'You're deliberately finding obstacles,' Stephen had muttered into his pint, as she'd swept off to speak to Frank Dillon. The security correspondent, who farmed a family holding at weekends, was gratified to be sought out by one of the most attractive women in the office until he discovred she wanted to quiz him about the revised expenses rates.

Still no sign of Helen. Molly glanced at her watch: 5.05 p.m. 'Hurry up, Helen,' she muttered. 'No point in squirting on the scent for my benefit.'

A sandy-haired man with a bold cast to his features emerged from the building and winked at Molly. 'Talking to yourself. Bad sign, peaches. The fellows in white coats will be after you if you don't watch out,' he advised in a north city accent. The sort of man who probably said he was Dublin bred and buttered. The sidelong glance he gave her smacked of promise.

You see, Helen – she mentally addressed her absent friend, taking care her lips didn't move in case she was overheard again – you're surrounded by men in your business. I bet he'd be a laugh.

Just then Helen appeared.

'Who's the lanky man in his thirties, reddish hair, talks like a taxi-driver and wears a navy Crombie?' Molly demanded.

Helen frowned. 'Sounds like Shane. Did he call you peaches?'

'Affirmative. Never been addressed as that before but it was quite endearing in him.'

Molly helped Helen find the sleeve of her coat as they walked.

'Middle management. Gay. Lives with a civil servant. The two of them are the life and soul of every party. Shane always refers to his boyfriend as his occasionally naked civil servant.'

Molly shrugged; win some, lose some. Anyway, she was only checking him out for Helen.

'Where are we headed? I can't make up my mind if I fancy a coffee or a drink.'

'Let's kill two birds with one stone and have a couple of Irish coffees,' suggested Helen.

'Plan A works for me,' agreed Molly. 'There'll be too many chancers I know in Doheny and Nesbitt's, will we move upmarket and flash our cash in the Shelbourne? I fancy the drawing room.'

They clattered past the bronze Egyptian torch-bearers on either side of the hotel's main entrance and steered right into an imposing room with floor-to-ceiling windows. A table with a pair of armchairs flanking it near the piano was vacant, and they sank into well-upholstered leather. Almost immediately a waiter took their order.

They sized up the other people in the room: inevitably they were tourists. Nearby were three Scottish women surrounded by Brown Thomas shopping bags, forming plans for the evening over gin and tonics – a visit to the Abbey to see Sebastian Barry's latest play seemed to be on the agenda. Down near the discreetly positioned till was a party of what they agreed must be North European men; Molly thought Dutch and Helen veered towards Belgian. They definitely weren't French.

'Still seeing Fionn?' Helen asked as the whiskey warmed her from the inside out.

'Sort of.'

Helen knew what 'sort of' meant in Molly's book: she couldn't decide if he were her boyfriend so she slept with him while she waited for elucidation. Helen pressed her lips together so she wouldn't be tempted to criticise Fionn but the whiskey loosened them.

'This man is trouble, Molly.'

'Which man isn't?'

'You were in smithereens after he left you. I was like someone trying to assemble a jigsaw minus a handful of pivotal pieces. You can't have forgotten how it felt. And what he did once he can do again. There's a wife on the sidelines somewhere. Who's to say he won't have his fun with you and then scamper home to her with his tail between his legs? Wives are comforting and men are gluttons for comfort.' Helen frowned as she leaned into her winged-back chair.

Molly stifled her indignation during this speech. Helen, fantasist *par excellence*, who was contemplating a dangerous liaison with her own brother, was lecturing her on sleeping with the enemy. The woman was delusional. If it weren't offensive it would be hilarious. However she didn't fancy an argument so she arced an eyebrow at Helen, who read a thousand words into the flicker.

'Didn't mean to climb into the pulpit, Molly. I just don't want to see you wind up hurt.'

'Snap.'

'You mean Patrick?'

'Unless there's another brother you fancy,' said Molly tartly. Immediately she regretted it when the hurt bloomed in Helen's eyes. 'Sorry, angel face. You rattled my cage on the Fionn front. You're absolutely right, he may well shag me senseless and then toddle off home to the Viking but

I'm enjoying the shagging senseless part of the scenario and I never believed in shagging sensibly (apart from condoms) so I've nothing to lose.'

The waiter, clearing a table close by them, found himself privy to so much personal information about a customer he couldn't help but hover in the hope of more – trying not to stare. Molly crossed her legs and overacted prim.

'You could lose your self-respect,' suggested Helen.

'Threw that out years ago. Next.'

'Your peace of mind.'

'It's a fair swap for someone to warm my feet on in bed. Next.'

'Your heart.'

'Ah.' Molly acknowledged defeat. 'Losing my heart once to Fionn McCullagh was unfortunate, twice would be careless.' She sighed and tipped back her glass. Then she rallied. 'We're forgetting I've already mislaid that wayward organ. It's in the indifferent keeping of the Greek. So I'm safe enough with Fionn, who may not be swarthily fascinating but at least he's available. Also interested in me, which counts for a lot currently.'

'You can't marry Fionn since he's already taken,' Helen pointed out. 'I thought you were preparing for a nuptial chapter; he's a plot deviation. You're dissipating your energies.'

'On the contrary, he provides light relief from the tedium of the chase. I'm nasty enough to dump him unceremoniously as soon as a husband materialises. But they're thin on the ground, these lads.'

'Except other people's.'

They finished their drinks, Molly scrutinising the Dutchmen from habit – the Scotswomen having rustled off in a plethora of bags – while Helen wondered why she found it so arduous to ventilate her relationship with Patrick. She'd broached the subject already, Molly knew how she felt about him and she needn't fear her friend would humiliate her in the middle of the Shelbourne by denouncing her as a libertine. That afternoon she had felt weightless with the promise of a burden shared when Molly agreed to meet her; now she couldn't frame the words. She envied people who opened their mouths and sounds flowed out, tongues clacking off palates to provide explanations.

'I feel like another Irish coffee without the coffee,' said Molly. 'I'm not fussy about the cream either, which only leaves the whiskey. How about you?'

'I'll have what you're having.' Decisions were beyond Helen.

'Ooh, you're like one of those women in romantic novels from years ago, who'd be whisked off to dinner and simper as the man masterfully ordered for both of them. Could we have two whiskeys, please?' Molly signalled to the barman.

She decided to pump Helen since she seemed reluctant to volunteer information. 'You lured me here under false pretences, Ms Sharkey,' she announced. 'I was promised an improper chat.'

Helen extended both palms outward in surrender. 'So I did. The case for the defence is that I was choosing my moment to introduce an unseemly element into what has been a singularly decorous encounter. Not.'

'Cheap shot,' laughed Molly. 'Now do you want to hear about Barry's connubial trials or shall I subside into silence and listen to you?'

Helen hesitated. She did want to discuss the Westport scheme with Molly but she needed a drink at her elbow first. And since she was embroiled in the Barry affair –

at Molly's behest – she was curious to know how her intervention might have shaped events.

'Give me a succinct update on developments relating to Barry – we can trawl ghoul-like through the details later – and then I'll explain what's happening with Patrick and myself,' she instructed.

The whiskey arrived, along with renewed supplies of nuts, and Helen popped one into her mouth before Molly did her usual trick of annexing the bowl.

'Chocolate is supposed to be fabulous with whiskey.' Molly leaned across and grabbed a handful, virtuously leaving the bowl in the centre of the table. 'Stephen on the newsdesk swears by the whiskey and chocolate combination. He says they complement each other because they're both sweet flavours. I keep meaning to try it out.'

'Interesting. Allow me to change the subject forthwith. Is Barry forgiven?'

Molly splashed lemonade into the glass, shading the amber whiskey to the colour of Helen's antique pine front door.

'Don't you love the clink of ice cubes in a glass? It's so grown up,' she remarked.

'Especially when they serve it in a glass with a stem.'

'That's the best part of gin and tonics, the lemon slice and ice cubes,' agreed Helen.

'Wrong, the gin's the best part,' Molly contradicted her, extracting clips from her bag and shoving them into her nest of hair to keep it out of her eyes. 'It wouldn't be much of a tonic without the gin. Now about Barry. The fiendish ploy I dreamed up in my plan meister's brain worked – up to a point. Your phone call left Kay palpitating with jealousy but it didn't make her kill the fatted calf and welcome Barry back under the Laura Ashley duvet cover. He's still languishing in the spare room, whining that she won't agree to let him have the electric blanket on alternate nights. However, she's suggested marriage guidance counselling, which is a sight more optimistic than divorce lawyers and bedsits.'

'How does Barry feel about marriage guidance?'

'Barry would go to a feng shui expert for a consultation if that's what Kay ordained,' said Molly, checking how securely fastened her clips were. 'They'd paint their garden walls two different colours, throw away spiky-leaved houseplants, attach curved handles on their kitchen cupboards and their life would be shiny-bright again. Marriage guidance is a result, the rest is up to him. Now what's happening with you and the brother?'

Helen winced. She wished Molly wouldn't refer to Patrick as her brother. She didn't think of their relationship in that way and it struck her as lewd when someone forced it on her notice.

'We're going away for the weekend.'

Molly's expression betrayed her surprise.

Helen took a steadying draught of whiskey and tugged viciously at a loose thread on the hem of her skirt. 'It's not what you're thinking.' A slap flared on each cheek.

'I'm not thinking anything.' Molly's facial muscles were back under control and she was impassive now.

'Yes, you are,' Helen contradicted. 'But this is something else entirely.'

'Oh?'

'It's love.'

Molly was silenced. Love she understood. Feelings for a brother which were inappropriate – make that illegal – were possibly explicable if you factored in love. She had Fionn on the go and she enjoyed making love with him – seriously enjoyed it – but she'd still throw him over in the morning at a word from Hercules, who might not even know where her erogenous zones were. Whereas Fionn had photocopied and memorised them. That could only mean she was unhinged . . . or in love. She certainly wasn't in love with Fionn, despite his pleasing attentiveness: he'd even turned up with a ceramic chicken toast rack for her collection the last time they met, a little six-inch-high fellow with a flirtatious eye.

Molly knew you couldn't choose who to love so Helen's two-word explanation made the most perfect imperfect sense. The friends sat in companionable silence, the other occupants in the room receding in search of evening meals. Helen mulled over Patrick's ability to take her grasp on reality and realign it to its antithesis, while Molly remembered how she'd superimposed Hercules' face on Fionn's the last time they'd made love and enhanced her own fervour. She made a mental pledge not to do it again, for she knew it was shabby, but it hadn't been premeditated; it had happened of its own accord and she'd reacted to it. Naturally she ought to have abrogated Hercules' trespass but it had caught her unawares. She'd veto it next time. Yes I will, she insisted, as a cynical subtext in her brain mocked the resolution.

'You really are a hussy,' remarked Molly.

Helen winced.

'Not you, angel face.' Molly patted her hand. 'Me. I'm talking to myself again.'

'I don't think there is a word for what I am,' said Helen. 'At least it's not in my lexicon. Corrupt. Aberrant. Debauched.'

'Don't be so hard on yourself.' Molly pulled her armchair closer to Helen's and strained towards her, intent on making a connection. 'You didn't choose to have these feelings and you're not a freak, however full of self-loathing you are.

You're not the only woman in the world to love her brother. It's happened before, it'll happen again. Lord Byron was supposed to be in love with his half-sister. There were even whispers that he fathered one of her children.'

'What happened to them?'

He was forced into exile. Better not share that with Helen.

'Can't remember, Helen. Sure you know I have a memory like a sieve.'

Helen thought about confiding how she'd spent a night with Patrick. It felt as though it had happened a few months ago instead of three years ago, for time adopted an erratic quality in her dealings with him. But she sensed it would be a betrayal to speak of it – their relationship was founded on love, not sex. Molly might misunderstand.

She continued her internal conversation aloud. 'I'm not convinced there needs to be anything physical between Patrick and me. We could always love one another platonically, isn't that an option? People do it.' Appeal haemorrhaged from Helen.

'It's possible,' conceded Molly.

Helen looked relieved but Molly felt she should be more outspoken in the interests of friendship.

'But could you really spend the rest of your life with someone you craved and not lay a finger on them, Helen? I know my own limitations: there's no way on earth I could manage that without imploding.'

Helen's eyes fastened on the curtainpole finials. 'I could if the option were not to spend my life with him at all,' she whispered.

Spare me from a love like that, wished Molly.

Spare me for a love like that, wished Helen.

'Plato probably had some unpleasant infection that made him favour Platonic love,' suggested Molly. It was a skewing of their conversation, she knew, but her brain needed respite. Just for a moment or two.

'I don't know why a journalist would use as a reference point a man who believed the spoken word was superior to the written.' Helen decided to leave after she'd finished her drink, if Molly was intent on drivelling on about a Greek who'd been dust for a couple of millennia instead of helping her through this emotional maze. Her discontent lapped out. 'Anyway this smacks of an elaborate ploy to turn the subject to Greeks. Or specifically your Greek.'

'He's not my Greek,' sighed Molly. Optimism intervened. 'But at least he doesn't appear to be anyone else's either so there's always hope.'

Hope. Helen quailed at the use of the word she was relying on as her own lodestar. There was only so much hope to go around. She needed the lion's share – Molly could manage on chutzpah.

Molly realised she should have encouraged her friend to talk through the permutations of her relationship with her brother. That's why they were meeting, after all.

'So you're going away with Patrick, any destination in mind?'

'Westport.'

'I'd have preferred Newport myself – the American one, not the Welsh fellow – but I suppose your entire weekend would be devoted to travelling there and back.' Molly beat the opening bars to the US national anthem against the tabletop.

'The idea of the weekend is to spend time together but preferably not in an airplane,' said Helen.

'Right, time together.' A pause. 'Didn't you do enough of that growing up?'

Silence settled oppressively on them.

But the nature of the hush altered during the course of ten minutes or so. It started as strained and progressed to a tacit truce.

'Helen Sharkey.' Molly guillotined the stillness.

'*Is mise*.' Helen acknowledged her name.

'We've eaten all the nuts and the pattern off the bowl to boot. Methinks 'tis time to sally forth, brave the dragons and run some nourishment to ground.'

Helen contemplated food. As Molly's notions went it wasn't the most suspect. Helen had eaten virtually nothing all day.

'Know what I fancy? Pecan pie, a massive slab of it.'

'I was considering something a little more substantial,' said Molly. 'By all means *il faut manger brioche* but not until after the *coq au vin*. Or veggie au vin in your case.'

'This sounds suspiciously like a ploy to carry on drinking,' said Helen.

'Since when did I need to resort to ploys? *Coq au vin* just entered my head but it could as easily have been a Guinness hot pot or a steak flambéd in brandy.'

'I detect a theme emerging, Moll.'

'Food?'

'Food doused in alcohol. Consumed with alcohol on the side, no doubt. And if there's chips you'll be asking for wine vinegar to sprinkle on them.'

Molly ignored Helen. 'Alternatively we could go somewhere for cocktails and eat the fruit out of them.'

'That would certainly take care of the hunger,' said Helen.

'It would?' Molly, having suggested the scheme, was overwhelmed by its flaws.

'Absolutely. A couple of cocktails apiece and we'd be so far gone we wouldn't know what to do with a plate of chips if they arrived carrying an "eat us" banner.'

'I can never imagine myself so pixilated that I wouldn't know how to decimate a plate of chips. Now, are we heading off in search of some stomach lining?'

'I'd still like a slice of pecan pie at some stage, possibly the pudding one.' There was a disconsolate note in Helen's voice.

'Have one if you must but I'd like you to know I've enrolled in the Save the Pecan Foundation and we take a dim view of nutivores like yourself scoffing endangered species.'

Helen stood. 'Molly, hunger has obviously left you deranged. Since it's too late to look for a new best friend let's go eat pasta.'

'Wait a minute.' Molly was earnest. She caught hold of Helen by the arm and pulled her back into her chair. 'Do you think it's wise to go off somewhere with Patrick? Are you sure it's what you truly want? Fine if you've thought it through and are prepared for the consequences but if he's pressurising you into it maybe you should reconsider. I'd hate to think of you taking an irrevocable step. I know you want to spend some time together but a weekend might be too protracted. Perhaps you should scale down – go away for the day.'

Helen chomped on her lower lip. 'You're right, it is precipitate. It made sense when I was with Patrick but now I'm not convinced. The idea was to get to know each other again, it's been three years since we spent any time together. We seem to know everything there is about one another on one level and scarcely anything at all on another. Does that sound ridiculous?'

'No,' lied Molly, who considered it smacked of insanity.

'I wish we could be together for a while, somewhere private that didn't involve actually going away. To be honest I'm a little wary about that, I suppose because there's always a risk of reality becoming obscured. I know I need to keep my feet on the ground.'

'Aha.' Molly sat upright so abruptly her bracelets jangled. 'Just call me your good fairy. I'm in a position to make your wish come true.'

'You are?'

'You can use my apartment. Fionn moved into his new place earlier this week and I can make an old man very happy, not to mention a bold man very soppy, by announcing my intention to empty his fridge and leave blonde hairs in his shower plughole. I'll clear out of number 16 by Friday lunchtime and stay away all the following day. From Sunday you can make your own arrangements. How does that grab you – does it transform you into Helen of Joy?'

Helen didn't respond immediately. Her lower lip, already brutally mauled, came in for further mistreatment while she pondered Molly's offer. It answered most of her reservations . . . but Molly had only a double bed. Her spare room was used as a study.

'There's a sofabed in the study,' said Molly. 'I don't need an Ouija board to divine that expression you're wearing.'

Helen thanked her so profusely that Molly raised her hands in capitulation.

'I know I'm the best friend in the world, I know I deserve a medal but I'd settle for dinner. Now I'm ready to sally forth, what's keeping you?'

'I'm sallying fifth,' said Helen.

'Let's go to Milano's,' suggested Molly as they passed the uniformed doorman.

'The Unicorn.' Helen's tone brooked no argument. 'I'm buying and I owe you more than a pizza.'

'You don't owe me anything. Except a decent burial if my stomach isn't introduced to some food soon.'

'We're on our way. I'll need to find a hole-in-the-wall machine but there should be a basket of bread in front of you within four minutes, three if we take our shoes off and sprint.'

CHAPTER 22

A phone call from Fionn left Molly fulminating. Helga was on a plane bound for Dublin to rescue their marriage and Fionn was relying on Molly to rescue him from Helga.

'Not my function,' she snarled.

'Do you want me or don't you?' he asked.

It was a bald question; Molly had no option but to prevaricate since she didn't know the answer. If in doubt, turn the tables.

'I'm not convinced it's me you want. Just someone to save you from your wife. You're terrified that Helga can do whatever she likes with you. She won't turn your willpower to stone with one look from her eyes; she's a woman not Medusa. But maybe you have no willpower where she's concerned.'

Injury radiated from his voice. And resignation. 'Perhaps I don't have much willpower. Helga, I mean Olga, is a singularly determined person. But you didn't answer my question and that's enlightening.'

Molly played for time. 'What was the question?'

'I think you know.'

She sighed. It was too early for cat-and-mouse games. Molly hadn't even finished her first cup of coffee of the day. And she'd be late for work at this rate. She was due to cover a tribunal in Dublin Castle starting at ten o'clock.

'Do I want the incomparable Fionn McCullagh or don't I? I'm not sure what I want. Yes I do, I know I don't want to be cast as a human parachute – simply pull and a soft landing is guaranteed.'

'You're still evading the question, Molly.'

'It's not a fair question.'

'I must know if there's a chance we can have a future together.'

'I don't see how we can discuss the future until you sort out the present.' Molly was rather pleased with the retort. She rewarded herself with a gulp of coffee.

'Olga belongs to the past.'

'So why's she broomstick-bound for Dublin even as we speak? Answers on a postcard, please.'

'For Christ's sake, Molly, I don't see why you have to be so flip about everything. It's offensive. This is my life you're reducing to snappy one-liners.'

Resentment roared through Molly. How dare Fionn criticise her when he was the one with a wife – not even an ex-wife – showing up to make her feel like the other woman in some cheap burlesque? Which she didn't consider herself to be. Not at all. He was her boyfriend before he was Helga's husband; she had a prior claim on him. And they were meant to be together for ever until Helga had muscled in, all Scandinavian and irresistible like an Ikea bargain basement.

'It's my life too,' she seethed. 'If you wanted me you could have had me four years ago instead of swanning off to design skyscrapers in Seattle and marrying a skyscraper wife to even it out. You put me through the wringer, you flattened me and now that I've fleshed myself out again you

346

emerge from the woodwork and say, "Hey, babe, I'm yours if you want me." So forgive me if I'm occasionally flip. I'd rather flip than flop. The fact is I appear to have developed a jaundiced view. Can't imagine how.'

She was panting by the time she finished and the silence on the other end of the phone line thickened to congealing point. Molly waited for a response. And waited.

'I see,' said Fionn.

That was worth holding her breath for. 'Is that it?'

'I have to clear up the flat and collect Olga from the airport. She'll be expecting me to meet her.'

And he always did what Olga expected. Molly slammed down the receiver with an entirely reasonable amount of force. It was a wonder the plastic didn't crack. Not the most mature behaviour but instant gratification had much to recommend it

As she stomped about the apartment preparing for work, a jarring realisation sent her deteriorating temper into freefall. With a wife in situ Molly couldn't camp out at Fionn's place while Helen used her flat as an unconsummated love nest. Actually, as far as she was concerned the celibate aspect wasn't carved in stone, so long as Helen knew what she was doing. But did anybody genuinely know what they were doing if they went to bed with their brother? Were they *compos mentis*? Molly shook her head until it vibrated to eject the questions cluttering it. She had enough on her mind, trying to find her mobile phone, mysteriously absent both from her handbag and the battery charger, and reach Dublin Castle by 10 a.m., never mind dwelling on sisters and brothers-in-arms. But there was still a clump of intruder thoughts irritating her. It couldn't be the change of plan affecting Helen and Patrick; Molly would be able still to lend them her flat. She'd crash with a friend from work if necessary. And if all else failed she could take a run home for the weekend. Granted, she wasn't long back from Derry but homes were intended as places to come and go from with cavalier irregularity; it was written into the parent/child charter. So what was rankling? As Molly dead-locked the door of her apartment she pinpointed the source of vexation: Helga was staying with Fionn. Which she'd every right to do as his wife. But Molly didn't have to like it. And neither she did; indeed, she realised with an emotion approaching alarm, she was feeling possessive.

This jaw-grinding response lasted as far as the ticket queue at the DART station until a cheering intervention to her temper came via the realisation it was Thursday. Which meant there'd be a lecture at the art gallery. She hadn't managed to attend for a fortnight. Perhaps Hercules was missing her – that's if he were still frequenting the talks. Defeatist attitude, there was every chance he'd be in Merrion Square tonight. Molly bolted back towards her flat – so what if she missed the beginning of the tribunal session, one of the other reporters would give her a shorthand note – and catapulted into the bedroom to find something more alluring to wear. She swapped her pinstriped trouser suit for a new suit in a colour the sales assistant insisted was bull's blood but which she thought of as burgundy. Crucially it had a wraparound skirt with a tendency to splice open. She'd sit beside Hercules crossing and uncrossing her legs until he turned the shade of her suit. Which meant she'd need to stop off at the hosiery department in Clery's first because these tights she was wearing were the denier of a black-out curtain. Crossing and uncrossing of legs required something a tad slinkier.

'Does anyone still actually call tights hosiery?' Molly

enquired of her keys as she dead-locked the front door for the second time.

'What's hosiery?' Elizabeth emerged from next door looking as though she'd managed two hours' sleep last night. Maximum.

'You just stick to the raspberry fishnets and you'll never need to worry, pet,' said Molly. 'Teamed today with slave sandals, ankle socks and striped capri pants, I note, as once again you push against the outer boundaries of conventional garb.'

Elizabeth was complacent. 'I seem to have a knack for throwing together a look. I reach into my wardrobe and the funkiest combinations leap out at me.'

'Inspired,' agreed Molly. 'Are you headed for the DART?'

Back in the office late afternoon, Molly was writing up her copy at breakneck speed – she needed to have her coat on and her pieces filed by ten past six to make the start of the lecture. Fortunately she'd managed to scribble one story at the back of her notebook over lunch and rough out the second during a boring tranche towards the close of the session as the lawyers wrangled over technicalities. If excess baggage on her credit card hadn't obliged her to collect a loan cheque from the Credit Union in Chronicle House she could have phoned or emailed her copy from Dublin Castle, avoided the office and been ahead of the game. But she should still be on time for Hercules if there were no distractions.

Barry had only just started a 4.30 p.m. shift, however, and was going to be in the office for the next eight hours. He was ready for a chat – their working hours hadn't coincided yet this week – and he wasn't deterred by Molly's harassed, 'I'm up against a deadline'. He knew it would be at least 7.30 p.m. before the subs started muttering they'd like to see the odd story if the next day's paper weren't to be peppered with empty spaces; in the meantime he had an inane grin on his face which he felt required explanation. Or at least some attention paid to it.

'Kay and I are getting on like a house on fire,' he said.

'Excellent.'

'Actually we can't keep our hands off each other.'

'Great.'

'We're like newlyweds.'

'Brilliant.'

'Jaw-jaw at marriage guidance led to paw-paw at home. Lubricated by a bottle of Baileys – can't stand the stuff myself but Kay has a weakness for it. Molly, are you listening to a word I'm saying? You haven't stopped typing.' Barry sounded aggrieved.

'You and Kay are having jiggery pokery in every room in the house. I'm deliriously happy for you. Now if you don't mind I have a date with destiny and I can't keep it until I file my copy.'

Barry decided to stop being peeved and start taking an interest in Molly's plans for the evening. He could always crow over the Lazarus-like resurrection of his love life when she wasn't pounding the keyboard and mumbling about checking the spelling of the tribunal lawyer's name.

'Anyone I know?' he asked.

'Who?'

'Your date.'

'No. Yes. Well, it's not exactly a date. Can you make yourself useful, Bar, and look up the spelling of MacCionnaith

350

in the library? It should be filed under the latest batch of tribunal stories.'

'I take it from your fever pitch of excitement it's not Fionn you're meeting.'

'No. Any chance of that spellcheck this side of first edition?'

Barry clicked on to the library file and read out the lawyer's surname to her. 'You OK with his first name?'

'Senan the usual way, right?'

'Right. Now about this not-exactly-a-date – does that mean he just said, "See you in the pub later," and you're not a hundred per cent sure if he fancies you or the idea of someone to have a jar with?'

Molly twisted her hair into a knot and slid a pen through it to keep it out of her face, then amended her spelling of MacCionnaith. 'Questions, questions. What are you, a journalist or something? A policeman wouldn't ask as much.'

'Just taking a friendly interest in your affairs of the heart. I like Fionn but it's a lose-lose situation for you, even if his wife is an ocean away. So who's his anonymous replacement and where are you meeting him?'

'At a lecture in the National Gallery.'

'I can see what you mean about it not being much of a date. A woman wouldn't know where she stood with a man who met her at an art gallery.'

Molly abandoned her story temporarily. 'Why ever not? It's a classy place to rendezvous.'

'Classy, possibly; open to misinterpretation, definitely.' Barry had the air of a man on terra firma. 'What's there to do in a gallery except wander around looking at paintings, many of which are pornographic or religious? And neither subject matter is conducive to a successful first date. You're safer with a restaurant; there's nothing pornographic or religious about food. Well, nothing obvious, anyway – you'd want to be really looking for it.'

Molly surrendered. 'Barry, I can see you'll give me no peace until you worm this out of me. It's not a date, let alone a first date. It's just that I wanted to make the art history lectures tonight on the off chance that my Greek god might be there. I'm a desperate case, I know, but that's love for you. Or concupiscence. The jury's out on this one. Now please, please, pretty please and all the trimmings, let me be until I file these stories. We'll have a coffee tomorrow and you can tell me all about yourself and Kay rekindling passion and igniting the electric blanket.'

Before Barry had a chance to answer, Stephen shouted down to him there was a caller on the line with a story about planning abuses worth checking out.

'A member of the public,' grizzled Barry as he picked up the line. 'Whoever it is will be giving out yards about their next-door neighbour's kitchen extension, not systematic corruption among the town planners.' He puckered his lips exaggeratedly at Molly. 'Slap on an extra layer of lipstick before you leave if you're determined to compete with a Raphael. Those Renaissance babes were the business.'

The National Gallery doesn't have any Raphaels, thought Molly as she scrutinised her shorthand for a half-remembered quote about cronyism. But she said nothing – she didn't want to kickstart Barry on to a discussion about the paintings on show. Which would inevitably involve him itemising Cork's superior collections.

Barry, meanwhile, managed to palm off his caller with a phone number for Dublin Corporation's planning office.

'Molly,' he said then, in quite a different tone to the one previously used.

'For pity's sake, Barry,' she complained, not noticing the alteration.

'Listen, I wanted to apologise for losing the head the other day and making a prize eejit of myself, trying to kiss you and everything.'

He had her attention now. She looked up from her tribunal report. 'Trying and succeeding.'

Barry ducked his head, then decided to play it honest and manly. 'Sure I'm only human,' he said. 'What man in his right mind wouldn't want to kiss you?'

Molly felt mollified, an emotion she preferred to avoid by and large because she felt it trailed syrupy behind her name.

'It was just the upset over Kay, it destabilised me,' he added. 'A shabby excuse but the truth is often pitiful. I could invent a more fetching lie but –' he was almost overcome with admiration for his own creativity at this point – 'you deserve the truth.'

'We'll say no more about it,' she said magnanimously. 'Just keep your lips to yourself in future.'

She made it to Merrion Square in time for a dawdle in the gift shop, since there was no sign of Hercules in the lecture hall, and pondered whether or not to buy a computer mousepad featuring William's Leech's first wife disguised as a novice nun. Gold star: she liked the Britanny convent garden; black mark: she wasn't convinced anyone's mousepad need a nun on it, especially one who appeared to be gazing skywards towards a vision of celestial hosts. Hercules' arrival acted as an instant solution – Molly abandoned the computer accessories, dithering terminated.

She strolled past the cash desk where he was paying, noticing but charitably overlooking his gun-metal grey fleece. Molly believed an *auto-da-fé* should be constructed especially for fleeces, an item of clothing she didn't so much scorn as long to see annihilated. Unreasonable, she knew, but logic disintegrated where the fleece was concerned. She must have it bad-bad-Leroy Brown for Hercules if she were prepared to ignore his fleece. Reassured by this proof of the panoramic scope of her feelings for him, Molly paused by the till so he'd notice her. Hercules, fumbling with his change, turned away without observing her. Good God above, he must be short-sighted as well as sartorially challenged; if Molly knew how to gnash her teeth she'd be doing it this very minute. She caught up with him by the staircase.

'Hey there, you, what's on the agenda tonight? Still life – how modernists moved it forward with the times?'

He favoured her with a look she could only interpret as cautious.

'Molly,' she said helpfully. 'I'm thinking of wearing a badge to remind people. I work with animals, my ambition is world peace and my star sign is Taurus, which might indicate I'm a bull in a china shop. But I'm not, I'm the most delicate piece of porcelain in the display case, it's just nobody seems to appreciate my true value. Now let me guess your name. The mists are parting, I see a G. Is it Genevieve?'

'Close but no cigar,' he laughed. 'Are you always so full on?'

She reflected. 'Sometimes I switch to automatic pilot, usually while I'm sleeping.'

They handed in their tickets and sat together in the second row from the back. Molly caught his eye on her knee as she crossed her legs: eureka! to quote another

Greek. But the lights dimmed and a Picasso flashed up on the screen, distracting her companion into more highbrow admiration.

'How's your beautiful friend?' he asked later over coffee.

'Joined a cult, relocated to a particularly inaccessible part of Canada.'

'That was quick,' he objected.

'OK, she's still in Dublin and hasn't signed herself over to a sect, but she's madly in love and contemplating a move to Ecuador.'

'Is Helen involved with a South American?'

Selective memory, thought Molly. He'd forget *her* name if she didn't remind him but Helen's is mentioned once and it's haunting him. She spooned up froth from her coffee, fantasising about telling Hercules who Helen was in love with. That should take care of Romeo's roaming eye. Prepare to be shocked, she'd say. How shocked? he'd ask. Think very shocked, she'd advise. Up a bit, up a bit, double it.

Molly sighed and decided to execute a graceful departure as soon as the coffee was finished. Of course she wasn't going to blab Helen's secret to their Greek and she'd need to be thick, say, a couple of paving slabs screwed together, to continue hurling herself at a man who had no intention of catching her. And who didn't appear to realise mouths were for kissing as well as pouring coffee down. Meanwhile, the man who *was* interested in her mouth, as well as every other part of her anatomy, was currently making love to his wife. Or at least ferrying her about and talking to her, sure that was nearly as bad.

'You never said whether Helen was involved with a South American.'

Molly forsook the froth. 'No, he's a local lad. A childhood sweetheart, you might say.'

Hercules looked downcast. She couldn't help but feel for him. 'Let me buy you a bun,' she offered. Food might not be as satisfying as requited love but it was infinitely more palatable than unrequited love. Molly thought there was every reason to believe his heart was no more than bruised when he brightened at the possibility of cake. However, he declined, somewhat reluctantly, because he was due at his sister's for a meal in half an hour and she catered with prodigal extravagance.

'Come with me,' he suggested on impulse.

Molly clattered her coffee mug against the sugar bowl. 'I couldn't,' she protested.

'Have you something else on?'

'No.' She thought of Fionn, who was probably leaving a series of increasingly indignant pronouncements on her phone messaging systems. 'No, I'm as free as a bird.'

'Well, then.'

'I can't just turn up unannounced at your sister's home and expect to be fed.'

'I'll ring her now so you're not unannounced. There's a callbox on the next floor, I'll be right back.'

Hercules left before she had a chance to proffer her mobile. Which she couldn't anyway because it was still buried under debris in her apartment. Molly finished her coffee in a daze. These Mediterranean types, even the watered-down south County Dublin versions, were insistent. Imperious even. She felt like the heroine in a Jane Austen novel. Except she couldn't remember his surname, let alone call him by it. 'Thank you so much for handing me into my carriage, Mr Popadopolis. I could never have managed that high step on my own.'

This was a wish come true. It was as though her fairy godmother had dropped by with a belated christening gift. Extremely belated. If this wasn't a date with the Greek god it was a sensational facsimile. It might not be dinner for two by candlelight but it was the same ballpark. Maybe not the Super Bowl but not the Little League either.

Hercules returned and helped Molly into her coat. 'She's delighted,' he said. 'We'll catch the DART over. She lives in Booterstown.'

'We'd need to stop by an off-licence so I can buy some wine.'

'No problem. I want to pick up a bottle of something myself.'

'And you're sure your sister doesn't mind?'

'Melina's enchanted. She wilts without company.'

They were on the street now and steering towards the train station.

Hercules continued: 'She doesn't get out much with the twins so it's a treat for her to meet someone new. She says she's put the babies down for the night but if one stirs they'll both wake so we might be lucky enough to see them. Anyhow, we can always creep into their bedroom for a peep.' He smiled self-consciously, teeth catching the pink flesh of his lower lip. 'I'm besotted with my nieces, I have to confess. You look like a woman who's fond of babies yourself.'

'Worship them,' said Molly, never having spared them much thought before. If he wanted her to be infatuated with his sister's babies she could dote with the best of them. So long as she wasn't actually required to change them. 'Should we bring some chocolate buttons or lollipops?'

'Too young, they're only four-and-a-half months old.

They're called Electra and Antigone, Lectric and Tiggy for short.'

Heavy names for a couple of infants. Molly did a double take while Hercules rummaged in his pocket for a DART ticket. Whatever happened to names people could spell, such as Louise and Donna? Or even something twinnish like Kelly and Shelley?

He slid his ticket into the machine after Molly and went on: 'Melina and Tim have a semi-basement apartment that suited perfectly when it was only the two of them but they're house-hunting at the moment because the twins' paraphernalia has overrun every nook and cranny. Buggies, high chairs, sterilising gadgets, piles of dirty washing, piles of clean washing, vast containers of disposable nappies . . .' He almost slavered with fondness.

The man of her dreams was turning into a baby bore. Much more of this and she'd stay on the DART to Blackrock. She scooped up a scowl that threatened to settle on her face, dressed it up in sheep's clothing as an interested expression and covertly watched a trailer for yet another *Star Wars* film on the platform screen. A couple more and George Lucas would have enough money to buy planets, never mind recreate them with special effects.

They each held a bottle by the neck as they walked towards a redbrick building with a cherry tree in the front garden.

'Can't ring the doorbell,' explained Hercules, tapping gently on a glass panel. 'Might waken the babies.'

The door was flung open by his sister, who carried off a somewhat unnatural-looking hennaed urchin cut despite her sultry colouring. She pounced on Molly in the hallway.

'Georgie never told us he had a girlfriend,' she beamed.

'It's been ages since he brought a woman over, hasn't it, Tim?'

Tim, invisible in the kitchen, mumbled something that could have been 'Yes' or could have been 'Where's the garlic presser?'

'She's not my girlfriend,' insisted Hercules. 'We go to the same art appreciation class, I'm only after telling you on the phone, Melina.' He pulled a face intended to convey apology to Molly. Meanwhile, on the other side of the narrow hallway, Melina was rolling the whites of her eyes at Molly in a manner which suggested her brother had asinine sensitivities.

'Friend, girlfriend, what does it matter? You're welcome here, Molly. I hope you're hungry. Tim's chef tonight and he always imagines he's feeding the five thousand although we offer a little more variety than loaves and fishes. Come in, let me prove we have a living room as well as a hallway. We've even managed to clear teething rings and teddy bears off the sofa so there's space to sit down.' She spotted a stray bib on the arm of the sofa and stuffed it into a trouser pocket without drawing breath. 'It's wonderful to see a new face – I'm crawling up the walls by the time Tim comes home from work. I have a horror I'll end up conversing with him in babytalk and neither of us will notice. Let me pour you a glass of wine, Molly. Better still, I'll send Georgie out to do it for me. You can have any colour you like as long as it's red.'

'I brought some white but red would be lovely.' Molly was warming by the second to Melina's surfeit of welcome.

'I've doubled my alcohol intake since the babies came along.' Melina tugged at her shirt hem in a vain attempt to cover her bottom. 'I have the gin bottle sitting on the table ready for Tim's key in the door. Of course, that's not the only reason I've stacked on the beef since the girls made their appearance but it's a contributory factor.' She adjusted her voice upwards a couple of octaves. 'Tim, is the virtuoso at a crucial stage of the culinary proceedings or could you step in to greet our guest?'

Tim, cheerful and balding, wearing a grey apron emblazoned with 'Silence, genius at work' that engulfed his skinny frame, popped his head around the door.

'Molly, glad you could make it. You may not realise it yet but you're providing a valuable social service to my terminally understimulated wife. Food will be ready in ten minutes. Here's Georgie behind me with the fruit of the vine.'

'Ignore anything she says about me,' instructed Hercules, doling out glasses.

'Even the part about you being a child with healing hands who made St Francis of Assisi look indifferent to animals?' Molly widened her eyes above the wine, realising she was going to relish the evening.

'No, you can believe that.'

'And what about the story about you giving all the pocket money you'd saved up for a mega-gears bicycle to the foreign missions?'

'Er, you can believe that too.'

Melina grinned and went into the kitchen to carry through a salad to the table in the corner of the living room. 'Georgie's in denial about the girlfriend bit. There's a science lab of chemistry sparking between the pair of them,' she whispered to Tim, popping a crouton into her mouth.

He patted her rump indulgently. 'Matchmaking again, Melina. Don't forget the tomato bread. I'll turn the oven off and follow you in.'

'She's just Georgie's type, he always had a weakness for blondes.'

'It's brunettes he favours.' Tim pushed the bread basket into her hand and turned back to his saucepans. 'Remember to light the candles on the table. If nothing else it should appeal to your romantic streak.'

In the living room Molly was dutifully admiring a silver-framed photo of the babies in christening gowns while Hercules explained how to tell the identical girls apart. 'Tiggy's nose is slightly snub whereas Lectric has a Roman one.'

Molly scrutinised a pair of Identikit noses.

'It's easier if you see them. Melina, we'll just nip into the babies' bedroom and Molly can have a look at the girls. I promise not to wake them.'

'You don't need to promise because you're not going anywhere. Dinner's ready, and since man cannot live by tomato bread alone I have your favourite Caesar salad here, Georgie. Now do you want Molly opposite you where you can admire her or beside you where you can hold her hand under the table?'

'You do realise,' said Hercules, 'this is the last time I'll invite a woman friend to your home. Molly, where would you be most comfortable sitting?'

'Oh no, does this mean I'm required to express an opinion?' said Molly. 'Anywhere's fine by me. I like being admired *and* having my hand held.'

Hercules checked her expression to gauge whether she was joking but couldn't decide.

Molly thought he looked particularly beguiling by candlelight. Mind you, she thought he looked tantalising in daylight too and, yes, 100-watt lightbulbs cast a certain glow on him. Especially since he'd shed the fleece to reveal a plain black T-shirt, her favourite sort on a man. No city names or beer advertisements.

As Hercules stacked plates after the first course, Molly was unable to withstand asking about a peculiar noise she'd noticed intermittently since sitting down.

'What's that snuffling sound?'

Tim pointed to a baby alarm near the table. 'Monitoring our heavy breathers next door. They do a lot of snorting for a pair of little ladies. It's better than a concert when Georgie goes in to sing them Greek lullabies. I keep waiting for the sound of smashing plates.' He smiled at Molly. 'Are you a student too?'

She must look young enough to be a student. I love this man, thought Molly. I love candlelight too.

'No, I'm a wage slave, a journalist.'

'Who do you work for? Would we recognise your name?' Melina perked up.

'The *Chronicle*.'

Melina's interest levels troughed. 'We read the *Enquirer*.'

By the time Tim's speciality curry was on the table the conversation had moved on to house-hunting.

'Melina and Tim are practising restraint on your behalf; they're one hundred per cent house-hunting bores,' said Georgie. 'It's a wonder they haven't quizzed you about prices in your area.'

'Where do you live, incidentally?' asked Melina.

'Blackrock. I'm only a few streets away from you.'

'Apartment or house?' Melina's eyes gleamed.

'Apartment.'

'Purpose-built or conversion?'

'Give her a break, Melina,' objected Hercules. 'And don't you dare ask how much she paid for it.'

'I suppose you snapped it up for a song years ago and it's

worth a fortune now.' Melina was wistful. 'We have a fair stack of equity in this place but houses are still beyond our reach unless we go right out to Greystones.'

'Your apartment is wonderful.' Molly's gaze travelled around the high ceiling, marble fireplace and elaborate cornicing of their late-Victorian home.

'We only have one bedroom, which is seriously over-crowded with two cots jammed in.' Melina passed mango chutney to Tim. 'We need a house and we need my salary. I'll be going back to work any day now –' Melina had an administrative job in the Department of Finance – 'although I hate the thought of leaving the babes.'

'Greystones is lovely,' said Molly.

'Commuting gives me the shivers.' Melina handed across a second helping of saffron rice to Tim; Molly wondered if they communicated by telepathy. 'Besides, I'm a Dub,' Melina carried on. 'I don't want to end up in Wicklow. That's the sticks.'

'You pays your money and you takes your choice,' said Hercules. 'Booterstown equals an apartment, Greystones equals a house. Tim's from Belturbet, Molly. Ask him to tell you some of his Cavan jokes.'

'Nice try, baby bro,' interjected Melina, 'but I'm nowhere near through obsessing about house prices. Molly, did it take you long to find your place?'

'Months,' shuddered Molly. 'I only bought it in the end so I could reclaim Saturday afternoons instead of spending them viewing properties. I also thought it might be agree-able occasionally to speak to people who weren't estate agents.'

'Georgie's not on the ladder yet,' sighed Melina. 'He doesn't know the horrors that lurk in wait for him.'

'I particularly like Tim's Cavan joke,' interrupted Hercules, 'about the fellow who berates God for not letting him win the Lotto and he makes such a pest of himself that finally God speaks to him. "Meet me halfway and buy a ticket," he says.'

'Only Cavan people are allowed to tell Cavan jokes,' protested Tim. 'Georgie, why don't you change the CD – we've all had enough of John Lee Hooker – and I'll clear the table while Melina establishes exactly how many rooms Molly has in her apartment and works out the market value of each one. By the way, don't even think about digging out the George Dolares CD. Anyway, you won't find it because it's been confiscated.'

Melina made eye contact with Molly. 'You see what I have to contend with? A husband who censors my CD collection.'

During a lull after coconut ice cream Hercules and Molly slipped next door to admire the twins, now whistling as they snored. In the bedroom he rested his arm on Molly's shoulders and she squirmed with pleasure.

'What do you think of my nieces?'

She squinted with limited interest at two lookalike bundles, one in a peach sleepsuit and the other in turquoise, dark curls clinging damply to the backs of their necks.

'Only gorgeous,' she pronounced, hoping it would be extravagant enough.

Georgie radiated gratification. 'They take after our side of the family.'

They returned to find Melina still contemptuous at the idea of living in what she insisted on calling a dormitory town.

'Greystones is a community in its own right,' Tim pointed out, but she wouldn't be gainsaid.

He smiled at Melina with such affection that Molly's

364

stomach churned with jealousy. So what if he were a balding dentist, he treasured his wife. Anyway, Barry had written a story the other week based on research showing that just over fifty per cent of Irish men aged twenty-two plus were subject to hirsute deprivation. Her gaze strayed to Hercules: no danger of an exposed crust there. Molly treated herself to a fleeting reverie in which she shampooed his black hair and combed it out.

'Do you think that's a good idea, Molly?' asked Tim.

She started. 'We're consenting adults; it doesn't hurt anyone.'

Three faces around the table expressed bewilderment.

'Do I think what's a good idea?' she added hurriedly.

'Asking my barber for a discount on the grounds he has less work to do on my scalp as I continue to moult,' explained Tim.

'Only if you're prepared for mockery in addition to rejection,' said Molly. 'Imagine if he claimed he should charge you more because of the search fee involved.'

Tim pretended to flinch. 'How did you find this one, Georgie?'

'Struck lucky, I guess.' Hercules leaned so close to Molly she could count the yellow flecks in his brown – make that espresso – eyes. 'Will we hit the road, Molly? I'll phone for a cab if you'd like to share one.'

Molly contemplated punching the air by way of answer but some degree of circumspection prevailed. 'Brilliant idea, ring straight away,' she beamed. 'We've kept Melina and Tim up late enough. They probably have an early start with the babies.'

'They'll wake at four a.m. demanding milk,' complained Melina. 'I'm going to have a hangover; I've been remiss about drinking water. In for a penny, in for a euro. Empty that bottle into my glass, Tim. The girls are sleeping so soundly you'd think we drugged them. Dipping their soothers into brandy doesn't count as drugging our children, does it?'

Tim shook his head in feigned despair. 'What if Molly thinks you really do that? You'd only have yourself to blame when the social services turn up on the doorstep tomorrow.'

Melina hugged him.

'I'll start the wash-up while we're waiting for our taxi,' Molly volunteered, gathering coffee cups as one of the candles spluttered out.

'I won't hear of it, not on your first visit,' Melina insisted, surfacing from her cuddle. 'The next time you come we'll have you sterilising nappies and scrubbing floors but tonight you're a guest.' She lowered her voice as Tim cleared the table and Hercules spoke to a taxi company from the phone in the hall. 'My brother seems smitten by you, Molly. He couldn't take his eyes off you.'

Molly was beguiled, although faintly incredulous. It was the twins he couldn't tear his gaze away from. She wasn't convinced Hercules had dribbled in her direction. She was certain she'd have noticed the pool of saliva at her feet.

'Have you been seeing each other long?' Melina was still *sotto vóce*.

'We're not really seeing one another. We just meet up at lectures in the National Gallery occasionally.'

Melina gave her a woman-to-woman look.

Molly shrugged. 'I think he's great,' she admitted. 'I'm probably a couple of years too old for him –'

'Nonsense.' Melina's dismissal was reassuringly swift. Molly noticed Hercules' voice was now coming from the kitchen rather than the hallway. He must be talking to Tim.

Melina added: 'Georgie's always preferred slightly older women. Girls his own age are too immature for him. Even as a kid he wanted to hang out with my friends and I'm four years older than he is. You must be about the same.'

'About the same,' parroted Molly, jettisoning three years without a qualm. Fibbing about your age didn't count as a lie.

Hercules returned, pulling the detested fleece over his T-shirt. 'The taxi should be here any minute. It makes sense to drop you first – you live in the centre of Blackrock, don't you? I'm further out. Great food, sis. You must ask Tim to teach you how to cook some day.' He bent over to kiss her cheek.

'That falls into the category of keeping a dog and barking yourself.' She kissed him back. 'Anyway, I do the maintenance cooking. That's where the real work lies. Anybody can manage the big production numbers. Pull the curtain back so you can watch the traffic, Georgie. The girls can sleep through fire and flood but a doorbell wakes them at the first peal.'

'Action stations, the cab's pulling up.' Hercules hustled Molly into her coat. 'Did you have any bags other than your handbag? Right, I'll direct the taxi-driver while you rub noses or whatever.'

Tim, who had finally remembered to take off his chef's apron, brushed his cheek against hers. Melina opened her arms wide for an embrace

'I can't remember when I've enjoyed an evening more,' said Molly. It was no embellishment.

*   *   *

367

As the taxi turned into her street she looked levelly at Hercules, seated a respectable distance away from her.

'Would you like to come in?' Molly invited. She didn't add 'for coffee'.

'Would you like me to?'

'Yes.' She didn't lower her gaze – although she remembered later that the taxi-driver reduced the volume on the radio so he could eavesdrop.

'I'm coffeed out,' said Hercules.

'Me too.' That was as direct as she was willing to be. She looked out of the window.

The cab pulled up outside Molly's block.

Hercules touched her elbow, recalling her eyes to his face. 'Let's pay him off here.'

CHAPTER 23

Helen was feeling abandoned by her friend. Resentment simmered as she rang her number for the third time in the space of forty-five minutes and was confronted with Molly's answerphone. No, she wouldn't like to leave a message. She was due to collect Patrick from the airport in a couple of hours and she needed all of Molly, not a disembodied voice. And wasn't she supposed to be dropping her keys around to Sandycove by lunchtime today – unless that offer of the loan of her apartment was no more than hot air.

Helen was in angst mode, arranging and rearranging the sofa cushions. She hadn't been able to face work that morning and had taken the entire day off instead of the agreed half-day. Tony hadn't sounded his usual accommodating self when she phoned to tell him of the change of plan. It was fair enough, conceded Helen, she'd given him zero hours' prior warning. But she'd been an exemplary employee until some weeks ago; that must count for something. And if it didn't, then to hell with J. J. Patterson and his entire management team. They could sack her for all she cared.

She trailed out to the kitchen and plugged in the kettle for want of something better to do. The prospective meeting with her brother was making her as jittery as a cat. When the doorbell rang Helen reacted as though she'd just lost one of her nine lives. Surely Patrick hadn't caught an earlier flight and decided to surprise her? Lucidity evaporating, she wondered about pretending there was no one home. Helen tried to peek out and check who was at the door without being seen. It wasn't possible. She'd rush out that very day and buy a mirror to position opposite her kitchen door so it would reflect the outline of callers, provided they stood to the side of the step where there was a glass panel. In the meantime she'd have to open the door without prior knowledge of her caller. Which she did, but with the gravest reservations.

It was Molly. Helen was so relieved she tripped standing back to allow her in.

'Been at the spirits already?' asked Molly. Without waiting for an answer she jingled her flat keys: 'Something for the weekend. Make yourself at home, help yourself to anything you want – wine, coffee, toyboys – oops no, I'm right out of them, I used the last one up yesterday. I wouldn't mind a mug of something before I head north. I'm off home to the mammy again this weekend. She'll start to imagine I have no life.'

Helen followed Molly into the kitchen, where she was inspecting the contents of her breadbin.

'Excellent, Helen, you have brown bread without the blue op art pattern splattered over it that mine has. I'll rustle myself up some cheese on toast before I brave Bus Aras.'

Helen watched her rooting in the fridge for cheese. 'Molly, are you going away especially to allow Patrick and myself to have your apartment?'

'Seems so. You can send off that promised testimonial to the Pope recommending me for canonisation any time you like. Although I suppose they'd have to make me a

370

Blessed first. Mind you, a weekend in Derry isn't so bad. I might see Mary-P again. She's postponed her wedding until the autumn so that some relatives from New Zealand can attend.' Molly wiped her hands on her corduroy jeans, belatedly snatched a length of kitchen roll to mop up the extraneous cheese shavings, and added: 'I may allow herself and Paul to whisk me off to view their own personal waterfall in Ardara. I could do with tossing in a coin and making a wish. A waterfall has to be even more effective than a fountain, superior pump action, and it's too long to wait for a full moon. The only problem with a trip to Derry is my mother's social life – that hits me where it hurts. She has a better one than I do. She's twenty-nine years older than me and doesn't even have all her own teeth. Does that sound fair to you? Don't bother to answer.'

Helen struggled with the cascade of gratitude that soared through her. She wanted to tell Molly how much she appreciated the gesture; all she could manage was a husky 'Thank you'.

'Don't mention it, angel face. Now, fasten your seat belt because I have something sensational to tell you as soon as I'm sitting at the table with a mug of coffee and a wedge of cheese on toast.'

Molly cut another slice of cheese off the block for nibbling while the grill heated and waited for Helen to quiz her. With a hint that juicy, nobody would be capable of containing themselves. Helen proved more than capable. She inspected her nails while Molly nibbled cheese.

'Something sensational involving a certain man we both know,' dangled Molly.

Helen nodded and burnished her nails against cream linen trousers.

'Are you flesh and blood at all, woman? You don't have an ounce of curiosity in you. It's unnatural.' She looked closer at Helen; she seemed paler than usual. Molly removed her snack from the grill and sat alongside her; Helen was obviously distracted about this get-together with Patrick. It was a waste, having such a luscious gobbet of news about Hercules to dollop on her plate; it wouldn't receive due attention. Exercise some restraint, Molly advised herself, and save telling her about the dinner until after the weekend.

'I went on a date with Georgie last night and he came back to my place.' She spewed toast crumbs from her mouth.

'Who's Georgie?' Helen abandoned her nails.

'The Greek, Hercules, the hunk from McDaid's off-licence.'

'He rang you up and invited you out?'

'No.' Molly wondered if she should make another slice of cheese on toast; this one had effected a vanishing trick. 'We met last night at the art lecture, had our usual cappuccino afterwards and then he asked me to go to his sister's with him for dinner.'

'You went on a first date and met his family, all in the one night?' Molly had every atom of Helen's attention now. 'I always knew you were an operator, Molloy, but this is big time. This is The Point as opposed to Vicar Street.'

Molly glowed.

'So what was his sister like and where does she live?'

'Never mind that,' said Molly, 'we can talk about her later. Cutting to the chase, we shared a taxi home afterwards and I invited him in for coffee.'

'So you grabbed him by the hair and dragged him off to bed. No wonder you look sated.'

'I'm not totally driven by animal impulses,' said Molly. Somewhat huffily, Helen noticed.

'Of course you're not,' she placated.

Molly sniffed and clattered about, making herself more cheese on toast.

'Did you get a snog at least?' asked Helen.

Molly nodded.

'With tongues?'

Molly nodded more vigorously.

'And did the earth move?'

Molly considered. She'd been so euphoric at finding herself soldered lip against lip with Hercules that she hadn't actually assessed whether all the chemistry was bubbling away in the appropriate test tubes. Now that she gave it some thought . . . he'd poked his nose into the corner of her eye more than once, his breath hadn't been exactly ambrosial after Tim's curry but hers probably hadn't either, the kissing had happened on the doorstep as they'd said good night and not on the comfort of the sofa, and he'd also managed to stand on her foot. Apart from that she had no complaints.

'Are you lost for words or lost in the memory of a snogorama?' enquired Helen.

Molly tapped her teeth. 'The jury's out on the boy's technique. I think I'll have to demand a rematch before I can make an informed decision. Let me see, it had, um, verve rather than polish. But hey, verve's good. I can teach him polish later.'

'So there's going to be a later?'

'All arranged. He wanted to meet up on Saturday night but obviously I'll be otherwise occupied, engrossed in chewing my nails to shreds while my mother debates which of her beaux to bestow her favours on.'

'Helen laid a hand on Molly's arm. 'You'd be going on another dream date with Hercules if it weren't for me.'

'More material for the sainthood,' shrugged Molly. 'Anyway, I don't want him thinking I'm available on Saturday nights with two days' notice – less if you consider it was after midnight.'

What was Molly planning to do about Fionn, wondered Helen. Molly shook her head in a 'you'll never credit what I'm about to tell you now' sort of way and brought her friend up to speed on Helga's unexpected arrival.

'Poor Fionn,' said Helen, for once taking his side.

'It's *caveat amator*,' objected Molly. 'I never led him on. I made it crystal clear this was nothing more than an interlude for me until I found a real boyfriend. One who wouldn't have a Scandinavian wife dropping by.'

'Is she a Finn?'

'Norwegian, why?'

'Just thought there'd be a certain symmetry to Fionn ending up with a Finn,' explained Helen.

'He hasn't ended up with her.' Molly shocked herself with the venom of her response.

Helen looked at her. Slowly she elevated one eyebrow and even more leisurely she arched the other. Molly pursed her lips defiantly. The kitchen clock struck the hour.

'Janey Mac,' squeaked Helen, 'I need to be behind the wheel in fifteen seconds if I'm to reach the airport on time to meet Patrick's plane.'

'Are you taking the toll road or driving through town? If you happened to be going via Gardiner Street you could drop me off at Bus Aras.'

Helen hesitated. The centre of town would be mobbed with traffic but it was the least she could do for Molly. If she ran short of time she could always abandon her car in the set-down only area outside Departures and sprint in for Patrick, instead of leaving it in the airport car park.

'Let yourself into the car while I set the burglar alarm, Molly.' She thrust the Golf keys at her friend and snatched up an overnight bag by the front door.

Helen meant to check her appearance in the bathroom mirror on her way out but was in such a panic that she forgot. Molly smiled as she saw her angle the car's rear-view mirror towards her at the first set of red traffic lights.

'A vision. As ever,' she told Helen, who pulled a face. 'Fionn sent me a gargantuan bouquet of flowers this morning,' added Molly. 'In case you're wondering why the flat looks like a florist's shop.'

'That was kind of him.'

'Guilty conscience,' retorted Molly.

'Any note with the blooms?'

'Three little words. No, not those words. "Sorry. Love Fionn." I'm not certain what he's sorry for. For ditching me in favour of his wife, or for his wife turning up? Usually I'm hounded by the man leaving messages on my answerphone but he hasn't rung once since he told me she was arriving. It would be courtesy to call and say he realised Helga was the love of his life and he didn't need me cluttering up their relationship any longer, but does he bother his head?' Molly rummaged aggressively in her bag and produced a packet of mints.

'You're being inconsistent,' said Helen as they sucked.

'So sue me.'

'What happened to *caveat amator*?'

Molly sucked aggressively. Two sets of traffic lights further on she conceded: 'It's true, I'm behaving a little strangely. Here I am with the Greek panting for a date – well, asking

375

me for one, anyway – and I'm not exactly ecstatic. Meanwhile, Fionn, about whom I've been less than enthusiastic from day one, only has to mention his wife wants him and I turn all territorial. Helen, I'm a mess.'

Join the club, thought Helen.

'But not as big a mess as you are,' added Molly.

Helen almost swerved into the path of an oncoming Jeep, which continued blaring its horn long after they were past. Molly decided it would be safer to muzzle herself regarding Helen's bubbling cauldron of a personal life. At least for as long as she were a passenger in her car.

At Gardiner Street Molly hesitated, one foot on the pavement. 'Don't let him force you or cajole you or even drug you into doing anything you'll regret,' she admonished.

Helen was aghast. 'Drug me? Molly, he's my brother.'

'Exactly.'

Helen searched Molly's eyes, ignoring the bus flashing its lights behind them because her hatchback was blocking its laneway.

Molly covered one of the hands on the steering wheel with her own. 'I'll say that again in capitals. HE'S YOUR BROTHER.'

'It's not too late to do a three-point-turn and go home,' panicked Helen. 'Maybe if he doesn't see me at the airport he'll realise I've changed my mind.'

The bus driver leaned on his horn as he pulled out past the green Golf.

'From what you've told me you'll have to face him sooner or later, Helen. Collect him, bring him to my flat – it's empty until Sunday night now – and thrash out whatever needs sorting between the two of you.'

Helen nodded, trance-like. Molly jumped out into the

street, then bent back through the passenger door towards Helen.

'Remember, Patrick's not the only one who loves you, Helen. I love you too. And I don't want to preach to you but, God knows, I'd hate to see you do something you'll live to repent.'

CHAPTER 24

Helen raced through Departures towards Arrivals. Her car was parked illegally and she needed to enter and exit the airport like a boomerang. She cut a determined path through the obstacle course of suitcases and baby buggies leading towards the escalator. Just before the stairs carried her downwards, Helen's eye was caught by a substantial blonde woman with a hairstyle that was either old-fashioned or ultra-modern, for it was a circlet of plaits at the crown of her head. As she watched, the woman laid her forehead against a man's and his arms snaked around to encircle her, fingers stroking the exposed neck beneath the golden plait. Helen smiled and then tensed: the man was Fionn.

She lost sight of them then, for the escalator was carrying her down to a floor below the lovers. Molly will be desolate, she thought, and then Molly was banished from her mind because Patrick was standing at the foot of the escalator watching her as though he knew she'd be arriving at precisely that moment.

'Helen.' Despite the distance still between them and the babble from milling crowds she heard her name clearly. Her heart acquired the properties of a combustion engine. She stepped off the escalator, gravitating towards his eyes; Helen had often heard of the look of love but never encountered it before now.

Patrick opened his arms and she hurtled into them.

In the car, as they drove to Blackrock, he angled sideways to watch her. The Friday afternoon traffic build-up was starting ever earlier and the journey was interminable – or maybe it just appeared that way to Helen, twisting first one hoop and then the other in her ear as the tailback stretched through Drumcondra. Patrick, by comparison, was blissfully unruffled. By nonverbal consent they avoided the usual small talk that marks the conclusion of a journey: did you eat on the plane? Did your flight leave on time? Did you manage with hand luggage or were you obliged to put a bag in the hold? Which left a mass of gaping space to fill. Helen found herself telling Patrick about seeing Fionn and Helga at the airport and how devastated Molly would be.

'It's her apartment we're borrowing, she's the journalist, isn't she? Excessive-looking – all curves and curls. If you were an artist you'd want to paint her, but only with a new set of oils. Doesn't she come from Fermanagh?'

'Derry,' Helen corrected him. 'Nobody comes from Fermanagh. It's all lakes and no people.'

'Never been there. Visited the English Lake District, though.'

'Shame on you.'

'It was lovely,' Patrick protested.

'So's Fermanagh. It's not pockmarked with dreary stee-ples at all, despite Churchill's verdict. It's two-thirds under water and –' she reflected – 'spiritual, for want of a better word. Full of ancient monuments, carvings inscribed in ogham script from pagan times and round towers from the Christian era. Although it's said the locals clung on to their old ways long after Christianity was introduced.'

'How do they know?' Patrick was scrolling through the music stations on the radio.

'Statues of the old gods were found in hallowed places, a classic case of hedging your bets. They probably prayed to a Síle na Gig as well as Our Lady.'

Helen and Molly had gone to see one of these primitive fertility symbols in situ – many have been moved to museums to protect them from the elements. She overlooked a river bridge in County Tipperary and they'd marvelled at her exaggerated vulva, which she held open as though it were a gateway. Which it was, the portal of life. The Síle na Gig, crudely hewn in rock but graphically representational in its celebration of birth and rebirth, had silenced both of them with its potency. Then Molly had remarked that their Celtic forebears certainly weren't prudish. Helen opted not to mention any of this to Patrick.

'Anyway,' Patrick was also thinking about Molly, 'I understood she wasn't keen on her ex, Fionn. I thought she was just putting in time with him.'

'She's more enamoured of him than she acknowledges but there's an impediment – Molly's set on getting married,' explained Helen.

'To anyone in particular or just for the sake of it?'

'There'd be grounds for imagining it's only for the dress and the honeymoon,' agreed Helen, 'but Molly's more complex than she pretends. Fionn's not really a contender right now because he's still married. To someone else. And he looked extremely married from what I saw at the airport. But to tell you the truth I'm not certain marriage is what Molly needs. You're supposed to be faithful and make certain vows when you say "I do" but she isn't one of life's naturally constant people. She's always imagining herself in love and that's fair enough when you're single but when you're married it's not so simple to say "I undo".'

'Is it fair enough to go around on a serial falling-in-love spree?'

Helen switched traffic lanes in the hopes of overtaking a dilatory An Post van and considered. 'Not at thirty-two it isn't. It shows a certain lack of control over your emotions. Too much control, however, is equally inappropriate; believe me, I know.' Lines materialised on either side of her mouth.

Patrick lowered the radio as the opening bars of Patsy Cline's Crazy came over the airwaves and reached for the place where Helen's shoulder joined her neck.

'Control can be jettisoned.' He said it matter of factly as he massaged. Helen turned left by the Auld Triangle and risked a glance at him, changing gear. He wasn't even looking at her. He seemed to be counting the storeys in the Georgian houses on his side of the road.

By the bridge at Connolly station she was ready to punctuate the silence again.

'Anyway, she has a Greek god to console her.'

'Wouldn't the consolation verge on the theoretical then?'

'He's not really a god. But he's not a geek either. He's about seven years younger than she is and works in her local off-licence to supplement his student grant.'

Patrick whistled softly. Helen thought the tune could be Yankee Doodle although equally it could be The Girl From Ipanema. She wasn't adept at recognising songs.

'She's not going to break her heart over Fionn with a younger man on the scene,' he remarked.

'Suppose not,' agreed Helen, far from convinced.

'Seven years is a fair-sized gap, all the same.'

'There's three years between us,' Helen pointed out.

'Irrelevant.'

'Is it?'

He laughed without any evidence of mirth. 'Compared to the other barriers we're facing it is.'

Helen felt darkness closing in on her. How could her emotions seesaw so violently from ebullience to woe in the space of a few miles? Patrick turned the radio back up and resumed stroking the knots at the base of her neck.

'Are you disappointed about Westport?' she asked.

'No. It was always about seeing you, where was irrelevant. An apartment in south Dublin, a hotel in the west of Ireland, I don't mind. So long as I have my s –'

'You were going to say "sister",' she interrupted, borderline hysterical.

'So long as I have my sweet Helen by my side.' His fingers kneaded more forcefully.

'You weren't going to say sister?'

'I don't think of you as my sister.'

'I don't think of you as my brother either.'

Patrick's smile blazed out. 'I do believe we're making progress. Now, how much further to your mate Molly's place?'

'We're here.'

Helen led the way through the foyer.

'I hope we bump into her neighbour Elizabeth. She's –' Helen fumbled for an appropriate description – 'a character. Makes Molly seem two-dimensional by comparison.' She turned the key in the lock, almost overpowered by the scent of flowers. 'This apartment has seen some action. If her walls could speak they'd be X-rated.' She caught Patrick grinning the wrong sort of grin and wished she'd considered the comment's implications.

She led the way into the kitchen. 'Coffee, tea or something stronger?'

'How about a pair of strong arms around your waist – or is that unacceptably brash?' He lifted her a few inches off the tiled floor.

'I thought we were going to talk,' she objected half-heartedly; to her disappointment he took her at her word and replaced her on the black-and-white tiles.

'Tea and talking it is. I take mine –'

'White, no sugar,' she finished for him.

'You do an excess of tea-drinking in this country,' Patrick observed while they were waiting for the kettle to boil.

'That has the ring of a man who's put some distance between himself and us.'

'I'm long enough over the water,' he shrugged. 'I don't feel English but neither do I feel particularly Irish any more.'

Helen produced Molly's rooster teapot and scalded it.

'I'm saddened by that,' she observed.

'You see me as having gone over to the enemy camp?' The last time she'd heard him use that barbed note he'd been speaking to Geraldine.

'They're not the enemy.' Helen's tone was no-nonsense. 'People are people. I simply think it's a shame that someone belonging to me has so little sense of his own identity that he feels neither fish nor fowl. Would you start believing you were a monkey if you set up house in a tree?' She slapped the teapot on the table between them and forgot to select the nearest approximation to matching mugs in Molly's pair-free universe.

'I'm not particularly interested in notions of nationality,' shrugged Patrick. 'It's every man for himself out there. What has Ireland ever done for me?'

'What have you ever done for Ireland?' she retorted.

Patrick changed the subject. 'I'll pour the tea – I don't think I've ever seen a chicken teapot before. What is it with your friend and the farmyard paraphernalia? There's a wall clock with fluffy yellow chicks instead of numerals, and, sweet Lord, I think I see a chicken toast rack beside the kettle.'

Helen prepared to meet him halfway. 'Molly has a minor mania about chickens. She says it's her rural genes asserting themselves – just because she was reared in a city doesn't mean countless generations of country forebears can be dismissed. Bizarre – but convenient when it comes to buying gifts. If I see anything with a hen on it I snap it up without hesitation and store it in my present box until the next birthday or Christmas.'

'What's a present box?' Patrick bit into a fig roll and smiled his lazy smile, the one he must use on Miriam too. Helen banished the thought.

'It's an oestrogen thing. Women buy gifts when we see something we like and then keep them for months until we find the right person to give them to, unlike men who purchase specifically for the occasion.'

'Women are strange beasts.' Patrick was on his second fig roll.

'It's a way of spending money without frittering it.' Helen added more biscuits from the packet to the plate.

'You've lost me there.'

'Sometimes you have this irresistible urge to spend, generally when you can least afford it, so it's damage limitation if you buy a present for someone you'd have to give a gift to anyhow, whether for their birthday or a house-warming.' Helen spelled it out patiently for those with learning difficulties.

'And did you buy Molly the teapot?'

'No, I think that was a birthday present from her god-mother. Anyone who knows Molly is aware of the chicken fixation. I can claim credit for a particularly funky rooster that squawks cock-a-doodle-do when your eggs are boiled. Once for soft-boiled, twice for hard.'

Patrick shook his head, dazed. 'I tend to dole out book and record tokens for presents myself.' A hoarse note edged into his voice. 'Helen, I watched the minutes tick past all week until we'd meet and now I can't believe we're discussing chickens.'

'Better than counting them, surely.'

He laughed. 'In case this weekend turns pear-shaped, which it won't because I believe in the power of positive thinking, I have a favour to ask up front.'

Helen waited, misgivings stirring.

'I'd like a photograph of you. I brought my camera with me.' Patrick conjured up an Instamatic from the tartan overnight bag at his feet. 'It won't bite,' he reassured her as she all but cowered into her chair. 'No need to fear white man's magic. I don't remember you being so camera-shy.'

'I don't like the way I look in photographs.' Helen folded her arms around her body, cradling the elbows. 'You must have loads of me. What about the graduation pictures? What about all those snaps Mammy took during the annual fortnight in Tramore?'

'If I was looking for a photograph of a skinny girl in shorts with occasional ringlets but more often a pudding basin haircut I'd ask Geraldine for one. She's keeper of the family albums. Ditto a photograph of a still skinny girl in mortar board and gown. What I want is a photograph of a beautiful woman in the prime of her life wearing a cream linen trousersuit and a gold necklace that would keep a family of six for a month if it's real.'

'It's not,' said Helen.

'I'll buy you necklaces studded with emeralds and rubies in Ecuador or Paraguay or wherever we wind up,' said Patrick. 'And if I can't find emeralds and rubies I'll glue green and red buttons onto the front. You won't mind, will you?'

Helen was laughing now, her arms no longer forming a stockade across her front. 'Not a bit, Patrick, I might even prefer them. You'll have to buy heat resistant glue, though, I wouldn't want my buttons to fall off if I were wearing one of the necklaces to a smart dinner.'

'No problem, my love. Now are you ready to face the lens?'

'Do I have to?'

'A quick click and it will be over.' He stroked her under the chin. 'One photograph, surely that's not too much to ask?'

Helen hovered between feeling cherished and apprehensive. She caught her reservations by the ear and decided to choose the flattered option. 'I'll need to comb my hair first.'

'Absolutely not. I prefer you slightly dishevelled, it's more natural.'

'Natural sucks. Now do you want this photo or don't you?' Patrick nodded. 'In which case I'm going to the bathroom to spend however long it takes making myself look natural. I may be some time.'

Safely behind a locked door she ran a desultory comb through her hair and then sat on the lavatory seat for a breather. This wasn't going according to plan. Come to think of it she didn't have a plan. Perhaps that's where she was going wrong. Concentrate on what you'd like to see happen and then go for it, she exhorted herself. Helen screwed her eyes tight shut and tried to project an image of herself living in Ecuador with Patrick. No pictures materialised. Then she attempted to visualise the two of them shopping for groceries, painting the spare room, choosing furniture. Still no pictures emerged. Finally she had a stab at imaging the two of them making love. Now she had pictures, dozens of them, each more beguiling and disturbing than the last. Helen knuckled her fists into her eyes, heedless of the mascara rings that would follow, and forced a sob back into her gut. Up it welled again. But no tears accompanied it, just a succession of dry, racking heaves.

'Helen.' Patrick knocked on the door and rattled the handle. His voice sounded panicky. 'Helen, open up.' She held her breath, sobs suspended. 'Helen, come out or I'll kick the door down. Don't shut me out, speak to me. There's two of us in this.' The pleading in his voice turned to grit. 'That's it, I'm breaking the door down. It's hardly more than plywood anyway.'

'No!' she screamed, then hesitated, taken aback by her own vehemence. 'No,' she said more moderately, 'we can't vandalise Molly's property. I'll come out.'

Helen clicked open the lock and faced him. He took her in his arms and she hung limply against his chest.

'I thought I could do this,' she said.

'You can.' He lulled her like a child, murmuring into her hair.

She noticed some of her black mascara was smeared on his mint-green shirt front and wondered what Miriam would make of that.

After a time Helen pushed him away. 'I'm fine now.' She walked ahead of him into the living room and slid on to the floor with her back to a sofa. 'I think we should decide what we're going to do with the rest of our lives, Patrick.'

He nodded. She saw – what? – resignation? lurking in the corners of his mouth. He approached to join her on the rug but thought better of it and sat on the sofa opposite.

The buzzer sounded; they looked at one another with consternation. It rang again more insistently, as though someone was leaning on it with their full weight.

'Does anyone know we're here?' Patrick mouthed.

'Only Molly, and she's on her way to Derry,' Helen whispered back.

The buzzing stopped but they continued to hold their breath. Just as they were relaxing, an authoritative pounding bullied the front door. Whoever had been ringing the buzzer was now outside the apartment.

'If no one knows we're here they'll go away soon enough.' Patrick crossed to Helen and took her hand.

'Molly,' bellowed a man's voice, 'I know you're in there. You can't duck me for ever.'

'What a racket. The neighbours will complain,' said Helen. 'You wait here and I'll deal with it.' She closed the living-room door behind her to block Patrick from view.

Fionn was standing on the doorstep, determination oozing from every brick-red pore. 'I knew you were in –' he began triumphantly, but ground to a halt when he recognised Helen. 'Oh, it's Helen, I'm looking for Molly.'

'I'd never have guessed it. Half the apartment block would never have guessed it either.' Icicles were suspended from her words.

'Sorry about roaring like that. Is she in?' Fionn looked abashed but stood his ground.

'No, she's gone away.'

Fionn stepped across the saddleboard, virtually nose to

nose with Helen, who was left with no option but to take a backwards pace and make space for him. 'She didn't tell me she was going away.' He sounded sceptical and she saw his eyes slide towards the closed living-room door.

Helen remembered why she'd never been a fan of Fionn McCullagh's: beneath that charming front was an obstinacy that told of someone implacable about having his way. He wanted to see Molly so Molly had to be in the apartment; no alternative existed.

Fionn crowded Helen, browbeating her into reversing her position by another few steps. 'Maybe you could give her a message for me.' He remembered the purported charisma and tacked on a 'please'.

Patrick opened the living-room door. 'Is there a situation here, Helen?'

'Not as far as I'm concerned,' said Helen. 'How about you, Fionn?' No response, although he did retreat a couple of paces. 'This is Fionn, a friend of Molly's – he was just leaving,' she added.

Fionn frowned from one to the other, then his brow cleared. 'He can only be your brother.'

It disconcerted them. Helen turned to Patrick, her grey eyes beseeching his grey-green ones. Do something, she pleaded silently. But Patrick seemed just as nonplussed. Fionn's surprise when they neither confirmed nor denied his deduction was visible. He sensed something amiss but was unable to quantify it. Instinct advised him to get off-side.

'We'll tell Molly you're looking for her.' Patrick's words were clipped.

Fionn addressed Helen, also sullen but in a less threatening way. 'When will she be back?'

'I'm not sure,' she lied for no reason she could think of.

'We just stopped in to drop off some belongings she left at my house. Actually, we need to get cracking ourselves because we have plans.'

Fionn's departure left her weak with relief. The tension which had kept her upright ebbed and she propelled her legs towards the living room before they folded.

'Who was that?' asked Patrick.

'The fellow I told you I saw at the airport hugging his wife. He's Molly's ex from years ago and they've been seeing each other again recently.'

'Idiot,' said Patrick. 'He'll lose both women playing fatuous games like that.'

'Juggling two women?' Helen averted her gaze as she posed the question. In case her face betrayed her.

'You can only keep it spinning for a short time, then gravity intervenes.' Patrick registered no awareness of the irony of which Helen was acutely conscious. 'I saw it with a guy at work,' he continued. 'We have an exchange programme with a firm of accountants in Washington. A woman came across for six months and he lost the head – lost the live-in girlfriend too. As for the live-out girlfriend, she went back to the US when her stint was finished. He was so traumatised he jacked in the job and hit the hippy trail.'

'Did you ever hear what happened to him?' Helen was interested in his fate, despite a sneaking conviction he probably deserved everything served up to him.

'He met a Spanish woman in Tangiers and moved to Madrid with her. They opened an antiques shop and had a couple of children.'

'And the moral is?' Helen's curiosity was replaced by vexation; the story hadn't developed as she'd foreseen.

'No moral. Stories aren't obliged to have them. Neither

are people. Or at least not the value system society at large would ascribe to; consensus isn't always healthy.' Patrick eased a hand round her shoulder and Helen realised that during the course of his tale he'd moved from the sofa opposite.

'But what about gravity intervening to smash your games?' she protested.

'That's not morality, that's common sense. He had to go off and find someone new to play with. Not a punishment but not necessarily what he wanted either.' Patrick bent his lips towards Helen, who watched their approach through lowered lashes.

'Molly always says common sense isn't so common,' she murmured, nerve ends tingling as his face neared. Her body leaned backwards on the sofa to make way for his.

A laugh bubbled at the back of his throat and he was so close now she could detect the auburn glint in the stubble already emerging on his jawline. Helen felt at once complaisant and irresolute about how to react but her body leapfrogged ahead of reason and made the decision. Helen's mouth parted.

'Never mind what Molly says. I'm more interested in Molly's friend,' he said, just before his mouth fastened on hers. Except it didn't.

She sat bolt upright, the movement pushing him upwards too. 'But can good and bad grow from the same tree? That's the question.'

Patrick blinked. 'I'm missing something here.'

'Crime and punishment,' she explained.

'I never said anything about crime.' A kernel of exasperation built within Patrick.

'That story about your workmate who cheated on his girlfriend and had to go into the wilderness for a time.'

'That was neither crime nor punishment. He was bored with his life and his girlfriend, had a fling with another woman, lost both and went walkabout for a while to clear his head. It's just sloughing off skins.' Patrick's vexation wasn't decreasing any. He chewed on a rag nail and wondered how Arsenal were faring in their away match at Anfield.

'So you don't think it was wrong of him to be unfaithful to his girlfriend? How long had they lived together? What did she do to deserve having her life split open like a pea pod?' Helen felt an unaccountable urge to weep for the unknown woman.

'I don't know how long they were together. I'm sorry I mentioned him; I can barely remember what the guy looks like.'

'But do you think what he did was wrong?' Helen persevered.

'No.' Patrick stood up and walked to the window; it was raining, one of those persistent drizzles which threatened to drag into the evening. He spoke with his back to her, watching the street below. 'It was clumsy, that's how he came a cropper. He was undecided – perhaps that's why he tried to see both women. He didn't know what he wanted. I believe you have to want something all the way, not let any impediments stand in your path.' He turned towards her, flint-faced. 'I know you're making comparisons with myself, thinking: "He's seesawing between Miriam and me and trying to have it all", but that's not the case. I want you, Helen; I've always wanted you. I'm prepared to take whatever repercussions are attached to spending a life loving you, what you must decide is whether you're willing to do as much.' He was speaking rapidly now. She frowned to keep pace with the words tumbling from him. 'I don't believe in crime and punishment. Or sin and damnation. I don't believe it's a sin to love you, Helen, because I can't accept this overwhelming sensation I have for you could be harmful. I feel nothing but positive life-enhancing emotions when I'm with you. I want to cherish you – and I will if you'll let me.'

She didn't answer for some time. When she spoke her voice was weary. 'I've been thinking about those reports of Nazi concentration camp commandants listening to Beethoven while the gas ovens were switched on. I used to believe it demonstrated how good and evil could grow side by side from the one branch but now I think it's that appreciation of beauty doesn't make you a decent person. You can be the most depraved person in the world and still love a Canaletto. Or your children.'

Patrick, floundering in his attempt to semaphore her thought processes, inclined his head cautiously.

Her eyes were moist as she continued, 'I don't believe in sin exactly, but I do believe in wrongdoing and in repercussions. So maybe some concentration camp commandants fled to South Africa or Chile and managed to evade justice. But natural justice would still have caught up with them. Either in sleepless nights and fractured peace of mind, or the loss of their identities, or even simply in lugging all that remorse and knowledge of transgression around with them for a lifetime.'

'What if they didn't feel guilty?'

'But they must have at some level, even if only in their epicentre. Otherwise why hide?'

'Self-preservation,' suggested Patrick. 'This conversation is morbid, Helen. Let's go for a walk, I think the weather might be clearing.' He peered from the window again but rain clouds continued to scud across the sky.

'I'm not talking about fugitive Nazis, Patrick.'

'I know. Now how about something to eat. Naked emotion always leaves me ravenous. You look a little peaky too. I'm going to fix us both a meal.'

Helen allowed him to change the subject because she was too jaded to do otherwise. She watched him walk into the kitchen annexe off the living room and examine the fridge.

'Lives sparingly, your friend.'

'Domesticity isn't high on Molly's priorities.'

'Don't need to be Inspector Morse to work that one out. Has she a bread bin, at least? Let's see if I can rustle us up a sandwich. Hmm, bread but no butter.'

'She's lending us her apartment, Patrick. Do you want room service as well?'

'Well yes, for preference I'd have liked a hotel but you altered the plan,' he said. 'Now, wait until you taste my superior scrambled eggs on toast, you'll marvel you subsisted so long on the substandard variety.'

He washed his hands splashily at the sink and set to work. Head against the sofa back, Helen's eyelids drifted downwards. A moment later, or so it seemed, he was caressing her cheek and leading her to the breakfast bench in a corner of the kitchen.

Helen thought she wouldn't be able to manage more than a mouthful but she found herself chewing and swallowing and enjoying the food with an appetite not experienced in months.

'Delicious. What's your secret ingredient?'

Patrick tapped the side of his nose. 'Chef's privilege. I told you I'd spoil you for other eggs.' He poured tea. 'I'll hit the shops later and replace Molly's provisions. Where would you like to eat dinner?'

'Not certain. Do you really want to go out?'

'I'm easy. I could order us in an Indian or whatever you prefer. We could watch television or I'll rent a video. It's probably not the most glamorous way you've ever spent an evening but it could be cosy.'

Helen smiled, grateful for the mundanity of it all. 'I'll come out with you. Even if it's still raining I could use the fresh air. I feel like watching an old Woody Allen film, maybe *Mighty Aphrodite*, or how about that one where he grows up in an apartment under one of the rides on Coney Island?'

'*Hannah and her Sisters*?'

'It's definitely not that one.'

Patrick clattered the plates. 'I'm not a Woody Allen fan. But if the lady fancies some New York angst, with a way-past-middle-aged man having relationships with nubile young beauties, then that's what she gets.'

'You forgot about the classic one-liners. It's always worth watching any Woody Allen film for those.'

'Such as?' Patrick collected their jackets and held Helen's out for her.

'He told Mariel Hemingway she was looking so attractive he could hardly keep his eye on the taxi meter.' Patrick chuckled. 'Diane Keaton didn't want to boil some live lobsters they'd bought and he asked her, "What do you want to do, bring them to the movies?"'

Patrick held open the door of the apartment, his mouth curved with merriment.

'I take it back, the man's a sage. Do you have the keys?'

Elizabeth was by the lift. 'Hey, Helen, who's the accessory?' She was wearing lederhosen and her hair spiked out in knotty cornrows.

'This is Patrick.' Helen introduced them as the girl scrutinised him unabashedly. 'Are you coming or going, Elizabeth?'

'Today was a working day, hence the dowdy attire,' explained Elizabeth. 'I'm meeting some of the gang in Pravda shortly but I thought I'd change into something funky and have a sandwich before going under starter's orders. Any more at home like you, Patrick?'

'You should meet my brother Seán, he's the looker in the family,' said Patrick.

'Send him up to Pravda any time after seven,' invited Elizabeth. 'They have more brands of vodka than you'd find in Moscow. I promise to wine him, win him and wear him out.' She winked as she closed the door of her flat.

'Girls were considerably less, um, assertive, when I was growing up,' he remarked.

'We're much improved,' Helen agreed.

'Did I say it was an improvement?'

'Didn't need to, I could read it in your eyes.'

'That, my love, was blind terror.'

'Still, the mythical Seán should be well able for Elizabeth,' said Helen.

'He's the man that could tackle her and a couple of her friends. Couldn't he hose them down if all else failed – one of the advantages of being a fireman.'

Emerging onto the street, Helen led him towards a Centra, promising a stopover at McDaid's so he could admire Hercules after the food was bought.

'I noticed something about Elizabeth next door,' Patrick remarked at the junction.

Helen was absentminded, watching for a break in the traffic.

'She didn't take us for brother and sister. In fact she

acted as though you were my girlfriend.' He measured her response.

Helen blanked him for a few seconds. Then a slow smile spread across her face, firing him with its irradiation, and he released his breath. Perhaps the evening might shape up to what he wished for after all . . .

CHAPTER 25

'So give it to me on the chin, is it good news or bad news? Are you going to Ecuador or staying in Sandycove? Am I losing a friend or gaining a penpal? Are you taking up with a boyfriend or retrieving your veil?'

Molly was back from her weekend in Derry and had wasted virtually no time in phoning Helen. The only delay was caused by an inspection of the apartment, which she examined – half hopeful and half apprehensive – for evidence of licentiousness but discovered nothing more incriminating than an empty Chablis bottle. There were also two full ones in her fridge by way of recompense.

'Too many options, you'll have to run them by me again,' prevaricated Helen.

'Basically I need to know whether the bonding session went Superglue or came unstuck.'

'Neither,' said Helen.

'Don't tell me you had a bout of brother-sister nostalgia, swapped childhood memories of scabbed knees and left it at that?' Molly was aggrieved. She slipped her index finger into the black coil of telephone wire and prepared to feel cheated.

'The last time we spoke you were warning me about Sodom and Gomorrah. Now you're scolding me because there wasn't enough sodoming and gomorrahing.' Helen's pitch matched Molly's in vexation. 'Patrick and I wanted to spend some time together and that's exactly what we did. We talked, we drank some wine and watched a video. It was pleasant.'

'Pleasant!' Molly spluttered over the word. 'Pleasant is tea and biscuits. Pleasant is finding a lost shoe under the bed. Pleasant is a seaside stroll. Pleasant is not spending a weekend with the love of your life.'

'Even if he's your brother' was left hanging in the air, unspoken.

'It was other things besides pleasant,' admitted Helen. 'It was frightening for a while, sporadically embarrassing, sometimes loving, nerve-racking on occasion but overall I'd have to stay with pleasant. That's why I love Patrick, we feel right together. Being suited doesn't necessarily mean fireworks exploding and corks popping. For some people it's like being wrapped in a duvet on a chilly night. I enjoy being with him and he enjoys being with me.' The acknowledgement was an opiate which injected tranquillity into Helen's voice. 'Let me tell you what the best part of our twenty-four hours together was. At one stage he was reading a newspaper with a glass of wine at his elbow and I was flicking through your CDs to find some background music and I looked up and felt overwhelmed just being with him. And almost as if he read my thoughts his eyes strayed from the newspaper and he watched me watching him.'

Molly stifled a seeding complaint; this didn't sound like her idea of a wild weekend. 'How come you were only together for twenty-four hours?'

'We'd made the decision we needed to by Saturday lunchtime and then he went back to London on an afternoon flight.'

'And that decision was?'

'I'd like to tell you about it face to face.'

Molly thought about pressurising her for a clue but abandoned the scheme; there was an inflexibility in Helen's voice that she recognised. Anyway, if she knew her girl it would be sublimation and self-sacrifice all the way; it's better to have loved and lost – prepare for desiccation – give up the ghost.

'Fair enough. I'll toddle off to bed now.'

'Did you find my note?' Helen delayed her.

'Which note?'

'The one by the kettle, it seemed the obvious place to leave it. People always fancy tea or coffee after a journey.'

'Didn't venture near the kettle, angel face. I found a couple of bottles of über-plonk in the fridge but that's all.'

'There's a useful lesson,' said Helen. 'The next time I leave you a note I'll pop it in the fridge. In the meantime, the message was to let you know Fionn called.'

'I can pick it up from the answerphone, it's no big deal,' shrugged Molly.

'No, I mean called to the apartment. Forced his way in, more or less. He seemed convinced you were skulking around the corner avoiding him and had a case of the Doubting Thomases, bent on putting his fingers in the holes.'

Molly was thrilled by his insistence. 'Pushy,' she breathed.

'Patrick thought he'd have to turn physical and eject him but he saw sense in the end,' said Helen. 'Look, I should tell you that I spotted him at the airport when I was collecting Patrick and he was in a clinch with a tall blonde.'

Molly waited for righteous indignation to sweep through her. It didn't. She waited for the misery of the deposed to sweep through her. It didn't. She waited for any emotion to sweep through her. It didn't. This meant she was well and truly over Fionn McCullagh – even evidence of perfidy failed to move her. Then she realised she was clutching two halves of a pencil left by the phone message pad and carbon smears from the broken strip of wood were daubed on her hands. If Helen said 'I told you so' she'd tear the telephone out of the socket.

'I'm sorry,' murmured Helen.

That bit deeper. Molly felt submerged beneath an exhaustion more draining than she'd experienced in her life; as though she'd given birth without painkillers or spent a week weeding or been floored by a wayward blow to the gut.

'I was semi-expecting it,' she lied. 'His wife flew over from Seattle to retrieve him. She doesn't sound like a woman who's easily fobbed off. Think I'll turn in now, Helen. I'll give you a call tomorrow when I work out my off-duty and we can arrange to meet up.'

'Are you sure you're fine?'

'Right as rain. Although what's right about rain is beyond me. Right as sunshine would be nearer the mark. I'm rambling, negative sign. I'm going to make myself some herbal tea and adjourn to my boudoir. Good night, Helen.'

Helen was loath to allow her to disconnect; she sensed Molly was more devastated by Fionn's betrayal than her blasé response indicated. 'Would you like me to drop by and have a cup of it with you?'

'Thanks but no thanks. I'll probably be dead to the world before the tea's brewed.'

'If you're certain . . .' Helen persisted.

'Completely. Utterly. Absolutely. Speak to you tomorrow.' Molly replaced the handset before Helen could fuss any more. Then she crumpled.

When she surfaced from the tears, nose threatening to disintegrate like an overblown rose, she thought: This serves me right for wishing I could make my mind up between Hercules and Fionn. Helga made her mind up first and beat me to it. Imagine losing him to her twice. I must be as dense as a peat briquette.'

Which didn't comfort Molly in the least but at least it galvanised her into heaving herself to her feet and going to bed. With her clothes on.

Next morning at work Barry gestured her towards the vacant seat next to him.

'Myself and some of the lads had a brainwave last night in The Kip,' he said. 'I'm just about to adjust all the numbers on the newsroom noticeboard. We've decided to rename the Garda Press Office the Garda Suppress Office because they're so tight-lipped.'

'And the rest,' muttered Stephen on his way to the water cooler.

'Inspirational,' said Molly. 'Are you going out for the coffees?'

'Another twenty minutes and I'll fetch them from the canteen. The classified girls will be on their breaks by then.'

'Have you learned nothing from the past few weeks?'

403

Molly, wearing glasses because her eyes were too sore from weeping to risk contact lenses, rounded on an astonished Barry. 'You were at your wits' end – although, come to think of it, that wouldn't take long – when Kay gave you your marching orders, and then two minutes after domestic harmony is restored you're eyeing up girls half your age. You disgust me, Barry Dalton. I wouldn't accept a coffee from you if my mental health depended on it.'

Stephen paused on his way back to the newsdesk to smirk at Barry's discomfort.

'And as for you,' began Molly.

'I've never lusted after an ad rep in my life, so help me God,' protested Stephen. 'I'm a happily married man.'

'That's a joke,' said Molly. 'You're all happily married men. But that doesn't stop you presenting yourself as idealists trapped within sterile marriages for the sake of the children when you're in a dim corner of The Kip talking to any gullible little creature with a pair of bright eyes.'

Stephen drew himself up to his full five feet six inches and adopted his chief news editor demeanour. 'Molly, I think you should remember whom you're addressing.'

'A happily married man – isn't that the claim you just made?' she said.

Barry forsook his fish expression and prodded Molly towards the back door.

'Where are you taking me and why are you manhandling me?' she demanded.

'For coffee and for the sake of your career.'

'Feck the career.'

'For the sake of your mortgage then,' Barry answered. 'And since when did a politically correct person like yourself use expressions such as manhandle?'

The disdain that dripped from Molly would have withered a hardy perennial. 'And since when did a woman like myself use expressions such as person-handle?'

Barry was impervious; Corkmen were accustomed to scornful women, he was fond of remarking. 'If you continue in that vein I'll start explaining to strangers you're menopausal,' he threatened, nudging her towards Café Aroma. 'Now, you can tell me why you're behaving like an unguided missile or you can tell me nothing, but we're shooting caffeine into your system at the speed of light. Possibly nicotine too if current behaviour persists. I'll make a decision on that further down the line.'

'I don't smoke any more,' said Molly.

'There's smoke drifting from your nostrils from where I'm standing.'

Against her will, Molly giggled.

'That's better.' Barry deposited her at a window table and went to the counter to order twin double espressos.

'Espresso makes me jumpy,' objected Molly.

'Not as jumpy as you make me when you're in this humour. So do you want to talk about it?'

'Not really.' Molly nodded her thanks to the teenager who placed coffee in front of her. 'My life's a disaster area and I don't know where to appeal for humanitarian relief aid.'

'I take it you mean your personal life.' Barry's eyes were kind behind his perennially smeared glasses.

Molly sipped at the espresso cream. 'What else. I'm going to die old and unloved without anyone to leave flowers on my grave.'

'You're always insisting you want to be cremated.'

Molly removed her spectacles and laid them on the table between them. 'Don't be so literal, Barry, I'll never manage a wallow with you correcting me at every turn around. Fionn's gone back to his wife and he's tormenting me to give him absolution. Well, I'm not doing it. I won't see him to give him the satisfaction of thinking there's no hard feelings because there are. I have grievances so solid about this you could quarry them.' She spotted a pear-shaped coffee stain on her jacket and tutted. 'I can't even be bothered asking for a glass of cold water to attack that piece of clumsiness. It can stand as a symbol of the state my life is in.'

Barry went to the counter and returned with water and a wedge of paper napkins. Molly automatically dipped and rubbed.

'He wasn't the worst in the world. I've seen you with pond life lower than Fionn,' said Barry, hand on his chin as he watched the mop-up.

'He was as far down the food chain as it's possible to date. Anyway, since when did you feel the impulse to defend Fionn McCullagh? The two of you were squaring up in my flat only a couple of weeks ago.'

'Rush of blood to the head.' Barry squirmed as he recalled his declarations to Molly. 'I wasn't in the whole of my health over this business with Kay.'

Molly thrust a note at Barry. 'Fetch us some more coffees, filter ones this time. My system couldn't negotiate another double espresso.'

She brooded while he placed the order.

'There's one thing I don't understand here.' Barry started to run his fingers through his hair but reconsidered because he'd combed it painstakingly to cover the spreading bald patch.

'Only one? You're streets ahead of me,' snarled Molly, with a wet oblong the size of Inishbofin across her front.

Barry thought to himself that he could be reading news-papers, answering telephones, he could even be work-ing. So how come he was sitting opposite a colleague who'd mutated into a porcupine? Oh yes, because she was a friend.

'What I don't understand,' he tried again, 'is why you're so bothered about Fionn going back to his wife. I thought you were girded for it from the outset. Whatever happened to shag him and shake him off?'

'That's exactly the problem,' Molly all but sobbed. 'I was meant to do the dumping, not him.'

Pique, thought Barry.

'Pig,' said Barry. 'A gentleman always allows the lady to believe she's ending their relationship.'

'I hate him,' said Molly.

If she did there wouldn't be half these histrionics, Barry reflected. He drank coffee, delighted with his cloudburst of insight into the female psyche. Perhaps all that drama with Kay had honed his intuition.

'In a fortnight or so you'll be over him, Molly. You'll look back on the way you're feeling today and be incredulous that he could churn you up like this,' he counselled. Then he lobbed in what he considered to be the killer gem, one she'd thank him for in time. 'And you know deep in your heart you're better off without him.'

Molly scowled. She preferred Barry when he was ogling advertising girlies.

Fortunately her mobile phone rang before she selected a thorn from the briar patch on the tip of her tongue with which to prick Barry's pomposity. It was Stephen, enquiring whether either of his reporters fancied doing some work that day.

'And don't tell me you're meeting contacts because I

know you and Dalton are gossiping over sticky buns in one or other of your coffeeshop haunts. Meanwhile, I have a newspaper that needs filling so make tracks back here pronto. And bring me a milky coffee while you're about it.'

Molly pulled a face at Barry. 'It's *il capo di tutti capi* placing his order for coffee. Suppose we ought to head back.'

'Suppose,' agreed Barry. 'Thought you were going to change that tune on your ringer. You said it was niggling you.'

'Never found the time.' She hurled the metallic blue phone back in her bag. 'Life's too short to sort out all your irks. Anyway, you need a few niggles to distract you from the predominant aggravations. Like your life swerving so far awry you can't remember how to heave it back on track.'

They collected Stephen's coffee and an apple slice to ingratiate themselves with him and strolled back through the GPO arcade to the office.

'What is that tune on your mobile anyway? Is it a film score?' asked Barry.

Molly snorted. Or it might have been an incipient sob. Some Day My Prince Will Come.

Helen was brimming over with verve. She compensated for previous weeks of inefficiency by lashing through outstanding work in a surfeit of energy. If Tony were there to observe it he'd have been impressed. However, he was on a couple of days' leave, bringing honour to his country as he high-stepped his way through a dynamic mambo in competition in Reykjavik. Helen discovered she was humming as she worked. The last time she'd caught herself doing that was Christmas Eve when someone had brought a CD player into the office and she'd warbled along, word perfect, to Wham!'s Last Christmas.

'You're in fine fettle,' commented Kevin Boylan at the desk next to her. 'Did your Lotto numbers come up at the weekend?'

Helen decided against telling him only mares were in fine fettle and she wasn't a horse the last time she'd checked in the mirror. Instead she responded: 'You must be psychic. I netted a seven-figure pay-out. I'm torn between a Ferrari and a Corvette Stingray. Believe me, Kevin, every cloud has a base-metal lining. It's wrecking my head trying to choose. And that's only the wheels. Then it's which island to buy. Let nobody convince you money strips a person of their responsibilities. There's a mammoth onus to spend to the hilt.'

'I know you're joking, because you wouldn't be here if you'd clicked on the Lotto.' He looked anything but certain.

'Just fulfilling my commitments before I pack my bags and jet off to the Caribbean. Now, I wonder where I left those holiday brochures.' She rummaged in her briefcase and produced the instruction manual for her microwave, while Kevin craned to see what she was reading.

He relaxed. 'You had me going for a minute there.'

Helen chortled. 'I don't even do the Lotto.'

'Something has you trilling, all the same.'

'Must be springtime and the sap rising.'

The arrival of the postboy concluded their exchange. Not that he ever had important communiqués to deliver – anything worth saying was transmitted by email – but they nevertheless ripped open their envelopes with misplaced expectancy.

'There's something different about you all the same today and I think I've worked out what's responsible for the sparkle,' said Kevin later. 'You have a date tonight.'

'I do,' confirmed Helen.

He was wrong-footed by her ready agreement, expecting prevarication. If not icicles. 'You do? I've never heard you mention dates before. Don't tell me, we're going to play the Lotto jackpot game. So the date's with a rock star. Let's see, who's playing in the RDS this week. Is it with Jim Corr?'

Helen contemplated stringing him along but decided he was too easy a target. 'It's with my friend Molly. We're going to eat noodles, drink Japanese beer and set the world to rights.'

'Japanese beer is very useful for setting-the-world-to-rights sessions,' said Kevin.

'I usually have the plum wine in these noodle bars but Molly said I had to expand my horizons.'

'Feel free to expand them in my direction if the impulse strikes you.' His glance at Helen was so forlorn she hesitated to slap him down.

Instead she chuckled as though it were a jest instead of a borderline invitation and logged off from her computer.

Helen and Molly met on the doorstep of Doheny and Nesbitt's, took one look at the heaving masses inside – who looked bound for a different kind of heaving soon enough from the amount of alcohol they were packing away – and by mutual consent exited simultaneously.

They crossed the road to O'Donoghue's, which was also cheek by jowl, although marginally less so.

'If we'd any sense we'd have stayed north of the river,' muttered Molly.

'This is only down the road from the noodle emporium,' Helen comforted her.

'What's a noodle emporium?'

'An extra large noodle bar. Now stop glaring and I'll buy you something alcoholic.'

Molly studied the bottles ranged along the back shelves of the bar for inspiration. 'A bacardi and pineapple juice topped up with white lemonade,' she decided.

'You order it, I'm not asking for that. You'll be wanting a cherry on a stick next.'

Molly added the cherry and a straw to her list of ingredients, the unshockable barman emitted indifference as he complied, and Helen succumbed to a blast of insanity and asked for the same.

'This is revolting,' she told Molly.

'But in a "here comes summer" sort of way,' said Molly. 'Remember we still have to decide on our holiday hot-spot destination.'

Helen ignored the latter remark. 'There was a hailstorm this afternoon. Summer's being dilatory.'

'All the more reason to toast it. Now, who goes first, your news or mine?'

'I didn't realise you had news, Molly. I expected the Spanish Inquisition about my weekend with Patrick. I have a bet with Kevin Boylan from work you'd be carrying thumbscrews in your shoulder bag.'

Molly bit her maraschino cherry in half and mumbled that she'd forgotten how delicious they tasted. 'I'm not anticipating tying you down and injecting you with a truth potion. But it seemed natural to assume that since I supplied the venue there might be a quid pro quo.'

'Molly,' said Helen, drinking deeply for Dutch courage, 'you can have three questions. The clock is ticking and away you go.'

Molly tapped a tooth with her fingernail. 'Did you make love?'

'No.'

'Are you intending to?'

'Yes.'

'What happens next?'

'You're not a journalist for nothing.' Helen retrieved her cherry by the stalk and dropped it into Molly's glass. 'We're going away together. I'm handing in my notice as soon as Tony is back in the office on Thursday. Patrick resigned from his job today. I'm not going to sell my house, that seems rash, but I'll rent it out and cover the mortgage.' The smile wasn't just coming from Helen's lips but from her eyes, her cheeks, her nose, even her eyebrows; her face was one extended grin.

'Where will you go?' Dazed though she was, Molly managed to probe further.

'That's question number four.' Helen was positively skittish as she tapped Molly's wrist reprovingly. 'But I'll grant you leeway. We're going to Australia. Patrick has a former colleague there with an accountancy firm who's looking for a partner. I have enough saved to give us a couple of months' grace and hopefully I should find work before too long. They must hire software programmers in Sydney as well as Dublin.'

Molly grabbed Helen by the arm and hauled her to her feet. 'I need air or food or both.'

They were at the corner of St Stephen's Green when

Molly realised she'd forgotten her jacket and they had to retrace their steps.

'More haste, less speed,' said Helen, stepping around a pile of discarded Harp cans.

'It's speed I need. Starvation will propel me into Abrakebabra for some fast food if there's any delay,' threatened Molly.

'Noodles are fast food. And you're the one holding us up.'

They cut across the side of the Green and minutes later were reading menus in Yamamori. Molly refused to comment on Helen's plans until she'd shovelled several overladen forkfuls into her mouth. Helen, meanwhile, swished her food around the bowl with chopsticks and waited for Molly to turn dissuader.

'You're throwing over your home, your job and your friends,' said Molly. 'Aren't you taking a chance? Just a diminutive one?'

'I've always wished for excitement and adventure – this is it.' Helen's breathing was shallow.

'You'll be financially dependent on him. He's the one with the job and the friend so at least he knows somebody else.' Molly stabbed the air with her fork between each group of three or four words.

'I'll find work, I'll make new friends. Anyway, I don't need anyone but Patrick.'

'Thanks for writing me out of your life so readily.' Molly returned to her noodles, lowering her face over the bowl to minimise distance between mouth and fork and thereby the potential for slurping accidents.

'I didn't mean it like that.' Helen reached out to touch one of Molly's blonde curls, hovered a few inches adrift of her shoulder and then patted her upper arm. 'Of course I'll never find another friend like you but we won't

413

lose contact. Say we won't, Molly.' Helen looked at her appealingly but Molly was sucking in noodles as though her life depended on it. 'You can come and visit us and I'll . . .' Her voice trailed off.

'You can't, can you?' Molly finally laid down the fork. 'You won't be able to come back here for holidays. You're burning your bridges. This really is the long goodbye. You're leaving behind everything you know.'

No dimmer switch could reduce Helen's happiness. 'Be glad for me, Molly. I'm in love. I'm only trying to follow my heart,' she whispered. 'Maybe it's a mistake to go but, God knows, it's a mistake not to – those hackneyed descriptions about being two halves of a whole and two hearts beating as one apply to Patrick and me. I know it sounds trite but that's how it is with us.'

Molly's own heart shrivelled. 'Oh, Helen, you're leaping into something so unquantifiable that I quail for you. It can't but turn out wrong, it's intrinsically unnatural. You'll have no luck from it, angel face. Please, if you feel anything for me, don't do this.'

Helen ground her knuckles into her mouth to stem the tears. 'I love you, Molly, but I love Patrick too and what I feel for him is more compelling. I –' her voice stumbled – 'I don't seem to have any choice in the matter.'

'But you *do* have a choice,' insisted Molly, glaring at a couple inclined to slide in alongside them on the bench seating. They took the hint and retreated.

'Helen, I'm not trying to stop you from doing what you honestly want to do, but I wouldn't be able to live with myself unless I emphasised all the drawbacks. What about Patrick's fiancée in London? What about Geraldine? What about the life you've made for yourself here? You're well thought of at work, you have a comfortable home, you have people who respect you and care about you. Surely all that must count for something?'

Helen traced the life line in the palm of her hand with a fingernail. There was an air of familiarity to Molly's words – she'd said them to herself often enough before the decision was taken.

'I hear what you're saying but the difficult part's over. I know the direction my life is headed in. I'm tired of swimming against the tide, I'm going to coast along with the current for a change.' She looked up from her palm doodling and dared Molly to continue arguing with her.

Molly changed tack. 'What if you get pregnant?'

Helen was stunned into silence.

Molly pressed home her advantage: 'You know the pill doesn't agree with you and condoms aren't completely safe. There's a chance you could end up carrying your own brother's child. Assuming you decided to have it, imagine the repercussions for the baby. Even if it's physically and intellectually unimpaired, which is by no means guaranteed, the mental ramifications are appalling. So while you gather ye rosebuds while ye may, remember there are aphids out there with a nasty habit of nipping blooms in the bud.'

She paused in case Helen had a contribution to make but her vocal cords had seized up. So she dredged deep for the *coup de grâce* and a quotation swam to the surface. 'One of those old Greek boys knew all about urging caution. He said: "One swallow does not make a summer. Similarly one brief time of happiness does not make a person entirely happy."' Molly was seized by a desperate compulsion to force Helen to see sense, to ram it into her. 'You may think it's a bower of bliss now but, trust me, you won't stay happy for long. I know you, Helen, I know you're too straight to live crook-edly.'

Helen stooped for her bag and threw her reefer jacket over her arm. 'I love Patrick and I'm going to make a life with him. I don't care about right and wrong or good and bad. I've been a good girl all my days and what has it achieved? A sterile life with a boring house, a boring job, a boring car and nothing in it to make me believe there's any rhyme or reason to this existence. Now I've found that something and I'm not going to lose it again. Not for Aristotle, not for convention and not for you, Molly.' Helen threw some cash on the table and walked towards the exit.

Molly's glance fell on her fork. She lifted it and propelled cold noodles towards her mouth. They tasted like cardboard but she ladled and chewed. Helen had made her position clear. Exhausted by the enormity of it all, Molly ate until the bowl was empty, and then she pulled Helen's discarded meal towards her and finished that.

She didn't even ask me what my news was. There wasn't a flicker of interest in the decision I've taken, Molly thought as she paid the bill. For all she knows or cares I could be emigrating to Seattle with Fionn or to Athens with Hercules. I could be setting up in a *ménage à trois* with Helga and Fionn. I could be planning to convert to the Greek Orthodox faith for an extravagant wedding. I could even have taken a head stagger and thrown in my lot with Barry. But she doesn't care and she didn't enquire. So she can wallow in ignorance and she needn't think I'll be keeping an eye on her house while she's gallivanting in Australia.

Bombarded with righteous indignation, Molly climbed the steps to the street. Helen was waiting there for her under a lamppost. Wordlessly she hugged Molly, who hugged her back.

'What's going to happen to us?' Helen asked when they emerged from the embrace.

Molly could find nothing that would pass muster for an answer.

CHAPTER 26

Molly failed to make it along to the art lecture, deliberately dawdling over her work, but she turned up in time for coffee with Hercules afterwards. She cringed when she saw his pleasure in her belated appearance.

'I thought you'd forgotten about our date,' he said.

She played for time until they were seated and had a modicum of privacy. 'Would I forget something as important as that?'

'I don't know.' The look he sent her way was measured.

Take a deep breath, she advised herself. 'There's someone else.'

Hercules' disappointment struck her as (a) guilt-inducing, (b) flattering and (c) disproportionate to their fledging relationship. They'd only been out once and shared a few intimacies and lattes. She'd been languishing over him for months and he hadn't even noticed her; her credit card balance would be infinitely more manageable if he hadn't proved so immune to her charms, thereby necessitating frequent return visits to his off-licence. Fortified by this lateral – and somewhat inaccurate – deduction, Molly resumed her Dear John.

'There's someone older,' she explained, 'closer to me in age. Not that you're a million miles away from it but you are

419

a little younger and, well, I feel more at ease with someone in my own age group.'

'So I'm too young for you this week,' said Hercules. 'I'm seven days older than I was last week when the age difference didn't matter.'

'I can't deny it,' agreed Molly. 'All I can tell you is that I've had a change of heart since last Thursday. Believe me, life would be infinitely less complicated if I could scoop you up and keep you but the fact is I realise I'm in love with someone else and I don't have the heart to carry on with this –' she gesticulated loosely – 'whatever this is between us.'

She rested her chin on the palm of her hand, where it still felt too heavy for her head. 'The joke of it is he doesn't even want me, he's married, but that appears not to alter my emotions for him, loser that I am. If anything it solidifies my feelings. When he wavered between myself and his wife I faltered too; when he indicated his choice I realised my decision had been made all along and I was too moronic or too obstinate or too –' she trawled for the description – 'clogged up with pride to recognise it. You see, he left me for her once before. And now I've lost him again. I wanted him then, I still do, but I can't have him. And that, Georgie, is my dilemma. But it needn't concern you and I'd be doing you no favours if I continued to see you under the circumstances. You're young, you're ravishing, you deserve to be with somebody who only has eyes for you instead of a preposterous woman wishing for the impossible.' Molly ground to a halt, suffused by emotion – a chunk of it self-pity.

Hercules behaved irreproachably. He told her if she ever changed her mind she should contact him, that she was exceptional and talented, that he appreciated her candour, that his sister rated her ('What's that got to do with the price of fish?' wondered the unromantic voice which occasionally surfaced in Molly's brain). They hugged briefly, bodies carefully not touching, and parted amicably. So amicably it was an anti-climax. Molly dallied along Nassau Street towards a taxi rank, reluctant to stand on a DART platform with Hercules now that ties were servered, and acknowledged there was never much in the way of lasting attraction from the outset. Face it, she scolded her reflection in the Celtic Notes music shop, she'd been moping over a handsomely presented package for months on end like a teenager. She didn't deserve a successful relationship because she was the thirty-two-year-old equivalent of a teen-mag reader. Comic strip emotions, comic strip dénouement.

Queuing for a taxi by the Bank of Ireland arts centre, she wondered whether she should behave like a big grown-up girl and meet Fionn, allow him to offer regretful apologies and make his escape with conscience salved. She'd been avoiding him since Helen told her about the scene with his wife at the airport and hadn't returned any of his calls. Elizabeth had knocked on her door at breakfast that morning and outlined gleefully how he'd camped out in the foyer of the apartment block last night when Molly was working until 1 a.m.

'I saw him when I came in from work to change at six, hanging around the letter boxes; he was still there an hour later when I went out to meet the gang except he was sitting on the steps near the lift,' Elizabeth had said. 'I had an early night and came home about midnight just in time to see him being escorted from the premises by the Guards after a couple of the residents complained.' She'd annexed one of Molly's rounds of toast. 'Lemon curd, haven't tasted that in years. He didn't appear to be drunk or on some chemical kick but you never know. You two had a row?'

'You could say that.' Molly had dropped more bread into the toaster and declined to elaborate.

'Work beckons.' Elizabeth had buttoned her wet look chessboard mac over paisley-patterned hotpants and simultaneously licked lemon curd from her fingers 'The tourists are going to have to compete very hard for my interest today.'

'Elizabeth, do you really work for Bord Fáilte or is it just a story you've devised for your own entertainment?'

'Why would I do that?'

'You look like someone who works in a record store or with a theatre group, maybe in an arts complex.' The timer on Molly's toaster had wound down and she'd collected the burned offerings. 'I imagined that people who dealt with tourists would have to play the Maureen O'Hara card. Maybe not dye your hair red but certainly conform a little more obviously to a stereotype.'

'I change into my *Riverdance* frock and slap on the orange wig and freckles at the office. Are you planning to eat all of that toast?'

'Allow me to bedeck one in lemon curd for you to eat on your way to the DART.' Molly had retrieved the knife she'd been using from the draining board.

Recalling that morning's conversation as she counted how many people were still ahead of her in the taxi queue, Molly weighed up the pros and cons of seeing Fionn one last time. The advantages were all on his side. He wanted to slope off to Seattle with an unmuddied conscience and couldn't do that while she played hide-and-seek. The only benefit to be gained for her was that cold comforter called Doing The Right Thing. Ah sure, for feck's sake get it out of the way and fire ahead with your life, she exhorted herself, and produced her mobile to ring Fionn then and there.

Yelling above the roar of the traffic, she arranged to meet him the following evening.

'Where are you now? It sounds like you're standing by the Anna Livia statue in O'Connell Street with juggernauts whizzing by,' said Fionn.

'Close. I'm on Dame Street waiting for that mythical beast, a taxi. A unicorn may come cantering by before an empty cab pulls up.'

'Listen, it's early yet, why don't I drive into town and meet you somewhere for a drink, say McDaid's at the top of Grafton Street? I should be able to find a parking space. I could be with you in twenty minutes or so.'

Molly shuddered at the suggestion of McDaid's – the coincidence of its shared name with Hercules' off-licence was too near the knuckle. 'Let's make it The Westbury,' she countered. 'I'll wander up there now.'

She paused to listen to a guitarist massacre The House of the Rising Sun, read her balance and order a cheque-book from a hole-in-the-wall machine, admire a cheongsam in Monsoon but admit she lacked the figure for it, and still reached The Westbury ahead of Fionn. She watched him race up the street towards the hotel, leather jacket flapping. We've played this scene before, thought Molly. I wonder if he'll use the same dialogue or produce a new set of lines. Cynicism was anaesthetising her for their encounter.

'You look well.' Fionn dropped a kiss on her cheek.

'So do you.'

'Can I buy you a drink?'

'I'm fine with the one I have.' She nursed her gin and tonic protectively.

Fionn didn't bother ordering for himself. 'Olga's gone home again,' he said. His expression was oblique.

Molly waited for him to tell her he was working out his notice and preparing to join his wife.

'She's filing for divorce,' he continued.

She held her breath.

'I'm staying in Dublin whether you'll have me or not. I've decided this is where I want to be.'

Molly realised her breathing was still suspended and decided suffocation held few attractions.

Fionn moved his chair closer but didn't touch her. 'I love you, Molly. I've loved you for years. What I felt for Olga was infatuation – with you it's a deeper, more lasting emotion, genuinely satisfying. But I've also meddled with your emotions and I can't defend myself. I've probably lost all chance of a present, of a future with you.' His eyes were blue-black and pleading for a reaction but she was back in breath-holding mode, which precluded speaking. Now he reached forward and attempted to lace his fingers through hers; she seized her glass in both hands to prevent him because her brain was whirring and she needed space to think. Gently he disengaged one of the hands and held it.

'It'll be a few months before Olga and I can be divorced. I may have to fly back to Seattle to tie up some loose ends but there's no reason why I can't put this behind me and move on.' Her hand felt safe inside his.

That's wonderful for you, Molly thought savagely, even as she admired his smooth, hairless hands. She didn't trust herself to speak so she nodded.

Fionn pulled his chair so close their breath mingled. The look he gave her combined anxiety with tenderness.

'I love you, Molly,' his voice was pillow soft. 'I need to know how you feel about me. Whether you think, in time, you could love me again. You did once before; it's not impossible that you might love me again – when you grow to trust me; when I prove I deserve your trust. Tell me how you're feeling, don't freeze me out like this.'

'I love you.' The words were torn from her but relief gushed through Molly as soon as she let them go.

There. She loved Fionn McCullagh. He knew it and she knew it.

Helen watched for the taxi that would carry her to the airport for her flight to Australia. Patrick should be in the air already and would be waiting at arrivals in Sydney for her. She glanced around the house. It no longer seemed like her home – already she'd disengaged from it. Perhaps the strangeness was due to the absence of so many of her personal belongings, for on the advice of a letting agent she contacted (but didn't use) she'd packed away ornaments, framed photographs and other personal items. Molly was minding her plants although her horticultural track record was pitted with the carcasses of everything from sweetheart to cheese plants. The only species to survive her ministrations was the cactus. But Molly insisted her luck was changing and Helen was moved to think of her plants trailing their spidery fronds across her friend's home. She lifted her airline ticket from the coffee table and checked the departure time again; the sale of her car had paid for it with enough left over for a float in her bank account for repairs to the house and to cover a few months of not working in Sydney if it took her a while to establish herself.

The new tenants would be moving in at the weekend, a couple from work. That's why she hadn't needed the letting agent. She'd been on nodding terms with Lorraine and Ted for a year or so and preferred to leave her home in the care of people she knew. Matching suitcases and a flight bag rested against a sofa. So much for the adage about having no more possessions than you can carry on your back. Then again, life had a way of tricking you into acquiring goods and chattels. For the twenty-third time she checked the window for a taxi drawing up, considered ringing the firm to confirm it was on its way but obliged herself to be patient. It wasn't due for another ten minutes. She couldn't sit, so she paced the living room and replayed her strained conversation of a few days earlier with Geraldine.

'But you never mentioned emigrating when we spoke in Galway,' Geraldine whined.

'It was an opportunity that came up unexpectedly. There was a vacancy with a sister firm in Oz that needed filling urgently. I only had a week to make up my mind.'

'But you can't even give me an address.' Geraldine was testy. 'You're behaving in a most peculiar fashion, Helen. One minute you're inviting me to Dublin for the weekend, the next you're jetting off to Australia and I've no way of knowing when I'll see you again.'

Helen avoided pointing out that the sisters weren't exactly confidantes; instead she placated Geraldine with false promises about sending her an address and dangled the prospect of a holiday which would never happen. Patrick wasn't mentioned until the end, when Geraldine asked: 'Any word on our brother's wedding plans?'

'Not a sausage,' lied Helen.

'Maybe I should ring him, establish the state of progress.'

Helen didn't want Geraldine talking to Miriam and discovering that Patrick was also going to Australia.

'I'd leave it, Geraldine. You know Patrick doesn't care to be interrogated about his movements. He'll give us dates and details when he's ready.'

'I suppose.' Geraldine's acquiescence was begruding but at least she agreed and Helen ended the conversation on the pretext of another call beeping on the line.

She twisted her watch around her wrist to read the dial and decided if the taxi weren't with her in two minutes she'd phone the company. A knock on the door forestalled her. It was Molly, breathless and perspiring.

'Caught you. Decided to share the taxi with you to the airport,' she panted.

'We said our goodbyes over a meal and a bottle of bubbly yesterday.' Helen was touched.

'I know, but I wanted to wave you off.' Molly slumped on the arm of the sofa. 'I thought I'd left it too late when I switched my alarm off and rolled over to sleep again but I belted down to the DART and there was a train on the platform. Have I time for a cold drink?'

'No, taxi's pulling up. Could you manage one of those suitcases while I dead-lock the front door.' Helen dropped her keys, picked them up and dropped them again, but finally the cab was hugging the coastline into town.

'I really appreciate this.' Helen squeezed Molly's hand as they sailed across the roundabout on the airport perimeter.

'What are friends for,' Molly responded. She hoped she wasn't going to bawl; airports always made her feel lachrymose but there was the added misery of losing the best friend she was ever likely to have. And to a future that could only be viewed as clandestine. If it weren't for Fionn in her life, reassuringly loving, she'd be weeping for herself as well as Helen.

'There's no need to come in,' said Helen to Molly, producing her purse to pay the taxi-driver.

'I want to see you on the plane,' insisted Molly. 'You're stuck with me until Passport Control.'

Helen smiled but Molly was unable to return it.

At the Aer Lingus check-in desk Helen was handed a note instructing her to ring a number urgently. She scrabbled for coins and Molly reached her mobile to her.

'I don't recognise the number.' Trepidation accelerated her pulse as she dialled the London code. Patrick answered it on the second peal; it was the direct line into his office.

'Miriam discovered what we were planning,' he explained, voice stealthy.

'Why aren't you in mid-air?' Helen asked. 'I'm at the airport. I was about to check in my bags when I received your message. I didn't know what was wrong.'

'I'm telling you what's wrong. Miriam learned what we intended. She threatened to tell my employers, the police, Geraldine, the village priest back home in Ballydoyle; she warned she'd take out an ad in the newspaper. She was hysterical. I had to promise not to go. At least not for now. I'd never be allowed to take up that position in Sydney.'

Helen listened dully to the words as they washed over her. She knew she should feel something – grief, betrayal, anything – but was conscious only of a flight information screen with flashing 'now boarding' lights for Budapest and Paris.

She tuned back in to Patrick, who was explaining this was only a delay, it didn't mean their plans were scrapped. He'd gone into work that morning, persuaded the boss to tear up his resignation letter and he'd start planning another escape route for them. Maybe Ecuador after all.

'Why were you still living with Miriam? Why didn't you move out into a hotel after we made our decision?' Helen sounded strangely unaltered to her own ears; you'd imagine there'd be a physical manifestation of the ground crumbling beneath your feet – a crack in the voice, at least, to match the chasm that had opened up. She ignored Molly's frantic eye signals appealing for information.

'Good question.' Patrick sighed. 'Unfortunately I don't have a good answer. I was being cowardly – I only told her last night.'

'You mean you allowed her to carry on for a month believing everything was fine between the two of you and the wedding plans were on track?'

Patrick didn't respond.

'You did, didn't you?' Helen insisted.

'Yes.'

'And how did she realise you were leaving her for me?'

'She wormed it out of me that there was another woman. You wouldn't believe the night we had, Helen. We sat through it crying and shouting and demolishing china. She even went for me with a pair of scissors – I didn't think she had so much passion in her. Anyway, she said something about you – she knows how attached we are to one another. I stupidly thought she realised more than she did and gave the game away. Basically she's blackmailing me not to go to you. I'm uncertain if it's because she imagines I'll stay with her or if it's because if she can't have me then nobody can.'

'You could always try calling her bluff.' Helen was hesitant but she made the suggestion anyway.

Patrick vetoed it instantly. 'The woman's deranged. She'd hound us, Helen. No, we have to draw breath and think this through. I'm not giving up on us but we need to pause a while.'

Helen focused on the flight information screen, now blinking a boarding light for Berlin. She'd never been to Germany, she realised. She'd travelled as far afield as Singapore but had never made it to a country just a few hours' flying time away.

'Helen? Helen, are you still there?' Patrick's voice whimpered in her ear.

'Goodbye, Patrick. Have a happy life. I won't be part of it.' She pressed the disconnect button.

Molly's face was a question mark.

'Creative ambiguities,' said Helen, and rested her head on her friend's shoulder.

CHAPTER 27

The gilt-edged wedding invitation arrived in the post with no prior warning.

Jenny Stewart-Browne and Patrick Sharkey
request the pleasure of
Helen Sharkey and guest
at their marriage in Rotherburn Parish Church, York
on June 26th at midday
and afterwards at the Old Coach House.

Helen studied it: the RSVP was to Patrick's old address in Camden Town, which meant he'd never moved. Same address, different girlfriend – he was useless on his own. Their last conversation had been two years previously at Dublin airport; she hadn't seen him since then. The time Helen labelled her Nearly Phase, when she'd nearly turned her life on its head, nearly left her home and job, nearly made a mistake – or not. She had no way of knowing.

Life was . . . stabilised now. She was still in the same house and working for the same firm, except she had Tony's job since he'd been head-hunted by a rival outfit. There was no man in her life but she had a sister in it; she made the effort to spend time with Geraldine and virtue had to be its own reward because she discovered that beneath her sister's prickly shell was a prickly individual. But one who nevertheless displayed occasional flashes of humour and whose company could be stimulating. Of course it could also be downright tedious but she only had the one sister, she may make the best of it.

Helen crumpled Patrick's wedding invitation in the kitchen bin and sighed as she realised Geraldine would harass her to go to York for the occasion. Well, she could plague her as much as she liked, Helen intended to be in Timbuktu if not Xanadu when 26 June wore around.

'Why not Quito?' she suggested to the packet of breakfast cereals, and when it didn't put up an argument she decided to make enquiries at a travel agency during her lunch break.

The phone rang.

'I hope you haven't forgotten you're coming to the antenatal clinic with me at lunchtime.' It was Molly.

'No,' fibbed Helen. 'I'll be at the Rotunda at twelve thirty. How's my godchild-to-be?'

'Alive and kicking, especially the kicking.'

'Have you settled into the new house yet? Worked out how to operate the dishwasher and appointed a cupboard for storing the crisps in and another for the baked beans?'

'Fionn's the organiser,' said Molly, 'I'm leaving all that to him. All I need to locate is the television remote control because it's too awkward to heave my vast bulk off the sofa when I want to change channels. Only one more week of work, thank heavens, then I can submit to the waves of sloth which are even now threatening to engulf me. I can't bend down to paint my toenails any more. Fionn sat me on the edge of the kitchen table and did them for me last night.'

'There's devotion. What sort of a fist did he make of it?'

'Not half bad. If this boyfriend of mine is ever made redundant as an architect I think we could set him up in business as a visiting beautician. Perhaps himself and Kay Dalton could go into partnership together. Barry's mad keen on entrepreneurial schemes at the moment. After twenty-odd years in journalism it's finally hit him that he'll never make his fortune from newspapers – unless he raises the finances to buy one, which is as likely as –'

'Patrick's getting married. An invitation came in this morning's post.' Helen heard Molly's intake of breath.

'Are you going?'

'No, I've decided to honour a prior commitment to kick up my heels in Quito.'

'How do you feel, Helen?'

'Sad, relieved, regretful, a pick 'n' mix of emotions. I don't suppose I'll ever marry. I can't believe he's able to shrug off our past so readily. Or maybe, unfortunately, I can. Anyway it seems as though it happened a long time ago to another person.'

Molly detected the loneliness in Helen's voice and wished she could find some way to mitigate it. 'I suppose it's useless telling you we have a new chief sub who's single – well, divorced – with all his own teeth and hair, and a fleeting resemblance to Patrick Bergin. Play your cards right and yours could be the face that launches a thousand headlines.'

'How fleeting a similarity to Patrick Bergin?'

'Imagine a jowlier, shorter brother. But I don't know why I'm even mentioning it, or the fact that he'll be in The Kip on Friday night, because you never agree to meet any of the men I suggest.' Molly's tone waxed towards indignation until she recalled Helen's wedding invitation.

'I'm happy as I am,' insisted Helen. 'Work's going well.

Sure they throw so much money at me I don't know what to spend it on, never mind contemplate cashing in the share options. I'm looking forward to a goddaughter to fritter some cash on.'

'Or godson.' Molly felt obliged to enter the addendum, although both were convinced she was carrying a girl.

'A godson will equally require bribes on the strict understanding that in years to come he'll visit me in my bath chair in the old folks' home. Possibly liberate me for a couple of hours every Christmas morning for a glass of sherry in the bosom of his family.'

'So that's how it works,' marvelled Molly.

'Indeed. Now I have work to go to even if you can use your pregnancy as an excuse to turn up late, Molly Molloy. I'll see you at the entrance to the Rotunda.'

Helen registered a wave of discontent as she fished out her briefcase from behind the sofa. The signs of affluence were more visible in her home now – a couple of paintings where framed prints had once hung; a pair of two-seater green chesterfields instead of elderly couches covered in cream throws. A silver Beetle was parked outside her front door. But her life wasn't exactly enthralling. She could only work so many hours . . . and then what?

She retraced her steps to the kitchen and ferreted out Patrick's wedding invitation. If he could press the fast forward button on life, why couldn't she?

'It still hurts, that's why,' she whispered.

Helen flipped open her briefcase and extracted a photograph from the back pocket. Patrick and herself grinned at the lens. He'd taken it that time she'd borrowed Molly's apartment, holding the camera at arm's length and snapping them both. It was slightly out of focus but their happiness was palpable.

Patrick was everything she'd ever wanted in a man. But then nobody was allowed to have everything, Helen reminded herself. Only last year she bought herself a gaudily painted wooden parrot as an *aide-mémoire* and kept it on her desk at work: its plumage was a sight to behold but it squawked. That's how nature operated and life took its cue from her.

'Defective dreams,' moped Helen, replacing the photograph in her briefcase.

Turning the ignition in the car, a thought struck her with such impetus that it winded her and she had to leave the engine idling while she digested it. People were given second chances – look at Molly and Fionn – why not dreams? They could be straightened out and tweaked in another direction. What was missing was the will to dream them. But she honestly wasn't certain if she had it in her.

Helen checked her rear-view mirror and pulled out, lecturing herself as she drove. So she wasn't likely to have the happy ending she'd have chosen for herself. But she didn't need to wallow all her life either. She could meet this chief sub-editor of Molly's on Friday, that would be a start. He might not be her knight in shining armour but she didn't think she could fit one of those fellows clanking into her living room, horse and all. Molly's colleague might distract her for an hour or a month. And if he didn't she'd be no worse off.

Helen swung her briefcase in her hand as she left her company car in its reserved parking space, an executive perk, and tested out the notion of meeting a man. It didn't seem utterly impossible. Maybe she could do it. If she could fly off to Quito on her own for a holiday she should be able to manage a drink with a person of the male persuasion. She imagined Molly's delight at lunchtime if she told her she was free to grace The Kip with her presence after all.

'A Patrick Bergin lookalike,' said Helen, 'that's promising. Just keep telling yourself, there's more than one Patrick in the world.'

She rolled the words around on her tongue, wondering if she believed them. Wishing she could. Faltering over wishing for anything.

'There's more than one Patrick in the world.'

Say the words and make them come true.